SPEARGRASS-OPIOID

DWAYNE CLAYDEN

BAD ALIBI PRESS

ALSO BY DWAYNE CLAYDEN

The Brad Coulter Thrillers

Crisis Point

Outlaw MC

Wolfman is Back

13 Days of Terror

Goddess of Justice

The Speargrass Thriller Series

Speargrass Opioid

Short Story

Hell Hath No Fury

AB Negative. An Anthology of Alberta Crime

dwayneclayden@gmail.com

DwayneClayden.com

Publisher's Note: This is a work of fiction. Names, characters, places, and incidents are a product of the author's imagination. Locales and public names are sometimes used for atmospheric purposes. Any resemblance to actual people, living or dead, or to businesses, companies, events, institutions, or locales is completely coincidental.

Published in Canada by Bad Alibi Press

Printed and bound in Canada

Cover Graphic by Travis Miles, Pro Book Covers

Editing by Taija Morgan

Proofing by Jonas Saul

Formatting by Dwayne Clayden

Speargrass-Opioid / Dwayne Clayden—1st print ed.

ISBN: 978-1-989912-00-3 (pbk), 978-1-989912–01-1 (e-book)

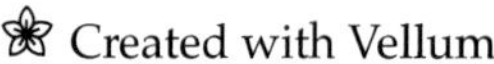 Created with Vellum

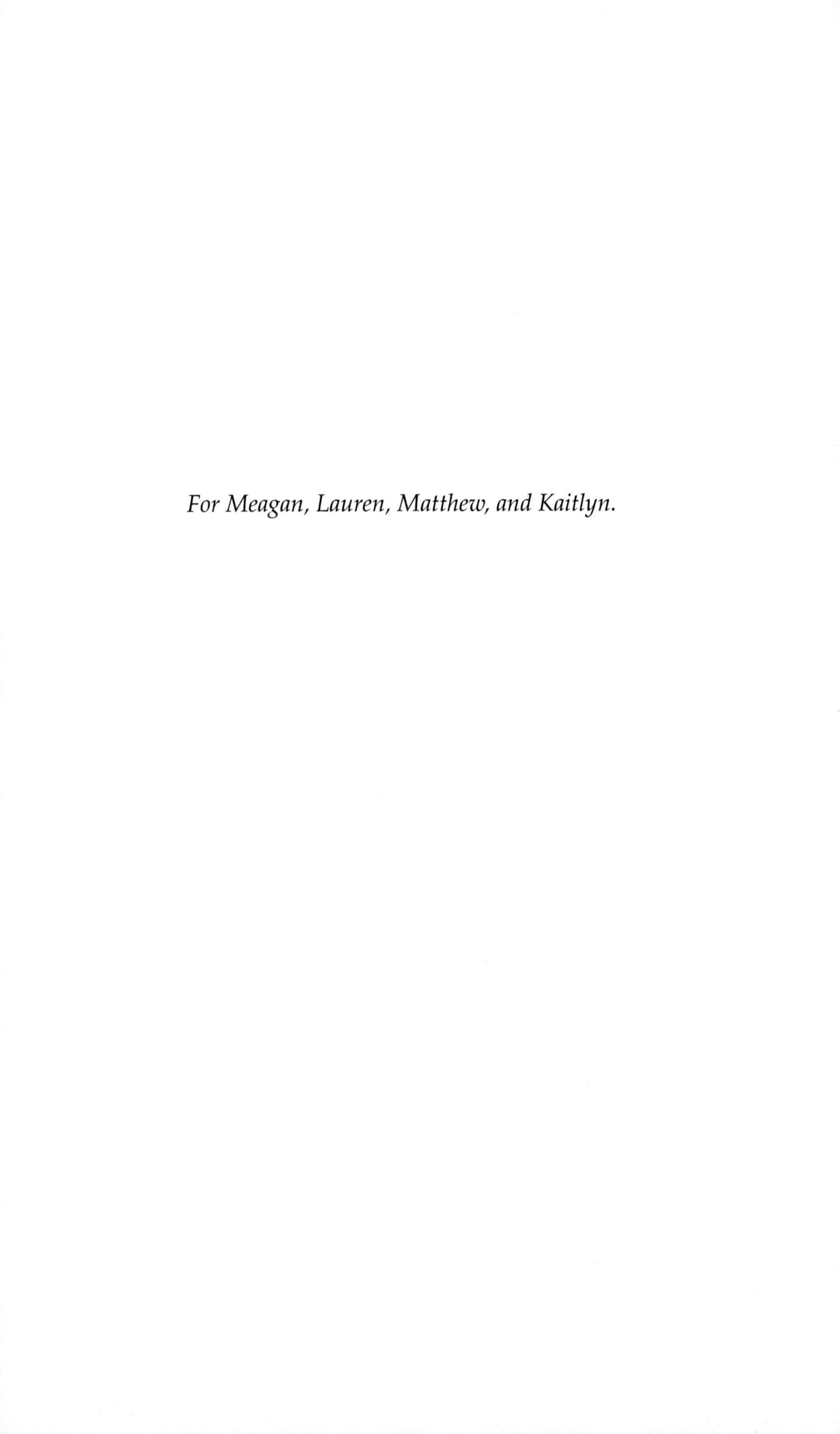

For Meagan, Lauren, Matthew, and Kaitlyn.

CHAPTER ONE

Franklyn Eaglechild slumped on the examination table, legs over the edge, and stared at the row of X-rays.

"Remind me, how many previous fractures?" the doctor asked.

"About fifty."

"All from rodeo?"

"No, some from hockey."

The doctor sighed. "The body wasn't meant to take this abuse. I'm amazed you're still walking."

"About that … the pain pills aren't doing a lot. I need something stronger."

The doctor turned and sighed. "Look, Franklyn, OxyContin is all I can prescribe. I shouldn't be doing that anymore."

"What's the option?"

"You gotta stop rodeo. Your next argument with a two-thousand-pound bull could be your last. Any subsequent fractures might not heal. Besides, you can hardly move. How would you dodge a bull?"

"Don't ride bulls anymore." Franklyn smirked. "Just steer wrestling."

"Oh great, so you jump off a speeding horse to wrestle five hundred pounds of steer to the ground." The doctor shook his head. "What could possibly go wrong with that?"

"Come on, doc, it's all I know."

"Why do you sell yourself short? A month ago, you said you were applying for a job. What happened with that?"

"It's back on the rez."

The doctor leaned against the wall and crossed his arms. "What's wrong with that?"

Franklyn shrugged. "I haven't been on the rez for twenty-five years."

"But it's home. You got folks there?"

"Nobody close. My parents died a long time ago. Grandparents, too. Don't know if I'd recognize anyone."

The doctor pushed off the wall and stepped over to Franklyn. "As I told you a month ago, rodeo is in your past. If you jump off another horse, it could cripple you for life."

"No options?"

The doctor rolled his eyes. "What about the job?"

"Speargrass Tribe advertised for an arena manager." Franklyn grinned. "But they offered me the job of sheriff.

"Are you kidding me?"

"Nope."

"You got any experience?"

"Some," Franklyn said. "I worked the Montana Highway Patrol. Primarily winter months after rodeo season."

"That's better than continuing rodeo and being crippled."

"I didn't think I'd get the job." Franklyn held out his shaking right hand. "Will I be able to hold a gun?"

"You'll be able to hold it, but I can't guarantee you'll be able to pull the trigger too many times. And you might not be accurate."

"About the pain?"

"I'll give you a two-month prescription for Oxy. But you must stop rodeo and take care of your body. Maybe try yoga."

"Are you insane?"

"Hey, pro athletes swear by it. Try it." The doctor grinned. "Lots of women go to yoga."

Franklyn's head jerked up. "Lots of women?"

"Lots."

Franklyn pulled out of the truck stop in Shelby, Montana, and headed east on Montana highway number eighty-nine. His Ford F350 effortlessly pulled the horse trailer. He'd stuffed his belongings into the camper—not a lot of stuff for a guy thirty-seven-years old. He had never needed a lot, just a noble horse, a few dollars in his pocket, and enough gas to get to the next rodeo. Now, he was headed back to the rez—a place he'd sworn never to return.

There had been nothing for him growing up on the rez, and little had changed. The Speargrass Indian Reserve covered land northeast of Great Falls, Montana. When he was ten or eleven, his grandfather drove him to Canada to go to the summer rodeos. They'd freely crossed the border at Aden or Wildhorse, but it could have been anywhere in between since the border wasn't patrolled.

Now, it was more challenging—a treaty card could get you into the States, but Canada required a US passport. That didn't mean there wasn't a hassle pretty much every time using the official crossings. Taking his horse back and forth provided an excuse for the border guards, in both countries, to give him grief.

The miles slipped away as he cruised south through endless fields of cattle. He drove with the window open and enjoyed the breeze.

The sound of a siren interrupted the quiet drive. Franklyn glanced in his mirror. Red-and-blue flashing lights of a Montana Cascade County Deputy Sheriff's cruiser. He vaguely remembered a cruiser passing him going west a few minutes ago. *Shit.*

Franklyn slowed the truck and pulled to the gravel shoulder. He'd been through this before. He stared straight ahead and kept his hands on the steering wheel.

He checked the mirror. The deputy was typing on his car computer. Finally, he exited the cruiser and marched to the truck.

"Afternoon, sir. Driver's license, registration, and insurance."

Franklyn reached across the truck and opened the glove box. From the corner of his eye, he noticed the deputy drop his hand to his gun. Franklyn slowly pulled a blue folder out of the glove box and handed it to the cop.

"Registration and insurance."

The cop nodded.

"My wallet is in my right back pocket. I'm getting that now."

Again, the deputy nodded. "You seem to know the routine. You been in trouble with the police?"

Franklyn pulled out his wallet, slid out his driver's license, and handed it to the cop. "Not in trouble, just stopped a lot." Franklyn eyed the deputy.

The deputy smiled, then his eyes peered at the driver's license. "You know why I stopped you?"

"Cuz I'm Indian?"

The cop scowled. "You getting smart with me?"

"If that's not the reason, then you tell me why *you* stopped me."

"You were crossing the centerline," the cop said. "You been drinking?"

"No. I have not been drinking."

"Step out of the truck, please." The deputy stood back a few feet, hand still on his gun. "I need to test you for impairment."

Franklyn stepped out of the truck. "I wasn't drinking."

"I want you to walk away from me in a straight line, one foot in front of the other, for ten feet, then turn and walk back to me."

Franklyn wobbled away from the deputy and muttered, "This is bullshit." He returned and stopped in front of the cop.

"You're wobbly," the cop said. "You sure you weren't drinking?"

"I have injured hips and knees from rodeo."

"Right." He held out a device with a mouthpiece. "This is a roadside breathalyzer. I need you to grip the mouthpiece between your teeth, form a tight seal with your lips, and blow."

Franklyn clenched his teeth, exhaled slowly through his nose and grabbed the device. He followed the deputy's request, one he'd given to others dozens of times in his own position as Montana Highway Patrol.

The deputy glanced at the reading. "Have a seat in the truck."

Franklyn slid into the seat and watched the cop march back to his cruiser.

Some things happened too regularly—like getting stopped because he was Indian and the assumption he'd been drinking. You'd think you'd get used to it, but you didn't. As Franklyn sat in his truck, he worked himself up. The anger typically buried deep bubbled to the surface.

The deputy tapped on the window. "Step out of the vehicle."

"What for?" Franklyn asked.

"You're under arrest."

"For what?"

"Driving while under the influence."

"I wasn't drinking. There's no way the breathalyzer showed any alcohol."

"Maybe, but I think you're high. Step out of the vehicle and keep your hands where I can see them."

Franklyn's hands shook. His heartbeat hammered in his neck. His jaw clenched.

One deputy. An empty stretch of roadway with the border an hour away. Franklyn could be in Canada before they found this guy. He wouldn't kill him. Just use his handcuffs against him.

Franklyn *could* tell the deputy he was going to the rez to be sheriff, but that wouldn't matter to this guy. Could say he had been MHP. This guy would laugh.

Franklyn opened the door and got out. He turned and faced the side of the truck and put his hands on his head.

"I knew you'd done this before." The cop yanked first one arm, then the second, and cinched the cuffs tight.

"My horse is in that trailer," Franklyn said.

"I've got a tow truck coming, and animal control will take

care of your horse while you're in jail." He shoved Franklyn toward his cruiser.

Franklyn sat on the wooden bench in the cell's corner, staring at the ceiling. Not his first time in a jail cell. Not the first time in jail when he had done nothing wrong. They'd given him the breathalyzer—he'd passed. They did more sobriety tests—most, he passed. He just didn't walk straight. The cop got excited when he found the pill bottle of Oxy. The deputy said he was adding a charge of possession of a narcotic. Franklyn finally convinced the cop to call his doctor. That had been two hours ago.

He stood and paced. The cell was the usual eight by eight, bars on three sides, and a brick wall at the back. There were six cells. Four of them held other Indians, all asleep. One was vacant.

His hip throbbed, and his knees creaked. First, from driving, then from the seventy-minute trip to Great Falls. He hoped walking would loosen his joints.

"Franklyn Eaglechild," a loud voice boomed.

Franklyn faced the cell door. The man at the door stared, an amused expression on this face. Franklyn stared back. There was something familiar about this tall, broad-shouldered man with short brown hair. He wore a dark leather jacket and jeans, a blue-checkered shirt, no tie, and cowboy boots. Franklyn cocked his head to the side.

The voice boomed again. "Don't tell me you don't remember your best friend?"

"Riley?"

Riley Briggs smiled. "Gibson, for Christ's sake, open the door."

Gibson stepped around Riley and opened the cell door. "Yes, sir."

Franklyn stepped out and glanced at the deputy's nametag: *BJ Gibson*. He'd remember that.

Franklyn rubbed his wrists. He wasn't sure what to do. Riley solved that with a bear hug. "What the hell are you doing in my cells?"

Franklyn glanced at Gibson. "He seems to think I'm impaired."

"Are you?" Riley asked.

"No." Franklyn gave Gibson an icy stare. Gibson's eyes followed the exchange—mouth open.

"I'm beat up from rodeo and hockey and don't walk too well. My back is stiff, and my hips feel like they're locked. He thinks I'm drunk cuz I'm Indian."

"No, that's not—"

Riley held up a hand. "Gibson lose that arrest report. Franklyn, come with me."

Franklyn followed Riley to a spacious corner office. "Fancy office."

"Cascade County Sheriff's office," Riley said.

"You're the sheriff?"

"No. He's away. He hates it when I use his office. I try to leave something to rot in his desk drawer."

"You always were spiteful."

"How long has it been?" Riley asked. "Twenty years?"

Franklyn laughed. "We're not that old. Maybe fifteen."

"How have you been?"

"I'm okay. You appear to be doing well. No uniform—

tailored jacket. Are you some big-wig in the sheriff's department?"

"I'm a Drug Enforcement Administration agent—the great and terrible DEA."

"Wow. A narc."

"Yup. I lead a drug task team. My partner, Leigh Blake, is FBI and there's an Alcohol, Tobacco and Firearms agent that steps in when I need him. Those ATF guys are serious about cracking down right now."

"Do they know about your teen years?"

"Nothing happened then."

"Uh-huh."

"I did my time in sheriff's offices in western Montana for ten years. Then DEA SWAT for seven. Now, I'm working out of Great Falls—back home."

"Some super cop."

Riley laughed. "Now and then I'd see your name in the paper setting some record for bull riding or steer wrestling and winning some show."

"Yeah, bull riding is in the past."

"Why?"

"I'm too beat up," Franklyn said. "Body parts don't move so well, and I hurt in places I didn't know I had places. Steer wrestling is over."

"What're you going to do?"

Franklyn grinned. "You won't believe me."

"Try me."

"I'm going to be the sheriff for the Speargrass Indian Reservation."

"I'll be damned." Riley burst out laughing. "That's if you get out of my jail."

"I did nothing wrong."

"Jeez, I've never heard that excuse before." Riley smiled. "What happened?"

"Your cop was going west. I was going east. He spotted an Indian driving a new truck with a fancy horse trailer and he U-turned. I wasn't speeding. He said I crossed the yellow line. Big deal. The road is straight till you hit Minneapolis."

Riley sat back in his chair. "Yeah, Gibson is a problem. He has an issue with Indians. He shouldn't be here or near any reserve, but no other sheriff's department will take him. Sometimes I get stuck using him."

"Guys like him make all cops appear rotten," Franklyn said. "Trust is low … doesn't exist at all."

"I heard you were working Montana Highway Patrol, but we were never in the same area at the same time."

"That's because every year when I'd come back from rodeo season, they'd send me to a new posting. MHP used my absence as a reason to ship me out. Each time it was further remote and more snow."

"Highway Patrol got you some experience, but nothing that will prepare you for working with the tribal council. This will differ from highway patrol."

"I know."

Riley leaned over the desk. "Being sheriff on the rez will not be easy."

"I need a job," Franklyn said. "It's either rodeo or cop. That's what I know."

"The politics will drive you crazy," Riley said. "Do you have any idea what you've agreed to?"

"It can't be too bad."

Riley laughed. "My friend. You'll be busier than I am. Montana hasn't got a town as wild as Speargrass."

"But they have tribal police. That's a good thing, isn't it?"

Riley shook his head. "Franklyn, nothing happens on that reserve without Chief Fox's okay. Sure, there are police, but it's selective enforcement. If you are for the chief, you're protected. If you're against the chief, well—"

"It's always been that way," Franklyn said. "It's the same anywhere you go—city or reserve, it doesn't matter."

"That's true. Just keep your eyes open, your back to the wall, your mouth shut, and trust no one."

"That's dramatic."

"Perhaps. Remember, you have a friend here. Whatever you need, just ask."

"I accept the offer if I don't get arrested coming here." Franklyn smirked.

"I'll take care of that." Riley stood. "Let's get your truck and horse trailer back and get you out of here."

CHAPTER TWO

THE SUN WAS SETTING WHEN FRANKLYN FINALLY DROVE INTO THE rez townsite. Not actually a town, never had been. There was a new school. The arena appeared the same, just older and in need of some serious repairs. That rink had been his salvation. If it hadn't been for hockey early on, he'd have nothing. Hockey in the fall and winter led to rodeo in the spring. Then the cycle repeated. He'd thought hockey was his ticket out. Funny how things don't work out according to plan. He'd been a decent hockey player and might have played in some minor pro league, but rodeo had been the right decision. Well, except for the broken bones, concussions, and the constant pain. He drove past a health center. It stood out from the surrounding buildings—fresher paint, a sign without graffiti. He would need to stop there soon and get a new doctor.

There was one vehicle at the administration office. He parked his truck and trailer along the fence and headed up the steps. He stepped inside the building into the expansive lobby.

The walls, decorated with tribal paintings, rose at least two stories to a half-dozen sun lights. Little light streamed in. At least half the lightbulbs were out. He checked to the left, then to the right, then strode straight ahead where a colossal buffalo head peered back.

There were no signs directing him to the chief's office. Franklyn had a choice of three halls. He nodded to the buffalo and strode straight ahead. He searched for names on the office doors, but there were none.

"We're closed."

Franklyn spun to the voice. A man wearing a dark uniform shirt and shoulder crests that said *Tribal Police* blocked the hallway. He was shorter than Franklyn with black hair and high cheekbones. Franklyn stared down at the skinny guy, reading the name on the shirt. "Crow, I'm here to see Chief Fox."

Crow crossed his arms. "He's not meeting anyone tonight."

"Well, tell him Franklyn Eaglechild is here to see him."

"You're late. Wait here." Crow turned and headed down the hall.

Franklyn scanned a bulletin board with job postings. Public works needed a grader operator, tribal police officers required, and the gas bar and *Subway* needed workers. The Speargrass Golden Nugget Casino had a dozen jobs posted. At least there were jobs. Twenty-five years ago, there were no jobs. The rez quickly slipped into poverty.

"Hey, Eaglechild," Crow said. "The chief will see you."

Crow led Franklyn down the hallway to a corner office. Two sides were all window and overlooked the river. It was an impressive view. In the pink light, he could see deer on the water's edge.

Chief Myron Fox turned away from the window. "Thanks,

Hiram. I've got this." He studied Franklyn. "Franklyn Eaglechild. Good to see you. You resemble your grandfather. I remember when he was chief. Not a lot older than you. Sit."

Franklyn slid into a padded chair.

Chief Fox sat behind an enormous oak desk. He crossed his arms, interlocking his fingers over his bulging belly. He puffed out his cheeks on an exhale, his tiny square glasses making his already chubby cheeks appear even chubbier. Franklyn clocked him as late fifties. The black hair was gray at the fringes like you get when you color your hair. At first glance, he appeared like someone's grandfather. Then you noticed the dark, piercing eyes and felt a chill.

"It was tough times for a long while. Oil royalties dropped to practically nil. Federal funding wasn't enough. Our people were in poverty. Hands out all the time. I knew it was for drugs. Our people were dying. Every week we had a funeral. Sometimes two. Drugs, suicide, murder."

Franklyn sat back. It was never respectable to interrupt a chief when he was pontificating. He'd let you know when it was your turn.

"The white man kept us begging. I wanted our trust fund—not in their hands, in ours. I wouldn't beg anymore. I wouldn't follow their rules. This was my tribe. I turned it around, not them."

The chief stared out the window at the orange glow from the setting sun. Finally, he swung back.

"What changed?" Franklyn asked.

"The casino. The feds wouldn't give money, but they loaned us money to build the casino. I accepted their money. We built a school and a health center. Now we had jobs. Next year we will build a new hockey arena."

"It sounds like things are going great."

"It is better. We have food and shelter. But white man's loans bring additional problems."

"Drugs?"

Fox nodded. "Too many like the money but not the work. For everyone with a job and working hard, there are two wanting to get money the easy way—shoplifting, assault, home burglary, car theft."

"It seems like there are jobs at the casino."

"Yes, many jobs. Not enough workers."

Fox stared out the window again. He was quiet for several minutes. When he turned back, the lines on his face were tight, and his dark eyes stared through Franklyn.

"You report to me. Tell me everything. Tomorrow, come back at nine. The Tribal Police office is on the upper level at the back. You have a receptionist and three constables. You've met Hiram Crow."

"Three? That's not a lot."

"It's what you get unless you can hire additional deputies. Good luck with that."

"About my pay?"

"Talk to Eva Redstone tomorrow. She runs Human Resources."

Franklyn nodded. "Where can I stay tonight? I've got a camper. Just need a place to park."

The chief shrugged. "Up to you. Park behind the building or at the arena." The chief opened a drawer and pulled out a large ring of keys. "Here. These are the keys to everything. One will fit the arena door. Stay there. There are bathrooms and showers —the best option for tonight. There's a house you can use when you get settled. One of your deputies, either Leroy Balam or

Hiram Crow can take you. It needs some work before moving in." The chief stood and faced the window. "Remember, I need to know everything."

Franklyn parked on the gravel outside the arena. He'd spent a lot of time here in his early teens—sunup to sundown. It was the gathering spot for kids. The one place for recreational activity. At one time, it was a safe haven for kids. Then the gangs formed, and the drugs were plentiful. Fewer and fewer children or teens played hockey. They toked up behind the arena, then came back in to watch the games. Soon harder drugs were available—heroin and crack. The arena was no longer safe. Then he was taken away from the rez. Managing the arena would have been a decent job. Maybe he could have restored it to a safe place for kids.

Franklyn grabbed a flashlight from the truck. At the main doors, he pulled out the ring of keys and tried them one by one. After about ten tries, the lock clicked.

He entered the dark arena. It was cool with the odor of strong cleaning products. He could have hiked around the arena blindfolded. He still remembered every nook and cranny. He followed the hall to the manager's office. Inside was the panel for lights.

Again, he tried several keys before he found the right one. He shone his flashlight on the panel. Someone had taken the time to label each breaker. He pushed all the switches and lights came on. A chair and an empty desk sat in one corner and a pile of hockey gear in another. It appeared as if the manager's office hadn't been used for a long time.

He headed back down the hall to the dressing rooms. The showers were stained from the hard water, but clean. The toilet was new. This wouldn't be an awful place to stay for a few nights if he had to. But he would stay one night and tomorrow move into the house.

He filled a bucket with water and headed back to the truck. He unlocked the trailer, and his horse backed out. Franklyn stroked his head and neck. The horse nuzzled into Franklyn's chest. "Hey, Diesel. Long day. Here's some water, then you can stretch your legs."

Diesel drained the bucket. Franklyn grabbed the flashlight and the reins and led Diesel around the arena. The back was fenced and housed a large water tank and the condenser. Big enough for the horse for tonight. They finished the circle around the arena. Franklyn filled the bucket and led Diesel to the back enclosure. He left the horse there and made two additional trips with some feed and hay.

He unhitched the trailer and drove to the combined gas bar and *Subway*. He fueled the truck and got a sub, chips, and Coke. Back at the arena he sat outside on the fresh-cut grass and ate. So, this was his lot in life. Full circle. He was back at the reservation he was forced to leave when he was twelve.

The lights outside the arena were smashed. He sat in the darkness staring at the stars. His head bobbed a few times.

One more trip into the arena and then to sleep. Something rustled the gravel as he neared the camper. He stopped and stared into the darkness. When his eyes adjusted, he glimpsed the glow of two eyes. They didn't move. When he stepped toward the eyes, they disappeared, only to reappear ten feet to the right. He could pick out the features of a dog. At least he hoped it was a dog. He stepped to the bumper of the truck and tossed the remnants of his sub. Franklyn knelt and waited. After about five minutes, the dog snuck out of the darkness to the food, ate hungrily, then disappeared.

Franklyn stood and stretched—his knees and back popping. Too much time sitting in the driver's seat, too many aches. Pain in his back, shoulders, knees—well, everywhere. He pulled a pill bottle out of the glove box and popped two Oxy with the last of the Coke, then lumbered to the arena, hoping there was hot water for a long shower.

CHAPTER THREE

RILEY BRIGGS DROVE DOWN THE GRAVEL ROAD SEARCHING FOR A signpost for the abandoned farm. He'd passed fields of cows for the last five miles. The landscape changed to tall pines. He found the signpost. He drove onto an overgrown farm trail and parked his Yukon at the side of the road behind the ambulance, three dark Suburbans, and a few Cascade County Deputy Sheriffs' Patrol cruisers. He jogged toward a DEA SWAT team standing beside a Suburban.

He held up a piece of paper. "Got the warrant."

"Any problems?" Leigh Blake asked. She was Riley's partner and an FBI Agent. At five foot four and not more than one hundred pounds, the redhead appeared tiny around this group of alpha males. She was an expert in martial arts, a marksman, and an avid dirt biker. Riley had yet to see her use any of those skills.

"Nope. The judge accepted the information. He's keen to get drugs off the street, so we're ready to go."

He turned to a hulking man in tactical gear. DEA SWAT Sergeant Hank Deaver was a veteran of the war in Afghanistan and the Iraq War as a member of Delta Force. He was one of the meanest men Riley knew. Deaver had the team ready for action.

"Deaver, have you checked the layout?"

"The farmhouse is about three hundred feet down this path. A truck and van are parked out front. Past the house is crumbling barn and another house that looks like it's been here for a hundred years. A path winds past two falling granaries and leads down the hill to the well. No one was awake when we checked the place out. Mind you, it was dark then."

"This time of day they'll be sleeping," Riley said. "My informant said there are four to six scumbags in the house. At least three males and they have extensive records for assault, guns, and drugs. Don't trust the women either. They'll scratch your eyes out if given a chance. Be alert for rifles and pistols, but they could have any weapon in there—and drugs. Tell your men to be alert and careful."

Deaver scowled. "They're always alert and careful. And as mean as a pack of rabid dogs. You worry about your sorry ass." He strode over to his team. "Gear up. We go in hard and fast."

Blake handed Riley a DEA ballistic vest and slipped on her own, FBI emblazoned on the front and back. "SWAT going to clear the house first?"

"Screw that," Riley said. "We're going in with them. It's six a.m. These shitheads are sleeping. We've got surprise on our side."

"It's policy to let SWAT go first."

"I'll let them go first, but we'll be second," Riley said. "You can stay out here with your nanny but you'll miss the fun.

Deaver, let's do this." Riley grabbed a shotgun from one of the sheriff's deputies. "You won't need this."

Riley followed SWAT close to the trees down the lane toward the farmhouse. SWAT split into two groups, one jogging to the back of the house, the other, led by Deaver, to the front. Riley followed Deaver, and Blake followed Riley.

When they reached the front of the farmhouse, Deaver counted down by lowering his fingers.

Three. Two. One.

A SWAT member swung a heavy battering ram. The door frame splintered, and the door swung open.

"Police. Search warrant," Riley and Blake yelled.

They heard a door breaking at the back of the house. More shouts. "SWAT. Search warrant."

Deaver and two SWAT veered left toward the kitchen. Riley and Blake to the right, toward the living room. A man on the floor crawled toward the couch.

"Don't move," Riley said.

The man hesitated.

Riley sensed movement from the right—a man charged at him. Riley struck him across the forehead with the butt of the shotgun.

The suspect collapsed to the floor. Riley stepped on the suspect's shoulder with his foot to pin him and swung the shotgun back to the living room.

The man on the floor reached frantically under the couch pillow, pulled out a pistol, and swung up his arm.

Riley leveled the shotgun and fired. The 00 buckshot pellets peppered the man's shoulder. He slumped against the couch, blood gushing from a half dozen holes.

The pinned man struggled to rise.

"Don't fucking move. Blake, cuff this guy and get that gun."

Deaver and his guys rushed into the living room.

"Get your medic to check this guy," Riley said.

"Medic up," Deaver shouted.

The SWAT medic knelt next to the suspect and applied a dressing to his shoulder.

The SWAT team from the back of the house pushed two men and two women in cuffs down the hallway to the living room.

"You four get on your knees." Deaver keyed his radio. "Send the sheriff's deputies here to transport the prisoners." He glanced to the suspect by the couch. "Get EMS heading here. Tell them one gunshot to the shoulder."

"Roger," dispatch replied.

"Okay," Riley said. "Let's see what we can find."

Riley, Blake, and Deaver searched the house. In the first bedroom, they found a .44 magnum under a pillow and a loaded shotgun behind the bedroom door. In the toilet tank, they discovered large baggies of marijuana.

SWAT searched the other bedroom and found a half dozen handguns, some marijuana, and a few baggies with pills, likely Oxy.

They met in the hall.

"We're missing something." Riley rubbed the stubble of his beard. "We'd find this shit in most dealers' homes."

"Nothing special here, Riley," Blake said. "No guns other than the ones these shitheads had. Nothing you can use to justify popping that scrote."

"I haven't heard anyone use scrote in ten years. Are you having a flashback? Is this retro Tuesday?"

Blake frowned. "Make all the jokes you want. That guy dies

and a baggie of marijuana is all we've got, they'll nuke your career."

"My career is already nuked. We're stationed in Great Falls, Montana. What's worse than that?"

"They could make you liaison to Speargrass," Deaver said.

"Okay, that would be worse. My snitch—"

"Confidential Informant," Blake said.

"My CI insisted they had drugs here for distribution."

Blake shrugged. "Maybe they were tipped off?"

Deaver shook his head. "If they knew we were coming this place would be cleaner than a Holiday Inn."

"I agree," Riley said. "Either the sni—CI is full of shit, or—"

Blake raised an eyebrow. "What?"

Riley snapped his fingers. "Say you're a dealer. You're hiding out on a farm. You wouldn't keep the drugs in your house. There are hundreds of places on a farm to hide stuff. Let's check the outbuildings."

They headed to the barn. The entire structure leaned to the right, the roof had collapsed in several places, and all the glass was broken. The door hung on one hinge. When Riley pulled, the door crashed to the ground.

"Hardly secure," Blake said.

The smell of manure and wet straw hung heavy in the air. Dust and bird crap littered outdated farm machinery. The stalls were covered with moldy straw mixed with horse shit. Riley kicked at a pile of straw and a half-dozen mice scattered. The other stalls were the same—moldy straw, shit, and scrambling mice.

Blake closed the door to a storeroom. "I checked all the shelves and drawers—no drugs or guns or anything illegal."

Riley climbed the homemade ladder to the loft. It was barren, except for bird shit and rats scattering as his boots stepped on the creaking floor. The open window provided a panoramic view of the farm—the farmhouse to the left, tilting granaries to the right and a lean-to. Everything was at least a hundred years old. Riley's stomach tightened. His gut was telling him something. He descended the ladder. "Let's check the granaries and the shed."

They checked a toolshed, two wooden granaries, and a lean-to with a rusting tractor and bailer—nothing.

"There has to be something here," Deaver said. "Back to the barn."

Riley stood in the middle of the barn floor and rotated in a full circle. "We found nothing on the main level, and I checked the loft—nada. Spread out in a line, and we'll work our way across the barn."

Blake stomped her foot on the floor. "I've got something." She stomped again. "Sounds hollow."

Riley knelt and, with a gloved hand, brushed away the dirt and straw—a trap door.

"Bingo." Riley used his knife to locate the sides.

Blake brushed away more straw. "I found a handle."

"Let's see what's down there," Riley said.

Deaver and Blake drew their pistols and aimed toward the opening.

Deaver nodded. "Ready."

Riley pulled the metal ring and swung the door upward. A blast of cool air escaped from the darkness. The top of a ladder was visible. Deaver cracked two glow sticks and tossed them into the hole.

"I'm going down." Riley, pistol in hand, stepped into the

opening and descended the ladder. The odor of wet loam was strong. He shone his flashlight around the pit. Two walls were nothing but dirt. On the third wall were several shelves. At least a half dozen crates were stacked against the fourth wall.

"It's clear," Riley said.

Deaver and Blake descended the ladder. There were seven wooden cases, approximately four feet long, two feet wide, and eighteen inches high, and two moving-style boxes. Deaver and Riley lifted the top crate off the pile and set it on the ground.

Deaver jammed a pry bar into the top of the crate and yanked. There was a screeching noise as the nails slid out of the wood. Riley pushed open the lid. Blake shone her flashlight into the crate. The container held twelve M4 assault rifles in two rows of six.

Riley whistled. "They're brand new."

Deaver nodded. "They're in better shape than our rifles. Maybe we could do a swap."

Riley's head jerked up, and then he noticed the grin on Deaver's face. The first time he'd seen Deaver smile or have a sense of humor.

"Had you for a minute," Deaver said.

Riley chuckled. "Check the other crates."

Two more crates held M4s. The fourth and fifth crates held two rows of pistols—Glock 22—40 Cal.

"I really want to trade," Deaver said.

They lifted the sixth crate onto the floor and removed the lid. AK47s, stacked two high, complete with the telltale banana magazines.

The seventh crate was jammed with ammunition—40 Cal. for the Glock, .223 for the M4, and 7.62 39 mm for the AK47s.

"Jeez," Blake said. "You could go to war with this stuff."

"That's what some gang intended," Deaver said.

"Who were these guys selling the guns to?" Blake asked.

Riley grabbed a Glock, pulled the slide back, and peered down the barrel. "Any criminal element—Red Demons or other outlaw motorcycle gangs, street gangs, or white supremacists."

"Where did the guns come from?" Blake asked.

"From the same source—an arms or gun dealer," Deaver said. "The M4s are new, and these are the original crates. The AKs aren't new, but the ammunition is in the original boxes."

"We'll be able to check the serial numbers," Riley said. "It's a place to start." He pulled out a knife and slit the tape at the top of one a box. "Well, lookie here."

Blake and Deaver peered over Riley's shoulder.

"Cell phones?" Blake raised an eyebrow.

"Not just any cell phones—BlackBerrys," Riley said.

"Does that mean something?" Blake eyed the phones.

"You bet," Riley said. "BlackBerrys are the choice of drug dealers and shitheads everywhere. In the good old days, all dealers had to worry about was cops pulling them over or tapping their home phone. Now they need to worry about cops or competition reading their text messages and emails. The NSA can remotely activate the cameras on cell phones and computers. That's a problem we should all worry about. The plan is to leave no digital footprint. Apple and Google harvest your information and share it with advertisers and the NSA. BlackBerry is better because it doesn't harvest your data—the software doesn't allow it. That's why you see most government employees carrying a BlackBerry because messages are strongly encrypted." Riley knelt next to the gun cases. "Oh, shit."

Deaver squatted beside him. "What's up?"

Riley pointed to indentations in the dirt. "There were more cases here."

"Are they hidden somewhere else?" Blake asked.

Riley stood and shook his head. "No. They already sold a few cases."

CHAPTER FOUR

FRANKLYN'S BODY SWAYED WITH THE MOTION OF THE BOAT. THE SKY was blue, and the air salty. The movement was soothing and … then he sat up. He wasn't in a boat. His camper was rocking back and forth. He threw open the door and was face to face with a horse. Not his horse. The rez had a few herds of wild horses. He pushed the horses away and jumped to the ground. About a dozen horses surrounded the truck and camper. At least half were rubbing against some part of the truck.

"Yeah, get away." A few moved. Most stared. He slapped one on the butt. It ambled toward the arena. The rest followed.

He watched as they lumbered around the corner of the building in no hurry. A black and silver dog slipped in behind them, casting several glances over his shoulder.

The sun was barely above the horizon. His watch said 5:45. He stretched and climbed back into the camper.

He slid into bed and tried to sleep. By 6:30, he gave up.

After a shower and shave, he pulled his clean hair back into a long braid and dressed for his first day on the job. He fed Diesel, filled the five-gallon water bucket, and headed to the administration building. His stomach growled, so he swung into the *Subway* parking lot—closed. *Damn.*

He parked at the back of the administration building, grabbed his battered briefcase, and headed to the door. Franklyn pulled out the ring of keys from the chief and tested a few, but his fingers kept fumbling, and his wrist shook until he dropped them. Screw it. He'd figure out which one worked later. He shouldn't be the first one here, anyway. He knocked on the glass door. No answer. He pounded on the door. Still no answer. He wandered to the back of the building and peered in the windows, ready to try the keys again. Through the second window, he noticed a guy in a tribal police shirt lying back in his chair, feet on the desk, sound asleep. Franklyn figured if he was up, the cop should be awake. He pounded on the window.

The cop leaned back in his chair as his head came forward. The backward momentum more than compensated for the slight rise in his head, and the officer fell onto the floor. He stumbled to his feet and glanced around. Franklyn pounded on the window again and pointed to the door.

The door opened, and a cop blocked the entrance. Franklyn glanced down at the dull eyes and pock-marked face with a rosacea-reddened nose. His hair was pulled back into a greasy ponytail.

"Office doesn't open till nine," the cop said. "Go away and come back later." He pulled the door.

Franklyn put his boot into the doorway and grabbed the handle. "I need to come in."

"I don't care what you need." The cop pulled on the door, but it didn't budge.

"What's your name?"

The cop eyed Franklyn, who was at least five inches taller and outweighed him by fifty pounds. "Leroy Balam—Tribal Police. Who the hell are you?"

"Your new boss." Franklyn yanked on the door and pushed past Balam. "Show me my office."

Paper coffee cups littered the desk, the tops of file cabinets, the windowsill, and around the wastebasket—which, ironically, was empty. Several stacks of assorted paperwork covered the desk. Any space not occupied by coffee cups had piles of file folders. He tossed his briefcase on the floor. At least this office appeared like they used it, unlike the arena manager's office.

Franklyn collected all the coffee cups and other garbage and filled two garbage bags. Then he selected the top three or four files off each stack and set them on a corner of his desk. The rest, he set on one of the two visitor chairs. Outside his office, he found a closet with cleaning supplies. He wiped the desk, phone, computer, monitor, and chair. He cleaned out the desk drawers. With a sense of accomplishment, he sat and turned on the computer. It asked for a login and password. *Perfect.* He headed to the reception area. "Balam. Balam."

The reception was empty, and another room with four desks facing each other, two by two, was vacant. His watch said 8:15. He filled a coffee pot from the bottled water dispenser and waited as the coffee brewed.

The office was musty and cluttered. The room the deputies used, with the four desks, was a disaster. The one sign of organization came from a desk by the reception counter.

Coffee brewed, he filled a paper cup and made a mental note to buy a mug–a big mug. He rocked back in his chair and enjoyed the first sip of heaven. He grabbed the first file and flipped it open—duty roster. Balam worked night shifts, midnight to 8 a.m. Hiram Crow worked days, 8-4. Calvin Lefebvre got the swing shift, 4 p.m. to midnight, and was the only cop listed to be called if help was needed after midnight. The computer-generated schedule also served as a timesheet.

The second file contained the crime stats for the last month. A lot of disturbances, frequent drunkenness, and a few fights. What was missing was arrests. Practically no arrests for the listed calls and not a single arrest for drugs—possession or trafficking. He'd seen some graffiti on the drive this morning. Yet there was no mention in the report about gang activity. Gangs meant trouble.

The third file was the budget for his departments. He quickly set that back on the desk. The fourth had handwritten notes. They all involved Balam. Complaints from reservation members and businesses. Notes about tardiness, missing shifts, and drunkenness at work. That matched Franklyn's first impression.

The door to their office closed with a thud. Franklyn needed a coffee anyway. He slipped around his desk and out into the reception area. A young woman wearing glasses, about five foot five with a long black braid like Franklyn's own, was staring at the coffee maker.

"Good morning," Franklyn said.

The woman shrieked and dropped her backpack. She spun, and after the moment of surprise, found her composure. "What are you doing here?"

"I work here." Franklyn was enjoying the game.

Not willing to back down, she said, "Okay, then who are you?" Her feet were set, her arms crossed.

"Franklyn Eaglechild."

She nodded. "You were to be here yesterday."

"I was delayed."

"Is this what I should expect? That you'll be here when you want to? Your own version of Indian time?"

She was someone he could work with. He immediately liked her. "Something like that. What's your name?"

"Paulette White Quills."

"What do you do here?"

"I keep you in line."

Franklyn smiled. "Full-time job."

She peered at the coffeemaker. "You made the coffee?"

"Yup."

"Is it any good?"

"Try it yourself," Franklyn said.

"I generally make coffee."

"Then you'll have to get here earlier." Franklyn refilled his cup and poured one for Paulette.

"No thanks, I don't drink coffee."

"You said you made—"

"I said I made the coffee. Not for me, though. Archie Gardner, the previous sheriff, said it was part of my job."

"Is it?"

"Not if you get here first. Let me get settled, and then I'll tell you about this place."

Ten minutes later, Paulette strode into Franklyn's office, set a box on the floor, and sat. "What do you want to know?"

"Everything."

Paulette stared over her glasses. "Is this the way it's going to be? One-word answers?"

"Maybe."

She leaned forward. "Look, funny guy. I can be your best asset or your worst enemy. You already got a bunch of enemies, so you'd best decide I'm your friend. Right now, your one friend. Let's start again. What do you want to know?"

Franklyn smirked. "Tell me about the staff."

"That's better. I'm your administrative assistant. That's the official term. I'm the receptionist, the dispatcher, I pay the bills, do the payroll, and tell you where you need to be and when. You always tell me where you are." She reached into the box. "Here's your cell phone. Always have that with you. Always." She reached into the box again. "Here is your portable radio. Always have that with you. The radio works on about sixty percent of the rez—the cell phone about ninety percent. That's why you have both."

Franklyn stared at the phone—it was new and fancy. It wasn't anything like his flip phone. He glanced at Paulette.

"It's a BlackBerry." She adjusted her glasses. "We all have them. The chief got a bargain on a case. I'll teach you how to use it. The radio is easy. It's on scan, so you'll hear our EMS and fire department, surrounding fire departments, and the Montana Highway Patrol. The Public Works department are on there, but they don't use the radio a lot."

Franklyn sighed. "Okay. What's next?"

"You have three officers—Hiram Crow, Leroy Balam, and Calvin Lefebvre."

"Lefebvre doesn't sound Indian."

"He's Métis. Young and keen and your best guy."

"What about the other guys?"

"We don't have enough time right now to talk about them."

"It's that shocking?"

"You can decide. EMS. You have sixteen full-time staff. The paramedics handle everything, so you don't have to worry about them. We don't have any Indian paramedics, so they are all from off the reserve. They work a ninety-six-hour shift, then head home. Most work shifts for other local ambulance services. They do their own purchasing of equipment, supplies, and drugs, and complete timesheets, payroll, and billing."

"Sounds like they're on top of things."

Paulette nodded. "The fire department—that's another story. There are a fire chief and two firefighters."

"Three firefighters?"

"That's on paper. They arrive at less than thirty percent of the calls. We rely heavily on the Fort Benton Fire Department about twenty minutes away—on a good day. If it's a big fire, we might have to call Great Falls."

"We call and they show up? Because they're upright guys?"

Paulette laughed. "Oh, no. They bill us."

"Do we have the budget for that?"

"Yup."

"But not the budget for additional firefighters."

"You're catching on."

"Okay, what else?"

"That's enough for day one. Oh, wait." She reached into the box and gingerly lifted out a gun and set it on the desk. Then she set three magazines on the desk. "I guess you'll need this."

Franklyn grabbed the gun, racked the action, peered into the chamber and down the barrel, ensuring it was not loaded, then held it in a shooting grip. "Nice. Colt 1911 .45 caliber."

"I know nothing about guns, but Archie wanted the best."

She tossed a keyring on the desk. "For your truck. Nothing special. It's a 2009 Ford Explorer SUV. We bought three from the MHP a few years ago. They were going to junk them. Archie got a smashing deal. Or so he thought. We spent a fortune getting them running. Yours is the newest one."

"Lovely. I'm going for a drive around the rez."

"Not yet." She stared at her notepad. "You have a meeting now with Eva Redstone in Human Resources. You know, get your paperwork signed so it's official. When you're done, come back, and I'll get the information technology guy to get you set up on the computer. Do you know how to use a computer?" She tipped her glasses down and smiled.

"Yes, Paulette. I know how to use a computer. Now get out of my office so I can get to my meeting."

Franklyn left the office and stepped out into the lobby. Then he realized he didn't have a clue where HR was. He turned back to his office but then had second thoughts. He wasn't going to ask Paulette for directions. He wandered down the hallway to another reception desk. "I'm here to meet with Human Resources."

The receptionist peered over a coffee mug. "Got a name?"

"Franklyn Eaglechild."

She glared at him. "I mean, who are you meeting."

"Oh, uh, I think it's Redstone, Eva Redstone."

"I'll let her know."

Franklyn knocked on the door, stepped inside, and stopped. Not what he expected. Seated at the desk was a Caucasian lady. "Sorry, I'm to meet Eva Redstone."

She peered up and smiled. "Did the name throw you off? Were you expecting someone with a tan?"

"No. Well, yes, I guess so."

"I'm Eva. Don't just stand there. Sit."

Franklyn put his Stetson on one chair and sat in the other.

Her eyebrows furrowed as she stared at the computer. "I know I saved your job offer."

Franklyn relaxed and admired the view. Long brown hair framed an attractive heart-shaped face. She had full lips and bright brown eyes. The light-blue T-shirt was providing a view of a lovely chest.

"Oh, here it is." She hit a button on the keyboard, and the printer sprung to life.

She swung her chair around and caught his stare. She slapped a document in front of him. "You'll like this. We offer competitive salaries and one hundred percent benefits coverage. For prescriptions, dental, massage, we cover it all. Nothing out of pocket for you."

One hundred percent coverage for prescriptions? That would come in handy. Franklyn flipped to the second page where the salary was listed. He kept his face neutral, but his brain was sparking. They were offering more than he had ever made.

"Chief Fox insisted we give you a generous offer. He wanted me to make sure you knew this was his idea."

Franklyn studied the page. "I applied to be the arena manager."

"We have a lot of vacant positions here." She leaned across the desk. Franklyn fought to keep eye contact. "So, anytime we get a résumé with terrific qualifications, we snap that person up, and we want them to stay. Your background with the Montana Highway Patrol was too good to pass on. Why waste your knowledge running the ice rink. The chief decided on your salary. You might not want to screw this up."

"I came here to do good work."

"Good for you." Eva shrugged again. "Sign here."

Franklyn headed back to his office. Under the buffalo head, an adolescent man sat, arms folded across his chest, rocking back and forth. His greasy hair hung to his shoulders.

"Are you okay?"

The head slowly lifted, eyes glazed, a faraway stare on his face. He appeared to be in his early twenties.

Franklyn peered down at the man. "What's your name?"

"Jesse."

"Jesse, what?"

"Jesse Ranger."

"You don't look well. Do you need help?"

"I'll be okay." Jesse's chin dropped to his chest. "Just got the shakes."

"Why do you have the shakes?"

Jesse shrugged. "I ain't got no drugs."

"Ah," Franklyn said. "That's a problem."

Jesse's head lifted—the vacant eyes blazed with fire. "You mocking me?"

Franklyn stepped back and held his hands up in defense. "Needing that next fix can be horrible."

"What do you know about it?"

"More than you'd believe." Franklyn glanced out the front door toward the *Subway*. "Do you need breakfast, coffee?"

Jesse's grin showed several missing teeth. "I'll take ten bucks."

"That's not negotiable. Breakfast or nothing."

Jesse's shoulders slumped. "Nah. Don't need no food."

Franklyn squeezed Jesse's shoulder. "Take care, Jesse."

Franklyn stepped into the police office and stopped beside Paulette. "What do you know about Jesse Ranger?"

She glanced up from her computer. "He's a strung-out drug addict who'll do anything to get his next fix. Why?"

"I just met him."

"You still got your wallet? Gun? Phone?"

"He seems okay."

Paulette grinned. "He conned you the first time you met him. You will have to do better, boss."

"What do you mean?"

"I don't trust him at all. He hangs out in the lobby. He's a nuisance. I get the deputies to kick him out when he becomes obnoxious."

"Good to know. Who's on duty today?"

"You." Paulette continued typing.

"Funny, smart ass. Who else?"

"Hiram Crow."

"Did he get here before me?"

Paulette laughed.

"He was here and left on patrol while I was at HR?"

Paulette shook her head.

Franklyn pulled a chair beside her desk and sat. "Okay, fill me in."

"Hiram is scheduled for day shifts, that's eight till four. He sometimes comes in by ten, occasionally."

"But I met him at about eight last night."

Paulette laughed again. "He's the chief's boy and a tribal councilor. Handpicked. Sometimes he's a bodyguard for the chief."

"The chief needs a bodyguard?"

"He's not popular with everyone."

"But last night—"

"That was for show. Chief wanted you to know he's important. He also wanted you to know Hiram Crow is *his* man."

"Call Crow and tell him I said he needs to get to work. Now."

"Okay, boss."

Franklyn turned toward his office, then stopped. "The chief said something about a house for me. You know anything about that?"

CHAPTER FIVE

RILEY AND BLAKE SAT ACROSS FROM EACH OTHER IN THE CRAMPED office writing arrest and evidence reports on the guns. They'd start by charging the suspects with possession of stolen firearms —enough to keep them in custody. The minor drug charges would come later.

"Do you have the serial numbers for the guns?" Riley asked.

"Deaver said they were nearly done," Blake said. "He'll email us a copy as soon as it's complete."

"He's taking his sweet time. Make sure you send the gun list to Dac Mahones in ATF. He'll find out where they were stolen. How's the scumbag I shot?"

"Lou Reynolds headed to surgery thirty minutes ago," Blake said. "We won't get to interview him until tomorrow morning."

"He'll have a cop at his door 24/7 until we can charge him and throw his ass in a cell." Riley entered his password into the computer. "I'll complete the report on the warrant. You work on the charges for the deputy county attorney."

"Briggs, my office."

Riley peered over his shoulder. Sheriff Jack MacDonald filled the doorway to his office, scowling under his salt-and-pepper mustache.

"You hard of hearing? I mean now." MacDonald stormed into his office.

Riley stood.

"Good luck," Blake whispered.

Riley raised his eyebrows and frowned. He sat opposite MacDonald's desk.

"Shut the fuckin' door," MacDonald ordered.

Riley pushed the door closed. "How's your day, Sheriff?"

"Don't start that shit with me, Briggs. What the hell did you think you were doing?"

"Executing a search warrant."

"Not that part, asshole. Why were you with the entry team? We have SWAT, so regular cops like you don't go rushing into dangerous situations."

"I'm not a regular cop," Riley said. "I'm a DEA special agent. I lead the drug task force. You know, the *n*arcotics *o*pioids *s*pecial *h*igh-*i*ntensity *t*askforce ..."

"Stop using that name." MacDonald's jowls jiggled as he shouted. "It's the Cascade County High-Intensity Drug Trafficking Area Program."

Riley grinned. "NO SHIT."

"Briggs!"

"Besides, I *was* SWAT—a SWAT commander. I know what I'm doing."

"I don't give a shit about what you've done before. In my county, you follow the command structure. You are not a commander anymore. You're under my authority, and you follow my rules—"

"I just use some office space here, Sheriff. Technically, I report to the president."

"Shut up." A prominent vein pulsed in MacDonald's forehead. "Your rogue days are over. That's what got you bounced out of SWAT. Blake is FBI. I don't need her complaining to her bosses."

"I'm confused here. Are you worried about me, or are you appearing stupid?"

The vein appeared on the verge of explosion.

"Blake doesn't need to get caught in your screwups and wild-west shootouts."

"Whether it was me or SWAT, that guy was going to get shot."

"If SWAT did the shooting, I wouldn't have to do an investigation. But you played John Wayne in my county. I need your officer-involved-shooting reports on my desk in two hours."

"I got a lot of paperwork to do on the arrests. Remember, the people we arrested with guns? That one?"

"Don't get smart with me, Briggs. Your end justifies the means isn't working. Blake can do the arrest reports."

"I can't dump that on her."

"You can, and you will. It's your screwup. Deal with it."

"But ..."

"Out, now," MacDonald bellowed. "Two hours."

Riley slid into his chair. "Sorry, partner. I have to do the officer-involved-shooting reports. Old MacDonald is on my case."

"Riley. You can't call him that."

"Everyone does."

"Not right outside his office."

"He's just making noise. He resents us being here. Reminds him his deputies lost control of drug trafficking here."

"I can't figure out if you have a death wish or you want to get bounced back to the Forest Ranger in Point Barrow, Alaska."

"He didn't hear me. Anyway, sorry. You're on your own to write the arrest reports for a few hours."

"It shouldn't take you that long to do the shooting report. You've done enough."

"Smartass."

CHAPTER SIX

FRANKLYN AND PAULETTE STOOD AT THE GATE. WELL, IT USED TO BE a gate—maybe twenty years ago. It barely hung from the top hinge. The fence was white at one time, now weathered, cracked, and gray. The dead grass lying flat on the ground was at least two feet long. In some places, shoots of green pushed through the thick overgrowth.

"We got a lawnmower at the office?" Franklyn asked.

Paulette shook her head. "Nope. Every spring we buy one. Every fall, it's gone. If you buy one, charge it to the tribe. Use it at your house, then bring it to the office. We need a new one, anyway."

Franklyn pushed the gate aside. The last screw failed, and the gate fell to the ground.

"Got potential." Paulette snickered.

"Real fixer-upper."

"This is one of the better homes." Paulette fought hard to keep a straight face.

Franklyn still hadn't figured out when she was messing with him. "Let's check inside."

A screen door leaned against an outer wall. The front door was open.

Franklyn stepped inside. Remnants of furniture littered what must be the living room. Most of the glass was smashed. The paint was peeling, and the smell of bird poop and mouse droppings overwhelmed them. "I have a lot of work to do."

"Take a week or so." Paulette rolled her eyes.

Franklyn wandered throughout the house. It didn't get better.

In the back was a three-rail corral. Like the rest of the place, at one time, it had been first rate. That would have to be the priority. Diesel needed a place to live.

"I'm going to need a lot of supplies," Franklyn said.

"A lot," Paulette replied. "I'll get you a hammer and some nails so you can fix the corral. The rest of the stuff you'll need will have to come from Great Falls."

"Do they deliver?"

Paulette laughed. "Sure, for a fee. A big fee. And they'll want cash first."

"I guess I'm going shopping."

Franklyn spent the afternoon repairing the fence. The original occupants knew how to build a fence. Despite the neglect of many years, it was in decent shape. The posts were deep. Some rails were rotten, so he discarded them. He didn't need a three-rail fence for Diesel—not like he would crawl under, so Franklyn finished with a secure, two-rail fence and an operating gate.

Diesel wandered around the yard, never straying far away, rooting out the green grass sprouts. He appeared to enjoy the freedom and being able to stretch his legs after two days of confinement.

Franklyn found an ancient scythe and file in the barn. He sharpened the long blade and then set to work hacking through the overgrown grass. When he finished, he had a heap of brown, brittle grass. Diesel had followed behind, nibbling on the exposed sweet grass.

Franklyn backed the truck beside the house on the east side, out of the path of the wind. He set the jacks on the camper and pulled the truck out. He'd need the truck bed and the horse trailer for the building supplies.

Pleased with an afternoon of work and some progress, he led Diesel into the corral, filled the water bucket, and headed to the arena for a shower. Then he'd drive into Great Falls and get supplies. He'd start the renovations on the weekend.

As he reached the corner of the arena, he caught movement by the corral. The dog slunk low to within five feet of Diesel, then dropped to the ground. Franklyn knelt, and they eyed each other.

CHAPTER SEVEN

Riley and Blake stood outside the interview room, watching the suspect on the video monitor.

"He's a juvenile," Blake said.

Riley glanced at the file folder he held. "Anthony Hart. He's twenty-four."

"Still, he looks like he's in his teens."

"That helps him get away with shit, but not today." Riley flipped through the pages. "He started in his teens—petty shoplifting, a purse snatching, and several underage in bars arrests. In his early twenties, drug charges appeared. He's nervous and twitchy."

Blake nodded. "He's been using. Probably ready for another hit."

"The drugs in that house were for personal use. Not enough there for trafficking. I'm sure they partied late into the morning. Until our wake-up call."

"While you were writing your essay on 'Why I Won't Shoot

Suspects Anymore,' SWAT went back through the house. They found cash in Tupperware containers in the freezer."

"Cold, hard cash."

Blake rolled her eyes. "They're still searching and counting, but so far, about twenty thousand."

"Likely from the sale of a case or two of guns."

Blake shrugged. "We don't know for sure they sold guns."

"I know," Riley said. "Let's see what our gunrunner has to say for himself."

They stepped inside the interview room. Riley threw a file on the table and sat. Blake stood by the door, arms crossed.

Riley opened the file and slowly flipped through the pages. He paused at the photographs and shook his head.

Hart fidgeted, as far as his hands cuffed to the table allowed.

Riley sat back in his chair. "Anthony Hart. Mind if I call you Tony? Of course, you don't. How's your head?"

"What do you think, asshole? You clubbed me with a gun."

"The way I remember it, you were running at me."

"I was running to get away."

"To get away from a house full of cops. How'd that work out?"

"Screw you." Hart tried to lean back in his chair, but he stopped as the handcuffs reached their full extension. He leaned forward.

"What can you tell me about the guns?"

"What guns?" Hart grinned.

"The ones in the barn."

"Don't know nothing about no guns in no barn."

"You don't know about the guns in the barn?" Riley mocked.

"I already said that."

"What will I find when the fingerprints come back?"

Hart stared at the table.

"I knocked you on your ass easily," Riley said. "Not a skilled fighter, are you? What do you weigh? Like a buck fifty?"

"'Bout that." Tony kept his head down.

"Guys who can't fight will not do well in jail. You know what that means?"

Tony's head popped up, eyes wide.

"A hardened criminal like yourself. That's federal time. Someone is going to look after you for a long time. Gunrunning. That's … how many years is that, Blake?"

"At least ten. Some guns were prohibited, so I don't know, maybe another five."

"Wow. Fifteen years, Tony. You're—" Riley stared at the papers. "You're twenty-four. You'd be thirty-nine when you got out. Hell, that's a long time." Riley shook his head, leaned back, and stared.

Tony wiggled in his chair, head down. He chewed on a lip and glanced up a few times. Riley stared back. Blake leaned against the wall, examining her nails.

Riley waited. There was a time, not that long ago, when he would have started the physical persuasion by now. That wasn't allowed anymore, and to his surprise, he'd found that time and silence were his friends. Give the suspect just enough to think about, let him think about it … wait.

Five minutes passed. Ten.

Tony lifted his head from the table. "Lawyer?"

Riley leaned forward so fast the chair nearly slipped out from under him. "What? I need names, dates, places."

"Lawyer," Tony said.

Riley snatched the file folder off the table and stalked out of the interview room with Blake close behind.

In the hall, Blake said, "How do you think that went?"

Riley noticed the smirk on Blake's face. "You could have done better?"

Blake shook her head. "Probably not, but you thought he would give you everything you wanted. The look on your face when he said 'lawyer' was priceless."

Riley headed down the hall. "Let's see what the other shit-head has to say." In the interview room, they adopted the same positions—Riley at the table, Blake by the door.

Riley set a file folder on the table and leaned back in his chair. The suspect sat straight in his chair, head and chin up. His eyes had followed Riley as he entered. This was Riley's first look at this suspect. SWAT had found him in a back bedroom with the two girls … ladies. Not what Riley had expected. He was clean-shaven, had styled hair, and a big grin.

"Graham Keane."

"Yes, sir," Keane said.

"We arrested you because you were in a house with known felons who had a stash of guns. What can you tell me about that?"

"I can tell you everything," Keane said.

Riley grinned and leaned back. "Great. Start at the beginning."

"A couple of days ago, I was hitchhiking east. No jobs in Seattle."

"Not any better in Montana," Blake said.

Riley swung to Blake and glared.

"I know. I wasn't hiking here. I'm going to Minnesota."

Riley nodded.

"I got a ride with a semi from Spokane to Great Falls. He was heading south, and I was going east. Anyway, I have my thumb up outside Great Falls when these guys stop in a van. You know the guys and chicks from the house. I get in. They're, like, drinking and using. They give me this stuff. I didn't know what it was and next thing I know, I'm in that farmhouse. The stuff was like Oxy, but better … or worse, I guess. Like, over the top powerful. Lou said I could earn some bucks to get east. They'll pay me well."

"Lou?"

"The guy you shot."

"Lou Reynolds. Right. What did you have to do?"

"Just drive a van and make deliveries."

"What were you delivering?"

"Lou didn't say. But he offered five hundred a day for the deliveries. He said sometimes I'd do pickups."

"What did you say?"

"I said it was a fair offer, and I'd think about it. Then we partied. There was booze and some of that powerful stuff. I don't remember a lot other than being in bed with the two chicks. Then the SWAT guys were dragging me out of bed and telling me to get dressed."

"You think I'm going to believe that story?" Riley asked.

Keane shrugged. "Look. I had no money. I'd stay the night and then leave the next morning. I figured they'd sleep until noon."

"Why didn't you want to stay?" Riley asked.

"Reynolds was crazy. I wanted to get away, but the girls said he'd kill me if I snuck out. I'm glad you shot him."

Back in their office, Riley stared at an empty file folder on his desk. "Keane has no record—not even a parking ticket. His driver's license shows an address in Spokane. It fits with his story. What did the girls say?"

"They backed Keane's story that he was hitching, and they picked him up. Keane was with them one night. They said they belonged to Reynolds but he told them to sleep with Keane."

"What makes Keane so special?"

Blake shrugged. "Hell if I know."

"What about the guns?"

"They knew nothing about guns, but both admitted to doing drugs."

Riley rubbed his whiskers. "They admitted to the drugs but not the guns."

"Let's face it, Riley, we aren't going to bust them for possession. It's a waste of time."

Riley tapped his fingers on his desk. "We've got no charges. Unless we get fingerprints off the gun cases, we've got less than zilch."

"That's a lot of guns off the street," Blake said.

Riley nodded and chewed his lip. "There's that. I'm worried about the guns they sold. When and where are they going to show up? We have to figure out how to nail them."

"We can interview Reynolds tomorrow. Maybe we'll get something from him."

"I doubt it. He'll lawyer up faster than Tony. Nothing we can do today. Tomorrow we'll talk to ATF about the guns, then interview Reynolds."

CHAPTER EIGHT

RILEY STEPPED THROUGH THE DOORWAY, DROPPED HIS KEYS IN A tray by the door, and headed to the bedroom. He pulled his Glock from his holster, dropped the magazine, and cleared the round in the chamber. He opened the closet door and placed the gun and magazines inside the safe, then locked the safe.

He wandered to the kitchen and opened the fridge—not a lot of selection. He pulled out the milk. When he poured it into the glass, it flowed like molasses, and a blob plopped out. A foul odor filled the room. He dumped the milk down the sink and left the hot water running.

He went back to the fridge—beer or Coke. He grabbed the Coke and filled a glass with ice. From the cupboard above the refrigerator, he pulled out the bottle of Captain Morgan's dark rum, poured a generous portion into the glass, and topped it off with Coke.

He flopped onto the couch, sipped the rum, and aimlessly clicked through the channels. He settled on *SportsCenter*. Lots of talk about the Stanley Cup. Riley endured the jabbering of the talking heads. Most hadn't played a single period of minor hockey, let alone NHL. Yet they were full of opinions. *Full of it.*

Riley had played a lot of hockey. None professional, but some junior, and he had a better idea of what would happen in the playoffs than these clowns. And don't even get him started on the eye candy the sports channels used as commentators. The commentators he respected were the guys who had played the pro game. Although, over time, they melded into a reporter instead of a retired player. Just once he'd like to see a former player tell the play-by-play guy he was talking out his ass. That brought a smile to his face. *Yup, just once.*

They all agreed that Boston would win the Stanley Cup. Ahead, two games to one over the St. Louis Blues, Riley was optimistic. A lifelong Boston fan, he'd suffered through a few Stanley Cup defeats. *I guess we'll see.*

He refilled his rum, sat at his computer and checked emails. He'd lost hope long ago, but he checked every day against all the odds that one of his kids had emailed—had answered the dozens of emails he'd sent—nothing today. There'd been nothing this week, this month.

Before he left Helena, before the shit storm that got him transferred, he'd see the kids twice a month. But visits were infrequent now.

He missed his kids. He was powerless to do anything. They didn't want contact with him except on Father's Day and Christmas. Even that was at a neutral, sterile restaurant. Christmas dinner with your kids in a restaurant was hardly the celebration they'd enjoyed for years. He'd hoped they'd still hang out after the separation. The job called him away at odd times and for days. But he'd been there for their piano recitals, awards ceremonies at school, and sports. Sometimes he'd driven like a wild man to get to a game, but he'd made it.

Family vacations were grand adventures with laughs in the pool or on the beach. I didn't matter to them now to them. He brought the glass to his lips. Empty. Time for another.

CHAPTER NINE

THE AMBULANCE BOUNCED AND SWAYED AS THEY TRAVELED OVER the rutted gravel road. Paramedic Eric Kennedy and his partner, Pam Taylor, rolled with each bump.

"The roads are getting worse," Kennedy said.

"These are roads?" Taylor replied.

Kennedy and his partner had worked together for years. She'd been his student and then his partner. She was keen, energetic, and typically good-natured. Lately, though, she'd become distant and less excited about work.

"Take the next right." Taylor tracked their progress on the Mobile Data Terminal. "Then, about a mile farther. The notes say it's not a house, but a field where some kids are partying. We'll see the campfire. Notes say one kid is passed out."

"Spring fire bans mean nothing," Kennedy replied.

The road swung sharply to the left. The faint light from a campfire was the only sign anyone was around. Kennedy found the opening in the fence and drove onto the field. As shoddy as the road had been, the field, untouched by humans since the beginning of time, had them bouncing off the ambulance roof.

About twenty people crowded around the fire. A few knelt next to a person on the ground ten feet away. Kennedy parked the ambulance so the side scene lights provided illumination.

Taylor grabbed the EMS kits and caught up to Kennedy at the front of the ambulance.

"Paramedics." Kennedy shone his flashlight on the patient. The group by the fire didn't move. The kids around the patient backed away.

"We can't wake him," a girl said.

"How long has he been like this?" Kennedy shone his flashlight toward the girl.

"I don't know," she said. "He came over here a while ago. I tried to wake him, but I couldn't. They said to let him sleep it off. When I came back, I still couldn't wake him. I got scared."

"You did the right thing." Taylor felt the boy's neck. "No pulse. I'll start compressions."

Kennedy grabbed his radio. "Dispatch, Speargrass One. Cardiac arrest. Need Speargrass Fire and Tribal Police."

"Roger, Speargrass One."

"Hey," Kennedy shouted. "We need some help. Anyone know CPR?"

No one answered.

"Fine, I need someone to hold the flashlights."

No one moved.

"Hey, you two." Kennedy pointed at the two closest teenagers. "Get over here. Now."

They stepped to him. "Hold one flashlight on his face. The other on his chest."

Kennedy passed the airway bag to Taylor. It would just be

the two of them. Not like Great Falls with ambulance backup minutes away, the fire department eager to respond, and all the cops you needed.

They were used to it. He'd trust the compressions and airway to Taylor. He'd take care of the IV and pushing the drugs. First, he connected the leads for the heart monitor and peered at the screen. *Damn.* Asystole. No heart activity at all. *He's been down awhile.*

Kennedy glanced at Taylor, who was also staring at the monitor. Their eyes met. They'd give it their best for twenty minutes, but the chances of survival were nil.

"What'd he take?" Kennedy asked the two flashlight holders.

"Don't know what you mean," the guy shining the light on the chest said.

"Let me make things clear for you," Kennedy said. "Your buddy is dead. He will stay dead unless you tell me what you were taking. That's his one chance. Tell me what drug he took."

"We don't know."

"That's bullshit." Kennedy glared past the flashlights. "What did he take?"

"No, you don't understand," the closest guy said. "Everyone brings pills to the party. We throw them in a bag and mix it up. Everyone grabs a handful. I don't know what the drug was."

"Are you shitting me?"

Flashlight Guy shrugged. "That's the truth."

Kennedy shook his head. "You must have some idea of what was in there."

"Maybe ecstasy, antidepressants, or whatever we can steal from our parents or grandparents."

"Those rarely kill people. What else?"

"I dunno." The two flashlight guys shared a glance.

"I'm tired of the bullshit. What else?"

"Probably Oxy."

Shit. "Check his pupils."

"Slow to react, but not pinpoint."

"I'll still give Naloxone. How's the airway?"

"Not great," Taylor said. "He has puked a lot. Suction didn't work. I swept out the chunks with my fingers. I have a tube in now."

"Likely aspirated. Nothing we can do about that. Just ventilate."

"Speargrass One, dispatch."

"Go ahead, dispatch," Kennedy replied.

"No answer from Speargrass Fire. I left a message for Tribal Police. No answer there either. Anyone else we can call?"

"No."

One teen who'd been watching from by the fire rushed over to Taylor. "I can do CPR."

"Great," Taylor said. "Just keep it fast."

The teen did compressions, Taylor squeezed the airway bag, and Kennedy administered medications. The Naloxone didn't reverse the effects of the opioid, Oxy. The epinephrine didn't restart the heart. The cardiac monitor continued to show a flat line.

Kennedy checked his watch. They'd been working on this patient for twenty minutes. He glanced at Taylor and shook his head. She nodded.

"Okay, let's stop."

Flashlight Guy said, "You can't stop, man. Keep trying."

"There's nothing we can do. He's gone."

"No way, man. Do something else. You can't stop until you get him back."

"We've tried everything. Your friend is dead."

"Then take him to the hospital."

"That won't help. He's dead. We've done everything they could do at the hospital."

"You didn't do everything. I've seen doctors on TV do other stuff. You're quitting because he's Indian."

Kennedy sighed. Not the first time he'd heard that.

He took a deep breath. "I'm sorry. Your friend died of an overdose from the pills. You're lucky more of you aren't dead. He's been dead a while. At least an hour."

Red-and-blue flashing lights bounced off the landscape, stopping the argument.

A Tribal Police officer stumbled toward them.

Balam. Kennedy frowned. *For once, Tribal Police show up, and it's Balam. I don't trust him. Especially around teens.*

"Hey, Balam," Kennedy said. "Probable overdose. He has been dead for more than an hour. We couldn't resuscitate him."

Balam nodded and stared at the body.

"The teens have a bag of drugs," Kennedy said. "You might want to get that."

"Yeah. Thanks for the advice on policing." Balam headed to the fire.

CHAPTER TEN

FRANKLYN ARRIVED AT THE OFFICE AT SEVEN-FORTY. HE'D FIGURED out that since *Subway* didn't open until seven-thirty, and unless he planned to cook in the camper, there was no sense getting to work early, then heading out to get breakfast. The coffee he could make at the office.

He figured out which key opened the back door, then headed to the security office. He knocked, but no one answered. *Where the hell is Balam?* He unlocked the office door. The lights were out and no one was around.

Franklyn locked the door and headed to his office. On the second try, he found the right key. He set the breakfast sandwich on his desk and got the coffee brewing. There was a piece of paper on Paulette's typically spotless desk. While the coffee brewed, he grabbed the paper. It was an incident report from early this morning—an overdose. The information was barely legible and incomplete. Most of the mandatory boxes were empty. All he could decipher was that a twenty-two-year-old male had overdosed in a field. EMS tried to resuscitate without success. They removed the body to a funeral home in Great Falls.

That was it.

He headed to the coffeemaker. Dang, he forgot to get a mug. He poured coffee into a paper cup, ate the sandwich in his office, and thought about how to handle the situation.

When Paulette came in at nine, Franklyn had worked himself into a foul mood.

"Get Leroy in here by ten," he barked. "Get Hiram and that other guy, Lefebvre. If they are late, they're fired."

He slammed his door.

Then he opened the door. "There was an overdose last night. I didn't get a phone call or called on the radio. What's with that?"

"The former sheriff didn't want to be disturbed after work," Paulette said. "Dispatch was told not to phone, and your radio goes to sleep at four p.m. and wakes at nine."

"That's stupid. Get that changed—today. I want to be notified, and I want the damn radio to work." He tossed the radio onto her desk. "Get it fixed." He closed the office door, gently this time.

CHAPTER ELEVEN

Riley parked at the emergency department entrance. Blake followed him to the elevators, and they rode to the fourth floor. Riley made a beeline for the nurse's station. "Riley Briggs. DEA. My partner, Leigh Blake. FBI. We're here to see Lou Reynolds."

A nurse peered up from her charts. "End of the hall and to the left. You can't miss the stormtroopers outside his room."

Riley showed his badge to the deputy sheriffs as he strode into the room and over to the bed. Lou Reynolds was sitting, eating yogurt, and watching the morning news. He glanced at Riley, then turned back to the TV.

"Lou Reynolds, I'm Agent Briggs, DEA. This is Agent Blake, FBI."

"I'm thrilled." Lou's eyes didn't leave the TV.

"We have some questions for you."

"I don't have answers."

"What were you doing at the farmhouse yesterday?"

Reynolds scowled. "I was sleeping, then some asshole broke into the house and shot me. He looked a lot like you."

"Maybe it was the gun you pointed at me."

"Self-defense, man. I didn't know who you were."

"DEA across the front of my vest and that we yelled, police, search warrant, didn't give you a hint?"

"Fuck, man. I was asleep. Then there were guys with guns in the house. Self-defense." Reynolds grabbed a cup of coffee, sipped, then glanced at Blake. "Now, if I'd seen ginger first, my reaction would have been different. Right, honey."

Blake headed toward the bed. Riley put his arm out and held her back.

"Uh, huh," Riley said. "Is that because the word FBI was more evident on her vest?"

Reynolds laughed. "Yeah. Let's go with that. I'm done talking. My lawyer told me to give you this when you showed up." Reynolds handed Riley a business card.

Riley kept a straight face and nodded. "No problem. Let me read you your rights." When Riley finished, he said, "Do you understand your rights as I have read them?"

"Fuckin' eh."

"I'll take that as a yes," Riley said. "See you in court, Lou."

After they visited the hospital, Riley and Blake headed back to their office.

"That was a waste of time," Blake said.

"Yeah." Riley grinned. "Terrible luck I shot him and gave his lawyer time to get to him."

"He lawyered up quickly."

"Awful luck for us on the lawyer." Riley slid into this chair.

"Why? Who is it?"

"His name is Dalton Frey." Riley tossed the business card to Blake.

She glanced at the card. "Is he any good?"

"One of the best." Riley frowned and gritted his teeth. "He likes high-profile cases."

Blake's eyes narrowed. "This isn't high profile."

"No, but his primary client is."

"Who's that?"

"The Red Demons Outlaw Motorcycle Club."

"Oh, shit." Then Blake cocked her head. "Why would Frey represent Reynolds?"

Riley leaned back in his chair with his hands behind his head. "That's the vital piece of information we got this morning. Reynolds and his gang are affiliated with the Red Demons. They have chapters all over the country, but Montana was one state they hadn't set up shop—until now." Riley reached for a file folder on his desk and read the contents. A grin crossed his face. "Well, I'll be."

Blake peered over the top of her computer monitor. "What?"

Riley held up the folder. "We got the preliminary fingerprint report. There's a match for four of our suspects. Graham Keane was lying to us. His name isn't Keane. It's Noel Bourget. He's the vice-president of the Red Demons MC in Spokane."

"There's the Red Demons connection," Blake said.

"Let's go down to the cells and talk to Bourget."

They stopped at the counter outside the holding cells. Riley nodded to the sergeant. "Morning, sarge. We need a few minutes with Graham Keane."

The sergeant glanced up. "Sorry, Briggs. He isn't here."

"What?" Riley did a double-take. "Where is he?"

"Released early this morning."

"What do you mean, released?"

"Kicked out, sent home. Shown the door."

Riley leaned on the counter. "He's a suspect in possession of some heavy artillery."

Sarge shrugged. "Can't help you there. They released him before I came on duty at seven. There was a sizable fight at the Mother Lode Bar around midnight, and they needed the cell space. Keane didn't have a record. He had a lawyer, so we sent him packing with a promise to appear."

"Let me guess, Dalton Frey is his lawyer."

Sarge sorted through a stack of paperwork, then pulled out one sheet. "Yup."

Riley slid his fingers through his hair. "Who authorized his release?"

Sarge read the paper. "Approved by Sheriff MacDonald."

"What does old man MacDonald have to do with this? Why is he screwing with my arrests?"

"Hey, I'm just the messenger." He stepped back from the counter. "We kicked the girls loose, too."

CHAPTER TWELVE

FRANKLYN WAS SORTING FILES WHEN THERE WAS A TENTATIVE KNOCK on the door.

"What?" Franklyn shouted.

The door opened about two inches, and Paulette peeked in. "Sorry. Leroy Balam doesn't answer his home phone or his cell. Hiram Crow is with the chief and won't be available until this afternoon. Calvin Lefebvre is here."

Franklyn strode to his office door and flung it open. Paulette scrambled to get out of the way. Franklyn headed to a cop standing by Paulette's desk.

"Lefebvre. I'm Franklyn." He thrust out a hand. Lefebvre was a few inches shorter than Franklyn, but at least six feet. He had a slim but toned build. His dark hair swept over his ears and well below his shirt collar. It appeared like Lefebvre was trying, unsuccessfully, to grow a beard and mustache.

Lefebvre grabbed Franklyn's hand in a firm grip. "Good to meet you, sir."

"We aren't doing the 'sir' crap. Do you know where Leroy Balam lives?"

"Yes si … Yes, I do."

"Great. Let's go." Franklyn tossed the keys to Lefebvre.

Lefebvre spun gravel as he accelerated out of the parking lot.

"He's not dying." Franklyn grabbed the dash.

"What?"

"Leroy," Franklyn said. "He's not dying—there's no rush."

"Sorry, boss." Lefebvre eased off the gas.

"What's your story?" Franklyn relaxed back into his seat.

"What?"

"Am I going to have to repeat every question?"

"No." Lefebvre paused and grinned. "It's just, well, no one here ever asked about my story."

"You're Métis?"

"Yup. My great-great-grandfather was a French-Canadian trapper. He'd trap all winter and then sell his furs at Fort Benton. On one trip, he met my great-great-grandmother. She was Blackfeet. When he went back into the mountains in late summer, she went with him. Every spring, they'd come back with the furs, and she dropped a baby in the summer before they went trapping in the fall. That happened for nine seasons. So, way back, I have a lot of relatives."

"How did you get hired?"

Lefebvre glanced at him. "They needed a cop. I was experienced. I was hired."

"No interview?"

"Nope."

"No background checks?"

"Nope." Lefebvre smirked. "As far as you know, I could be a serial killer."

Franklyn stared out the window and deadpanned. "Oh, I doubt there'd be two of us in the same car."

Lefebvre pounded the steering wheel and laughed.

"Why are you a cop?"

"I read everything about fur trappers and the old west." Lefebvre swung onto a gravel road. "It sounded like a magnificent time to be alive. At first, I thought I'd be a mountain man. But I watched every western movie made. Especially the ones where the marshal or sheriff was against a massive gang and outnumbered."

"Seems odd that you'd be a cop." Franklyn glanced at Lefebvre. "Indians didn't do so well in those movies."

"True, but if you want to make a difference, and I do, then you've got to break stereotypes. I want to prove Indians can do this job."

Franklyn nodded. "Is being Métis held against you?"

"Sure, repeatedly I'm told I'm not a real Indian, that I don't belong." Lefebvre shrugged. "I just ignore that and do the best I can." He spun the steering wheel to the right. The SUV slid sideways toward the ditch. Just as Franklyn was sure they were going off the road, Lefebvre hit the gas, and they sped down another gravel road.

"Where'd you learn to drive like this?"

Lefebvre smirked. "I've always had a lead foot. Nearly kept me out of Montana Highway Patrol. I had some demerits, and then I got stopped speeding a couple of weeks before training started. If they gave me a ticket, I'd have too many demerits, and I would have been disqualified before I got in."

"So, what did you do?"

"I begged."

Franklyn's eyebrow rose. "And it worked?"

"Yup. I also owed him a bottle of decent whiskey."

"You survived the training. Where were you posted?"

"Little Big Horn."

Franklyn's head jerked toward Lefebvre. "What?"

"I requested it."

"You're kidding?"

"Oh, yeah." Lefebvre chuckled. "Significant history there."

"How did you end up in Speargrass? Not exactly the go-to place for cops."

"I'd been at Little Big Horn four years, and they were going to transfer me to Missoula to get some city time. I'd worked with some great Indians at Little Big Horn. One of them told me about this job. I came here to check it out, and they hired me on the spot. I drove back to Little Big Horn, loaded my stuff in my truck, got my dog, and drove here."

"Aside from your blue eyes, I figured you were full Indian," Franklyn said. "I can see why they hired you."

"One of the cousins."

They hit a large bump. Franklyn's head hit the roof, and he shouted as he dropped back into his seat. "Shit. A spring just went up my ass."

"Sorry."

"Are we close? I want to be alive when we get there."

"Another mile."

"Tell me about Balam."

"Ah, boss. I can't do that. I'm not gonna talk about someone behind their back."

"Something? Anything? I need to know what I'm dealing with."

"Oh, you'll know soon enough." Lefebvre pulled into a trail

that led to a dilapidated house with a Tribal Police SUV parked out front.

"He takes the SUV home all the time?"

"Yup. Crow, too."

"What do you drive?"

"Well, most of the time I drove this truck. The former sheriff, Archie Gardner, didn't take it home. He left work about the time I started, so it worked well."

"Why do they take them home?"

"So they can respond if they get called when they're off duty."

"Do they respond when they're off duty?"

Lefebvre laughed. "Nope. Only me."

Franklyn marched to the front door and pounded. "Leroy Balam, open the door."

No response.

"This is bullshit." He pounded again. "Balam, open the goddamned door." He tried the doorknob—it rotated.

"This is illegal, isn't it, Sheriff?"

"Thought I heard someone call for help. Didn't you?"

Lefebvre scratched his head and gazed away. "Ah, Sheriff. You're putting me in a terrible spot."

Franklyn stepped back from the door. The kid had integrity—Franklyn couldn't fault that. "How about this? Balam came home before his shift ended and doesn't answer his phone. Maybe he's sick or dying. As his boss, I should make sure he's okay."

Lefebvre nodded. "I can live with that."

Franklyn opened the door, and they stepped inside. Beer bottles, liquor bottles, and junk littered the house. Franklyn made his way to the back bedroom.

Balam was lying naked on the bed. The room stank of marijuana smoke and sweat.

Franklyn stepped to the bed and slapped Balam's legs. He kicked his legs and rolled over. Franklyn stepped to the head of the bed and leaned toward Balam's face. "Shithead, get up."

Balam's eyes slowly opened. He stared and blinked. "What the fuck do you want?"

"I need to know about the overdose last night."

"Check the report." Balam pulled up a blanket and rolled over.

"There isn't anything in that report. Get your ass out of bed and do a proper report."

"I'll do it when I get in tonight." Balam curled into a ball.

Franklyn stepped to the other side of the bed, lifted the mattress, and flipped Balam onto the floor. "Now, asshole."

Franklyn glanced around the room. He noticed a .38 revolver and holster, badge and case, and radio on the night table. Franklyn noticed a paper bag as he turned to leave. He opened the bag—it was full of pills. "Where'd you get this bag?"

"At the overdose this morning," Balam mumbled.

Franklyn stood over him. "You mean the pills that killed a kid?"

"Yeah."

"Why aren't these locked away in evidence?"

"By the time I got back to the station, it was time to quit," Balam said. "I was gonna do that tonight."

"I should charge you for neglect of duty," Franklyn said. "Be at the station at eleven. You show up at a second past eleven, you're fired."

Franklyn reclined in his chair, put his feet on his desk and hands behind his head. *One heck of a morning.*

Paulette called out, "Chief Fox on line one."

It just got worse.

He sighed, dropped his feet to the floor, and grabbed the phone. "Good morning, Chief."

"Franklyn, what the hell are you doing? You can't break into people's homes."

Franklyn leaned forward, one hand holding the phone, the other holding his forehead. "Ah, I see you've talked to Balam."

"He called me fifteen minutes ago. He said you broke into his house, stole his stuff, and embarrassed him."

"That's close. I went to his house because he didn't answer his phone and I needed to know about a death early this morning. The door was open, and he didn't answer. I found him in bed. The bag of pills from the death that he didn't put into evidence was on his night table. I should have fired his ass and thrown him in jail."

"Eaglechild. Two days ago, I told you to report to me—to check with me. I want you to back off with Balam. He needs the job."

"If he needs the job, then he needs to do the work. He can explain that to me when he gets here at eleven. If he's late, he's fired. I won't have him working for me. You can find something else for him."

"You're not listening, Eaglechild. I'm telling you he works for you. Back off." Fox paused. "One last thing. Balam will be in at one. Not earlier."

Franklyn heard a click and then the dial tone. He stared at the phone, then hung up. Either he'd made his point, or he was unemployed. He stood, coffee would be great, but rum would be better. He limped around his desk. His hip was seizing, and the pain was shooting down his leg. He grabbed a paper cup and filled it with coffee.

He opened the top drawer of his desk, pulled out the pill bottle, and tapped an Oxy into his hand. He washed it down with coffee. He closed his eyes and sat back, waiting for relief. When he opened his eyes, he eyeballed the bag of pills he'd seized from Balam's house. He picked up the bag and dumped the contents on his desk. At least a half-dozen distinct shapes and sizes. He sorted the pills and filled in an evidence tag. When he got to the OxyContin pills, his pen hesitated above the label. He had a two-month supply of Oxy, and he was frequently taking double what he was prescribed. They'd last a month, if he was lucky.

He stared at the pills, then logged the OxyContin and sealed the evidence bag. He carried the evidence bags to Paulette. "What do I do with these?"

"They go in the evidence room." She pointed to a door in the office's corner.

"We have an evidence room?"

"No, it's a closet."

"The closet? Is there a lockbox in there?"

"Nope."

Franklyn glanced from Paulette to the closet door and back. "Anyone can get in there?"

Paulette peered over her glasses. "If you have a key."

"Do I have a key?"

She swung away from her desk and held her arms wide. "You have a key to everything."

That afternoon a knock on the door awoke Franklyn. He slid his boots off the desk. "Yup."

The door opened a few inches.

"Oh dammit, Paulette. I'm sorry. Come in. I won't yell or bite or kick or swear. Well, I'll likely swear."

Paulette smirked. "Here's your radio. It is on all the time. Just so you know, that means you will hear every fire call, every police call, and every EMS call. The paramedics are busy at night."

"Well, let's give it a try."

Paulette handed Franklyn a note. "Chief Fox called back. He needs Hiram for the day. You'll have to meet with Crow tomorrow—or maybe Monday. Possibly Tuesday." She adjusted her glasses, grinning.

"Who does Crow work for, the chief or me."

"Did you want me to answer that?"

Franklyn laughed. "No, I guess not. I already know."

"Leroy Balam is here."

"Great, send him in."

Balam slunk into the office. He was in uniform—barely. Neither the shirt nor pants were clean. His black boots appeared gray from a lack of polish and care. His braided hair had a greasy shine.

Franklyn pointed to a chair. "Take a seat."

Balam flopped into the chair, folded his arms, and mumbled, "Why am I here? I thought the chief called you."

"He did and bought you two extra hours of sleep. That's it." Franklyn leaned forward. "I don't care how things were done before I arrived. There are new rules. First, clean that uniform and polish your boots. Have pride. Second, you report to work on time, and do your job. I'm not picking up the slack for you and Hiram Crow. Third, reports are completed before you leave at the end of your shift. If you don't have them done, then you stay until they are done. I want every box checked and a narrative, so I have a clue what happened." Franklyn grabbed a piece of paper. "This is useless." He threw the it on the desk. "Evidence is properly collected, marked, and put into the evidence locker. You never, ever, take evidence home. That bag of pills is useless as evidence because you brought them home. I wasn't kidding. Next time this happens, I'll have the county attorney charge you. That will be the end of your police career. I won't have to fire you. The state will." Franklyn handed the report to Balam. "Go to your desk and do this properly. You're dismissed."

Balam stormed out of the office.

Franklyn stood and marched past Paulette. "I'm going to go do some stress management. I'll be at the house and doing some demolition. Call if you need me."

Balam quietly slipped into the chief's office, closed the door, and grabbed a chair.

"What the hell are you doing here?" Fox asked.

"I thought you'd want a report of my meeting with Eaglechild."

"Not in the middle of the day. Are you insane?"

"Relax." Balam pulled out his hunting knife and trimmed a fingernail. "No one will care. Besides, I'm in uniform." He did an air quote. "Official police business."

"Fine. Make it quick."

"He's making a show of being in charge. Ragged on me for

my uniform. He's bossing everyone around. Paulette is running around getting him radios and cell phones. I overheard him complain that you keep Hiram Crow busy, and he has to do all the work."

"Any signs he'll be a problem?"

Balam shook his head and cracked his knuckles. "Nothing yet. He's in over his head. Between learning police work and trying to salvage that falling-down rodent-infested house, he'll have no time for police work."

"Okay. Keep me informed—not during the day."

CHAPTER THIRTEEN

RILEY STEPPED INTO THE INTERVIEW ROOM AND SAT ACROSS FROM Tony Hart. Blake grabbed the chair next to Riley and set a file folder on the table.

Riley leaned back and put his hands behind his head. Hart was skinny, with stringy blond hair and a foul body odor. His body practically vibrated.

"Tony, how was your night in cells?"

He stared at his hands.

"Consider last night a peaceful night. From now on, they get, well, more challenging. How much meth are you using daily? Did you get the shakes last night? It looks like you have them now. Chills? What about pain? Tonight, it will be worse. Then the night after—"

Tony's eyes stared at his shaking hands. "Lawyer."

"Yeah, I understand he talked to you last night. The funny thing is, you're still here. He didn't get you out on bail. I'll bet he promised a lot."

"I'm not supposed to talk to you without my lawyer."

Riley held up his hands. "I get that. You don't have to talk without your lawyer. You don't have to say a thing. I just came by to see if you were okay."

Tony eyeballed Riley and snorted.

"Some guys get freaked out their first night in jail. I wondered if it freaked you out. Of course, being locked in cells here is a lot different from federal prison."

"I don't care."

"You might not care today, but when those cell doors clang shut and you know you aren't going to be free for years, you'll care then. But heck, I'm just here talking. You don't have to say anything. Takes a tough man to face federal time. Maybe in a few years, you'll bulk up and be able to defend yourself." Riley leaned forward. "Tell me about the guns."

"Don't know about no guns."

Blake flipped open a file. "When you told Special Agent Briggs you didn't know about the guns, he thought, well, maybe Tony is telling the truth."

"I was."

"This morning, I came into work, and this file was waiting. Do you know what's in this?"

"Fuck if I care."

"Come on, you care. Hell, you're worried. What could these dumb cops have on me? Let me show you." Blake pushed a piece of paper the size of a postcard across the table.

Tony glanced at the paper, then stared at the wall.

"Those, my twitchy friend, are fingerprints." Blake tapped a finger on the prints. "Those are the fingerprints from when you were arrested." Blake pulled some papers out of the folder.

"This is the report of the fingerprints on the box of cell phones. What do you think is the connection?"

Tony tossed the fingerprint postcard back. "You're the cop, you tell me."

"Absolutely." Blake leaned forward.

Tony leaned back.

Blake grinned. "They match. They belong to the same guy —you."

Tony groaned, sank in his chair, and lowered his head.

"The weird thing is, we didn't find prints on the cases of guns or the ammunition, just on the box of cell phones. Got me wondering." Riley rubbed his whiskers. "Why is that? Then I checked the box of cell phones. There was an uneven number. That was weird. Then I checked your belongings. I was amazed to see you had several brand-new cell phones. I was gobsmacked when I realized they were BlackBerry's, the same make as the phones in the box. I was beyond words when I found out the serial numbers on the phones were in sequence with the other stolen phones."

"Ah, shit."

"Right, now, Tony," Riley said, "you're the one I can connect to the stolen guns, ammunition, and cell phones. I can charge you for all of it, that would be the simple thing to do. But I'll give you one chance. I don't want you to take this the wrong way, but you aren't the mastermind behind the guns. You know, maybe you were hanging out. Maybe you went for a walk and found the stash. Nice BlackBerry phone is hard to resist. I can't get a conviction for a few cell phones. Of course, that's if I present the case that way. More likely, I'll say the phones were part of a box that was with ammunition, that was with guns. That's a whole different story to a judge. I can tell you aren't an evil guy. Otherwise, you would have taken a gun or two. I'm confident I can help you, but you will need to help me. I'll give you a few minutes to think about this. When I come back, why don't you tell me what happened." Riley stood and grinned at Tony, then he and Blake left the room.

They headed back to their office.

"Why are we leaving?" Blake asked. "You had him."

"Not yet," Riley said. "I want him twitchy. We'll give him two hours."

Riley opened his eyes and leaned forward in his desk chair. "Is it time?"

"You've been sleeping for ninety minutes," Blake said. "You feel better?"

Riley jumped to his feet. "Feel like a million bucks. Let's see how Tony is doing."

Tony glanced up as they entered the interview room. His hair was wet and stuck to his head. His shirt soaked through at the armpits and chest. He squirmed in his seat as much as he could handcuffed to the table.

Riley grabbed a seat. "You look like shit, Tony." Riley leaned back and crossed his arms.

Tony's head twitched to the side, his eyes blinked, and he wiggled like his chair was on fire. "You said you'd help me."

Riley nodded. "Damn straight. You don't need to suffer. Tell me a story, and I'll get you out of here."

Tony tried to rub his sleeves on his forehead. "You swear I'll get out of here."

Riley held up his right hand, three fingers extended, and his thumb over his pinky finger. "Scout's honor."

"I was in the back of the van. We drove around for a while. Then we stopped and loaded two boxes in the back with me. Reynolds said they were new cell phones."

"Who did you get the phones from?" Riley asked.

"I didn't see anyone. The boxes were hidden beside the road. Then we drove back to the farm. I carried the boxes to the barn and noticed the stacked crates."

"You didn't know what was in the crates?"

"Not then. I went back later that night and stole phones. I figured I could trade them for drugs. I got curious and I opened one crate. When I glimpsed the guns, I closed the crate and beat it out of there."

"That's all you have?"

"I told you what I know. You'll still help me, right?"

CHAPTER FOURTEEN

FRANKLYN LET DIESEL OUT OF HIS CORRAL TO WANDER. HE SLIPPED off his Tribal Police shirt, hung it on the truck mirror, but kept his T-shirt on. He pulled the toolbox out of the truck, selected a large crowbar, and a claw hammer and stomped into the house. Might as well start at the front. He slid on buffalo-hide gloves.

He dug the end of the crowbar into the plaster and pried. The plaster came loose easily and littered the floor. As he got lower, the plaster crumbled and fell apart, from moisture and the smell was overwhelming. He went back to his truck, got a bandana, and tied it around his nose and mouth. He got on his knees and pulled the plaster back with his gloved hands. At the bottom, he came across mouse bones and rotting mouse corpses. He went back to the truck and grabbed a wide grain shovel and tarp. He laid out the tarp in front of the house and scooped the plaster and mouse parts onto it. He pulled out the insulation and piled it into the tarp.

As he dragged gyprock panels to the pile, he heard a whimper. Outside the corral, the dog crouched in the grass. In daylight, his fur shimmered black and silver. Franklyn moved toward the dog, but he scrambled backward. "Hey, it's okay. I'm friendly." Franklyn moved slowly, but the dog still retreated. Franklyn went to the cooler in the camper and pulled out beef jerky and cheese. That was all he had. He put the cheese and beef on a paper plate and set it by the corral. A few trips later, the dog was eating.

By late afternoon he had made five trips to the dump and had the entrance and living room stripped to the studs. He was filling the tarp with a sixth load when he heard the crunch of tires outside. He stepped onto the porch, crowbar in hand.

An ambulance came to a stop beside his truck, and the paramedics climbed out. The driver was mid-thirties, five foot eight, two hundred pounds with sandy-white hair. His partner was the early thirties, long brown hair, and athletic with a slim build. She was taller than her partner by at least two inches.

The driver strode to Franklyn and extended his hand. "Eric Kennedy."

Franklyn slid off a glove and grabbed the hand. "Franklyn Eaglechild."

"I hear you're our new boss."

Franklyn nodded. "Guess I am."

"This is my partner Pam Taylor."

Taylor stepped forward and shook his hand. "Pam."

Franklyn glanced over his shoulder. "They spared no expense on my accommodation. A fixer-upper."

Kennedy flipped the keyring in his hand. "We stopped by your office to see you. Paulette said you were here. When she told me the alarm number, I knew you had some work ahead of you. We stopped and picked up some drinks and sandwiches. Care to dine with us?"

"That sounds great. I'd invite you into the dining room, but—"

"Yeah. I'll pass on that," Kennedy said. "We can sit on the porch."

Taylor brought the sandwiches and soda from the ambulance. She tossed Franklyn a plastic container of sanitary wipes. "You might want to clean up before you eat."

They sat on the porch and ate.

"I appreciate this," Franklyn said. "Got no place to cook, except the camper. Not going to cook here for a while."

A whimper sounded from the corral again.

"That your dog?" Pam asked.

"No. He showed up my first night."

Pam glanced at Franklyn, then lowered her eyes. "Looks like he's yours. You know you're accepted when you get a rez dog."

Franklyn tossed part of a sandwich toward the corral. The dog crawled forward, devoured it in two bites, then wagged his tail.

"What do you think so far?" Kennedy asked.

Franklyn tossed another piece of the sandwich to the dog. "Well, it's an eye-opener. In some respects, just like I remember. But some things are worse—houses, poverty, the dead eyes of some people and the issues with Tribal Police. I've made some waves. I already got a call from Chief Fox."

"We wanted to talk to you about a few problems we have." Kennedy was flipping the keys again. "Is that okay?"

"Sure." Franklyn braced himself. "Fire away."

"We were at an overdose in a field about four this morning."

"I read Balam's report." Franklyn sipped the Coke. "Or what little there was."

"We're on our own most of the time." Kennedy glanced at Taylor, then back to Franklyn. "All the paramedics are white. Generally, that's not a problem. But sometimes there are a lot of people in the homes or at the parties. We call for Tribal Police backup, but no one comes. Or if they do, it's long after we needed them. We're creative at solving our own problems. We can diffuse most incidents. But it would be great to count on police presence."

"I didn't hear that call this morning," Franklyn said. "I found out my radio is asleep most of the time. I got that fixed. When I'm around, you can count on me."

"That's fair," Kennedy said. "That will help. But, well, we have a problem with one of your cops."

"Who?"

"Leroy Balam."

"That shouldn't be a problem. I talked to Balam today. I gave him shit. I told him he's fired if he doesn't get his act together."

Kennedy held his sandwich halfway to his mouth. "You disciplined him? Does the chief know?"

"The chief is pissed. But I made my point."

"You got large ones." Kennedy drank the soda. "Balam is as slimy as they come. He uses his position as a cop to do all sorts of bad stuff."

"Like what?"

"I have no proof, just a lot of things we see or hear, but he's probably into teen prostitution and drug trafficking. If it's illegal, he's involved."

"He doesn't seem smart enough."

"No, he's not. Someone is telling him what to do."

Franklyn's jaw tightened. His sandwich sat like lead in his stomach. "Do you know who the big man is?"

Kennedy glanced at his partner. "No. We've tried to figure it out."

"Fair enough." Franklyn nodded to Taylor. "Your partner ever talk?"

Kennedy laughed. "Enjoy it while you can. Once she gets talking, she never stops. Not to pile things on you, but the fire department is never around. They don't back us up either. We could have used them this morning."

Franklyn sighed, wiping the back of his hand across his mouth. "I haven't met with them yet. Guess I need to do that tomorrow."

"Thanks. Just don't expect them to be at the station. We share the building with them and never see them. Call us anytime. There's always a crew on duty." Kennedy balled up the trash from lunch.

Franklyn stood and glanced at the house. "I gotta get back to work. This place isn't going to repair itself. Thanks for lunch."

The paramedics waved as they left, but the pressure Franklyn felt didn't leave with them.

CHAPTER FIFTEEN

THE SUN WAS SETTING AS FRANKLYN UNLOADED THE LAST OF THE insulation and gyprock. If all went well, he'd have the entrance and living room finished by Sunday. He could move into the living room while he worked on the rest of the house. He'd have to track down a bed and other furniture.

Franklyn was stepping out of the shower when the radio emitted tones. "Speargrass 1, respond to alarm number 2246 for an unconscious person."

"Speargrass 1, roger."

Franklyn listened while he toweled off, shaved, and changed.

"Dispatch. Speargrass 1 is on scene."

Thirty seconds later, Speargrass 1 was back on the radio. "Dispatch, Speargrass 1, we have a cardiac arrest. Need Tribal Police and Fire."

"Roger, Speargrass 1."

Franklyn was already heading to his SUV when the tone

blared out of the radio. "Speargrass Tribal Police and Fire respond to assist EMS at alarm 2246."

Franklyn keyed the radio as he opened the SUV door. "Tribal Sheriff responding."

"Uh, roger ... Tribal Sheriff."

Franklyn smiled. *That will have them talking.*

Franklyn checked the call on his Mobile Data Terminal. The GPS automatically provided directions. The roads got worse the closer he got to the house.

Ahead, the ambulance lights flashed in the dark night. He parked beside the ambulance and entered the house. It was a bungalow—living room to the left, hallway to bedrooms to the right, and kitchen straight ahead. A crowd gathered in the kitchen—voices getting louder.

Kennedy and Taylor were kneeling on the living room floor beside a woman in her early forties. Taylor was squeezing the airway bag. A man was doing CPR. Kennedy opened boxes of medications and empty syringes piled up.

Franklyn called out to them. "What can I do?"

"We're not sure what happened," Kennedy said. "Can you talk to the family?"

"Sure." Franklyn's eyes searched the room. "Who knows this woman?"

A man stepped out of the kitchen. "That's ... that's my wife."

"Come back into the kitchen where we can talk." Franklyn pulled out a notebook. "What's your name?"

"Wendell. Wendell Green. That's my wife, Shirley."

"Tell me what happened," Franklyn said.

"She's been upset all day. Our son died this morning. He—"

"What?"

"Our son. He died of an overdose this morning. We're suffering, but my wife has been inconsolable. He was only twenty-two. We've been grieving all day. Shirley said she wanted to lay down and went to the bedroom. That was about seven." He glanced at his watch. "Two hours ago. When I came in to see if she was okay, I couldn't wake her. She was cold. Someone called 911. We helped the paramedics bring her to the living room. The paramedics said it was easier to work there."

Franklyn glanced at Kennedy and Taylor. They were working hard on the patient, and no one was interfering. "Wendell, can you take me to the bedroom?"

Franklyn scrutinized the room. He grabbed a pill bottle off the night table and held it to the light. Oxy. "Who's Randall Smoke?"

"That's my father-in-law," Wendell said.

"Why does Shirley have these pills?"

Wendell swallowed hard and stared at the floor. "Those are the ones your cop brought here this morning after the overdose. He said they were in our son's jacket."

"My cop?"

"Yeah, Leroy Balam."

Franklyn's eyes grew wide. "He gave them to your wife?"

"Yes."

"Where did your son get them?"

Wendell sighed, and his shoulders slumped. "He has a drug problem. He steals from his grandfather. Sometimes, Randall sells them to him."

"And your wife?"

"Same problem."

Franklyn strode back to the living room and knelt next to Taylor. "I found a pill bottle of Oxy. It's empty."

Taylor nodded. "That's what we figured. We've already

given Naloxone. It didn't work. She's been down awhile. We aren't getting her back. We'll go another couple of minutes, but—"

Family members crowded into the living room.

Franklyn stood and waved them back. "The paramedics need space to work. Can you all move into the kitchen."

"Franklyn." Taylor glanced up. "Look for other pills. If the Naloxone didn't work, she must have taken something else."

"Sure, I'll check." Franklyn headed back to the bedroom. He returned quickly with two pill bottles. He handed them to Taylor. "They're empty."

"Shit," Taylor said. "Gabapentin and Mogadon."

"Is that harmful?" Franklyn pursed his lips.

"Yup," she whispered. "There's no antidote for these two. We see this combination with OxyContin frequently. Always fatal."

Franklyn winced, then headed to the kitchen. Family members stared at him expectantly. "Shirley swallowed some pills—a few different ones. The paramedics have tried everything they have. She has passed on. I'm sorry."

An older woman pushed in front of Franklyn. "Are these the same paramedics that came to my grandson?"

"Yes."

She glared at Franklyn. "They're racist."

"Why do you say that?"

"They asked about drugs and alcohol. They think because we're Indians we all drink and do drugs. They're racist."

"They have to ask those questions," Franklyn said. "It's part of what they—"

Wendell put his hand on the woman's shoulder. "I've been watching them for over twenty minutes working to bring my wife back. They've done everything they could. Don't pretend the problems are anything but our own. As elders, we should be stepping in. This is on Shirley, and the drugs she took."

"She was a wonderful daughter. A terrific mother who lost her son." The woman elbowed past Franklyn and into the living room. "Get out," she shouted at the paramedics. "Leave my daughter be. Get out."

"Ma'am," Kennedy said.

"Get out!"

Franklyn stepped between the elder and the paramedics. "They are getting their equipment. Give them a minute."

She glared at Franklyn with eyes ablaze. "You're the sheriff. Get these white people off our reserve. They have no business here."

Franklyn escorted the paramedics to the ambulance. "That was dangerous."

"We're used to it," Kennedy said.

"You're kidding?"

"No." Kennedy set the heart monitor in the ambulance. "Meet us at the station. We'll get you a coffee."

Franklyn parked beside the metal Quonset and followed the ambulance inside. There was a second ambulance, two firetrucks, and two other vehicles—a Ford 150 and Forerunner.

When Kennedy and Taylor slid out of the ambulance, Franklyn was staring at the F150 and Forerunner. "You've got better response vehicles than I do."

"Not response vehicles." Taylor grinned and pointed to the Forerunner. "Our personal vehicles."

"You park inside?"

"Yup." Taylor shrugged. "If we left them outside, they'd get vandalized."

"I have to park outside."

"Sucks to be you." She chuckled and pointed to a doorway. "That's the fire department's offices. Not that you'll find firefighters there."

Franklyn wandered over to the door, found it unlocked, and opened it. The office was in darkness. "They ever here?"

"Seldom," Kennedy said.

Franklyn faced them, eyes wide. "And they don't back you up on calls?"

Taylor glanced at Kennedy. "I don't remember them being on an EMS call with us for months."

"Often, we're at fires, and they aren't," Kennedy said. "We sit and watch the building burn while waiting for the Fort Benton volunteer department to arrive."

Franklyn glanced from one to the other. "You're messing with me."

"Nope," Kennedy said. "A few years ago, Speargrass had a volunteer department. A house fire came in, so we went. We watched it burn for about thirty minutes, then Fort Benton Fire Department arrived. They worked for three hours, letting it burn to the ground and making sure it didn't become a grass or brush fire. That's all they can do. The next day there was a sign-in sheet sent to payroll. There were twenty names on the Speargrass Fire Department sign-in sheet saying they had been at the fire for five hours. Two things wrong with that. They had twelve volunteers, and no one showed up. That was the end of the volunteer department."

"Incredible." Franklyn glanced at the fire trucks. "So, now the firefighters are full-time?"

Taylor laughed as she led them through the maze of vehicles. "Well, full-time paid, but part-time working. There's one guy we haven't seen for months."

Franklyn held his hands wide. "What does the fire chief do about it?"

"Nothing," Kennedy said. "He's here maybe half the time. He's young and has limited experience. The other guy is new, he's keen, but when the veteran guy never comes to work, and the fire chief is here half the time … he just gave in. Now, he's as guilty as the other two."

Taylor opened another door. "Come upstairs and we'll get you that coffee."

Franklyn rubbed his head. "Forget the coffee. I need rum."

CHAPTER SIXTEEN

THE HEALTH CENTER OPENED AT EIGHT, AND FRANKLYN PLANNED TO be the first one there. He strode into the crowded center and stopped at the reception desk. A partition divided the waiting room from the rest of the clinic. On top of the counter was six-foot-high Plexiglas that appeared thick enough to stop a bullet. There was a tiny opening, not more than half a foot square. The lady behind the counter kept working on some paperwork. Franklyn tapped a toe while he waited and thought of all the things he needed to accomplish today.

A few minutes passed, and there was still no acknowledgment. Franklyn coughed. No response. "Excuse me."

The lady glanced up, glared, and went back to her paperwork.

"I'm Franklyn Eaglechild—"

"Well, isn't that special."

"I'm the new sheriff—"

"Extra special."

Franklyn glanced at her nametag, placed both arms on the counter, and stuck his face into the opening. "Look, Violet. I need to see the doctor. I don't have all day to wait for you to finish whatever it is you're doing."

Violet raised her head, her dark eyes glared. "I was trying to figure out how to get all these people taken care of by the doctor in the limited time he has here today."

"I don't need a lot of his time."

"You're not going to sit quietly in the waiting room, are you?"

Franklyn shook his head.

Violet dropped her pen. "Fine. I'll take you back, you being the sheriff and all. Don't expect this level of service in the future. Follow me."

She led Franklyn to an examination room and slammed the door behind her.

The examination room was like most—examination table, computer in the corner, and posters warning of the harmful effects of smoking, unprotected sex, and drugs.

The door opened, and a thin man in his fifties came in, wearing a white coat. He extended his hand. "I'm Dr. Dillard. How can I help you …?" He glanced at Franklyn.

"Franklyn Eaglechild."

Dillard sat and entered the information into the computer. "You haven't been here before."

"I'm the new sheriff here."

"You have your work cut out for you." He swung his chair toward Franklyn. "What's the problem?"

"No problem yet, doc. I thought I should come in. You see, I rodeoed for twenty years, and my body is beaten up. I'm in pain most of the time. My last doctor gave me a prescription for Oxy.

It will run out at the end of the month." Franklyn coughed, hoping the doctor wouldn't check the dates on his prescription. "I figured I should get to know you, and then when I need a prescription refill, I won't be a stranger."

Dillard pursed his lips and nodded. "Every day I have a dozen, maybe *dozens* of people needing Oxy. It's the one drug that gets asked for by name. I'm sure your previous doctor told you that generally we are not prescribing Oxy. Only in the most serious instances."

"I understand, doc, but I'm in awful shape. I brought my X-rays so you can see I've broken a lot of bones. Maybe fifty."

Dillard's eyebrows raised. Then he accepted the envelope from Franklyn. He placed a few of the X-rays on the viewing monitor. "This is old school. Few people print X-rays anymore. Everything is digital."

"I've collected them after each injury."

Dillard turned back from the X-rays. "Look, Franklyn, there's no doubt you've abused your body. I don't question that you are in pain. We need to find another solution. That will take more time than I have today. Make an appointment for next week, and I will create a treatment plan."

"But, doc—"

Dillard held up his hand. "No time today. See me next week."

As Franklyn stormed past the reception desk, Violet said, "Hey, do you want to schedule a follow-up appointment?"

"No." Franklyn slammed the door behind him.

CHAPTER SEVENTEEN

Riley and Blake sat at a boardroom table across from Alcohol, Tobacco, and Firearms Special Agent Dac Mahones. The ATF boardroom was furnished with the typical lack of imagination of most government organizations. The table was solid wood, but the chairs were well-worn and uncomfortable. The walls had a selection of prints with no apparent theme, nor recognizable people, locations or objects.

Mahones worked undercover for the ATF and looked the part. His skin was light brown, and his hair and beard black. Riley figured Mahones could pass for several nationalities, which made him the ideal undercover agent. His build was slim, but his shoulders were broad, and biceps stretched the sleeves of his black T-shirt.

Mahones flipped through the information Riley had given him. "We'll run serial numbers. Did your suspects say where they got the guns?"

"They lawyered up fast," Riley said. "Tony Hart wrote some

rambling story about them going somewhere to pick up something and take it somewhere else. So, we got nada from him. He's a meth head needing the next fix."

"They're all low end," Mahones said. "The delivery guys. They might not know where the guns came from. The farm is a convenient place to store contraband. Whoever thought about exploring under the barn is brilliant."

Riley grinned. Blake rolled her eyes.

"Who owns the farm?" Mahones asked.

"The county, I guess," Riley said. "Ten years ago, the widower who owned the place died. It's abandoned now. He had no next of kin or a will. What's *your* guess on where the guns came from?"

"The M4s and Glocks are likely stolen from a military base."

"Malmstrom Air Force Base is just east of Great Falls," Riley said. "Could they have come from there?"

"Nice and convenient. The AKs will show up as confiscated overseas and shipped back here—legally or illegally. I'd bet they were stored at the base and scheduled for destruction. The phones might be legit. Anyone could place an order overseas, and a week later, you've got a box of phones. Of course, they could be stolen. I'll know by tomorrow at the latest."

"So, we can turn this file over to you?" Riley slid his chair away from the table.

Mahones laughed. "Not so fast, Riley. That might be a lot of guns to you, but to the ATF, that's the equivalent of an ounce of marijuana. If you found ten times as many guns, then I might be interested."

"I haven't dealt with gun trafficking before," Riley said. "Where do we start?"

"Treat this like a minor drug bust," Mahones said. "What would you do?"

"I'd squeeze the little fish hoping to get a bigger fish," Riley said.

"Bingo," Mahones said. "Call me if you need advice, or you find more stolen guns. I'll run the serial numbers. If you get suspects, send their names, and I'll see if they're in our files."

"I think there was at least one additional case of guns," Riley said. "Should I be worried there's a case of guns missing?"

"You should be shitting your pants."

Riley kept the SUV above ninety as they raced back to Great Falls.

"In a rush?" Blake asked.

"We've got a lot to do. The information from Mahones was interesting but didn't help a lot. That's two hours we won't get back."

"If the information is solid, it will be worth the time."

"We'll see." Riley tapped the steering wheel. "Why did you join the FBI?"

"You asking because I'm a girl?"

Riley rolled his eyes. "It's a partner question. I couldn't care less if you were a girl or a Klingon. Do your job, cover my ass, and we'll get along fine. I'll try another question. Where are you from?"

"Mesa, Arizona. I went to University at Brigham Young University."

Riley's head jerked toward Blake. "You Mormon?"

"Um, no."

"Is there a story?"

"Isn't there always?" Blake gazed out the side window and twirled her hair. "The FBI recruits heavily at BYU. They like the clean-cut Mormon boys. They're already used to white shirts and suits."

"But they recruited you."

"Yup. The first semester, second year, they had a job fair. I thought I'd check it out. Next thing I know the FBI has checked *me* out and the full-court press was on. They paid for my last two years. I graduated in June and started the academy in September."

"How did you get this assignment?"

"I majored in chemistry and minored in martial arts."

Riley did a double-take. "You can minor in martial arts?"

"It was more of a hobby, but I went to competitions."

"You any good?"

"Respectable." Blake glanced at Riley and grinned. "I won a few matches."

"Why martial arts?"

"I hated my three older brothers beating the crap out of me. I started when I was six."

"Ah, so you were a tomboy. Who wins the fights now?"

Blake smirked. "Me. Always. They've backed off. But I still go dirt biking with them. There are hundreds of trails in Mesa."

"Well, there you go. Now I know."

"What about you?" Blake asked. "Family?"

"Divorced. Two kids, Chris and Robyn."

"Do they live in Great Falls?"

"Nope, Helena."

"We should have stopped to see them."

Riley stared out the window, and his voice grew cold. "That's not possible."

"Sorry."

They drove in silence, then Blake asked, "How did you get to DEA?"

"First, I was a deputy sheriff in western Montana and then DEA SWAT. After SWAT, I was assigned here as an agent for the DEA."

"What's the deal with you and SWAT?"

"What?"

"I heard Sheriff MacDonald mention you were kicked out of SWAT. What's the story?"

Riley's jaw tightened, and his hands gripped the steering wheel so tight, his knuckles went white. "That's not a discussion we're going to have." Riley felt the heat in his face as he drove, his eyes glued straight ahead. Then Riley slowed as they descended the hill into Speargrass. The river rushed through the valley, splitting the towering pines into a north and south bank. He drove right and parked at the back of the Tribal Administration building.

"Why are we here?" Blake asked.

"Got a warrant to execute."

"You didn't say anything earlier—" Blake jogged to catch up to Riley.

He strode into the sheriff's office and stared at a lady sitting at a desk. "We need to see Franklyn Eaglechild."

"Can I tell him what it's about?"

"What's your name?" Riley stared.

"Paulette."

"Well, Paulette, just get him." Riley stepped close to Paulette and glared down at her.

Paulette pushed her glasses up her nose and crossed her arms. "Not until I know what it's about."

Riley glanced at Blake, shrugged, and showed his badge. "Fine, have it your way. We're here to arrest Eaglechild for drunk and disorderly and failing to appear. Tell him to get his ass out here."

"Tell them to come and get me," Franklyn yelled from his office.

"Have it your way, asshole." Riley pulled out his handcuffs as he pushed past Paulette.

Blake and Paulette followed.

Franklyn was sitting with his feet on his desk. Riley knocked Franklyn's feet to the floor. "Get up, asshole."

"You've called me that a few times. I'm starting to get a complex." Franklyn stood, glared at Riley, and scratched his ear. "Here's what I want you to do. You and your ginger partner should go back out, get on your posse horses and get off my rez. You have no authority here."

"The warrant for your arrest says I have authority," Riley said. "So, do you come quietly, or do we do this the hard way?"

Franklyn peered past Riley. "Just the two of you?"

"Yup."

Franklyn grinned. "Then I guess it's the hard way."

Blake grabbed Riley's arm. "Let's double-check the warrant."

"Wait, Franklyn," Paulette said. "There must be some mistake. Don't make trouble."

"You should listen to her," Riley said.

"She makes sense, occasionally." Franklyn rubbed his chin. "Perhaps there is another way. Buy you a coffee?"

Riley slid the handcuffs onto his belt. "Sure."

"Paulette." Franklyn winked. "Mind getting us some coffee?"

Paulette stared, her mouth wide open. "But … I thought … what was … damn you. He's right. You are an asshole."

Paulette delivered the coffees and said to Blake. "Come sit with me. We can compare notes on what jerks our bosses are."

"He thinks he's my boss." Blake chuckled. "Do we have that much time?"

Coffee in hand, Franklyn leaned back in his chair and motioned with his cup. "What brings you to the rez?"

Riley sipped and made a face. "Not the coffee."

Franklyn smiled. "I like it strong."

"It's not just strong, it's thick. Like drinking motor oil." He set the cup down and told Franklyn about the gun bust and the Red Demons connection. "How were your first few days?"

Franklyn filled Riley in on the overdoses, his deputies, and his house project.

"Are you sure the house is habitable?" Riley asked.

"By the time I'm done with renovations, it'll practically be a new house."

Riley appeared skeptical. "Do you need some help?"

"I've seen your handyman skills."

"I'm better skilled now."

"Seriously?" Franklyn smirked.

"No."

"I thought maybe you'd learn something while playing house," Franklyn said. "I heard that relationship went to crapola."

"Yeah. I screwed that up." Riley swirled his coffee. "I could blame the job or shift work. I love this job. It's my life. And that's not helpful for a relationship."

"Kids?"

"Two," Riley said. "Boy, Chris, fourteen. Girl, Robyn, eleven."

"Do you see them regularly?"

That was a gut punch. He seldom saw them, and even emails were rare. He hated it when this topic came up. Franklyn was simply curious—brothers catching up. "No. They're in Helena, but …" Riley squirmed in his seat. "What about you? A lengthy line of former Mrs. Eaglechilds?"

Franklyn laughed. "Nope. I might have shacked up with a few buckle bunnies during rodeo season, and a few might have spilled over into the long, cold Montana winter."

"Kids?" Riley raised an eyebrow.

"None a lawyer has told me about."

"Just as well. The last thing we need is more like you." Riley set the coffee cup on Franklyn's desk and stood. "The real cops have work to do. Stay in touch."

CHAPTER EIGHTEEN

RILEY STEPPED INTO THE BAR AND WAITED FOR HIS EYES TO ADJUST to the dim light. Like virtually every bar in Montana, this one had a western theme. The light fixtures were antique lanterns. The floor was wood plank and littered with peanut shells. The walls were worn barn board with wanted posters for Jesse James, the Hole in the Wall Gang, and a dozen other villains of the wild west. Above the bar were revolvers that were purported to have belonged to Wyatt Earp, Buffalo Bill Cody, and Pat Garrett. Although it was unlikely any of them had ever been close to Montana.

Riley spotted Deaver and his SWAT team in a back corner. He pulled up a chair and joined them—all conversation stopped.

Deaver rolled his beer bottle on the table. "We weren't expecting you."

"I'm a special agent. I find people." Riley signaled to the

waitress for a tray of beer. "That was a bit of luck finding the guns."

No one responded.

"Good thing those assholes were asleep," Riley said. "They had enough firepower to make it a shit show."

One SWAT member eyed Riley. "You'd know all about shit shows."

Deaver glared. "That's enough, Taggert."

Riley ignored the comment but felt the sting. "I wasn't sure if this was still your regular watering hole."

"We come here once in a while," Deaver said.

"You know, team members come here," Taggert said. "A way of making sure we've got each other's backs."

Riley felt the heat race up his neck. Coming here was stupid. He knew that, but he'd come anyway. The raid had gone well. He thought the time had healed the wounds.

The waitress set a tray of beer on the table. Riley grabbed one and drank half the bottle. His jaw clenched, and he felt the tension in his shoulders. Time won't heal some wounds. His hadn't. Never would. Why did he think it would be different for these guys? "Getting those guns before they hit the street is a win."

"Yeah," Taggert said. "The only one shot this time was that puke. Riley playing the cowboy, shoot out at the O.K. Corral."

"You got something you want to say, Taggert, spit it out." Riley stood.

"You're a hazard, Riley." Taggert stood. "You're a danger to anyone who works with you. I pity your partner—what's her name, Blake?"

Riley moved toward Taggert. "Better still, let's take this outside and settle it."

"My fucking pleasure." Taggert lunged toward Riley.

Deaver was on his feet, hands on Taggert's chest, pushing him back. Another SWAT member dragged Riley away from the table.

"Riley, you need to leave," Deaver said.

Taggert sneered over Deaver's shoulder toward Riley. "Thanks for the beer."

"Screw you, Taggert."

Riley slammed the door as he entered his house. He tossed his keys on the counter—they slid across and onto the floor. He tugged at his holster and dropped his gun on the kitchen table. *I need to lock it up.* Fuck it. In two steps, he was at a cupboard and pulling out a bottle of Captain Morgan's rum. Less than an inch swirled in the bottom. He set the bottle on the counter, opened the pantry door, and slid out a box. Inside were three bottles of rum. *Damn.* Tomorrow he'd need to get another case.

He grabbed a glass mason jar out of the sink, rinsed it, filled it with ice and poured the last of the rum from the bottle, and a healthy portion from a new bottle. He flopped down in his recliner, drank two large gulps, let the fire in his throat decrease, then swallowed another gulp. He closed his eyes and took deep breaths to calm down. The encounter with SWAT and Taggert still ate away at him. He'd had no problem taking the heat for the training disaster. He was the commander—the team was his responsibility. But he'd never have believed the team would abandon him, that they'd lay the sole blame on him.

Another long drink. Taggert was an arrogant prick, always had been. But he was an excellent tactical cop. He believed he did no wrong, and his holier-than-thou attitude needed reining in. Riley wasn't there to do it, and Deaver wouldn't. No way he would rock the boat with the team—his team now.

Riley refilled the empty jar, slumped back in his chair, and clicked on the TV. The Boston Bruins better beat St. Louis tonight, or the day was a total loss.

CHAPTER NINETEEN

By mid-Saturday afternoon Franklyn was making progress. The gyprock was hung in the entrance and living room. He had installed a sizeable bay window and built a nook at the back of the house with French doors giving a magnificent view to the west. Once he hung the front door, he would call it a day. His reward was the largest steak Golden Nugget Casino had.

The dog had followed him around as he worked and even allowed a pat or two on his head. If Franklyn was working at the front of the house, the dog watched from a foot away. When Franklyn was working on the nook and installing the French doors, the dog oversaw the work from the porch.

I can't keep saying, "the dog." I need to give him a name. But a name didn't come to him. *Wild Dog* was the closest he got—not a lot of improvement.

Franklyn gathered his tools and locked them in the truck. His routine had changed slightly. When he got water for Diesel, he got water for Wild Dog. When he fed Diesel, he fed Wild Dog.

Instead of giving the dog scraps, he'd purchased a bag of dog food. With the animals happily munching on dinner, Franklyn headed to his truck. He opened his glove box, pulled out his pill bottle, and tapped two pills into his palm, and swallowed. Franklyn drove to the arena for a shower, a change of clothes, and then dinner at the casino.

CHAPTER TWENTY

Franklyn had made significant progress on the house on the weekend and needed supplies. Lefebvre helped him load four-by-eight sheets of gyprock into the truck, then slid boxes of screws, mud, and tape on top of the gyprock. Lefebvre set four pails of paint into the back of the cab along with brushes, tape, and rollers. They jumped into the truck for the drive back to Franklyn's house.

"I'm making one stop." Franklyn parked at the main entrance to the Cascade County Sheriff's Office. Lefebvre followed Franklyn up the steps to the reception counter. A lady eyed them. "Can I help you?"

"I'm here to see Riley Briggs."

"Does he know you're coming?" She appeared determined to end the conversation and get back to whatever she'd been working on.

"Nope."

She sighed. "And you are?"

Franklyn grinned. "Sheriff Franklyn Eaglechild. Speargrass Tribal Police."

She grabbed the phone. "I'll see if he is here." She punched three numbers, then said, "Sheriff Eaglechild to see Briggs. I see. Can you talk to him?" She hung up. "Riley isn't here. But one of our deputies will be right out."

Franklyn and Lefebvre stared at the array of wanted posters on a corkboard. A few had red lines drawn through them—no longer wanted. Franklyn turned when a door opened. Facing him was Gibson, arms crossed and a loopy grin on his face.

"Did you come back to see if your room was still available?" Gibson chewed a wooden match, spit out some fragments, and glared at Franklyn.

Franklyn stepped toward Gibson, forcing him to backpedal. "You never give up, do you?"

Gibson collided with a wall. "You'd better watch yourself. I've got witnesses."

Franklyn smirked. "So do I. Where's Riley? I didn't come here to talk to you."

"He's following up on a case."

"What case?"

"That's confidential. I'm not sharing that with you." Gibson straightened, apparently feeling comfortable withholding information.

Franklyn stepped back. "Tell Riley to call me as soon as he can."

"What do I say it's about?"

"That's confidential. Be sure *he* gets the message."

Back in the truck, Lefebvre asked, "What was that about?"

Franklyn told Lefebvre about Gibson stopping him for impaired driving on a trumped-up charge.

Lefebvre shook his head. "You'd think we'd be rid of assholes like that. They give all white cops a bad name."

Franklyn nodded. "That they do."

Riley Briggs slumped in his chair. "That was a royal waste of time."

Blake glanced at him. "Where were you?"

"Checking with some of my sni—confidential informants to see if they've heard about new guns for sale on the street. They haven't heard a thing."

"Or they're not telling you."

"Oh, they'd tell me."

"Now what?" Blake asked.

"I'll call Franklyn in Speargrass. Maybe he can find out what happened."

Gibson wandered over and crossed his arms. "Are you sure you want to do that? Tribal Police aren't known for having answers or being cooperative."

"Well, it's worth a shot." Riley grabbed the phone and dialed.

"Speargrass Tribal Police," a male voice said.

"This is Special Agent Riley Briggs of the DEA. I need to talk to Sheriff Eaglechild."

"He's not here."

"When will he be back?"

"Not a clue."

"Can I leave a message?" Riley asked.

"Sure, if you want to."

"Have him call Riley Briggs as soon as he can."

"Yeah."

Riley heard a dial tone. He stared at the phone, then slammed it back in place.

"Let me guess," Gibson said. "Less than helpful. Get used to it. They don't tell us shit."

"Maybe if you didn't hassle them with bogus vehicle stops, we'd get more cooperation."

"You'll figure it out, Riley. They hate us. You being buddy-buddy with the Speargrass sheriff will make things worse. They'll hate him like they hate us." Gibson headed to the door. "I'm gonna go out and hassle me some Indians."

Riley shook his head as Gibson left the office. "What an ass."

"You know he does that to get under your skin," Blake said.

"Maybe, but he *will* hassle the Indians."

"Ignore Gibson." Blake handed Riley a note. "Dac Mahones called for you."

"Does he have information for us?"

"We have an appointment tomorrow at Malmstrom Airforce Base with Major Donovan Leavitt. He wants his guns back."

CHAPTER TWENTY-ONE

That the Golden Nugget Casino restaurant would be an excellent place to go for breakfast had eluded Franklyn. You'd think after a week of *Subway* breakfasts he'd have caught on. *Too many concussions from butting heads with bulls.*

At seven, the restaurant was half full, mainly seniors. Must be another tour passing through. The corner table was vacant, and he sat facing the entrance. He peered at the paintings on the walls, all done by local artists. Most were nature scenes, some excellent.

The early breakfast meeting was with the school superintendent, Preston Thunder. Now that Franklyn was wearing a Tribal Police shirt, Preston should find him quickly enough. The waitress poured coffee and left menus. Franklyn leaned back and enjoyed the first cup of the day. He held the cup at his mouth after the first sip. Hmmm. *Not as flavorful as office coffee.* He shrugged and took another sip.

A distinguished man, matching Franklyn's height and

weight, stopped at the restaurant entrance and glanced around. He had carefully cut black hair, piercing dark eyes, and carried himself with confidence. He spotted Franklyn and headed to the table, hand held out. "Preston Thunder."

"Franklyn. Thanks for suggesting this. I'm counting on a decent breakfast." They sat. "What's tasty?"

"It's all good. If you're starving, the buffet is terrific. But you have to be starving to get your money's worth."

"Good to know."

The waitress poured a coffee for Preston and refilled Franklyn's cup.

"Are you from around here?" Franklyn asked. "I don't remember the name Thunder."

"No, northwest—Blackfeet. I have been here a year. You?"

"I grew up here," Franklyn said. "Well, born here. My older brother, sister, and I lived with my grandparents until I was twelve. I was a bit of a handful. My grandparents couldn't handle me, so I ended up in foster care. I went through a few homes in Great Falls before I stuck in one. It worked out for the best. They gave me the structure I needed."

"By structure, do you mean discipline?"

Franklyn chuckled. "Yeah, discipline. They were so tough. I was constantly in trouble for about two months. Then, I don't know, something in me snapped. I realized what they were doing. I knew they cared. That they loved me. They were white. I thought all white people were evil. That's what I'd been taught —they stole from us. Our heritage, our lifestyle, our land. But here was a family who cared. They didn't see Indian—they saw a kid and cared."

Preston nodded. "I was lucky. I had a great family around

me. Lots of love. We had nothing, but I didn't know. My father became a councilor, then chief. We lived better then."

The waitress was back and took their orders.

Franklyn sipped his coffee. "You've done well. School superintendent."

"My father was a wise man. He knew education was the key. We always went to school. Most of my friends skipped school—a lot. I thought that would be fun, so I skipped school with them when I was in grade nine—once." Preston grinned. "The leather belt came off, and I didn't sit for a week. Then my father took me to a drug and alcohol rehabilitation center for American Indians in Missoula. We went there at lunch, and we helped serve the meal. I observed the empty eyes of the men. Some barely teenagers. Vacant, nothing there. No emotion and certainly no hope. We didn't talk on the way home. We didn't need to. The lesson was clear. I have a master's in education."

"Good for you. Your father is a smart man."

"He is."

"Is he still chief there?"

"No." Preston sighed and stared at a painting behind Franklyn. "In his third term, he decided we needed to get out of poverty. That we needed to stop holding our hands out and asking the government to do everything for us. If my people needed money, he put them to work—cleaning the arena, picking up garbage, painting over graffiti—stuff like that. At the next election, his rival campaigned by saying my father had made them slaves. That he would not make them work to feed themselves. The rival even handed out money for votes. My father lost, and the new chief shamed my father. The new chief and council and their followers shunned him."

"That's harsh."

"It was difficult for my father. He is a proud man. He was doing what he thought his people needed. There was nothing in it for him. He was successful and owned a grocery store. But after the election, people stopped shopping at his store. Driving many miles away to stores with poorer quality food." Preston smiled weakly. "How about you? You grew out of your rebellion?"

"Not immediately. That first year they grounded me more than I care to remember. They tried to channel my energy … and anger. Basketball was a terrible idea. I liked to throw elbows. Hockey was next. I played on a team with my foster brother. He was a decent hockey player. Riley liked having me on the team because if anyone touched him, I would kill them. The league suggested I not play the next year. My foster parents knew they needed to find something for me. Then we went to a rodeo. It was love at first sight. So, they got me into rodeoing. I focused my anger and aggression toward the bulls. It worked out for everyone."

The waitress set their breakfasts in front of him. Franklyn dug into the eggs and hash browns. "This is great."

"You act like you're starving."

"I'm living out of a camper." Franklyn wiped his mouth with a napkin and sat back. "Sorry. Not very polite. When I'm hungry, I dive in."

"Don't worry about it." Preston spread grape jelly on his toast. "How did you become a cop?"

"My foster brother, Riley, wanted to be a cop. That was his goal since he could walk. That's all he talked about. So, when he went through the recruiting process for the Montana Highway Patrol, I thought, what the heck, and I applied. Few Indians in the MHP, so I had the inside track. We were both accepted and were scheduled to start training in September. Riley decided he'd prefer to work for a sheriff's department and headed to western Montana. The weekend before training started, I was at a rodeo. I won the bull riding and went to the bar to celebrate. While we were drinking, a guy came over to me. He said he would sponsor me in the pro-rodeo circuit. He talked a good story with lots of money involved. I was naïve. But I loved rodeo, so I said yes and signed a contract. It didn't take long for me to realize he was getting most of my rodeo winnings. It took years, but I finally got out of that contract."

"Let me guess, white guy." Preston chewed on his toast.

"I was broke and needed an offseason job. I was at a rodeo in Browning. The Montana Highway Patrol was hiring troopers. I was in great shape and Indian. Since I had already been accepted once, they hired me. I worked part-time as a trooper for ten years. When rodeo season was in full swing, I'd take a leave. When I came back to duty, though, each time I was transferred. Even though the brass wanted an Indian officer, most of the detachments didn't. Moving around was beneficial, though, I gained experience, and it wasn't just highway patrol. I did some city stuff, too. I can't rodeo anymore, and I needed a job. So, here I am."

"What does your foster brother do?"

"He's a special agent with the DEA."

"And now you're the sheriff. Do you have any experience with drugs?"

"Some, why? Do you have a drug problem?"

"*We* have a drug problem. I'm not sure the gangs are significant. There's a lot of Oxy for sale. Particularly at the three trailers by the arena, across from the schools. Sometimes at the gas bars. We've chased some guys away from the school. The dealers live in those trailers. I won't let them on the grounds, but the kids head there at lunch."

"I'll check into it. What about the gangs?"

Preston shook his head. "Wannabes. We shut that down. I banned gang colors and ball caps and suspended a few. But like I said, the dealers sell right out of their trailers. That's where your actual problem is. That and the administration building."

Franklyn's eyebrow rose. "Where I work?"

Preston nodded. "Right under your nose."

CHAPTER TWENTY-TWO

RILEY SHOWED HIS AND BLAKE'S IDS AT THE GATE TO MALMSTROM Air Force Base. The military police guard pointed them to the Military Police Building. Riley parked out front and hiked up the steps to the main door where another MP met them.

Riley showed his ID again. "We're here to see Major Donovan Leavitt."

The MP nodded. "Follow me." He led them to a door. "Step inside, sir, and ma'am. Major Leavitt will be right out." He closed the door behind them.

Riley and Blake were in a clear booth between two doors. Riley pushed the second door, but it was locked. He realized they were trapped. They were being X-rayed and scanned for chemicals.

An MP with buzz-cut salt-and-pepper hair, a bushy mustache, and an immaculate uniform, approached and opened the door.

The major was built like a middle linebacker for the Denver

Broncos. Riley's hand disappeared into the giant paw the major extended. "Welcome to Malmstrom Air Force Base," a voice, not unlike Sam Elliott, drawled. "I'm Major Donovan Leavitt. You must be Riley Briggs." He nodded to Blake. "Ma'am. You must be Leigh Blake. Come on back to my office."

They followed Leavitt through a maze of hallways to a spacious corner office. "Please, have a seat." Leavitt sat behind his desk. "Dac Mahones says you found my guns."

Riley grinned. "I guess that's for you to tell us if they're yours. We seized Glocks, M4s, and AK47s."

Leavitt steepled his fingers under his chin. "We're like a FedEx hub. All types of stuff flows through here. Some of it new, some not. Some on its way for deployment practically anywhere. Some on its way to be disposed of. The serial numbers you gave Mahones match our inventory. But when we checked, the guns were missing."

"How did they go missing?"

"I wish I could say we have stringent controls and nothing ever goes unaccounted for. But there's a lot of stuff coming and going every day. If one percent went missing, that would still be a lot of stuff. Even FedEx doesn't have one hundred percent accuracy. The guys working the warehouse typically have a low education in a minimum-paying job. When the opportunity comes to make some extra cash, they jump at it. I'm not saying they all do that, but all it takes is a few. To make it worse, the gangs, particularly the biker gangs, know bases like this are like a garage sale. Anything you need is here. So, they get their members into the military. Once through training, these guys apply for jobs like shipping and receiving. We're dumb enough to give them that assignment because no one wants those jobs. When someone volunteers, we grab them."

"Don't the guys from the gangs have criminal records?"

"Sure, some do. But we're willing to forgive those crimes for someone who wants to turn their lives around and serve their country."

"Sounds like a bunch of crap," Blake said.

Leavitt grinned. "Sure, it is. You know that, I know that, but we need the bodies."

"There must be a record of what comes in and what goes out," Blake said.

"You bet," Leavitt said. "The guys the gangs install here aren't stupid. Some of them are wizards with a computer. A quick check of our computer records and everything looks hunky-dory. Unless we suspect something is wrong and get our computer forensic nerds to check it out, stuff like the guns you confiscated goes unnoticed."

"What about the BlackBerrys?" Blake asked.

Leavitt shrugged. "Everything you can think of passes through here. BlackBerrys are the cell phone of the government. The feds like the encryption. I'll bet we have thousands of boxes coming and going every month."

"What were you doing with the AK47s?" Riley asked.

"I'll check, but my guess is they were confiscated overseas and sent here for destruction. I'm sure the bikers and gangs think they'll look cool with them. I'll take an M4 any day."

"What's the next step?" Riley asked.

"I need to find out who is stealing United States property. I'll get a team on that today. I'll give you a statement declaring the guns and BlackBerrys were the property of the United States of America and stolen. You should have an easy time getting convictions."

"We could get convictions if the judge hadn't released them."

"I could say I'm surprised," Leavitt said, "but I'm not."

"I'll get warrants for their arrest, and we'll search for them." Riley raised a finger. "One more thing."

"What's that?" Leavitt asked.

"There's a Red Demons connection. One guy we arrested had an excellent fake ID, so he was cut loose right away. When his prints came back, we found out he was high up in the northwest Red Demons."

"There you go," Leavitt said. "That helps me. I'll investigate the background of the shipping guys and see who has Red Demons connections. I might close my side of this by lunch."

"Lucky you. I've got five shitheads in the wind. They could be thousands of miles from here by now."

"That's true," Leavitt said. "I'd bet they have some unfinished business here. I doubt the Red Demons are thrilled about losing the guns. Your shitheads will have to make amends to the Red Demons, or something unpleasant will happen to them. If I get anything out of the guys on this side of the theft, I'll let you know right away."

CHAPTER TWENTY-THREE

FRANKLYN PARKED OUTSIDE THE EMERGENCY SERVICES QUONSET and strode to a door marked *Fire.* It was locked. Franklyn checked his watch—9:30. He wandered around the building and found another door marked *EMS.* He was about to knock, then stopped. They were probably sleeping. He continued around the building to the back. The immense overhead door was closed. There were two man doors on the side, but they hadn't opened for years. As he reached the front of the building, the EMS door opened.

"How did you know I was here?"

Eric Kennedy pointed skyward. "Cameras. I watched you walk around the building. Did you come for coffee?"

"I came to meet the firefighters."

Eric laughed. "I won't see them until maybe ten-thirty or eleven. Come in for a coffee."

Franklyn followed Eric up the stairs to a room that was a combination kitchen and living room. It couldn't be more than twelve by fourteen. Eric handed Franklyn a coffee and sat on the couch. Franklyn scanned the cramped room. "Not a lot of space here." He sat in a recliner.

"A bit crowded, but we call it home."

Franklyn sipped. "This is excellent."

"Special blend. One of the few comforts we have."

"You're awake early," Franklyn said.

"I don't sleep a lot," Eric said. "I'm on the computer most of the time."

"Was this always the fire and EMS building?"

"No. It was a temporary structure built for highway work here about fifteen years ago. The rez got it when they left. For years, we were bounced around. We even lived at the casino with the ambulance parked outside. In the winter, we'd plug it in but have to start it every couple of hours. The ambulance had a lot of vandalism. So they moved us here. This was a temporary office space. We converted it to bedrooms."

"Is it safe?"

"Well, aside from the fact there's only one route out of here in a fire, the diesel from the outdated firetrucks drifts here, and the mice scratching in the walls when we are trying to sleep—other than that, yeah, it's safe."

Franklyn laughed. "Where's your partner?"

"Unlike me, she likes to sleep. Won't see her until noon unless there's a call. So, what do you think of the rez? Is it what you remember?"

Franklyn took another sip. "That was a long time ago. I don't think a lot has changed and that's depressing. I see the same defeated looks in the eyes of the elders. But now I see it in people of my generation. The worst thing is I see it in the youth. That's what scares me. I've been gone for close to twenty-five years. There still aren't many businesses. Sure, there's the casino, gas bar, and *Subway*. But the best jobs go to the chief and councilors' families."

Franklyn shook his head.

"There are jobs in Great Falls or Helena. But how would you get there? You don't have money for a car because you don't have a job. If you had a job it would be here, so you wouldn't need a car. It's just round and round."

"There's a lot of hitchhiking," Eric said.

"Yeah. I've seen that. Not a safe way to get to and from work. Not reliable. If you missed a few shifts or were late, you'd be fired."

Eric nodded. "We've picked up a few hitchhikers. Typically in the winter, when it's minus one hundred. It doesn't bother me, but I worry about the ladies. Sometimes we have two lady paramedics working together. I don't like it when I hear they picked up a guy."

"That's not a safe idea."

"I know," Eric said. "I tell them, but when it's freezing, what can they do?"

"I remember my older brother would hitchhike to Helena," Franklyn said. "He'd have his girlfriend stand on the highway. When someone stopped to pick her up, he'd jump out of the ditch and climb into the vehicle too. He'd laugh when he told the story. It always pissed off the drivers."

"They still do that. One night we stopped, and I swear a dozen people came out of the ditch. We packed them in and brought them back to the rez. Where's your brother now?"

"He died about ten years ago. Traffic accident."

The sound of the bay door opening interrupted their conversation. Then the rumble of a diesel engine starting.

"Firefighters are early," Eric said.

"Well, I guess I should go say hi," Franklyn said. "Thanks for the coffee."

"Anytime."

Franklyn followed engine noise and the smoke back to the emergency vehicles. The firetruck was belching purple smoke. A lanky man in a blue shirt and pants stood outside the overhead door smoking. Franklyn headed to him. "I'm Franklyn Eaglechild, the sheriff."

The man exhaled smoke and stared. Finally, he shook the extended hand. "Jay Littlebear. Fire chief." He stared past Franklyn to the trees and took a long drag on the cigarette. "I hear I gotta report to you now."

"That's what they want," Franklyn said. "Don't think of it as working for me. We can work together."

"You got any firefighting experience?"

"I'm handy at starting campfires," Franklyn said.

"I got enough arsonists here." Littlebear stomped out the cigarette. "Don't need another."

Franklyn wasn't sure where to take this conversation. Littlebear was creating a wall. Franklyn wasn't sure if it was because Littlebear didn't like reporting to him, or Littlebear didn't like reporting to anyone. "Look, Littlebear. I have no firefighting experience. That's up to you. I'll take care of the budget and get you the equipment you need. At fires, you're the boss."

"Sure, works for me." He pushed past Franklyn toward the running firetruck.

"Where are your other guys?" Franklyn asked.

"Not sure." Littlebear kept walking.

Franklyn jogged to catch up. "When do they generally get here?"

"They don't come in unless there's a fire."

Franklyn crossed his arms and stared. "I thought you three were full time."

"We flex our hours cuz most fires are at night."

"Do they check in with you?"

"Sometimes."

Franklyn gritted his teeth. Simple-sentence answers. He was giving minimal information. "Do you start the truck every day?"

"Pretty much."

"You run it inside?"

"Yup."

"You know the paramedics are upstairs trying to sleep, and the diesel exhaust drifts up there?"

"Not my problem."

"Maybe you could move the truck outside while it's running."

"I suppose I could."

"How about every day, that's what you do."

"Didn't take you long to tell me what to do, did it?" Littlebear brushed past Franklyn, climbed into the truck, and drove out of the bay. He continued out onto the highway and headed to the townsite.

That went well.

CHAPTER TWENTY-FOUR

FRANKLYN PARKED BESIDE THE ARENA AT ELEVEN FORTY-FIVE. HE wasn't trying to hide, but he wasn't in the open either. Shortly after noon, three teens sauntered across the school parking lot, past the arena, and up the hill to the trailers. Within minutes Franklyn's count was at twenty, with more coming across the parking lot. He figured they stayed about three minutes, then headed to the school playground where they sat against the fence. By twelve forty-five, the flow of students had stopped. When the school bell went at twelve fifty-five, they strolled toward the school. Franklyn watched the last of them enter the school.

A knock at the window surprised him. He lowered the window to see Jesse's gap-toothed grin. "Hey, man, what're you doing here?"

"Just some policing."

Jesse glanced at the trailers. "You watching the kids buy drugs?"

"You know about that?"

"Sure, man. They sell to the kids all the time."

"What do they sell?"

Jesse shrugged. "Whatever. You know. If the dealers get Oxy, they sell that. If they get some meth, they sell that. Like, whatever they have."

"Are you thinking about buying some of their product?"

Jesse smiled the toothless smile. "Not from them. They won't sell to me."

"Why not? Dealers don't care who they sell to."

Jesse bounced back and forth. "I ripped them off … a few times."

"That would piss them off."

"That's how I lost my teeth—well, some of them." Jesse's smile widened, exposing the gaps.

"What do you do, Jesse?"

"I'm an artist."

Franklyn's eyes widened. "You didn't tell me that when we met."

"I don't remember when we met."

"Are you talented?"

Jesse set down a pack, pulled out a sketch pad, and handed it to Franklyn. He flipped through the drawings. *They're outstanding.* "You've got talent, Jesse."

"You want to buy one? Fifty bucks."

"They're first-rate, but that's too expensive for a sketch." Franklyn pointed to a drawing. "What's this?"

"Sitting Bull running Custer through with Custer's sword."

Franklyn handed the sketch pad back to Jesse. "That didn't happen, did it?"

"Does it matter?"

Franklyn shrugged. "I guess not. Get in. I'll take you to *Subway* and buy you lunch."

"I'd rather have the money."

"I know you would." Franklyn smiled. "You said that last time. Lunch or no deal."

"Lunch, I guess."

CHAPTER TWENTY-FIVE

Riley stopped at the gate and watched the military police officer approach. He scrutinized Riley's SUV while a second MP slid a mirror on an extendable pole under the vehicle. Then he approached the open driver's window. "Identification."

Riley handed his and Blake's ID to the MP. He compared Riley's picture to the ID. He headed to the passenger side and examined the FBI ID, his eyes on Blake most of the time.

He marched back to Riley. "You two armed?"

"Yep," Riley said. "We both have pistols, and I have a backup. Ankle holster."

"What's the purpose of your visit?" The MP stared stone-faced at Riley.

"We're meeting with Major Leavitt."

"What's the nature of your visit?"

Riley sighed. "Talk to Leavitt. He invited us."

The MP stared at Riley while he tapped their ID in his hand.

Finally, the MP handed Riley their identification and strode to the guard shack.

The gate arm lifted, and Riley accelerated through, then slowed when he was past the MPs.

Blake shoved her ID back into her pocket. "What was that about?"

"Hell if I know."

They entered the Military Police Building, and things got worse. First, they emptied their pockets and placed their guns and phones in a tray. This time when they entered the glass room, they were held there for five minutes. When they were released, an MP waved a wand over them. Then they were escorted to the full-body X-ray and scanned.

An MP grabbed their guns and cell phones. "We'll keep these safe while you're here."

Riley wanted to protest but decided it wasn't worth the argument that he would lose.

Another MP escorted them to the elevator and accompanied them. Leavitt met them as they exited onto his floor. "You got here fast."

"We would have been quicker if we hadn't been treated like terrorists by your MPs at the gate and downstairs."

"Sorry about that. After you told me about the stolen guns, I increased security."

Riley explained the search conducted downstairs.

Leavitt pursed his lips and crossed his arms. "I guess word got out you two had a role in getting guys on base arrested. That's their way of saying they don't approve of outsiders. I'll have a word with them."

"You arrested two guys?" Blake asked.

Leavitt nodded. "It didn't take long. I had my best IT geek

check the computer files for all shipping and receiving involving guns. It took him about ninety seconds to find the fake computer records and another five seconds to find the clerk involved. I checked who his friends were, and we got his accomplice."

Riley stepped closer. "Have you interviewed them?"

"No. We made a show of the arrest. Never hurts to put the fear of Uncle Sam in their heads. They've been biding their time in separate cells. We waited until you got here to interview."

"I'd like to be in the interview room," Riley said.

"No can do. Not yet, anyway. They'll be tried in a military court. I don't want their JAG lawyer claiming there's inappropriate pressure from outside law enforcement. Nothing personal."

"None taken," Riley said.

"We'll get the information we need. If there's anything we miss, let me know, and I'll let you talk to them."

Leavitt led them to the elevator and pushed the button for the basement. When the elevator doors opened, two armed MPs were waiting, and they were taken to a room that looked like NASA's Mission Control. It was the size of a basketball court. Monitors covered three walls, and computer screens sat on every desk.

"Wow," Blake said. "It's impressive."

"We monitor the entire base from here—entrances to the base, every building, warehouses, the hangars, runways—everything you can think of. Which makes it impressive they got cases of guns off the base."

"I'm not sure *impressive* is the word I'd use," Riley said. "But certainly creative."

Leavitt led them to a room at the far end of mission control. A giant screen covered one wall. On display were a dozen images from around the base. Riley, Blake, and Leavitt sat in chairs facing the screen. Not just any chairs, but recliners with various controls on the armrests.

"Are we here to watch the latest Fast and Furious movie?" Riley asked. "I need a Coke and popcorn."

Leavitt laughed. "I'm not saying that does or doesn't happen. This is a multi-purpose room. Some interrogations take hours. Other events of a strategic and tactical nature can go on for days. It is enjoyable watching an interrogation in comfort. This is also the most secure room." Leavitt pressed a button on the arm of his chair. "Bring up the live feed from the interrogation rooms. We're ready."

The jumbo screen went blank, then images from two interview rooms appeared, side by side. The rooms were identical—a table with one chair on one side and two chairs on the other. In both rooms, a prisoner sat handcuffed to a table. The door to room one opened, and two men dressed in MP uniforms entered and sat across from the prisoner. He glared at the MPs.

"I'm Lieutenant Watson." The MP nodded to his partner. "This is Sergeant Hudson. Do you know why you're here?"

The prisoner shrugged. "They said I sold guns or something. I don't know what they're talking about."

"I have a few questions about your job on the base."

The prisoner tried to lean back in his chair, but the handcuffs kept him in place. So, he stretched out his legs. "Ask me anything."

Watson tapped a file folder on the table. "You work in shipping and receiving."

"Yeah, so?"

"Your job is to track everything that comes in or goes out and enter it into the computer?"

"Yup." He yawned and glanced at the camera mounted on the wall.

"Where did you get your computer skills?"

"Prison."

Lieutenant Watson flipped through the file. "You were in prison for selling drugs to school kids."

"Yeah."

"How did you get into the forces?"

"I was a model prisoner. I went to classes and stuff. I'm skilled with computers. They offered me a deal. If I joined the forces, they'd let me out of prison. I wanted out."

"Tell me about your tattoos. Where did you get them?"

"Some before prison, some in prison, and some this year."

"Tell me about the biker tattoos."

"What do you mean?"

"The one on your left bicep—Red Demons."

"I got that before prison."

"Did they have anything to do with the drugs you were selling then?"

"I don't want to answer. Besides, I didn't know where the drugs came from. I was just a dealer."

"For the Red Demons?"

"That was then. I work for the military now."

"Do you associate with any gang?"

"I'm over that."

Watson slid a photo over the table. The suspect glanced at it and shoved the picture away.

"Look again." Watson slid the picture back. "That's you playing pool last night with your buddy. The bar is packed, and the bikers are wearing the colors. Wait, you have a biker vest, too."

"Shit." The prisoner put his head onto his hands. The MPs left the room.

The screen switched to the other interview room. The MPs entered—they sat as before.

Prisoner two worked at the loading dock of shipping and receiving. This interview proceeded like the first. But he provided a fresh piece of information. They were contacted in prison by the Demons and coached on what to do to get out on good behavior. The bikers arranged for an ex-military guy to teach them about the army and how to get the right assignments. The interviews took three hours, with the MPs moving between rooms. Riley could barely keep his eyes open, and then he heard the first suspect say, "If I cooperate, what's in it for me?"

Watson leaned back in his chair, quiet, as if bored.

"I've got the info you need."

The prisoner had Riley's full attention.

"We can't make promises," Watson said. "That's up to the Judge Advocate General's office." He glanced at his partner. "We don't have any problem talking to JAG about how helpful you were."

"You'll really talk to JAG?"

"Absolutely."

The suspect squeezed his nose and sniffled. Watson waited.

"Come on, come on," Riley said under his breath.

"Here's how we did it."

Riley grinned. *Bingo.*

For the next hour, the prisoner detailed the plan. The planes coming back from Iraq and Afghanistan were loaded with weapons. The warehouse was always jam-packed. The paperwork with the guns was marginal. The bottom line: the armed forces had no clue how many firearms went to Iraq and Afghanistan, let alone how many came back. Cases labeled M16s were a mix of M16s, M4s, and AK47s.

They'd tried to sort the guns into groups. That made it worse —guns all over the warehouse floor, and then there was no way to track where the weapons had come from.

One night over beers and games of pool, they had talked about how screwed up the military was. A few weeks later, they met in a private room at the bar. The local biker president was there with another biker interested in the guns.

"With the mess of guns all over the base, I had the shipping guys sort out the new rifles and pistols and stack them in one area—the working guns in another—and the wrecked weapons in the third pile. Those were to be destroyed. We had thousands of cases stacked throughout the warehouse. At night I changed the computer records and moved cases of new guns to the 'to be destroyed' pile. I loaded them on pallets, wrapped them in plastic, and changed the labels. I entered a disposal company name into the federal system, but it was run by the bikers. They came before six a.m. when I was about to go off shift, but before the day shift came in. I added the new guns to the disposal files and printed off the paperwork, which would appear legit if the MPs checked the truck and double-checked with the computer. It would all match."

"How many loads did they haul away?"

"About twenty—two loads a week."

Twenty. Riley shook his head in amazement.

"How long have you been doing this?" Watson asked.

"About three months."

"How many cases to a load?"

"Four pallets, with about twenty cases per pallet."

"How many guns per case?"

"Typically, twenty rifles. More if it was handguns."

Riley did the math in his head—1600 rifles a load! He dropped back into his chair. He glanced at Blake, who stared open-mouthed at the screen.

"Where do the guns go after they leave the warehouse?"

The prisoner shook his head. "I heard the Red Demons needed guys to drive trucks all over the US—to white supremacists, local militias and survivalists. There were loads to Canada and Mexico. Some sizable shipments went to Los Angeles, Chicago, Detroit, and New Orleans."

Riley, Blake, and Leavitt stared at the screen. No one knew what to say.

Riley was shaking his head. "Holy shit."

Leavitt punched a button on his chair and issued orders. "I've got the warehouse on lockdown, and everyone who works there confined to quarters. Any that live off base will be picked up and confined to base. It'll take weeks—months—to unravel this."

"That's an understatement," Riley said. "And I was excited about finding a few cases of guns."

"I owe you two a medal, but we don't give them to civilians. We can do drinks. If you ever need anything, call me."

"It wouldn't hurt if the governor and attorney general knew our part in this."

"Riley has a public relations problem," Blake said. "He needs all the gold stars he can get."

Leavitt laughed. "I'll mention it to my wife. She's the chief of staff for the governor."

"I'd like to talk to the suspect for a minute—no longer," Riley said.

"Sure," Leavitt said. "We have the information we need. Follow me." They left the room and followed Leavitt down a hall. He knocked twice on the door, and it opened. Lieutenant Watson blocked the way.

"Special Agent Briggs has a few questions," Leavitt said. "I said it would be okay." Watson stepped aside.

Riley entered the room. "I'm Special Agent Riley Briggs. Why did the BlackBerrys get shipped out with the guns?"

"That was a special order. The other biker wanted Black-Berrys for his guys. I adjusted the computer record."

Riley slapped a photo on the table. "I'd like you to look at that picture and tell me if you know him or have seen him."

The suspect nodded. "Yeah. That's the guy I met in the bar. He's the one with the plan."

"Do you know his name?" Riley asked.

"I'm not sure anyone said it."

CHAPTER TWENTY-SIX

FRANKLYN PARKED BESIDE THE ARENA AND USED HIS BINOCULARS TO check on the trailers. He couldn't see anything useful—no sign of anyone awake. At eleven-fifty, a guy came out of the first trailer and wandered over to the second. Knocked once and entered. A few minutes later, he was back with a grocery bag. Shortly after twelve, the first students crossed in front of Franklyn. The teens didn't give him a second look. Either they didn't see him, or they weren't scared. That they weren't worried about the cops seeing them buy drugs was a problem.

Same as before, they were at the trailer a few minutes and then strolled back to the school. Franklyn stepped out of the SUV and snuck along the side of the arena. When he was out of sight of the trailers, he waited. As the teens strolled past, Franklyn called to them. "Sheriff. Come here."

They glanced at each other, then to the schoolyard.

"Don't even think of that," Franklyn said. "You're not faster than a bullet."

"You can't shoot us."

"You want to find out? Just get over here."

They shuffled over to Franklyn. The one who'd done the talking was older, maybe sixteen. The other younger, maybe thirteen.

"What're your names?"

The older one said, "Johnny Hunter. He's my cousin, Kellan Hunter. Who're you?"

"Franklyn Eaglechild. Sheriff."

"Where's the other sheriff?" Johnny asked.

"I don't know," Franklyn said. "He left, I guess."

Johnny shuffled foot to foot. "What about Leroy?"

"What about Leroy?" Franklyn countered.

Johnny shrugged. "He doesn't give us no hassle."

"I'm sure he doesn't," Franklyn said. "What were you doing at the trailer?"

Johnny glanced toward the school. "Just talking to a friend."

"That friend got a name?"

"I ain't sayin'," Johnny said.

"Why not?"

"I don't know you, man. I shouldn't have given you my name."

"Yet you did," Franklyn said. "I'm the police. You have to."

"You got no authority here."

Franklyn's jaw dropped. "I'm the police."

"That don't mean nothing," Johnny said.

Franklyn ground his teeth. He was tired of dealing with Johnny's attitude. "You got five seconds to tell me the name or I'm arresting you for possession."

"Possession of what?"

"Whatever I find when I search you."

"That's an illegal search."

"You a fricken' lawyer?" Franklyn said. "I caught you coming out of a trailer of known drug dealers." Franklyn grabbed Johnny by the arm, swung him against the wall of the arena, and applied handcuffs.

Kellan backed away.

"Stay where you are."

Kellan froze. Franklyn grabbed his second set of cuffs and slapped them on Kellan. Franklyn pushed Kellan against the wall beside his cousin.

"Am I going to find anything sharp in any of your pockets?"

"Kiss my ass, man," Johnny said.

Franklyn leaned harder against Johnny.

"If I get hurt, you'll be sorry."

"I'm scared shitless."

Franklyn searched Johnny and found a four-inch gravity knife and two baggies of pills—seemed like Oxy. "You got a prescription for these?"

"Of course."

The search of Kellan produced two baggies of pills and a switchblade.

"You two want to tell me who's selling from the trailers?" Franklyn asked. "Or do you want to go to jail? Your call. You have ten seconds."

Silence.

"Five seconds."

"I don't want to go to jail," Kellan whimpered.

"He's bluffing," Johnny said. "Maybe me. But you're too young."

"Your cousin's right," Franklyn said. "He'll go to jail. You'll go to foster care. That's worse."

Kellan was in full body-racking sobs. "I'll … I'll tell you."

"Shut—"

Franklyn's meaty hand pushed Johnny's face against the wall.

"Go on, Kellan," Franklyn said.

"They're brothers or cousins. Lonnie, Torin, and Zeke Lamont."

"They live together?"

"No. They each have a trailer."

"How do you know which one to go to?"

"In the window," Kellan said. "Each day they put a red bandana in the front window. That's where the drugs are."

"Why a red bandana?"

"You know, they're Red Demons, man."

Franklyn nodded. "Since you two have been cooperative, I'll cut you a break. I'll keep the knives and the drugs. You can go back to school."

"I don't have to go to foster care?" Kellan asked.

"Nope." Franklyn undid the handcuffs. "Get in my truck."

"Why?" Johnny asked.

"I'm taking you back to school."

"It's okay," Johnny said. "We know the way."

"Get in. I need to make sure you talk to Superintendent Thunder."

CHAPTER TWENTY-SEVEN

As Franklyn entered the office, Paulette's phone rang. "Yup. He's here. Okay. Now? Okay."

"Boss, you're wanted in HR right away. Eva needs to talk with you."

Franklyn turned on his heel and headed downstairs to Eva's office. He knocked once, then strode in. He stretched out in a chair, tossed his Stetson onto another chair, and put his hands behind his head. "I knew you'd be calling to see me."

Eva raised an eyebrow. "How did you know?"

"I just knew. From our last conversation."

"Our one conversation," Eva said.

Franklyn grinned. "Yeah, that one."

"I received a call from Chief Fox," Eva said. "He's agitated."

"I'm sorry," Franklyn said. "Did you do something wrong?"

"Not me, you idiot." Eva rolled her eyes and glared at Franklyn. "You hassled the fire chief."

"Littlebear treats the job like it's an inconvenience. I still haven't seen the other firefighters and Littlebear has no clue where they are."

"The chief wants me to remind you he expects you to use discretion in dealing with your staff," Eva said. "This isn't the way he wants you to handle things."

Franklyn folded his arms across his chest. "Why doesn't the chief tell me?"

"Well, he feels this is a human relations problem that I can handle it."

"Can you?"

"Can I what?"

"Handle me." Franklyn watched the red flush start on her chest and up her neck to her cheeks.

"That's not, I mean, what I meant ..." Eva stopped, inhaled deeply, then sighed. Franklyn nearly laughed out loud.

"You have to play by the rules," she said.

"Whose rules? The chief or the constitution?"

"What?"

"Do I enact the laws of the United States or the chief's whims."

"Both, I guess."

Franklyn slapped his thigh and grabbed his Stetson. "Let's go for dinner tonight."

"What? No. Franklyn. This is serious."

"I am serious."

"You'll lose your job," Eva said.

"For having dinner with you?"

"You're impossible."

"Are you worried about me?" Franklyn stood. "Tell me over dinner."

"Franklyn—"

He grabbed a pen off her desk. "Write your address. I'll pick you up at five. Wear something fancy."

CHAPTER TWENTY-EIGHT

FRANKLYN ENTERED THE OFFICE AND STOPPED AT PAULETTE'S DESK. "What can you tell me about the previous sheriff?"

Paulette peered up from her computer. "What do you want to know?"

"Why did he leave?"

She tilted her head to the side and chewed her lip. "Quick answer is he and the chief didn't get along."

"They fired him?"

"Humiliated. There's a lesson for you."

Franklyn nodded. "I want to review the incident reports and arrests related to drugs for the past two years. Can you get them for me?"

"Sure," Paulette replied. "There's an elder who wants to see you."

"Tell him I'm busy. Make an appointment for next week."

"Uh, boss, he's right here."

Franklyn glanced at the waiting area. An older man with

silver-white hair sat at one chair. His posture was perfect, and he smiled at Franklyn with gleaming white teeth.

"No time for an elder." The man shook his head. "We will have to work on your manners, my son." He stood and strode toward Franklyn. "Silas Powderhorn." He extended a hand.

"My apologies. I'm—"

"Yes, I know. Franklyn Eaglechild. Son of Clarence, grandson of my friend Isaac."

"Come to my office." Franklyn turned back to Paulette. "Can you get those files for me, please?"

The elder sat.

Franklyn tossed his Stetson onto the top of the file cabinet. "Can I get you anything? Coffee?"

Powderface held up a hand. "No, I am fine. Your delightful assistant provided for my needs while I waited."

"I hope you weren't here long." Franklyn sat.

"An hour or more."

"I am sorry. Paulette should have called me."

Powderhorn shrugged. "She offered, but I am an elderly man. I had nowhere else to be. I enjoyed my conversation with her."

"How can I help you?"

"Oh, you can't do anything for me. I am here to help you."

"How so?"

Powderhorn leaned forward. "I was chairman of the Justice Committee for many years. I oversaw the Tribal Police."

"I didn't know there is a Justice Committee."

"There isn't anymore." Powderhorn snorted. "Chief Fox didn't want others telling him what to do. He wanted control of the police, so he disbanded the committee ten years ago."

"Chief Fox has total control? There's no oversight?"

"An interesting choice, you are."

"How so?"

"Typically, he has sheriffs who owe him or who have a terrible secret only he knows. Men he can control."

"What happened to the last sheriff? Paulette said he and the chief didn't get along."

"His secret was that he's an alcoholic. He was drunk one night at a wake and told Chief Fox he was an insufferable prick, a liar, a fornicator, and a cheat."

Franklyn shook his head. "Not a smart idea."

"The next day, a few of the chief's men came to this office, dragged him out, beat him, and stripped him of his clothes. He staggered away in humiliation."

"I'll remember to keep a spare set of clothes here."

Powderhorn laughed. "Yes. Excellent idea."

"Why would Chief Fox hire me?"

"You must have a secret he can exploit." Powderhorn cocked his head to the side. "Have you thought about what that is?"

"I'm just a worn-out rodeo cowboy," Franklyn said. "What you see is what I am."

"I see an honest man." Powderhorn smiled, then lowered his eyes. "But none of us is so pure as not to have secrets. My warning to you is, be ready for the day he uses your secret against you. Decide now how you will handle that. You will stand up to him, no matter the consequences, or he will own you. And everything you believe in will be compromised."

Franklyn frowned. "I can handle the chief."

Powderhorn stood and smiled weakly. "Many before thought the same thing. One last warning. Trust no one."

Franklyn scrambled out of his chair and extended a hand.

Powderhorn accepted Franklyn's hand with both of his. "Thank you for your valuable time. Good day."

Franklyn dropped into his chair after Powderhorn left. He leaned back and put his boots on his desk. He closed his eyes and thought about the warnings. Secrets. There was no way the chief could know.

CHAPTER TWENTY-NINE

Franklyn parked outside Eva's house in Fort Benton. It was a bungalow that, at one time, had been part of the married quarters for the Air Force Base. It was in excellent condition. He wondered if there was a man's touch to the yard.

He'd rushed home after four, grabbed some clean clothes, jeans, a checked shirt, and his snakeskin cowboy boots. He raced to the arena for a shower and shave. He nearly forgot to feed Diesel. As he was about to leave, Wild Dog lurked around the corner. Franklyn scooped dog food into a bowl and set it by the corral. It appeared the dog was his for life.

He was barely out of the car when Eva appeared at the door in a navy blouse, dark pants, and low heels. He held the car door open. "You look great."

She smiled. "I see you changed into your cleanest, same-looking outfit."

Franklyn glanced at his clothes. Maybe he should do some clothes shopping in Great Falls.

Once Eva had the seatbelt on, she glanced around the truck. Franklyn realized that while he'd cleaned himself well, he'd forgotten about the truck. "Umm, sorry. I didn't think of cleaning the truck."

"No problem. I love the smell of horse manure mixed with man sweat." She grinned and punched him lightly on the arm. "Don't worry about it. I've been in worse."

"That's hard to imagine."

"Have you been inside Balam's SUV? There's stuff growing in there."

Franklyn gave Eva a sideways glance. "I'll check into that."

"Where are we going for dinner?"

"Great Falls," Franklyn said. "It's best we are away from the rez."

"Are you worried about my reputation?" Eva asked.

Franklyn grinned. "No, mine."

Franklyn stared across the table as Eva sipped her red wine, then swallowed a gulp of his rum and Coke. *That hit the spot.* They sat at a corner table so Franklyn had a view of the entrance. The table was laid out with a white tablecloth and napkins, more utensils than he would need, and a selection of glasses, some for water, others for wine. Not that he knew which wine went with which glass.

"I still don't get it. Other than being here with me, you seem bright, good at what you do. Any business would be ecstatic to have you. Why work on the rez?"

Eva set her wineglass down and sat back. "It was a 'get started' job. I'd graduated from college and didn't have any experience. I applied for lots of jobs, but the rez was my only offer. If you want to get your feet wet in Human Resources, the rez is a place to learn. After a few years, I bought the house in Fort Benton. I got comfortable with life."

"What do you do in your job?"

"Everything from hiring to firing." She pulled her hair off her shoulder. "Lots of people want jobs—well, they want the paycheck, but not the work. Every department is a revolving door of employees. Late for work or not showing up at all are issues. In some departments, it's not a problem. But if we don't have police or fire, that can be significant."

"I know." Franklyn nodded and furrowed his eyebrows. "The police need a lot of work, but the fire department—I don't even know where to start. I need to hire at least one, maybe two additional deputies."

"If you've got the budget." She leaned toward Franklyn. "I can help."

Franklyn cleared his throat. "At least EMS seems dialed in."

"You won't have issues with EMS. When you get called to your first fire here, you'll see what I mean. Anyway, after a few years, I had an excellent grasp of the job and the culture here. The position of Human Resources director was available, and I got it.

The waitress set menus in front of them.

"Thank you." Franklyn glanced at Eva. "We'll have another round of drinks before we order."

Eva sipped her wine and peered over her glass. "Why did you come back?"

"I needed a job." His chin dropped, and he stared at his hands. "I'm broke. Rodeo doesn't give you too many career opportunities."

"Why didn't you go back to Montana Highway Patrol?"

"That was an option, but I was fed up with getting bumped around. I wanted to settle in one place."

Eva's grin was wide, an amused expression on her face. "And you picked Speargrass?"

Franklyn rubbed the back of his neck and laughed. "Doesn't make sense, does it?"

"Did you want to get back to your culture?" Eva reached across the table and slid her fingers across Franklyn's hand.

"I don't think I thought of that until I got here." Franklyn pulled his hand back and rubbed it on his pants. "I was a kid when social services hauled me away. But when I got back here, I realized not a lot had changed. There was still poverty, contaminated water, and it was like everyone had given up."

Eva leaned forward, meeting his gaze. "Do you want to change that?"

"I'd like to."

"That's noble, but after ten years here, I don't have a clue what the solution is."

The waitress placed fresh drinks in front of them.

Eva opened her menu. "Should we order dinner?"

"Good plan."

They ordered and sipped their drinks. Franklyn rubbed his chin. "Baby steps. I'll work on Tribal Police first. Then the fire department."

"Good luck." Eva tilted her wine to him.

Franklyn tapped her glass. "When you aren't working, what do you do?"

"I like mountain biking."

Franklyn glanced out the restaurant window. "Few mountains here."

"Well, maybe not mountains, unless I'm on vacation. Then I go to Moab in Utah or Kananaskis in Alberta. What about you?"

"No real hobbies, I guess." He spun the drink in his hands. "The rodeo was both a hobby and a job. It takes hard work to get to the top and stay there. Once I'm settled, I'll ride my horse. My hobby is rebuilding a house."

Eva's eyes sparkled. "Any Mrs. Eaglechild or ex-Mrs. Eaglechild?"

"Nope, neither of those. And no tiny Eaglechilds—as far as I know."

Eva smirked. "No ladies in your life?"

"Oh, I didn't say that." Franklyn chuckled. "Well, not now, but on the rodeo circuit—"

"I'm sorry I brought that up." Eva stared down her nose. "Some things a girl just doesn't want to hear."

"What about you? Pretty lady, impressive job. You'd be a catch and a half on the rez."

Eva chuckled. "Don't think the men haven't tried. Frequently, married men. The young guys are too scared."

"The chief speaks highly of you." Franklyn flashed a broad grin.

"Don't think he hasn't tried a thousand different ways—the two of us going to meetings outside Speargrass. One hotel room booked. Or a meeting in Las Vegas, except he and I were the only ones there. When sneakiness and charm didn't work, he flat out threatened my job. I told him to fire me. He kicked me out of his office. He still tries, just not as frequently."

Franklyn flexed a bicep. "I'll protect you."

Eva's eyes flashed over her wine glass. "You think you are man enough for the job?"

Riley parked outside the restaurant. With little food in his house and the hectic pace of the last few days, he was starving. Nothing a rare thick steak couldn't cure. He licked his lips in anticipation. A double rum and Coke would hit the spot.

He called Regan on his cell phone. It rang two times before she answered. "Are you finished for the day?"

"Nothing pending until tomorrow."

"Great," Regan said. "So, we've got the night together? You're not going to dine and dash?"

"I'm all yours for at least twelve hours." Riley headed down the sidewalk. "I'm at the restaurant. I'll get a table. Do you want a glass of Chardonnay?"

"Oh, yes. A large glass."

"That shitty of a day?"

"You won't believe it when I tell you. See you in fifteen."

Riley tucked his phone in his pocket and headed into the restaurant where the hostess met him. "For one?" She grabbed a menu.

"For two," Riley said. "I would prefer a quiet corner."

"I'll see what we have." She peered at a diagram of the restaurant.

Out of habit, Riley's eyes scanned the room. He'd been here many times, but he still located the exits, perused the occupants of every table and … what the—

It couldn't be, but it was. Franklyn Eaglechild was at a corner table with a gorgeous lady with long brown hair.

"I have a table for you," the hostess said.

"I've changed my mind." Riley exited the restaurant.

He redialed. "Regan, the restaurant is out."

"Why?"

"I'll explain later."

"How about you come to my place then," she said. "Grab something on your way over. I'll have a rum and Coke waiting for you."

"That's an even better plan."

CHAPTER THIRTY

FRANKLYN WAS AT THE OFFICE SHORTLY AFTER SIX. THE INFLATABLE mattress he'd thrown on the bed was more uncomfortable than the camper. Franklyn needed to buy a real mattress soon. His back was screaming by four. He finally gave in to the pain at five and popped two Oxy. When the pain lessened to a dull ache, he drove to the arena for a shower. He still didn't have running water at his house, just water he had to pump from a well.

With a fresh coffee in hand, he pulled the reports on drug activity and arrests on the rez out of his briefcase and sat back to read. The bottom line: there were few reports and fewer arrests.

He picked up the next file labeled, "Dispatch Reports." Franklyn hadn't asked Paulette for this information, but she knew he'd need it. The file contained at least fifty pages of dispatch reports.

It was apparent there were more dispatched calls to drugs than there were arrests or even reports. He tried to link the reports and apprehensions with the dispatched calls, but he couldn't make it work. He ended up with paper all over his office.

At eight-thirty, the outer door opened. Franklyn dropped his feet off the desk and hobbled to the reception area. "Hey, Paulette. You're in early."

It wasn't Paulette.

"Crow, you finally came to work?"

"Chief doesn't need me this morning."

"Good. I need all the information we have on the residents of those three trailers across from the arena. A lot of activity there during the day from the school kids."

"Sounds like a job for Paulette. I'm not your secretary."

"You haven't been a cop, either. This is the first time in two weeks I've seen you in the morning. You're scheduled for day shifts."

"Chief keeps me busy."

"Yeah, well, I pay your salary. From now on, you check in with me every morning. If I have stuff for you to do, the chief will have to wait."

"He isn't going to like that," Crow said.

"That's between the chief and me," Franklyn said. "About those reports—by tomorrow, noon. No later."

Crow stomped out of the office.

Franklyn topped up his coffee and went back to reading the reports.

When Paulette came in at nine, Franklyn's office was a disaster. Files and paper littered every available space, including the floor.

Paulette glanced around, adjusting her glasses. "I see you've been redecorating. I like it. The busy executive look."

"I don't need you being a smartass in the morning." Franklyn drank the last of his coffee.

"Would you like more coffee?" Paulette asked.

"That would be great."

"There's still some in the pot. Help yourself." Paulette grinned and headed back to her desk.

"Okay, smartass. I'll get my own coffee."

Franklyn refilled his cup, then sipped the coffee as he stared at the mess of papers on his desk.

"Would you like some help with this?" Paulette asked.

"I guess. I can't match the dispatched calls to arrests and reports. I tried sorting them into piles, but that didn't work."

"No kidding." Paulette smirked. "That would work if this was 1950. I'll type the information into a spreadsheet and let the computer sort it."

"You can do that? The computer will do the work?"

"It's a neat thing that got popular, oh, about thirty years ago." She glanced at the worn leather bag on the floor. "About the time your briefcase was popular."

CHAPTER THIRTY-ONE

FRANKLYN WAS MUNCHING HIS TOAST WHEN HIS CELL PHONE RANG. "Eaglechild."

"Franklyn, it's Preston."

"Hey, how's it going? Come over to the Golden Nugget and have breakfast with me."

"Can't. Sorry. I'm meeting with the school principals this morning. But this afternoon, the kids at the elementary school will be dancing. You should stop by."

"I'll be there."

"Have you parked by the trailers over the lunch hour?"

"Yup. All week. Ever since you told me about the drug dealing. No one is buying drugs there anymore."

"That's because they moved their distribution."

"What?"

"The Lamont boys stay at the trailer to watch you while you're watching them."

"Where did they move to?"

"The gas bar and *Subway*. They've got some minor gang bangers parked in the back corner selling drugs. The kids walk from the school to the *Subway* for lunch. That's what I'm hearing. But the drug sales are now at the gas bar. Then the kids get high and come back to school or pass out in the schoolyard."

"I'll be darned."

"Thought you'd like to know."

Franklyn grabbed his Stetson on his way out of the office. Hiram Crow and Calvin Lefebvre were coming the other way. "Crow, head out to the trailers by the arena. Make sure the school kids stay away during the lunch hour. Park by the arena, but in plain sight."

Crow stared. "Sure."

When Crow left, Franklyn said, "Lefebvre, you're with me."

"Where are we going, boss?"

"The gas bar."

"You need to top up the tank?" Lefebvre asked.

"That's what I want them to think," Franklyn said. "We're shutting down some drug deals."

"You sent Crow to do that."

"I want the guys in the trailer to see the police SUV there. They've moved operations. They're selling at the gas bar now."

"How do you know this?"

"I have connections."

Franklyn pulled to the pumps. "Lefebvre, fill it up. I'll be right back." He strode into the gas bar. "Is the manager here?"

The woman behind the counter pointed toward the back office.

"How are you doing? I'm Franklyn Eaglechild. New sheriff. Sorry we haven't met sooner. My fault."

The man stood and extended a hand. "Ike. Nice to meet you. What can I do for you?"

"Just following up on a complaint. I was told there's some drug dealing happening in your parking lot over the lunch hour. Any truth to that?"

"Yeah. Over the past week, it's gotten busy. I try to chase them off, but they don't listen to me. And if they leave, they're back the next day."

"Do you have any security cameras here?"

"You bet. The place is surrounded by cameras."

"Mind if I review the film from yesterday, say noon on."

"Be my guest." Ike sat at his desk and brought up the surveillance video from the day before. "Do you know how to run this?"

"No," Franklyn said. "Can you run it, and I'll watch?"

Ike cued the video. At twelve-fourteen, three teens approached a ten-year-old, blue, four-door sedan in the corner of the parking lot. About a minute later, they strolled away. Franklyn watched the video for another couple of minutes. Four groups of teens approached the car. As the last group left, Franklyn said, "Can you zoom in?"

"It'll be fuzzy."

"I want to see their hands."

"Sure." Ike zoomed in. It was fuzzy, but Franklyn was sure two of the teens were holding plastic bags. Good enough for him.

"Thanks, Ike. We'll get them out of your hair."

Franklyn headed back to the SUV. Lefebvre was killing time cleaning the windows. "Let's go. The guys in the blue car are dealing. I'll take the driver's side. You watch the passenger. They've probably got guns, so keep alert."

Franklyn marched to the driver's window. "Driver's license, registration, and insurance."

"You can't hassle us," the driver said. "We aren't doin' nothing wrong. We're just sitting here."

"See that sign behind you? It says no loitering. You've been here for over twenty minutes—that's loitering. Get those documents."

He handed over his driver's license, then fumbled in the glove box. He pulled out a worn, plastic folder, the type insurance companies hand out. Franklyn checked the documents. "This registration is for a Buick—this isn't a Buick."

"Yeah, about that. I just bought this. I haven't changed the registration yet."

Franklyn tossed the driver's license to Lefebvre. "Call Paulette and have her run the name. Get ID from the passenger."

"That's against the law."

"Step out of the car, please." Franklyn stepped back, his hand rested shakily on his pistol.

The driver stepped out.

"Hands on the hood."

When the driver complied, Franklyn kicked his legs apart. "You got anything sharp in your pockets?"

"That's for you to find out."

"If my partner or I get hurt, that's going to be a gigantic problem for you."

"Yeah. I'm terrified."

Franklyn searched the driver, finding a lighter, penknife, and a wad of bills. "You have a thick stack of money here. You like fives?"

"Just what the machine gives me."

"Interesting. It always gives me twenties. Keep your legs spread." Franklyn finished the search. Nothing that would give him a reason to search the car.

"Boss," Lefebvre said. "The passenger has a warrant for failing to appear and an outstanding charge for possession for the purpose."

"Well, now. It looks like we have a reason to search. Cuff him." Franklyn applied the cuffs to the driver and pushed him over the hood of the car. "Leave your guy here. I'll watch them. Search the car."

Lefebvre crawled into the passenger side. "Are we going to find anything you want to tell me about now?"

"Go to hell."

"That's not a polite way to talk to my deputy. Any luck?"

Lefebvre backed out of the car, smiling. He held a large plastic bag that contained a bunch of smaller packs. "Looks like Oxy." In his other hand he held two dark objects. "Looks like brand new Glocks."

Franklyn smirked. "Hey, assholes, you're under arrest."

Franklyn left the arrests and interviews for Lefebvre to do and drove to the school. He was a few minutes late, and the dancing had already started. He watched from the doorway.

The dancers couldn't be more than five years old. They wore the brightest outfits and were putting everything into their moves. A trio of drums kept a steady rhythm. He couldn't help but smile. This was the best thing he'd seen since he'd been back —joyful kids performing in their tradition.

The students clapped along with the drums and gave hearty applause when the dance was complete. For the next hour, students from every age group performed. Each group trying to outdo the one before.

Franklyn sighed. He felt at peace, like the worries of the days lifted from his shoulders. He closed his eyes and let the waves of the beat sweep over him.

Crow burst into the office as Franklyn arrived back from the school. "What was that?" Crow shouted.

"What are you talking about?"

"You sent me to be the decoy while you made the arrest."

Franklyn shrugged. "Well, I needed the dealers to think we were still watching them. Yes, you were a decoy."

"Then why didn't you tell me about the plan."

"It was need-to-know, and at that point, you didn't need to know."

Crow's eyes were wide, and his nostrils flared. "I'm your deputy. I have a right to know."

"I'm the sheriff, and I decide who gets to know. Head down to cells and see if Lefebvre needs any help with fingerprinting or processing those two shitheads. They can stay in cells for the weekend. We'll take them to Great Falls on Monday."

Hiram Crow headed toward the door.

"One more thing, where's the info on the trailer boys?" Franklyn asked.

"Check your fucking email."

Franklyn opened the email from Crow. It wasn't a surprise that the Lamont brothers had a record—it was the extent of the record. Although their crimes were only documented from their sixteenth birthday onward, they'd been awfully busy.

Pages of charges and not a day in jail for various reasons—evidence misplaced or lacking continuity, arresting officer failing to appear, and judges throwing out the charges. He shook his head and leaned back in his chair. He had learned nothing he didn't expect. He closed his eyes.

Franklyn awoke when his door slammed into the wall. His feet hit the floor, and he nearly launched out of the chair.

Lefebvre stood in the doorway, his face reddening. "Sorry, boss."

Franklyn rubbed his eyes. "Some quiet would be enjoyable. What's up?"

"The passenger from our drug bust wanted to talk. He has a few priors and is worried he'll 'go to the big house,' as he said." Lefebvre shrugged. "I let him think that would happen."

Franklyn yawned and rubbed his eyes.

"Anyway, I got him into an interview room. Your door was closed, so I thought you were busy. I got Paulette to sit in the interview with me. I recorded it, and Paulette wrote notes."

Franklyn stretched and yawned again. "Is this story going anywhere?"

"Right. Okay. To the point. He told me all about the drug operation. Where the drugs are hidden, the cash is and how they were watching you all week. The Lamont boys thought you were watching them when it was Crow. So, they didn't warn the guys at the gas bar."

"Do you think you have enough for a search warrant?"

"Yeah, the information is golden."

Franklyn swung his legs off the desk, stood, and grabbed his Stetson. "You need to tell this to Special Agent Riley Briggs."

CHAPTER THIRTY-TWO

After the trip to Great Falls, Franklyn parked the SUV, strolled across the parking lot, and entered the administration building. Jesse was sitting in his usual place under the buffalo. Franklyn was about to sit with Jesse when his cell phone rang.

"Boss," Paulette whispered, "so you're aware, Chief Fox is in your office."

"Thanks." Franklyn straightened. "Later, Jesse." He lumbered up the stairs and down the hall to his office. He wondered why he was in such a hurry to see the chief. It wouldn't be a friendly visit.

"Good to see you, Chief." He placed his Stetson on top of the file cabinet and extended his hand. "What can I do for you?"

"Franklyn." Chief Fox spoke slowly, eyes glaring, ignoring Franklyn's hand. He set his arms across his gut and clasped his fingers. "Where were you?"

"I was in Great Falls." Franklyn rounded his desk and sat.

"The purpose?"

"I needed some new clothes and to meet with a few people."

The chief's eyes bore into Franklyn. "You do that instead of working?"

"The people I needed to see work during the day."

"I see." Fox nodded and pursed his lips. "How is your friend, Special Agent Riley Briggs? That is the person you met with, isn't it?"

"It was a courtesy call. Our areas share a border. I may need their help."

Fox leaned forward and pointed a finger at Franklyn. "We do not allow the feds on our land. We have Tribal Police. You and your fine officers. You take care of my people. We handle our own problems. You've been here, what, two weeks?"

"Not quite," Franklyn said.

The chief nodded, sat back, and stared over Franklyn's shoulder. "Not enough to know your staff or your job or re-learn our customs. You've been away for many years and have lived with the whites. You learned many wayward habits. When you arrived, I told you to seek me before you made any decisions. Yet, you have not done that. You embarrassed me."

"Chief you hired me to—"

Chief Fox held up his hand. "You do not interrupt an elder. You do not interrupt your chief. You have lost your way. You do not remember our customs. I am the father of this nation. The Great Spirit saw fit for the people to elect me to watch over them, as a father would his children. You are back in the family, my son. I do not like to do this, but sometimes my children need scolding—need re-direction. Perhaps a sweat is what you need. It will help you gain back your focus. Until then," the chief stood. "Hear me now. If you continue on this path, if you continue to force the white man's law on my people, there will be consequences."

At the office door, he turned back. "You should also reconsider your decision to take a white woman to dinner in Great Falls. Do not think you can hide things from me."

CHAPTER THIRTY-THREE

RILEY ROLLED OVER IN BED, ENJOYING THE HEAT OF THE SUN. HE opened one eye and stared at the clock radio: 8:45. He was sure he'd checked the clock every hour as he tossed and turned. He vaguely remembered glimpsing the clock at five-thirty. It had been a while since he slept this late. He lay on his back with his arms over his eyes, wishing for Monday morning. He listened to the steady beat of his heart, willing it to slow. A relaxation technique he'd learned as a sniper.

Sunday. Father's Day. His heart raced. So much for the relaxation. Riley glanced at his cell phone on the nightstand. He held onto the hope that there'd be a message—*come for dinner … can we come over for dinner?*

It didn't hurt to dream. Well, it did hurt. It hurts a lot when the dream doesn't come true. When it's not even close.

With excitement and reluctance, he grabbed the phone and punched in his code. His finger hesitated over the email app—he wanted to know and didn't. He hit the button. Air Miles sent coupons and Las Vegas wanted him back. Some random people wanted to join him on LinkedIn. Nothing from the kids. He tossed the phone on the bed.

In the kitchen, he brewed a coffee and poured in a healthy amount of Bailey's Irish Cream. Coffee in hand and two Tylenol, he retrieved the Sunday paper from the front step and settled into his living room chair.

Sitting around the house was not a smart idea. Too long with your own thoughts. Too long with demons visiting. He packed a bag and headed to the gym.

Ninety minutes later, he was both exhausted and refreshed. One thing he missed about SWAT was the five-thirty a.m. runs followed by weights. It wasn't the same on your own.

After showering, Riley stopped at *Appleby's* for breakfast. He glanced at the heart-healthy options and ordered three eggs over easy, double bacon, double sausage, five buttermilk pancakes, a cold glass of milk and a coffee. Pulling out his cell phone, he checked for texts or emails. Nada.

He sipped the hot coffee—black, like most cops—and checked out the restaurant from his booth. There were a few families dressed in their Sunday finest catching breakfast after church. A few tables had men with kids—celebrating Father's Day in a restaurant. That was a shitty way to spend Father's Day, but he'd settle for it.

Breakfast arrived, and he polished it off in record time. He lived by the motto, "never miss an opportunity to eat or pee." Hearing your stomach growl on a stakeout or enduring the immense pressure in your bladder happened once. You learned from that. He left a decent tip and smiled at the young waitress as she turned away. He hoped she'd be with her father later.

On his way home, he'd bought a case of Captain Morgan's

Spiced Rum. He settled in for an evening with the Captain and ESPN. The talking heads droned on about hockey free agents come July first and what team needed a specific style of player that would ensure a cup next season. His other options were soccer or golf. He thought he'd give soccer a shot.

The cell phone rang, shocking him awake. He'd been deep asleep, aided by half a bottle of rum. He shook his head a few times and grabbed his phone.

"Hello," he said, happier than he felt.

"Did I wake you? You sound groggy."

He slumped back into the chair. "Sorry. Yeah, I was asleep. The phone woke me."

"No call from the kids?"

"Nope."

"Let me take you out for dinner," Regan said.

"It's too early for dinner," Riley said.

She laughed. "It's nearly five-thirty."

Riley rubbed his eyes and focused on the clock on his mantel. "Damn. I slept most of the afternoon."

"Doesn't sound like you're in a condition to drive. How about I make dinner at your place?"

After dinner, Riley drifted off to sleep, a full stomach, and a dizzy head from the bottle of rum he'd polished off. Regan had made pasta and homemade sauce. Good thing she brought the ingredients. His fridge and cupboards were bare. She'd packaged the leftovers. At least he'd have something to eat tomorrow. It was still one of his worst days, but somehow, she'd made it bearable. God, he missed the kids.

He vaguely remembered the voice of an angel telling him to wake up, that she couldn't get him to bed. Why did an angel want him in bed? He grinned at the possibilities.

The sound of a door closing awoke him. He peered around the dark living room, pulled the fleece blanket around him, and drifted off, snoring within seconds.

CHAPTER THIRTY-FOUR

FRANKLYN STOOD AT THE BACK OF HIS SUV, CHECKING HIS GUN AND spare magazines, then slipped on the ballistic vest. He headed over to Lefebvre, Kennedy, and Taylor outside the Emergency Services Quonset.

"Kennedy. Can you have dispatch send another ambulance? Not that we'll need it, but better safe than sorry."

Kennedy nodded.

Riley Briggs, Leigh Blake, and Cascade County Deputies, Faith Bennett and Brian Gibson checked their gear at Riley's unmarked Yukon. Sergeant Hank Deaver and four members of SWAT geared up at their trucks.

Gravel flew as Leroy Balam and Hiram Crow skidded to a stop. Balam marched over to Franklyn. "What the hell is going on?"

"Drug raid," Franklyn said.

"Where?"

"Trailers by the arena."

Balam tilted up his chin and sneered. "What's the DEA doing here?"

Franklyn narrowed his eyes. "I called them."

"They can't operate on the rez without permission," Balam said. "Permission has to come from the chief."

"I am the chief ... well, sheriff."

"Not you." Balam rolled his eyes. "Chief Fox."

Franklyn shook his head and smirked. "I don't think so. Policing is my responsibility."

"I'm calling the chief." Balam pulled out his cell phone.

Franklyn grabbed the phone from his hand. "Communication silence from now on."

Balam glared. "You'll pay for this." He stomped away.

Crow stood beside Franklyn, arms crossed. "Why didn't you tell Balam and me this morning about this?"

"I wasn't sure it would happen."

"You didn't want us to know," Crow said. "You don't trust us, only your white friends."

Franklyn scrutinized Crow. "Should I trust you? Prove it. Get your gear ready. We leave in ten."

Franklyn watched Crow stalk away. Then Crow and Balam had an animated discussion.

Riley wandered over. "Trouble in paradise?"

"Just being safe. The fewer people who know about this, the better." Franklyn stared at Riley. "You look like shit."

"I'll be fine."

"He's oozing booze," Blake said. "Wait until he sweats."

Riley scowled. "Do you have the warrant?"

Blake held up a document. "DEA certified by a federal judge."

Franklyn nodded toward the cruisers. "Are you kidding me?

Gibson is the guy you brought?"

"He's on duty."

"Gibson hates Indians, especially me."

Riley grinned. "I promise he won't arrest you today."

Franklyn shook his head. "You better be right." Franklyn and Lefebvre headed over to Crow and Balam to tell them the plan, then the four of them met with Riley.

Deaver and his team marched over. "We're ready."

When they'd gathered around Riley, he nodded to Franklyn.

"There are three occupied trailers. There's a front door and another door at the back on the other side. Expect resistance and guns. The trailer with a red bandana in the window is the one selling drugs today."

"Riley and I will drive by the trailers in Riley's SUV," Franklyn said. "Once I see the red bandana, Riley will tell SWAT that's their trailer. Riley and his guys ..."

"... and gal." Riley grinned.

"Ya, ya, and gal, will take one trailer. I'll take Tribal Police to the other trailer."

"Arrest everyone," Riley said. "Cuff them, search them, and bring them out front. Then we'll search the trailers for drugs and guns."

"Sounds like a plan," Deaver said.

"Kennedy, keep the ambulances out of sight, but close," Franklyn said. "I'll phone if we need you."

Kennedy nodded.

"Mount up," Riley said.

At eleven forty, Franklyn jumped into Riley's truck. Riley sped down the hill, dust swirling behind, drove left toward the arena, and then left again to the dirt road leading to the trailers. Franklyn spotted the red bandana in the window of the middle trailer. Riley phoned SWAT to take the middle trailer, and his team to take the first one on the left. Franklyn called Lefebvre and told him to come to the trailer on the far right. Within a minute, the vehicles raced up the dirt road.

Franklyn kicked in the front door. He and Crow swept into the living room. They stepped over empty bottles and assorted garbage and sidestepped down the hall to the bedrooms. Franklyn glimpsed Lefebvre and Balam heading to the kitchen. He scanned the first bedroom—an empty bed and clutter. No one in the bathroom. The bedroom door at the end of the hall was closed. He tried the knob—unlocked. He slowly twisted the knob, then flung the door open. "Police."

The room stunk of dope, and clothes littered the floor. Two people—a man and a woman—sat up in bed. The woman pulled the sheet around her.

"Hands." Franklyn pointed his pistol at them. "I need to see your hands."

The man raised his hands. The woman said, "I can't—the sheet will fall."

"Tough." Franklyn pulled the sheet away. "On your feet."

Lefebvre and Balam entered the room.

"The rest of the trailer is clear," Lefebvre said.

"Great," Franklyn said. "Crow, get her some clothes and cuff her. Balam cuff him. Get them out front."

Riley and his team raced to their assigned trailer. "Blake, take the back door. Gibson and Bennett, you're with me."

"The back door? Are you kidding me?"

Riley shrugged. "That's the best spot. No time to argue, let's go." He gave her a minute to get in place.

Riley hiked up the steps to the front door two at a time, then put his shoulder into the door which easily gave way. Riley entered, his eyes following his pistol around the living room. He pointed to the left, and Gibson and Bennett headed down the hall to the bathroom and bedrooms.

The living room was sparsely furnished with a ragged couch, an armchair with the stuffing falling out in several places, and a coffee table with three legs propped up with a ten-gallon pail where the fourth leg should have been. He turned to the right and stepped toward the kitchen. Moving those few steps brought a wave of disgusting odors to his nose from rotting food, stacks of dirty dishes, and overflowing garbage.

"Police. Freeze," Gibson shouted from the far end of the trailer. Riley sprinted in that direction, colliding with Gibson as he rushed past. The suspect bolted out the back door and vaulted over the railing. Riley sprinted out the door in time to see the suspect crash into Blake.

They tumbled to the ground, rolling several times before stopping with the man on top of her. He was a foot taller and at least a hundred pounds heavier. With his weight on her, she would have trouble breathing. He put one hand around her throat, brought the other hand back, and swung at her head.

Riley headed to the steps.

Blake got a knee free and landed a blow to the suspect's nuts. He groaned, released his grasp, and rolled to the side.

Blake struggled to her knees, then stood. The man staggered

toward her and swung a wide arcing punch toward her skull. She caught his fist, twisted his arm to the side, and kneed him in the ribs.

He cried out and stumbled back. It wasn't enough to stop him. He charged again.

He threw two halfhearted punches—off the mark. As he brought his arm back, preparing for another hit, Blake's fist struck the assailant's windpipe.

He gasped, made squeaking sounds, and fell to the ground, his fist punching dirt.

Blake rotated his arm, and his body followed as he rolled face down in the dirt. Blake held the arm while dropping both knees onto his back. The assailant squeaked louder.

She cuffed one arm and wrenched the other back, applying the second cuff. She stood, dusted off her hands and dragged the suspect to his feet.

Riley grinned and clapped, slowly at first, then faster. He nodded to Blake, then headed back into the trailer.

Riley stood in front of the trailers as they brought the suspects out. SWAT were marching four men out of the middle trailer, including the Lamont brothers. Blake was shoving her prisoner around the trailer. Gibson and Bennett pushed two suspects over, and Lefebvre and Crow brought another two to the group.

"Okay, nine arrested," Riley said. "Not a shoddy morning's work. Let's see what treats they have for us."

Riley led Franklyn and Blake into the middle trailer. Like the others, empty bottles and cans littered the floor, and fast-food containers overflowed garbage cans. The place stank of stale food, sweat, tobacco, and weed.

On a coffee table in the living room, they found containers about the size of a shoebox. Inside were plastic baggies containing various numbers of green pills. Franklyn put on examination gloves and grabbed one bag. "Oxy." He selected a pack of pills from another box. "Not sure what this is."

Riley stepped over and examined the package. "That's meth."

In the third box, Blake found stacks of five-dollar bills. "This is a terrific start."

Franklyn headed toward the kitchen, but Riley grabbed his arm. "Not yet."

Riley knelt next to the coffee table. There were three legs and a pail where the fourth leg should be. Just like the other trailer. Riley lifted the corner of the table and pulled the bucket out. He knocked the pail on its side. Dozens of bags of drugs littered the floor.

"Jackpot," Franklyn said.

Riley tapped Blake on the shoulder. "Start bagging this evidence."

"We've got it," Franklyn said. "This is my jurisdiction. I'll get Lefebvre. We'll record the evidence and store it in our evidence locker."

Riley glanced at Franklyn and frowned. "This is a lot of drugs. We can do it, and there won't be any problems in court."

Franklyn glared at Riley. "You don't think I can do my job?"

Riley held out his hands. "Whoa, big fella. I'm just offering to help. At least let Blake help."

Franklyn called Lefebvre, who sprinted into the trailer. "You're in charge of the evidence. Everything inventoried, bagged, and labeled." Franklyn glanced at Blake. "She can help."

Riley followed Franklyn to the kitchen. On the table were a scale and more plastic baggies. Beside the table was a box filled with green leaves.

"Grass, weed, marijuana, pot," Franklyn said. "Whatever you want to call it doesn't matter. Still illegal. This is better than I imagined."

"We haven't even started searching yet," Riley said. "Follow me."

Under the coatrack at the back door sat a bowl of water and a bag of dog food.

"Notice anything strange here?" Riley asked.

Franklyn shook his head. "Food and water for a dog."

"Do you see any dogs?" Riley pulled the large dog food bag away from the wall, reached inside and dug around, then pulled out his hand holding an ice cream bucket. He set the bucket on the floor and popped the lid—more baggies of drugs.

CHAPTER THIRTY-FIVE

TWO DAYS LATER, FRANKLYN MET RILEY AT THE COURTHOUSE AT nine a.m. Riley said they were first on the docket. They had found nothing of significance in the two outside trailers. Still, they'd laid the serious charges on the four occupants from the middle trailer, a list of charges including possession for the purpose of trafficking and weapons offenses, and two had outstanding warrants.

"Where's the Deputy County Attorney?" Franklyn asked Riley.

Riley pointed to the table on the left. "That's her. Shoulder-length brown hair pulled to the side."

"Kinda cute. I'm going to say hello and get her phone number."

"Good luck with that," Riley said.

"You don't think I can get it?"

"Nope. She's all business. Want to bet?"

"Sure," Franklyn said. "Ten bucks?"

Riley laughed. "Not a chance. One hundred."

They shook hands.

Franklyn approached the DCA and stood at the side of the table. The blue blazer over a white blouse and gray skirt gave the impression of power. Franklyn was impressed for other reasons. "Excuse me. I'm Franklyn Eaglechild. I'm the sheriff on the Speargrass Reservation."

The DCA's gray eyes surveyed Franklyn. "Ms. Quinn, Deputy County Attorney. This is quite the arrest. How long have you been sheriff in Speargrass?"

"About two weeks."

"Two weeks, huh? Impressive. Just a formality this morning. The charges will be read. They'll be remanded to custody, and a court date will be set. All the boring stuff. Court routine and all. I don't expect you'll be needed. I understand you did the raid with the DEA and FBI. Is this your case?"

"Yes. The DEA Special Agent is here as well in case you need him. He's at the back. Riley Briggs."

Quinn glanced at the back of the courtroom. "Right, I know him. An ass if you ask me. Way too high on himself, if you know what I mean."

Franklyn grinned. "He's confident and cocky, that's for sure."

"That's an understatement. If I need anyone, I'll call you. But we should be okay today." She focused on her files. Franklyn was dismissed. He sat with Lefebvre and Riley in the back row.

Riley held out a hand. "You owe me a hundred bucks."

Franklyn shook his head. "We didn't put a timeline on the bet. This wasn't the right time, but she likes me."

"Yeah, right."

"She isn't impressed with you, though." Franklyn smiled.

Riley's eyebrows raised. "And how do you know?"

"Some things she said. I'll have that phone number next time I see her."

Franklyn felt a tap on his shoulder. *Chief Fox.*

"Chief, what're you doing here?" Franklyn stood.

"These are my people. No matter what they have done, I am here for them." The chief leaned close and hissed. "You had no right. No right at all. You'll regret this."

Chief Fox stalked across the aisle and selected a seat behind the defense desk.

The bailiff entered from a door at the front of the courtroom. "All rise. Justice Leery presiding."

They rose.

"Be seated," Leery said. "I see we have an honored guest. Welcome, Chief Fox."

Chief Fox stood. "Thank you, Your Honor. It is my pleasure to be in your court."

The courtroom doors opened, and a man in a stylish suit carrying a briefcase rushed to the front. "My apologies, Your Honor. I am Dalton Frey representing the four accused."

"Welcome, Mr. Frey," Justice Leery said. "Bailiff, please bring in the accused so we can get started."

Two court guards escorted the four accused into the courtroom to seats next to Frey.

Justice Leery put on reading glasses and peered at several stacks of paper. "These are serious charges." Leery gazed at the DCA. "Ms. Quinn?"

"Yes, Your Honor. Monday morning at eleven forty-five Speargrass Tribal Police, along with agents from the DEA, FBI, and SWAT executed search warrants on three trailers on the Speargrass Indian Reservation. They had detained nine occupants of the trailers. The four accused appearing before you today were arrested and charged with the listed offenses."

Quinn paused and glanced at the justice.

"Ms. Quinn. I'm far from confused, continue."

Quinn nodded. "A search of the trailers found several pounds of marijuana, Ziplock bags of OxyContin pills, Ecstasy pills and methamphetamine. Several prohibited knives and firearms were discovered. Two of the accused have outstanding warrants."

Dalton Frey stood. "If I may, Your Honor, I'd like to speak to the search warrant and DEA search."

"Proceed, Mr. Frey."

"Your Honor, the defense contends the search of their trailers and arrests are illegal."

"On what grounds, Mr. Frey?"

"Because the DEA has no jurisdiction on the Speargrass Indian Reservation and therefore any search, discovery, or arrest by them is illegal."

Quinn was on her feet. "Your Honor, the Speargrass sheriff asked the DEA and FBI to assist and get a search warrant. That is his prerogative as sheriff. There is a Memorandum Of Understanding between the FBI and Speargrass, where the FBI has jurisdiction in serious situations, of which drug-related crimes are included. This is the procedure on every Indian Reservation. As the Speargrass Tribal Police has four members, it was imperative for officer safety in the execution of this lawful search warrant on three trailers, that help was requested."

Frey rose from his seat. "I object, Your Honor. The one person who can ask the DEA to enter the Indian Reservation is the Tribal Chief, not the sheriff."

"Not so, Your Honor," Quinn said. "This is a federal and FBI matter, and the sheriff must be able to ask for assistance without first getting permission from the Tribal Chief. It is outlined in the MOU. I can provide a copy to my learned colleague for his education."

Justice Leery held up his hand. "This is an interesting discussion. I concur the sheriff must be able to request assistance in serious situations. I don't know simple drug dealing fits into this category. The execution of the search warrant was not a matter of immediate public safety. The Tribal Chief could have been consulted."

"Your Honor," Quinn said. "That illegal weapons were found justifies the need for additional police support."

"Come now, Ms. Quinn. Are you suggesting the end justifies the means?"

"Of course not, Your Honor. Sheriff Eaglechild had a reasonable suspicion weapons would be found. That is outlined in the search warrant."

"The DEA search warrant," Frey said.

Quinn didn't give Frey the benefit of a glance. "Even if weapons had not been discovered, it is reasonable to assume gang members who sell illegal drugs have weapons."

"Making assumptions, are you?"

"Your Honor—"

"If I may, Your Honor," Frey interrupted. "Perhaps it would be worthwhile to hear from the Tribal Chief. He is here with us today."

"Objection, Your Honor," Quinn said. "This is a hearing to have the charges read, the accused to make a plea, bail, and set a trial date. We are not here to debate matters of interpretation of the law."

"Thank you for that lesson in criminal law, Ms. Quinn. I am

well versed in that area. I don't think it will hurt to hear from our guest. Chief Fox, please step forward and take the stand."

"For the record, I object." Quinn slumped in her chair.

"Objection noted," Leery replied. "Chief Fox, as this is not a formal part of the process, you will not be under oath. However, what you say will become part of the court record. I encourage you to be truthful. Can you please tell the court your position and role?"

"I am Myron Fox, Tribal Chief of the Speargrass Tribe. I am responsible for five thousand of my children."

"Thank you, Chief," Leery said. "In your role as Tribal Chief, do you also oversee the Tribal Police?"

"All departments are my responsibility."

"Did Sheriff Eaglechild apprise you of the search warrants?" Leery asked.

"No, he did not."

"Is that unusual?"

"Yes," Fox said. "In the past, my sheriffs have always consulted me on serious matters."

"Why didn't the sheriff consult with you?"

Quinn slapped a file against her wooden desk. "Objection, Your Honor. Calls for speculation."

Leery leaned forward and glared at Quinn. "May I remind you, Ms. Quinn, this is not a formal part of the proceedings and, therefore, your objection has no foundation and is overruled."

"Your Honor, we can ask Sheriff Eaglechild," Dalton Frey said. "He is in the courtroom."

"I am interested in what Chief Fox has to say. Why didn't your sheriff consult with you?"

"Eaglechild is new. He does not have the experience as a police officer I thought he had when we hired him. He needs additional training and does not understand tribal tradition or criminal law."

"Thank you, Chief."

Franklyn clenched and unclenched his hands. His jaw ached. He started to rise, but Riley pulled him down. "Not worth it."

He jerked away from Riley's grasp. Franklyn bit his lower lip. When the initial wave of tension faded, his face heated, and his gut churned. He shrunk down in this seat. They were treating him like a naughty child and talking like he wasn't there.

"If I may, Your Honor?" Chief Fox asked.

"Of course, sir."

"These are wayward boys. I admit to that. I offer my support to them." The chief faced the accused with open arms.

Should get an Oscar for that act, Franklyn thought.

"If you see fit, I'd like them released into my custody, so I may have the elders provide restorative justice in our tribe where they will be nurtured."

Quinn was on her feet again. "Objection, Your Honor. This is outrageous. The charges, the serious charges, have not been read. The court cannot support their release back into the community."

"Objection overruled. Again, Ms. Quinn, this not a formal part of the proceedings."

"But, Your Honor, you are treating this like it is," Quinn pleaded. "There is no sworn testimony before you. I ask that we return to the formal proceedings and have the charges read."

"Very well, Ms. Quinn. I will read the charges. Will the accused please stand."

Justice Leery read the extensive list of charges for each defendant. Each entered a plea of not guilty.

"Now, to the issue of bail."

"Your Honor," Quinn said. "I request no bail. They are accused of selling drugs to school kids. Sheriff Eaglechild observed this. Their residence is within walking distance of the school. That they will re-offend is absolute. I request they are remanded to custody."

Mr. Frey slowly stood. He smoothed his jacket and fastened the buttons. "Your Honor. I believe we have a satisfactory compromise. That the defendants are released into the care of the Tribal Chief, and he directs his elders to work on rehabilitating these boys."

"Objection, Your Honor. I object to these men continually being called boys. They are in their twenties, men who know right from wrong and must remain in custody."

Mr. Frey said, "As I was saying before my learned colleague's outburst, I believe it is in the best interest of these bo—*men* and the Speargrass Tribe that tribal restorative justice is used. After all, it is the Tribal Chief who is welcoming them back and accepting this enormous responsibility."

Leery sighed, slid off his glasses, and peered down from the bench. "I am concerned over the use of the DEA. This matter requires thought and research. I will consult with my colleagues. For now, the warrant, search, exhibits, and use of the DEA will stand. However, I caution the Speargrass Sheriff about doing this again until I have made my decision. Any further use of the DEA without the consent of the Tribal Chief unless it is clearly an urgent situation, is forbidden."

Leery looked up from his notes to glare at Franklyn and Riley.

"Further, I release the four accused into the custody of Chief Fox for the purpose of imposing Speargrass restorative justice as deemed appropriate by the chief and his elders. Once I have made my decision on the search warrant, DEA, et cetera, we will reconvene to address the charges before this court. Court is dismissed for a fifteen-minute recess."

Dalton Frey shook Chief Fox's hand and strode out of the courtroom. The chief talked to the four accused.

Franklyn and Riley approached Quinn. Her face was red, and she shoved files into her briefcase.

"What the hell was that?" Riley asked.

"Leery was elected last year," Quinn replied. "He's going be soft on offenders. You better bring in airtight cases." She glared at Riley. "Especially you, *Special Agent*."

Franklyn glanced at Riley and raised an eyebrow.

Quinn slammed her briefcase closed and glared at them. "If you don't, Judge Leery will throw the cases out."

Riley and Franklyn sat on a park bench and watched as the Missouri River cut through the city. Riley tossed pieces of French fries onto the grass and watched the pigeons fight for the scraps. He dipped every third or fourth chip in ketchup and munched.

Franklyn threw his burger onto the bench.

"Don't like the burger?" Riley asked.

"The chicken is chewy."

"Not chicken," Riley droned. "Probably pigeon."

"That's disgusting."

Riley shrugged. "You should have had the mystery meat burger. With enough condiments, it tastes fine." He watched the Missouri River winding its way through the park. "I like it here. My place to come and decompress."

"Do you come here regularly?"

"Not enough. My ex, Cory and I would take the kids to parks in Helena or out into the country on Sundays. We'd let them run until they dropped. Then we'd have a quiet Sunday night together. It seems like a century ago." Riley watched a mom pushing a stroller while two kids, maybe four or five, raced ahead. *A century ago.*

"Have you seen the kids lately?" Franklyn grabbed a few of Riley's fries.

Riley stared at the river and sighed. "Nope. They don't contact me often even though I know they have a cell phone permanently attached to a hand."

Franklyn tapped Riley on the shoulder and pointed. Chief Fox, Dalton Frey, and Justice Leery were heading down the path on the other side of the park. The conversation was animated, and laughter drifted across the river.

"Best of friends," Riley said.

"Is that the way court works here?"

Riley munched a few fries. "Nah, usually I'm the one the justice is yelling at."

"Seriously."

Riley faced Franklyn. "Our system is great until it isn't. One corrupt idea is having elected judges. Hell, elected sheriffs are an awful idea. But it's what we're stuck with. This is the worst I've seen. Petty stuff gets tossed out. When it comes to drugs and guns, they generally do the right thing. We have to work harder, different."

"What can we do?"

Riley tossed a few fries. "Not sure yet."

Franklyn picked at his burger, checked the contents, and tossed it back on the bench. "There is one thing."

"What's that?"

"If your aim was better, Reynolds would be dead. That'd be one problem solved."

"Yeah. It's just a lot of paperwork." Riley glanced at his watch. "Time for my case. You coming?"

They stood, and Franklyn said, "I better head back to Speargrass and be ready for the wrath of the chief."

CHAPTER THIRTY-SIX

THE BAILIFF CALLED COURT BACK INTO SESSION AS JUSTICE LEERY entered.

"Be seated." Leery peered down at Ms. Quinn. "I hope your next case is better prepared."

Riley watched Quinn turn a bright red.

Quinn stood. "Yes, Your Honor."

The bailiff called Lou Reynolds, Riley's gunrunner, into the courtroom.

Leery flipped through the pages in front of him. He slid his glasses off and stared at Reynolds. "Mr. Reynolds, these are serious charges. You have been busy. The first charges are for possession of stolen firearms and cell phones, and an assault on a police officer."

Dalton Frey stood and buttoned his jacket. "Your Honor, if you please."

Leery sat back and nodded. "Go ahead, Mr. Frey."

"My client had the misfortune of being in the wrong place, with the wrong people, at the wrong time."

"Oh my god. Are you serious?"

Leery glared at Quinn. "Councilor."

Frey grinned and continued. "My client has no job. No home. No vehicle. He relies on the generosity of others. He admits his choice of acquaintances is lacking. But he doesn't have a lot of options."

Quinn jumped to her feet. "Your Honor. The defendant's guilt or innocence will be decided later. At that time, I will present our case, which includes fingerprint evidence and a sworn statement from a witness. Can we move to the reading of the charges and have the accused make his plea? Mr. Frey can save his theatrics and excuses for the next court date."

"Ms. Quinn, please be seated. Mr. Frey, I am concerned Mr. Reynolds was found with the guns and drugs."

Frey spread his arms wide. "My client is a drug addict and cannot get treatment. It has forced him to seek drugs wherever he can. He doesn't deny he was in that farmhouse."

"Please, Your Honor, can we get to entering a plea," Quinn said.

Frey shook his head. "Your Honor, my client was asleep when men with guns burst into the house. He was groggy and still under the influence of drugs—his untreated addiction—and was afraid for his life. He knows he lives a nomadic life with dangerous people. My client not only fears for his life from the drug dealers but also the police." Frey spun and pointed at Riley. "After all, that officer shot him. My client thought they would kill him."

Quinn jumped out of her chair so hard it fell back onto the floor with a loud crash, startling Leery. "There is no evidence before the court on any of this. We are not at the trial stage. At the right time, I will present my case. Until then, I request Mr. Reynolds be held without bail. He is charged with serious offenses, and as my learned colleague has stated, Mr. Reynolds has no job, no residence, and no ties to the community. He is the definition of a flight risk."

"Mr. Frey, I agree with the prosecution," Leery said. "These are serious charges, and I see his potential as a flight risk."

"If I may suggest, Your Honor, a compromise suitable to both parties. A concerned citizen is willing to post a one-million-dollar bond and sponsor Mr. Reynolds in a private addiction center."

"That is not satisfactory," Quinn said. "Mr. Reynolds needs to be behind bars until he answers these charges and I present our case. At that time, Mr. Frey, you can present the case for the defense."

"Your Honor," Reynolds said, "I'd like to get some help." Reynolds wept and slumped into his chair.

Leery stared at Reynolds for a moment, wiped a tear from his eye, and sniffled.

"Mr. Reynolds. I could not live with myself if I didn't have compassion for someone who is asking for help. I grant bail on the conditions Mr. Frey outlined. The prisoner is free to go to addiction rehab. This case is set over for one month when I expect a report on Mr. Reynolds' treatment and progress."

Quinn would not win today. He feared there would be many days when she wouldn't succeed. It appeared Leery would believe any cock-and-bull story presented before him. *We're in the worst opioid addiction crisis ever, and Reynolds, the guy in the middle of it, is sent to rehab.* Riley had a hundred dollars Reynolds wouldn't ever see the door of the rehab center.

CHAPTER THIRTY-SEVEN

Chief Fox sat at his antique desk, a glass of whiskey on ice swirling in his hand. Leroy Balam sat on the couch.

"What do you think of Eaglechild?" Chief Fox asked.

"He's a pain in the ass," Balam said. "I knew that right from the start."

The chief swirled his glass and sighed. "The reports I got said he was down and out. Defeated. His rodeo career was over. He was beaten up and could barely move."

Balam nodded. "We got lucky with the judge."

"Find out what he drinks and send him a case, compliments of me. Maybe a high-quality box of cigars, if he likes them. Hell, even if he doesn't, send them anyway."

Balam grinned. "After the embarrassment in court today, Eaglechild will slink home with his tail between his legs."

"Anything else?"

"You already know he and Eva went out for a romantic dinner in Great Falls," Balam said. "She asked him in when he brought her home. If you do this right, she could become valuable to us."

"Anything else?" Chief Fox asked.

"He confiscated a lot of drugs from the Lamont brothers. Some of it was Oxy."

"Find out if the drugs are still in evidence."

"If they aren't?"

The chief smirked and sipped his whiskey.

CHAPTER THIRTY-EIGHT

RILEY LEANED AGAINST THE BED'S HEADBOARD. THE SMELL OF Chinese food and sex hung in the air. From his spot, he could see into the en suite. Regan Quinn brushed her brown hair. She swung her head backward, flicking her hair behind her. She padded back into the bedroom.

He could watch her walk toward him naked, or away for that matter, all night.

She climbed onto the bed and on top of him.

"What were you thinking?" she asked.

"That you look good naked."

She pouted. "Only good?"

"Amazing. This is the way to forget about a ghastly day in court."

"Why did you bring that up?" She pounded on his chest with her fists. "My worst day in court, ever."

"I'm sorry," he said. "You are hot when you're pissed off."

"Like I am now?"

"Yup, exactly like that."

She grabbed his arms and pinned them to the bed. "Punishment must be commensurate to the crime."

"Oh, gosh, Ms. County Attorney. That there's an awfully multitudinous word."

She leaned down and kissed him. "You've been a naughty boy." She kissed him again.

"Guilty as charged." He felt the stirrings deep inside as his hands roamed over her back and down to her ass. She had a great ass.

Regan lay motionless as they enjoyed being connected. Slow at first that built into full hip swings. Her hair hung in Riley's face, her perky breasts just out of reach. She was immersed in the passion and brought them both to a powerful climax. She collapsed onto his chest. "Wow," she said.

"Yeah."

She pushed up. "Yeah. That's it? Just yeah?" She pounded on his chest.

He grabbed her arms and swung her over on the bed. He pinned her arms beside her head. "I don't know why you start this. You always lose."

She smiled. "Maybe I like it?"

Riley laughed. "I don't think there is any maybe to it—I know you do."

"Not right now, though. I can't feel my arms."

Riley rolled off and lay on his side with his head supported by his arm. "You are beautiful."

"You're just saying that because I screwed your brains out."

"That you did. Twice. Doesn't change the fact you're beautiful."

"You're not so hard on the eyes yourself."

"Warts and all?"

Regan's hands roamed over his chest. "Nope. No warts. Just scars."

"Funny. Warts, baggage, whatever they call it now."

"We've all got baggage. I'm sure these scars each have a story."

"They do."

Regan traced her finger over the scars. "Maybe sometime you'll share?"

He nodded. "Someday."

"Something on your mind?"

"Just thinking."

"About last Sunday and Father's Day?"

Riley stared at the ceiling. At work, he was cold as ice. Dispassionate, some said. Iceman. Nothing got to him. Just one thing. His kids. From the day he left, they were against him. His ex-wife was a master at misdirection and the art of the unspoken word. The kids said she hadn't said a word against him. But she didn't have to say anything—it would be insinuated. Two years later, it still hurt. Every day was a challenge of some sort, but there were a few days he could barely keep it together—Christmas, birthdays, and Father's Day.

"They didn't call? Send you a card and a present? Offer to take you to dinner?"

Riley shook his head. "The first year, they had me over and prepared the meal—all my favorites. After that, it was an email late in the day. Then I'd hear from one of them. 'Happy Father's Day. I hope it's an enjoyable day.' How can it be enjoyable when I don't see or hear from them?"

Riley rolled off the bed and headed to the bathroom. He sat on the toilet. Not because he needed to go—well, he did, but he needed to be alone to get his shit together. He was an idiot. In bed with a gorgeous woman who wanted to be with him, who wanted to bang his brains out, had banged his brains out, and now he was moping. *I hate it when I do that.*

He grabbed some Kleenex and blew his nose. *What the fuck.* He stood and lifted the toilet lid.

He slid back into bed. Regan rested her head on his chest. "I'm sorry."

"Me too. I'll be all right. I always am when I'm with you."

"I know it hurts. You don't have to hide it from me. I care. I'll be here for you—today, tomorrow, and all the tough days."

"Thank you." He stroked her hair and kissed her cheek. "I love you."

Regan snuggled closer. "I know."

CHAPTER THIRTY-NINE

FRANKLYN SAT IN THE CORNER OF THE CASINO RESTAURANT. THE table was littered with the charts, graphs, and spreadsheets Paulette had created. What she'd done was terrific.

She'd explained the spreadsheets to him and said it would be easy to spot some trends. Easy for her, maybe. The more he studied the spreadsheets, the less he understood. He sat back and rubbed his eyes. The waitress refilled his cup. He sipped the coffee. Staring at the pages didn't help. He gathered the spreadsheets and charts that showed the complaints by the time of day. There were few calls in the morning, and the calls increased by mid-afternoon. The peak time for calls was after midnight. *That made sense.*

Next, he studied the spreadsheet that listed the location of the calls. This one was easier—Paulette had sorted by location and included a map. Franklyn highlighted a dozen frequent locations. The top three were the rodeo grounds, the quad, and the gas station-*Subway*. Again, that made sense.

He leaned back in his chair. What had he learned?

He checked the time of the complaints—most of the complaints were after midnight. A few came in on the weekends during rodeos or when there was a ball game at the quad. The calls at the gas station-*Subway* came in between 11:30 and 12:30, and 3:30 to 4:30—when the kids weren't in school.

What was interesting was the lack of complaints about the three trailers. Interesting, but what did it mean? That the kids weren't going to complain.

Farther down the list were complaints from the school, with Preston as the complainant. It was easy to spot the complaints from the Tribal Building—most of the complaints came from Paulette. He'd need to ask her about that.

When Franklyn read the report for arrests, his eyes widened. There were a few arrests. Less than five in any month, despite the average number of complaints being over sixty. None of the arrests had occurred between midnight and eight a.m., despite nearly fifty percent of the complaints occurring at that time.

Franklyn dropped the papers. His jaw tightened. "What else has that son of a bitch been doing behind my back? I'll kill him." Balam was the one cop on duty after midnight.

He leaned back in his chair and clasped his hands behind his head. Excellent information, but what would he do with it? He could move Balam to an earlier shift. But that meant Lefebvre would have to work night shifts. There was no way Crow would work night shifts—the chief wouldn't allow it. Franklyn would not work night shifts because, well, because he was the sheriff. He was needed during the day.

Franklyn checked his watch—eleven-thirty. Perfect time to visit the trailers. The judge may have put the Lamont boys on the street, but there was no way he was letting them sell to school kids again.

This time he parked his SUV on the driveway to the trailers. He slid out and leaned against the door. By noon, the first of the students started across the playground. When they reached the arena, their steps slowed. A few ventured closer, hesitated, then reversed course. By twelve-fifteen, the students were gathered at the edge of the playground, trying to figure out what to do.

The door to the middle trailer opened, and Ronnie Lamont, the oldest brother, stood on the porch, glaring at Franklyn. "What the fuck do you want, pig?"

"Pig? That's retro. Did you just arrive from 1976? Just admiring the view from here."

"Fuck off. This is private property."

"It's not." Franklyn grinned. "All the rez is tribal land. No one owns the land or the house. Since I'm the sheriff of the rez, I can go anywhere I want. I can stop and park anywhere I want. Today, I'm parking here."

Lamont turned into the trailer and slammed the door.

Franklyn chuckled, then called Lefebvre on the radio. "Anything happening at the gas station?"

"Nope," Lefebvre said. "Before noon, a few cars arrived. They cruised through the parking lot, gave me the finger, then sped off. Shortly after noon, a dozen kids came across the highway from the school. When they spotted me standing there, they went into the *Subway*. They ignored me, left the store around twelve forty-five, and headed back to school."

At three-thirty, Franklyn met Lefebvre at the trailers. They parked in front of the trailers and activated the lights. Lefebvre handed Franklyn a coffee then leaned against Franklyn's SUV. The school kids didn't even cross the playground.

CHAPTER FORTY

Pam Taylor held the steering wheel tight in both hands as the ambulance bounced and shuddered on the unlit gravel road. Eric Kennedy had one hand on the dash and the other holding the armrest. "Slow down."

"If I go any slower, we'll be standing still," Taylor said. "Just when you think you've been on the worst roads possible, you find this cattle trail. Anything new in the notes from dispatch?"

"Just that people at this house aren't feeling well. Maybe food poisoning."

Taylor swung the ambulance into the driveway and dodged the cows wandering down the lane. She parked the ambulance, so it was pointed back out the way they'd come in. It was a safety measure so they could speed away if they had to, but it also put the ambulance at the back door facing the house, so it was easy to load and unload the stretcher.

Kennedy grabbed the EMS kits, and they strode to the door. They stepped over kids' toys, bottles, and car parts.

On the garbage-littered porch, a screen door hung by one hinge. The wooden door was open, with a gaping hole about a foot from the bottom.

"Paramedics," Taylor shouted.

"In here," a faint voice replied.

They followed the sound of voices through the kitchen, skirting empty beer cases while fighting off mangy dogs.

They jammed the living room with at least eight people. A woman was slumped in an overstuffed chair. A man lay on the floor, and another was motionless on the couch. The others closed around them, chattering in Blackfoot.

Taylor knelt by the man on the couch and reached for a pulse.

Kennedy went to the woman slumped in the overstuffed chair. "What happened?"

"We had a party," a woman, mid-fifties or older, said. She wore thick tortoiseshell glasses. "They won't wake up."

"No pulse," Taylor said.

Kennedy shook his head. "None here either." Eric glanced at the woman. "When did the party end?"

"It hasn't."

"When did it start?"

The woman with tortoiseshell glasses, arms across her chest, glared at Kennedy. "Yesterday afternoon."

"When were they last awake? Talking?"

"Tonight, before dark."

"An hour? Two hours ago?"

She shrugged. "Maybe more."

Taylor knelt by the man on the floor and checked for a pulse. She glanced at Kennedy and shook her head. The two she'd assessed had been dead for a while—hours.

Taylor stood and faced the group. "I'm sorry, they're dead."

"You have to do something." A giant man in a blue shirt pushed to the front. "You're paramedics. Wake them up."

"We can't," Taylor said. "They've been dead too long."

"I know there are drugs you can give." Blue Shirt guy pressed close to Taylor, the heat from his skin rolling off him. The rank beer and cigarettes on his breath churned her stomach. "Help them now."

"You don't understand," Taylor pleaded. "We want to help. But it's too late. They died hours ago."

"You're racist," Tortoiseshell Glasses said.

As Taylor glanced toward their escape out the back door, Blue Shirt grabbed her, threw her to the floor, and hissed, "Help them."

Kennedy keyed his radio. "Speargrass 1, code 200 red."

The radio crackled. "Speargrass 1, repeat the last message."

"Speargrass 1, code 200 red."

"Speargrass 1, you are unreadable. Call on your cell."

As Kennedy pulled the cell phone out of his pocket, Blue Shirt swung, his punch knocking Kennedy to the floor.

"Help her."

Kennedy rolled away as Blue Shirt kicked his boot at Kennedy's side. The cell phone slid across the floor and under a chair.

Kennedy pulled the woman onto the floor and started chest compressions. He pushed the red button on the radio.

Taylor's tears wouldn't stop. Blue Shirt kept yelling, telling her to give drugs—to use the shock machine. She watched Kennedy stop compressions and stagger to his feet.

"It's no use." The punches came fast until Kennedy fell, then he was kicked in the ribs and stomach. Kennedy stopped moving.

Tears streamed as Taylor stared at her motionless partner and did chest compressions. Her arms ached, and her hands shook as she defibrillated the corpse. She wasn't sure how long she could continue this charade—she was out of medications. She'd given the cardiac drugs first well, it didn't matter, and every few minutes she'd grab a drug and push it into the IV line.

No one was coming. Soon, they would take it out on her.

Franklyn woke with a start. He peered around the darkness, wondering what had awoken him. The phone rang, and he fumbled for it on the night table.

"Sheriff Eaglechild."

"Sheriff, this is EMS dispatch. We've lost contact with your ambulance crew. They responded to multiple sick people. That was about twenty-five minutes ago. Two minutes ago, they called in, but the transmission was garbled. We just received a distress beacon. It comes and goes, but it identifies to their radio."

"What's the alarm number?"

"5666."

Franklyn jumped out of bed and yelled, "Send two ambulances and get my deputies Leroy Balam and Calvin Lefebvre responding."

Franklyn raced out of the house, tripping over Wild Dog and stumbling to his SUV. The paramedics were five minutes away as the crow flies, but at least twelve with the windy roads and loose gravel. He called Balam and Lefebvre on the radio, but neither answered.

The SUV bucked. If he'd learned nothing else from bull riding, it was balance. He remained firmly perched in his seat. Franklyn spotted the ambulance ahead, but no sign of Balam or Lefebvre. Franklyn pressed harder on the gas, then hit the brakes and slid sideways toward the ambulance. He threw the gearshift into park before the truck had stopped moving. He grabbed a flashlight and raced through the door.

A large man in a blue T-shirt in his thirties stood over Taylor. Her hands covered her head. He had a handful of hair in one hand and with the other, tore at her shirt, popping the buttons.

In two strides, Franklyn was beside him, swinging the flashlight. Blood sprayed from the cut on his temple.

He staggered backward but didn't fall. With blood streaming from his face, he dove at Franklyn, and both men crashed into a wall. The man was immense, but Franklyn was heavier, and he shoved him away.

The man came back at Franklyn, fist swinging. Franklyn sidestepped and swung the flashlight across the side of the guy's head. He crumpled to the ground.

A chair smashed against Franklyn's back, and searing pain raced up his spine. Before he could recover, someone grabbed a leg of the broken chair and swung at Franklyn's hip. Pain ripped through his side as he fell against the wall.

Another man with a baseball bat high above his head raced toward Franklyn, swinging downward.

Franklyn had nowhere to go—trapped between the wall and the assailant.

A gunshot echoed. Blood burst from the man's shoulder, and

the bat fell to the floor. Lefebvre stepped in, Glock raised. "You okay, boss?"

The room filled with screams.

Someone yelled, "Murderer."

Franklyn drew his pistol and, with Lefebvre, positioned themselves in front of the paramedics. A male voice said he was getting his rifle.

Another voice boomed in Blackfoot. The room quieted.

Hiram Crow strode to the group, trapping them in the room's corner. He glanced over his shoulder to Franklyn. "You'd better get the paramedics out of here fast. I can't hold them here much longer."

Lefebvre assisted Kennedy to his feet, and they hustled out of the house. Franklyn reached down and pulled Taylor to her feet. He worried if he knelt, he wouldn't get up again. Once Taylor was on her feet, Franklyn grabbed her around the waist and dragged her out.

Sheriff's deputies' cruisers led two Great Falls ambulances into the yard. Gibson and Bennett got out and raced toward Franklyn.

"Gunshot wound and another with a head wound," Franklyn said. "Escort the paramedics in, but tell them they need to get their patients and get out quickly. All hell's breaking loose."

Paramedics hustled to Kennedy and Taylor and guided them to an ambulance. Once the back doors were closed, the ambulance raced off.

Franklyn watched them disappear in the dust and darkness.

Despite Justice Leery's edict that Riley had to stay off the rez, an officer-involved shooting brought Riley and Blake back. Riley interviewed Calvin Lefebvre and Hiram Crow. To avoid future questions about conflict of interest, Riley had Blake interview Franklyn.

Franklyn sat at his desk with his boots on the surface. Riley sat opposite him.

"Hell of a night." Riley brought a coffee to his lips. "The paramedics going to be okay?"

"I talked to the hospital a while ago. They're keeping them both for observation. Eric has a concussion and bruised ribs."

"His partner?"

"Bruises to her face, eyes black and a split lip. Emotionally, she's a mess."

"The paramedics were lucky the dispatcher was on the ball and called you."

"It wouldn't have mattered to any of us if Lefebvre hadn't arrived. That guy was about to cave in my head. We'd all be dead if Hiram Crow hadn't stepped in. I don't know why he was there. I didn't call him, and he wasn't on duty."

"Not your time," Riley said.

Franklyn leaned back and closed his eyes. He glimpsed the bat coming toward him. Then the assailant's shoulder exploded.

His eyes popped open, and he swung his feet to the floor. "It was a righteous shooting."

"I know."

"Lefebvre's an excellent shot. A marksman. That bullet went where he wanted it to go. He didn't aim center mass. He aimed for the shoulder and hit it."

Riley nodded. "I know. Forensics will figure that out. The

problem is, it won't make a difference. Métis cop shoots an Indian man. You're going to have problems."

"They'd beaten two paramedics ..."

"White paramedics."

"... and assaulted me."

"They think you're white," Riley said.

Franklyn frowned.

"It would be worse if you'd fired the shot."

"I was too late getting my gun out," Franklyn said. "It happened fast."

"Frequently does."

"The shooting was legitimate."

"You and I know that." Riley shrugged. "The members here don't. They're not going to let the facts get in the way. The shit is going to fly."

"I've got a thick hide," Franklyn said.

"You might need it. We've got another problem."

"What?"

"There's a more powerful drug on the streets. An opioid, fentanyl. We've both had overdoses in our area. Let me know if you hear anything." Riley stood. "I'm going to get some sleep."

"Me too," Franklyn said. "You better let me know what you learn."

"Deal." Riley waved as he headed out the door.

CHAPTER FORTY-ONE

Franklyn didn't knock and didn't break stride as he straight-armed the front door open and barged through the house into the bedroom. Lefebvre rushed to catch up.

Balam was lying face down on the bed, between two naked teens. None of them moved as Franklyn stood over them. "Wake up." One girl rolled over onto her back, still not seeing Franklyn.

"Balam," Franklyn repeated. "Get up, you useless piece of shit."

The teen on her back opened her eyes, screamed, grabbed a sheet, and pulled it over her body. The other teen, squirmed, opened her eyes and squinted as she tried to focus on Franklyn. She gave up and rolled over.

Franklyn grabbed a glass sitting next to an empty bottle of whiskey and tossed the liquid on Balam's face. He bolted upright, ready for a fight. When he recognized Franklyn, he said, "Get the fuck out of my house."

"You're still on duty. It's four a.m., and you're home in bed. You got anything to say?"

"Not feelin' well," Balam said.

"Let me rephrase," Franklyn said. "You got anything to say that isn't bullshit? Too sick to work but not too sick to party with underage teens?" Franklyn leaned close. "You're drunk, not sick. I warned you if you screwed up again, I'd fire you." Franklyn stepped to a dresser and grabbed a badge, radio, pistol, and magazines. He glared at Balam. "You're fired."

Franklyn opened each dresser drawer and rifled through the contents—socks, underwear, condoms, loose change, and a bag of pills.

Franklyn waved the bag. "I'll take these. Give me a day to decide whether I arrest you for possession. Should be enough to charge you with trafficking. Have a nice day."

Franklyn nodded to Lefebvre. "Get the girls dressed and take them home. Use Balam's SUV. He won't need it anymore."

Franklyn returned to the office, made coffee, and slumped in his office chair. *Son of a bitch.* That was one heck of a night.

He sipped coffee and eyed the bag of drugs from Balam's. They were useless in court, but it might be worth it to have that hanging over Balam's head. It would make life miserable for Balam, at least for a few months.

He leaned forward in his chair and grabbed the bag. He slid the drugs around inside the plastic. He was getting proficient at recognizing the various drugs used on the rez. The green Oxy was easily identifiable. There were E, Ecstasy, Tylenol 3s and 4s, and another half-dozen he didn't recognize.

"Morning, boss."

Franklyn dropped the bag. "Morning, Paulette."

"Another drug bust?"

"Balam had these at home. I fired him and confiscated the pills." He eyed the bag. "Can you enter these into evidence with the drugs from a few weeks ago?"

She picked up the bag. "What's the case number?"

"I haven't got one yet. I'm not sure if I'll charge him."

She nodded. "Okay, but I require a case number, or I must destroy them."

Franklyn stared at the bag in her hands. "Destroy them."

"No problem, boss."

CHAPTER FORTY-TWO

Riley slid into the booth across from Dac Mahones. He was sipping a beer—two others sat on the table. Riley grabbed one.

"What's got you slumming in our neighborhood?" Riley asked.

"Sure, help yourself to my beer."

"Don't mind if I do," Blake said.

"Fine, but you're buying the next round," Mahones said.

"I figure you've got something important to tell us. If it's useful, I'll buy all night," Riley said.

Mahones nodded and leaned forward. "You two have stepped in a whopping shit pile."

"He's used to it," Blake said and clinked bottles with Mahones.

"This might be a deeper pile than he's ever been in."

"Do tell." Riley inhaled half the beer.

"The Red Demons Motorcycle Club is moving into Montana."

"I already figured that out. A guy by the name of Noel Bourget is hanging around."

"Noel Bourget is an important dude in the Red Demons. They sent him here to organize it. That's why his ID and cover were excellent. They might not be counterfeit. It might be the genuine thing. If they have someone in motor vehicles, well, the driver's licenses won't show up as fake cuz they're legit."

"I didn't think the Red Demons were an item in Montana," Riley said.

"They're not," Mahones said. "But they want to be. Every year the Demons have a large ride across Montana heading to the huge biker get-together in Sturgis."

"That I know about," Riley said. "The highway patrol crap their breeches every year, expecting the worst to happen."

"The Demons are too smart to do something in the open. It's a show of strength."

"But it's never amounted to anything significant," Riley said.

"Nope. There's an active Mongrel presence in Helena. That's why Bourget is avoiding Helena and targeting Great Falls. In 2008 ATF had a guy undercover with the Mongrels for two years. That led to over one hundred arrests and over one hundred and fifty search warrants. They were banned from wearing colors for ten years. In the last year, they've come out from under a rock and are wearing gang colors and making their presence known."

"Who controlled criminal activity if the Mongrels were out of commission?" Blake asked.

"The Warlords are still the dominant club. They have a bunch of rules. Every member must sell drugs and own at least one handgun they carry at all times. They work in pairs to avoid screw-ups that might embarrass the club. If you see one

Warlord, search for another one. A lone biker is a tempting target for punks trying to prove their worth to another club."

"Are we expecting a war? The Warlords versus the Mongrels versus the Red Demons?"

"Nope. The Warlords and Mongrels motorcycle gangs have an agreement—they'll do anything to keep the Demons out of Montana. If the Red Demons have chosen Great Falls as their Montana HQ, the drugs on your streets will explode. A motorcycle gang war will follow."

CHAPTER FORTY-THREE

Franklyn twisted in bed. The chanting and beat of drums bounced around in his head. Too many pills gave him nightmares. The noise grew louder.

Sweat dripped from his face, pouring from his body. Had he gone to a sweat with the elders? A pow wow? The noise grew louder, his sweat now a steady flow. The heat was intense.

Wood crackled, accompanied by the shooting of sparks. Embers burned his face.

The chanting changed.

In his mind, he witnessed the singers change from humans to animals—a dog howling, a horse whinnying in terror. Behind them, the flames from the fire grew. The heat was unbearable.

Franklyn's eyes sprung open. The fire roared through his house.

He jumped to his feet and was hit by the intense heat. He dropped to the floor and crawled.

Sparks hit his bareback, and tiny spikes of pain rippled across his shoulders. He coughed and crawled.

The smoke was thick on the floor. He hit a wall, crawled left, and found the open bedroom door.

He squirmed across the living room floor. The fire above him roared, and the heat from the floor rolled over him in waves. He inched forward, disoriented.

Then he heard barking. Through the smoke, he spotted Wild Dog, low on his haunches, slowly crawling backward.

Franklyn scrambled to keep the dog in sight. He hit something solid.

He reached upward and found a handle. He opened the door and rolled onto the porch, then down the stairs. He lay on his back, coughing, tears pouring from his eyes, washing away the smoke and grit.

A warm tongue licked his face, then a bark. He opened his eyes.

Wild Dog was inches away, rocking from side to side, barking. He'd run a few feet away, stop and bark. Over the roar of the fire, Franklyn heard Diesel. The horse's cries were frantic.

Barefoot, Franklyn loped around the burning house to the corral. He flipped the latch on the gate, and Diesel shot past, running a hundred yards into the pasture, the dog at his side.

Headlights bounced toward him, red lights flashing. His hope that the fire department had arrived were dashed—it was the ambulance.

The passenger door opened, and a lady paramedic he didn't recognize stepped out. She rushed toward him, her eyes assessing him. "Uh, you want a blanket?"

Franklyn stared at her, confused by her question. Then he glanced down. Aside from his boxers, he wore nothing. When he spun back to the paramedic, she placed a blanket over his shoulders. "Are you okay?"

Franklyn coughed. "Yeah. I was asleep. Dreaming." He coughed again. "I'm Franklyn Eaglechild, the new sheriff. We haven't met."

"I've heard about you. I'm Kathy. Adam and I work in Great Falls."

"Where's the Speargrass ambulance?"

"They're heading to Great Falls Hospital with an imminent delivery. So, we're covering for them. In fact, we spend half our time on the rez. I need to complete an assessment. Walk with me to the ambulance."

"Wait." Franklyn stared at the burning house. "Is the Speargrass Fire Department on the way?"

"No one was at the station when we got the call. I haven't heard them on the radio. Fort Benton Fire is on the way. But they'll be another ten minutes."

"Too fucking late," Franklyn said.

"Let's get you checked out," Kathy said.

"I've got some clothes in the camper." He stumbled and limped over the uneven ground and the sharp prairie grass. Kathy followed behind.

In the camper, he found a well-worn T-shirt, jeans, and sneakers. His cowboy boots and Stetson had burned in the fire.

When he stepped out of the camper, Kathy was standing with Diesel. His ears perked up when he spotted Franklyn. He gave the horse a big hug and rubbed his forehead. There was a yelp at his feet, and he knelt. A soft tongue licked at this hand. "You saved my life, Wild Dog."

"That's his name, Wild Dog?" Kathy asked.

"I haven't found the right name."

"You have to give him a name."

"Doubt he'd come if I called him."

"How about Ember?"

Franklyn nodded. "Yeah, I like that. How about you, Ember?"

The dog licked his face.

"It's settled then." Franklyn and Kathy headed to the ambulance. Diesel and Ember trailed behind. Franklyn coughed and coughed.

While Franklyn watched his hard work go up in flames, Kathy jumped into the back of the ambulance and came out with an oxygen tank and mask. They sat on the bumper. "Breathe this for a while. It will help."

Kathy pointed to a man in a paramedic's uniform walking toward them. "This is my partner, Adam."

Franklyn slipped the oxygen mask off his face. "Hi, Adam." He coughed. "I'm Sheriff Franklyn Eaglechild."

Adam nodded. "This your place?"

Franklyn stared at the burning building. "Yup."

"Dang," was all Adam said.

Over the roar of the fire, Franklyn heard the chirp of a siren and watched two firetrucks rumble past the ambulance. They parked on opposite sides of the house. In a well-practiced routine, firefighters wearing self-contained breathing apparatuses pulled hoses and started the pumps. Within a minute of their arrival, water was raining on the house. Adam wandered over to the firetrucks.

A firefighter in a white helmet approached. He ignored Franklyn and headed to Kathy.

"We gotta stop meeting like this," he said. "My wife gets suspicious when I leave in the middle of the night."

"In your dreams." Kathy pointed to Franklyn. "Fire Chief Ron Wilson, this is Sheriff Franklyn Eaglechild. He's new. This is … *was* his house."

Wilson held out his hand. "Pleasure to meet you." He eyed the fire. "Not great circumstances, though. I'm sorry about your house. I see your fire department didn't show again."

"No, they didn't."

Franklyn faced Kathy. "Can I borrow your phone? Mine is, well mine was in my house."

Kathy handed her cell phone to Franklyn, who dialed Fire Chief Littlebear. It went to the voice message. He thought for a moment, then dialed the fire hall. The phone rang about fifteen times before he hung up. Next, he called fire dispatch.

"Fire dispatch, non-emergency."

"Hi, this is Franklyn Eaglechild, I'm the sheriff of Speargrass Indian Reservation. I'm at a house fire. The Speargrass firefighters haven't arrived. Can you tell me why they weren't dispatched?"

"Sure, Sheriff. We called the fire hall phone number per protocol. It just rang, and no one answered. We tried several times. We were getting a lot of calls about the fire. We paged Fort Benton Fire. We know they'll always respond."

"Do you always call Fort Benton?"

"Look, Sheriff, we gotta cover our butts. If something goes to crap, we'd be liable. So, yeah, we always call Fort Benton for every fire call on the rez. That way, we know someone is responding."

"Okay, thanks. Have a good night."

Franklyn headed back to Wilson. "Dispatch says they called Speargrass Fire, but no one answered."

"That's the trend," Wilson said. "We see them on maybe

twenty percent of the calls on the rez. On most of those, we're first on the scene even though we have a twenty-minute drive. Not counting the time to get to the station from home and geared up."

"I appreciate what you guys are doing."

"Aside from the fact it's two a.m., no problem. It's what we do. We respond to more fire calls on the rez than in our town. You pay us well for this service. We're a volunteer service, and we always have new people. We get our best training fighting fires on the rez."

"Sounds like you should pay me," Franklyn said.

"That's one way of looking at it. You know we're not going to save anything."

"Yeah. I've been renovating for two weeks. About half done."

"Any idea how this started?"

"Nope. I got home at about midnight. Everything was fine. When I woke up, the fire was roaring. I crawled out under the smoke."

"You doing your own electrical?"

"Some."

"Do you know what you're doing?"

"I know my shit, Chief Wilson." Franklyn's jaw was set, and he glared at Wilson. "This isn't an electrical fire. This place went up fast."

"You're saying arson?"

"Isn't that what you think?"

"Well, once we get the fire knocked down, I'll inspect for an accelerant. A fire investigator will make an ultimate decision."

"Don't you do that?"

Wilson laughed. "Nope, that would cost you even more

money. Your fire chief will do it, or he'll hire a buddy of his. Don't hold your breath waiting for a report."

"Don't you have to be certified to do investigations?"

"Yup. Your fire chief isn't certified. That's why he gets his buddy to do it. But that guy seldom shows, and you'll never see the report."

Franklyn sighed. "Ah, hell."

"You're gonna have a battle with your insurance company."

"I didn't have much. I can replace the Stetson and boots."

Red-and-blue lights bounced over the driveway. Lefebvre got out and sprinted over to Franklyn. "Boss. What happened?"

"Some shithead torched my house, that's what happened."

Lefebvre glanced at the house. "Sorry, yeah, I see that. I mean … you okay?"

"Yeah, I'm fine."

"Diesel?"

Franklyn pointed to the ambulance where Diesel and Ember were getting attention from Kathy. "He's fine."

"Who'd do this?"

"The list is lengthy and getting longer."

"Want me to do a track?" Lefebvre asked.

"A what?"

"A track. I'll get my dog and see what we can find."

"You've got a tracking dog? We've got a K9 Unit?"

Lefebvre smirked. "Well, just me training him. But he's reliable. It's worth a shot."

"Go for it," Franklyn said.

Lefebvre sprinted to his SUV and raced off.

Franklyn headed back to the ambulance and sat on the bumper with Kathy.

"You two don't need to stay," Franklyn said. "Go get some sleep."

"We have to stay until the fire is out. We're here for the firefighters. Adam wants to be a firefighter, so he hangs out with them."

"You do this regularly?"

"We respond to fires on the rez three or four times a month."

"How many times does Speargrass Fire respond?"

She laughed. "Maybe one."

"One?"

"Yup. If it's during the day, which none are, it's not cold, and it's not hunting season. Sometimes one guy shows up. Not much he can do."

"So, we rely on Fort Benton?"

"That you do. They come to everything because even when Speargrass Fire says they are responding, frequently it's just the one guy, Scout Ryder. He's keen, but he's also wondering why he busts his ass when the fire chief and the other firefighters don't give a damn. Nothing Scout Ryder can do when he arrives alone. When it's a house fire, Speargrass Fire would need Fort Benton Fire anyway. If it's out of control, Great Falls Fire responds."

Franklyn shook his head. "Incredible."

"Life on the rez."

"If you don't mind me asking," Franklyn said, "why do you work here? I'm not trying to be sexist, but the rez is a tough place for anyone, let alone a woman."

"We don't have a choice. It's part of a mutual aid agreement. Speargrass EMS would help in Great Falls if we were overloaded with calls. But most of the time, we're out here taking calls. My friends ask me the same thing. It's hard to explain. After what happened to Pam and Eric, I'm having second thoughts. The calls are nothing, like a toothache or a hangover, or holy shit calls, like the overdoses."

A dark Chevy Yukon SUV with flashing blue lights pulled in behind the ambulance. Franklyn headed over. Riley Briggs climbed out and stared at the fire. "Holy smoke."

"You could say that," Franklyn said.

"I noticed one of your SUVs racing away from here, lights flashing. Do you know who did this?"

Franklyn shook his head. "Nah, I don't know. That's Lefebvre. He's getting his dog to do a track. Maybe see where the arsonists came from."

"Three cops and one of them is K9," Riley said. "That's impressive."

"More of a hobby. I have two cops now."

"What?" Riley asked.

"I fired one. That's a story for later."

Riley watched the firefighters pour water on the frame. The roof was missing, walls were burned, and the inside was a mess of charred floating debris. "It's worse than a fixer-upper now."

"No shit."

"Will you rebuild?"

Franklyn shook his head. "No."

"You can't live in your camper."

"For now, I guess I have to."

"Stay at the casino," Riley said. "I'm sure you can get a deal being the sheriff and all. At least for tonight, maybe a week. Then you can search for a better place."

"There's nothing on the reserve. At least nothing that's in any better shape than this was. I don't have it in me to start over."

"I've got room. You could stay with me."

"That would be outstanding." Franklyn glared at Riley. "Me rooming with a white federal cop. It would ruin my reputation."

Riley pointed to the fire. "I hear it's not that spectacular, anyway."

"I'll figure it out. I've got options."

"Like the lovely lady I spotted you dining with a few weeks ago."

"What? How?"

"I'm the police." Riley shrugged. "A lot of farmers around here are retiring and moving into the towns. I'll bet you can buy or rent a suitable place with a few acres and a barn for Diesel. Rent for now until you figure it out."

"That's a terrific idea."

"Not just a pretty face," Riley said.

Franklyn laughed. "I going to make a call and see if I can get a room at the casino, at least for a night or two."

Franklyn headed over to Fire Chief Wilson and introduced Riley. Wilson nodded to Riley. "I found where the fire started. You want to see it?"

"You bet," Franklyn said.

They headed to the back of the house where Franklyn had stacked debris from his renovation.

"I'm guessing you had a pile of wood and other scraps from your renovation," Wilson said. "If I were a betting man, I'd say they brought a bale of straw over from the horse corral. Doused the straw in gas and off it went. With the dry straw, piles of pasteboard with lots of glue, this would have ignited quickly, raced up the outer wall to the roof and fanned out from there. I'll bet it wasn't set more than fifteen minutes before you woke up. Maybe less."

"Arson," Franklyn muttered.

"Arson," Wilson confirmed. "Who'd you piss off this week?"

Franklyn frowned. "It's a long list."

"I'd say the sheriff has an arson to solve with a vested interest in finding out who did this," Wilson said.

Riley scanned the charred remains. "That he does."

"We're done," Wilson said. "I don't think there are any hot spots. But get your fire department to put several tanks of water on this tomorrow."

"Thanks, Chief Wilson." Franklyn shook his hand.

"Franklyn. Franklyn, are you okay?" Paulette raced across the yard, threw herself into him and wrapped her arms around his neck. Franklyn stepped back with the force of her hug and peered over her shoulder at Riley, who had a sizable shit-eating grin on his face.

"Paulette, I'm okay."

She released her grasp, stepped back a wiped away a tear. "Diesel and Wild Dog?"

"They're fine. Wild Dog saved Diesel and me. He has a new name, Ember."

"Better than Wild Dog." Paulette sniffled, then scrutinized the emergency vehicles. "Where's Speargrass Fire?"

"Your guess is as good as mine."

"Those fuckers." Paulette threw her hand over her mouth. "I'm sorry. I don't normally swear, but, well, those motherfuckers."

Franklyn grinned. "I had those same thoughts."

"I'm going take off," Riley said. "If you need anything or a place to stay, call me. Take care of the timeworn cowboy, Paulette." Riley winked at Franklyn, then headed to his SUV.

Paulette grabbed his arm. "What happened? How did it start? How'd you get out?"

"I'll tell you everything tomorrow. It's been a long night."

They headed to Diesel and Ember.

"What will you do with these guys?" Paulette asked.

"Good question. I hadn't thought about that."

"I'll get my dad to help me," Paulette said. "We'll take Diesel back to the corral at the arena."

Franklyn put his arm around Paulette's shoulder. "Thank you."

She smiled. "Taking care of you is a full-time job. I'll get Diesel settled. You won't have to worry about him. I'll take Ember as well if he comes with me. I suppose you're back to sleeping in your camper at the arena."

"Not tonight. I called Eva. She got me a hotel room at the casino. I'll stay there tonight and maybe for a few more days until I figure out what to do."

Paulette stepped back, her voice cold. "Eva arranged it? I see."

She marched away from Franklyn and called Diesel. He headed toward her.

Franklyn scratched his head as she marched away.

Franklyn left his truck at the house and drove his department SUV to the casino. Tomorrow he'd load the camper and move back to the arena. Franklyn hauled his briefcase and a duffle bag of clothes and toiletries he'd grabbed from his camper into the casino.

Eva met him at reception. "As soon as you called, I phoned the manager of the hotel and arranged a room for the week."

Franklyn's phone rang.

"I'll check you in," Eva said. "Take the call."

"Franklyn."

"Boss, we got a great track." Lefebvre's breath came in gasps.

"You don't say. Where does it lead?"

"You won't believe this."

"I'm not in the mood for games."

"Right, boss. Sorry. The track was perfect. Pax latched onto a scent behind your house, raced toward the school, past the arena, and then up the hill to the three trailers. Pax stopped in front of the trailer on the right."

"Son of a bitch."

"What do you want to do?"

Franklyn glanced over to where Eva and the receptionist were engaged in an animated conversation. "Is your dog certified in K9?"

Lefebvre paused. "No, sorry, boss."

"The courts might not accept your track as reasonable cause to get a search warrant. At least we know who we're dealing with."

"What're you going to do?"

"Think about it tonight," Franklyn said. "We'll talk tomorrow."

Franklyn headed back to the reception desk.

"Your room is ready," Eva said. "I got you two keys. I know you're always losing things."

The receptionist grinned.

Franklyn grabbed his briefcase. Eva slung a duffel bag over her shoulder.

"I can get that," Franklyn said. "You should get home and back to bed."

"I'll help get you settled. Make sure there are no problems with your room."

Eva led Franklyn down a hallway to the left. Franklyn followed. She opened the door, and he followed her into the room. Not a low-end motel room like on the rodeo circuit. He scanned the sizeable room with a king-sized bed, desk, LCD TV, coffeemaker, and bar fridge. The bathroom was nearly as large as the bedroom with a walk-in shower and hot tub.

He set the briefcase on the desk, grabbed the duffel bag from Eva, and tossed it into the corner. They stood facing each other. Franklyn knew what he wanted to do but having Eva stay was a dangerous idea. "The room looks great. I don't think there'll be any problems here I can't handle. I smell like a campfire. I'm going to shower and sleep for what's left of tonight. See you later today." He headed into the bathroom and closed the door.

Franklyn let the water warm and then stepped in. The water felt like soft fingers on his back, and the heat penetrated his aching muscles. He had unfamiliar aches and pains from the fight at the overdose. The last thing he needed was more pain.

He shampooed his hair, washing the soot and smoke away. He turned the water hotter. It stung at first, then felt great.

He faced the showerhead and let the water flow over his head. He hoped the hotel had a large hot water system because he could shower for hours. The moist air was soothing on his throat. The sound of the water was peaceful, like listening to a spring rainstorm. As fatigue overwhelmed him, he decided he'd better get out of the shower before he fell asleep and knocked himself out on the shower floor. The image of the paramedics finding him there was not pleasant and something he'd never live down.

He dried off, wrapped the towel around his waist, and wandered toward the bed.

Eva smiled shyly back from under a sheet. "It was too late for me to drive home. I hope you don't mind. I stayed."

Franklyn's brain processed what was happening.

Eva let go of the sheet and tapped the bed. "Come, sit. Let me give you a massage."

Franklyn's brain and other body parts kicked in. Eva, in glorious nakedness, was waiting for him. He forgot about the exhaustion.

Her soft hands rolled across his shoulders, over his back, and down his ribs.

"My god. Your shoulders and back are a mass of scars. Do you have a death wish?"

"Years of rodeo takes its toll."

"Those are fresh bruises. Are they painful?"

"I had a fight at an overdose call."

"Let me see if I can ease that pain." Her fingers dug deep into his muscles, avoiding the bruises. She found spots that sent electric shocks through him. Under her skillful fingers, the knots released. Her hands reached around to his chest. He felt her breasts press into his back, nipples sliding across his skin. Her hands moved from his chest, across his stomach, and still lower. She nibbled his neck. He grabbed her and pushed her onto the bed.

Franklyn's hands slid down her back to her butt. He grasped the firm buttocks. *Yup, she was a bike rider.*

Franklyn leaned against the headboard. "I can't believe my house burned."

"A lot of these houses are breeding pits for every insect, rodent, and disease known to mankind," Eva said. "Bed bugs, lice, whatever."

"You think it's good my house burned?"

"Well, you were getting it into decent shape. It was practically new. I would have recommended a few feral cats to keep the mice and rats away."

"I can't stand rats."

"What? The tough policeman is scared of rats."

Franklyn grunted.

She leaned onto her elbow, stared into his eyes. "You're thinking about the fire, aren't you?"

"Uh, no."

"You are." Eva sat up. "Okay, let's get this out of the way. Do you know who did it?"

Franklyn cocked his head. "Lefebvre and his dog got a great track to the trailers. It's the Lamont brothers."

"What will you do?"

"I need to get a search warrant, but the court isn't on my side."

"You're doing nothing?"

"I didn't say that. When I work this out, they'll pay."

"Can we forget about the Lamont brothers for a while?"

He slid over to Eva.

She stroked his jaw. "You have a strong jawline."

"Thank you."

She leaned in and kissed him. "You have delicious lips." She kissed down his neck. "Tasty neck." She nibbled across his chest. "This isn't bad either." She flicked her tongue in his belly button.

Franklyn leaned back with anticipation.

CHAPTER FORTY-FOUR

FRANKLYN AWOKE TO A PHONE RINGING. HE RUBBED HIS EYES AND glanced around the room—not his camper and not the house. A bedroom with two night tables, a mirror across from the bed, and a TV on top of a dresser. Where was he? The phone rang again. He grabbed the receiver. "Sheriff Eaglechild."

"This is your wake-up call. Have a pleasant day."

Franklyn hung up and rolled over in bed. The blanket and sheet were in a tangle at the end of the bed. Scattered towels led to the bathroom.

He sat up and rubbed his eyes. Body aching, Franklyn stretched, exhausted from lack of sleep. He glanced at the clock on the night table. Seven. Eva finally let him sleep about three. He had no idea when she left. Four hours of sleep would have to be enough.

Stumbling to the bathroom, Franklyn opened his shaving kit. *Oh, shit.* Most of his Oxy had burned in the fire. All that was left was a few pills in the truck.

He leaned onto the counter and stared at his haggard face What the hell was he going to do?

Franklyn started the shower and let the warm water ease his aches—neck, shoulders, back, hips, heck, his entire body. He increased the heat as high as it would go. He'd burn away the pain. When he couldn't stand it any longer, he reduced the heat and finished with an icy shower. He wandered out of the bathroom and stared at the bed. He grinned, thinking about the events after his last shower.

Then he remembered the fire. *All my hard work*. Someone tried to kill him. And Diesel.

When Wilson asked him if he had enemies, he'd said the list was getting longer. *Did I make that many enemies in a few weeks?*

At first, he thought it was the family of the man Lefebvre shot. Around here, a family could mean near a hundred people.

But Lefebvre's dog tracked straight to the trailers. He'd put a dent in their distribution. Sitting outside their trailers had cut the traffic from the school kids to zero. Having Lefebvre park there in the evenings slowed the drug trade.

The list didn't end there. Leroy Balam and Hiram Crow hated him. Would Leroy torch Franklyn's house because he got fired? People have killed for a lot less. Crow just didn't like him.

He was being played by everyone from Chief Fox down. There was no doubt, right from their first meeting, that the chief wanted someone he could control. Someone to do as he was told. That had never been Franklyn. That's what got him into foster care and bounced around inside the system. Riley's father channeled that stubbornness into rodeo. Franklyn had always done it his way. Not always the right way, but still his way.

And where the hell was Speargrass Fire Department? They'd suffer the wrath of Franklyn.

He'd finished more than one bar fight he hadn't started. He didn't blink staring down a two-thousand-pound bull. No man or men would scare him. Not even the chief. By the time he was dressed, he was ready to go to war.

Franklyn's first stop was at the arena. Ember raced toward him. Franklyn knelt, and Ember smothered him with slobbery licks. Ember stayed at his side as Franklyn wandered over to the corral. Diesel ambled over and nuzzled Franklyn's face.

He filled the water barrel, threw out some fresh hay, and held a bucket of feed as Diesel devoured his breakfast. Franklyn filled Ember's bowl with kibble. The dog that once shyly accepted food dove into the bowl like it was raw meat.

When Diesel had licked the bucket clean, Franklyn brushed him, examining for burns or injuries. Diesel had survived the fire without a scratch. Franklyn would have the vet stop by and check Diesel anyway.

Satisfied the animals were okay, he drove to the house.

Franklyn wandered around the perimeter of his house. His sneakers sunk into the soaked ground and piled ashes. The odor of charred wood was heavy in the air. Wisps of smoke reached skyward from dozens of hot spots.

He shook his head. Total loss. Nothing to be salvaged. On the good side, he hadn't moved his personal stuff into the house. His clothing, boots, Stetsons and bedding were ashes now. Worse, almost all of his prescription. The pills were worth more than all his possessions. The clothes could be replaced. The Oxy could not.

He stared at the pit of burned lumber and water, at the fragments of the walls that hadn't collapsed. He placed his hands on his knees and hunched over. Was this worth it?

Franklyn headed out to settle a few scores.

The fire station was in darkness when Franklyn arrived. The office area empty. He wandered out to the bays. They had parked two ambulances inside, one behind the other. Both firetrucks, the engine and the tender, were parked inside. The hose beds on the engine were bare, and hoses lay in piles over the floor. Not a single length of hose was in place. He climbed into the cab and turned the ignition. The fuel gauge read less than a quarter tank. He eyed the gauges and dials on the side of the engine. If he was reading them right, the engine had no water.

The fuel gauge in the tender registered below a quarter tank. The indicator showed there was no water. Neither truck was ready. Franklyn wasn't a firefighter, but he was sure water and hoses were important to firefighting.

Franklyn spotted a phone on the wall and called Littlebear.

A groggy voice answered. "Hello."

"Chief Littlebear?"

"Yeah."

"It's Eaglechild. Why aren't you at work?"

"Oh, I don't feel too good."

"There was a house fire last night. Dispatch says they called, but no one answered. Who was the phone transferred to?"

"Me."

"Why didn't you answer?"

"I felt a cold come on, so I shut off my cell phone."

Franklyn's jaw tightened, and his pulse pounded in his temples. "You what?"

"I shut it off."

Franklyn stared at his phone in disbelief. "Did you transfer it to someone else?"

"No."

"Did you tell fire dispatch Speargrass was out of service?"

"No."

"Why not?" Franklyn wanted to scream.

"I just didn't. I was sick."

"I want you and your firefighters at the station within thirty minutes. I want both those trucks loaded with the hose, the water tanks filled, and the gas tanks full. Then get over to my place, the one that burned, and make sure there aren't any hot spots. Fort Benton Fire Department has already left the scene."

CHAPTER FORTY-FIVE

By the time Franklyn arrived at work at seven forty-five, a crowd had gathered outside the entrance to the administration building. He parked, joined the group, and followed their gaze. Big red-and-blue letters scrawled across the wall read:

Apple, go back to your white home!

No French Cops

A few people laughed as they watched Franklyn. Bile rose in his throat. His heart raced, and blood flooded his brain.

Jesse staggered up beside Franklyn. "Hey, you get it? Apple. Red on the outside, white on the inside. That's you, man. They don't think you Indian no more. Too long with the white folk."

"What do you think, Jesse?"

"You're okay." Jesse shrugged. "You treat me fair. Even when you make me mad." Jesse grabbed Franklyn's arm. "Buy me breakfast."

Franklyn shook him off. "Later, Jesse. I'm busy."

He stomped into the office.

"Morning, Paulette."

She barely raised her head from her desk. "How did you sleep?"

"Uneasy."

"I'm surprised you got any sleep at all." The coldness was back in her voice. "How are your burns?"

"They're okay. It didn't take a lot to treat them."

"I'm sure it didn't. How's the house?"

What was going on with Paulette? He was missing something. "House is a total loss. Diesel and I would have died if Ember hadn't saved us. By then, the house was consumed with flames and smoke. Ember led the way out. Then I opened the corral gate for Diesel. Thank you for looking after them last night."

"I wish I could have done more, but you were already being cared for. They were content to be back at the arena. How'd the fire start?"

"What do you think?"

"Arson?"

"Arson."

"Who?"

"The Lamont brothers. I need to do some shopping today." Franklyn glanced at his outfit. "Everything I owned except these clothes burned. Oh, I need a new cell phone and a new radio."

"Sure, I can get you a phone. We've got a box full. I'll set it up for you. The radio might take a few days. Use Balam's until I get you a new one."

Lefebvre staggered into the office. Paulette turned, then gasped. "Oh, my god."

Franklyn stared, his jaw dropped. The man wearing a Speargrass Police uniform was barely recognizable. Tape covered his nose, both eyes were black and puffy, and his lip was split and swollen.

"Mornin', Sheriff." Lefebvre tried to smile but his lips barely moved. There was a gap where a tooth should have been.

"What the hell happened?" Franklyn asked.

Paulette pulled out her chair and guided Lefebvre to it. Franklyn sat across from Lefebvre.

"After Pax and I did the track to the trailers, we went home. I was tired and wasn't paying attention. When we got home, I got out of the SUV and shut the door. That's when two guys jumped me and shoved me to the ground. I didn't have a chance to grab pepper spray or a baton—nothin'. One guy hit me with something, a baseball bat, I guess. The other put the boots to my face. I tried to crawl under the SUV, but they pulled me back and kept thumping away. Then Pax came flying around the front of the truck and jumped the guy with the bat. Both guys were swearing, and the guy with the bat was yelling, 'get the cop's gun and shoot the dog.' I curled up so they couldn't get my gun. Pax yelped, and then I heard a vehicle start and gravel flying everywhere."

Paulette gasped and put her hands over her mouth. "Oh, god. How's Pax?"

"He seems okay. I dropped him off at the vet. Maybe some bruised ribs."

"The vet's going be busy today." Franklyn frowned. "Who was it?"

"Too dark and happened too quickly. They were in a truck, but that narrows it down to everyone."

"Who patched you up?" Paulette asked.

"I stopped at the health center. Dr. Dillard wanted me to go to Great Falls for X-rays. I said no."

"Might be a sound idea," Franklyn said. "At least go home, take the day off."

"No, boss. They came after both of us. We can't let that go unchallenged. We can't show weakness by feeling sorry for ourselves."

"All right. Take it easy for a while. I'm sure Paulette would make you a coffee."

"I'd love to." Paulette grabbed a mug, filled it, and handed it to Lefebvre.

Franklyn stared at his empty coffee mug as Paulette placed the pot on the burner. Paulette smirked as she headed to her desk.

Franklyn filled his mug. "I'll be in my office." He stopped in the doorway and stared at his chair. There was a hole the size of a quarter in the headrest. He focused on the window. There was another hole, the size of a dime, with cracks spreading out. His eyes moved from the window to the chair and followed the bullet path to the far wall. Another hole, the size of a fingertip, and many smaller holes—pinpricks. The bullet had broken apart after the collisions with the window, chair, and wall. He used his pocketknife to dig into the wall around the largest hole and pulled out a tiny piece of lead.

"What're you doing, boss?" Paulette stood at his door, arms across her chest, frowning.

"Someone shot at me."

"What? Now? You're joking, right?"

"Nope. Possibly a hunting rifle. They shot right where I'd be sitting."

"Holy," Paulette said. "When did it happen? How did it miss you?"

"I don't know when it happened, but luckily I wasn't here.

Can you pull the surveillance cameras from last night to this morning, please?"

The three of them watched Paulette's monitor as she played the video from several cameras located around the building. After twenty minutes, they found what they were searching for. At seven-forty that morning, a black truck raced in front of the building and stopped. A rifle barrel poked out of the window, and a single muzzle flashed. Then the truck raced off.

Seven-forty. Most days he was at his desk by then. Most days. Not today.

CHAPTER FORTY-SIX

Chief Fox sat at his antique desk, a glass of whiskey on ice swirling in his hand. "How's Eaglechild?"

"He's fricken' lucky." Leroy Balam sat on the couch, trimming his nails with a hunting knife. "How he got out of the fire is a mystery."

"Such a shame." Chief Fox laughed. "He was doing a fine job renovating the rat-infested house I gave him. Until it became a bonfire."

"Any problems with the fire investigation?" The chief swallowed a gulp of whiskey.

"No. The fire investigator we use still hasn't been to the scene. Public Works is knocking down what's left and hauling it away. If the inspector ever shows, there'll be nothing but a hole."

"Fort Benton Fire gonna be a problem?"

Leroy shook his head. "They like the money we pay for fighting our fires. They won't raise any stink."

"Who shot at Eaglechild's office?"

"Damned if I know," Leroy said.

"You have no idea?"

"Revenge for the shooting. It would have solved our problem of Eaglechild escaping the fire."

Chief Fox snorted. "I wonder who it is."

"Someone kicked the shit out of Lefebvre and his dog." Balam worked on a thumbnail. "My money is on the Lamont boys."

"Eaglechild is using up his luck." The chief swirled the whiskey in his glass and watched the ice spin in rapid circles. "That's two strikes. Next time he won't be so lucky."

"You should fire him," Balam said.

Fox sipped the whiskey. "Any sign Franklyn's addiction problem is back?"

"Don't think it ever left, but it's not showing. He walks with a limp and wobble, but that's from injuries, not drugs. He drinks rum and Coke, but nothing excessive."

"But he's still taking Oxy, right?"

"Oh, yeah. He carries a bottle in his truck. If the rest of his pills burned, he's gonna be in withdrawal soon. If he hits low enough, he will take the pills he confiscated from me. If he takes too many, he'll seal his own fate."

The chief nodded. "Possibly. Why not help him along and replace a pill or two with the stronger ones?"

"I like the way you think." Balam grinned. "Eaglechild talked to Eva about posting for two deputies. With me gone, that leaves Hiram Crow to keep things in line. I don't trust him."

"Don't worry about Crow." The chief swiveled his chair and stared out the window. "He wants to be chief someday. He'll do the right thing."

"If Franklyn hires his own guys, we'll lose all control. We can't let that happened."

"I already talked to Eva," the chief said. "She'll slow the hiring process."

"Eva stayed the night with Franklyn after the fire."

"I know." The chief swung his chair back to Balam. "She told me."

"The Métis boy's dog followed the Lamont boys back to their trailer."

The chief shook his head and closed his eyes. "Are they incompetent?"

Balam chuckled. "They're not the smartest, that's for sure. What's Franklyn gonna do?"

"She says he's not doing anything, at least right now."

"I'll tell the Lamont brothers to keep a low profile." Balam slid the hunting knife back into its sheath.

CHAPTER FORTY-SEVEN

FRANKLYN STOPPED BY HIS HOUSE ON HIS WAY TO GREAT FALLS TO do some shopping. He hadn't heard from Littlebear or a fire inspector, so he thought he'd see if he could find anything that tied the fire to the Lamont brothers.

As he passed the last of the trees, he stomped on the brakes, threw the truck in park, jumped out. He headed to Littlebear, who was watching a public works loader push the remnants of Franklyn's house into a pile.

Franklyn glanced at the loader, then back to Littlebear. "What the hell are you doing?"

"The house was a safety hazard. I didn't want the kids coming here and getting hurt." Littlebear sucked on a piece of grass. "The walls were unstable, and the floor destroyed. The roof was hanging by a nail or two."

"Did you do an investigation?"

Littlebear shrugged. "Nothing to investigate. The cause of the fire was obvious."

"What do you mean?" Franklyn loomed over Littlebear.

Littlebear stepped back. "Chief Wilson told me you'd been replacing the electrical during renovations. I see this all the time. Some handyman does his own work, gets sloppy, next thing you know there's a fully involved fire."

"It was arson," Franklyn yelled. "The Lamont brothers stacked straw against the wall, used an accelerant, and lit the straw. Wilson showed me where it started."

"I talked to Wilson," Littlebear said. "It was dark, and he wasn't sure what started the fire. He didn't want you to feel guilty about your screw-up with the electrical wrecking your house. Truly a shame. I hear it was coming along nicely. It'll be in my report to the fire commissioner."

"Report?" Franklyn's hands balled into fists. "You're not a qualified fire investigator."

"Sure, but they accept my reports. We have a lot of fires here."

"But you don't go to any of them."

Littlebear grinned and strolled away.

CHAPTER FORTY-EIGHT

RILEY WAS LEANING BACK IN HIS CHAIR, HANDS BEHIND HIS HEAD, when Blake stepped into the office. "Hard at it, I see."

"I'm doing research."

"With your eyes closed?" She grabbed her chair and pulled it next to his. "What type of research?"

Riley leaned forward and pointed to the computer. "The Lamont brothers."

"I thought Franklyn already did that."

"He did, but he didn't give me the details. After the arson, I wanted to know about those cocksuckers."

"Wow. You sound angry."

"Hey, they went after my brother."

"What'd you find?"

"They are brothers. Twenty-two, twenty-four, and twenty-six."

"There's skillful family planning."

Riley glared at Blake. "Check out their rap sheet."

Blake leaned closer as Riley scrolled through pages of criminal charges. "That's not possible. They all have two pages of charges."

"And not one day in jail. Heck, I can't find a conviction. The list goes back to when they were sixteen. Who knows what trouble they were in before?"

"Not unusual for future criminals to start with arson. Franklyn's house might not have been the first."

"I'm sure it wasn't."

"Why didn't the charges stick?"

Riley hit the print button, and the printer spat out six sheets of paper. He shuffled through the pages and highlighted a few sections. "The one pattern I see is that the court released them to the Tribal Chief in recent cases. On a few others, the arresting officer failed to show, and evidence was missing or improperly cataloged."

"Who were the officers?"

Riley circled a name on all the pages. "One officer responsible for all three brothers' arrests."

"Who?"

"Leroy Balam. Speargrass Tribal Police."

"The guy Franklyn fired right before the fire?"

"One and the same."

"No wonder the chief knew how to get them released. He's done this dozens of times before. And Balam happens to know three arsonists."

CHAPTER FORTY-NINE

LIGHT STREAMED THROUGH THE CAMPER WINDOW AS FRANKLYN rolled off the bed onto the floor. He grabbed the stove handle to pull himself up. His back seized, and he could barely move his legs. He'd decided to stay in the camper close to Diesel and Ember after finding the bullet hole in his office, in case anyone tried to hurt them. Leaving the comfortable bed at the hotel was a mistake.

He dressed and staggered out to the truck. He snatched the pill bottle from the glove box and poured two Oxy into his hands. He tossed them into his mouth and swallowed. He gagged on the dry pills but choked them down.

It was a strain to carry feed and water to Diesel. He would have to ask Paulette to take care of the horse. He couldn't lift bales, and carrying a full bucket of water was impossible.

The next morning Franklyn limped into the health center and headed straight to reception. "Sheriff. How can I help you, Sheriff?" Violet asked.

"I need to see a doctor. I'm in a lot of pain."

Violet rolled her eyes. "Of course you do. Weren't you supposed to make an appointment last time you were here?"

"Yeah, I got busy."

"But not busy today?" Violet glared at Franklyn. "Have a seat, and I'll see if I can get you in."

Franklyn stumbled to the waiting room but decided to stand. As painful as that was, he was worried if he sat, he'd never be able to stand. The Oxy from the morning wasn't having an effect.

The wait was brief, and she showed him into an examination room. He used a stool to get onto the table. A few minutes later, the door opened, and Dr. Dillard came in.

"Franklyn, you're finally back. I said to schedule a follow-up with me in a week—been a lot longer. How's your deputy?"

"He's doing okay."

"He got an old-fashioned shit-kicking. What brings you here?"

"I can barely move. My back, hips, and knees won't work. I could hardly get out of bed this morning. My supply of Oxy burned with my house last night." No sense telling him about the dozen left in the truck.

"That was your place?"

"Yup."

"You were inside?"

"Yup."

"Take off your shirt." Dillard listened to Franklyn's chest. "I don't hear any breathing problems. Did you inhale a lot of smoke?"

"Yup, a lot."

"Well, your lungs are okay. We should do an X-ray, anyway." Dillard examined Franklyn's back. "You're in spasm."

"Doc, can you replace my Oxy?" *Just one more time.*

"I could, but we should start getting you off opioids. I can give you an injection that will ease the spasms."

Franklyn's brow rose. "That's it?"

"What do you mean?" Dillard folded his arms.

"Doc, I'm seized up. I'm in agony."

"Once the injection takes hold, you'll be better. Tylenol Extra Strength will help. I'll also give you a prescription for Voltaren. Take one morning and one at night. Tylenol and Voltaren should give you relief."

"What about tomorrow? I come back for another injection?"

Dillard shook his head. "Oh, no. I can give the injection once a month."

"And the pain?" *God, no, I can't handle the pain.*

"I'd suggest a massage today."

Maybe Eva can take care of that. "Doc, I can't function without Oxy. I don't abuse it. I need it to make it through the day."

"That's the definition of abuse or certainly addiction."

"Is it wrong to need medication to live?" Anger replaced frustration. "If I had diabetes, would you prescribe insulin? Would I need that for the rest of my life? Is that addiction or abuse, or is that treating the problem?"

"That's a different scenario. Without insulin, the person would die."

"Without pain relief, I can't function."

Dillard sighed. "Franklyn, do you want to beat your dependence on Oxy?"

"Sure." *Not really.*

"I can help. Other than the Tylenol and Voltaren combo, there are two options. Methadone, which is a substitute for OxyContin. You have fewer cravings, it lasts longer, and you experience fewer highs and lows. The second option, and the one I recommend, is to get the opioid completely out of your system—total detoxification. I can get you into a treatment center. They can help you while you detoxify."

"Doc, I can't. There's a lot going on here."

Dillard handed him a card. "Then at least talk to this counselor. He's here tomorrow afternoon." Dillard drew up the medication and gave the injection. "Give this a few minutes to work, then you're free to go. Give the Tylenol and Voltaren a chance."

Franklyn watched the doctor leave the exam room. He was screwed. He stared at his knees and wrung his hands. *Oh shit.* He straightened, drew in a deep breath, and slid off the exam table.

He ignored Violet's calls for another appointment as he stormed out of the clinic, tossing the card for the counselor in an ashtray. In his truck, he opened the glove box, pulled out the pill bottle, and poured the pills into his hand. As awful as he'd thought—twelve pills. Three days max unless he stretched them out, say two a day. He shook his head and tossed two into his mouth, swallowed, and put his head in his hands.

CHAPTER FIFTY

As Riley swung out of the parking lot, he grabbed his phone and dialed. He accelerated through the yellow light.

"Hello."

"I'm on my way to your house."

"Sounds great, but should I believe it?" Regan asked.

"No fresh leads to follow. I'm at a dead-end right now. I can use a quiet night."

"It won't all be quiet."

"I'm looking forward to that." His phone buzzed.

"Hang on a second. I've got another call." He clicked to the other call. "Briggs."

"Riley. It's Gibson. I'm at a suspicious death. Two deaths. You need to get over here."

"Call Blake. She can handle this."

"Blake is on her way, but you need to be here. This is bigger than she can handle. I'll send the details and address to your phone."

Riley sighed and opened the text. *Shit.* He clicked back to Regan.

"Let me guess," she said. "Duty calls."

"Yeah. Two dead—husband and wife. I'll call you later."

"I won't wait up."

Paramedics were coming out of the house without a patient as Riley arrived. One of them shook his head. Riley paused and surveyed the large two-story house with a quadruple-car garage. To the right were a barn and stable. A few horses chased each other around a corral. The yard around the house was landscaped—none of this fit with two overdose deaths. He slipped under the police tape and headed to the open front door. Blake and Gibson stood just inside the entryway, staring into the living room. Riley followed Blake's wide eyes.

A man and a woman lay on the carpeted floor, about four feet apart. Around their bodies were the signs the paramedics had worked hard on the couple. Intravenous lines were still connected to IV solutions, and the catheters taped in place. The ends of the laryngeal mask airway stuck out of the corner of their mouths. Ordinarily, the paramedics cleaned up their wrappers, boxes, and syringes, but Riley had told Gibson over the radio to make sure the paramedics left everything as it was. *Damn.* He should have talked to the paramedics before they left.

Riley glanced around the living room. "Where did the 911 call come from?"

"From the house," Gibson said. "Dispatch said the caller was a child, and she said Mommy and Daddy were sleeping and wouldn't wake up. Then hung up."

"Oh, jeez." Riley shook his head.

"Six years old," Gibson said. "Dispatch called back, but the kids didn't answer the phone. I got here at the same time as EMS. We found the parents on the couch, unconscious and unresponsive. The kids were watching TV. Like nothing had happened."

"Where are the kids now?" Riley asked.

"They're in the kitchen with Deputy Faith Bennett," Gibson said.

"Did you call child services?"

"Bennett did. She'll stay with the kids until child services arrive."

"Blake, check on the kids and talk to Bennett. See what information you can get." Riley scanned the living room. The house was clean and respectable. Not the crack houses he was used to walking into in situations like this.

The one thing amiss was Mom and Dad on the floor—dead. Riley glanced at the family photos on the mantel over the fireplace. Another wall held two picture frames with the kids' school photos.

Riley knelt next to the bodies—a young couple—mid-thirties. They were ghostly in appearance. Their lips blue—blood pooling in their backs. Staring into those dead milky eyes sent shivers up his spine. He closed their eyes.

Riley checked their arms—no track marks. They didn't inject anything, at least not into their arms. During the autopsy, the coroner would search for injection sites in other places like between the toes.

Riley stood. "Gibson. Did you check for medications? Did the paramedics find any?"

"The paramedics didn't ask me to," Gibson said.

"Show some initiative, Gibson. I'll check." Riley headed down the hall. On his right was the bathroom. There were no medications on the counter. The bottom shelf of the medicine cabinet was filled with pill bottles. The regular stuff—Tylenol, Advil, Aspirin, birth control pills, and hemorrhoid cream—nothing that causes overdoses.

Riley left the bathroom and headed further down the hall to the master bedroom. The room was neat—the bed made, and no clothes strewn around the floor. Something on the night table on the other side of the bed caught his eye. Riley searched around the bed. He slipped on gloves and grabbed a baggie that contained about a dozen green pills. He slid one pill to the side of the baggie. There was writing on one side, and an eighty on the other side—*OxyContin.* Might be his eyes, but the imprint appeared off to him. Like it wasn't centered.

He slipped the baggie into his jacket and searched the drawers of the night table. He rifled through the clothing drawers, opened the closet, and moved the clothes to the side. He checked to see if there were any secret panels—nothing out of the ordinary.

Riley headed back to the living room and stopped next to Gibson. "All right, until we know more, these are suspicious deaths."

"Looks like a double suicide to me," Gibson said.

"We'll see," Riley said. "Get the forensics guys over here to check everything. I found a baggy of pills in the bedroom. My bet is these aren't ordinary pills. I need you to drive it to the forensics lab in Missoula."

"That will take the rest of my shift."

"Did you get a name for family members or anything like that?"

"No. Bennett is working on that with the kids."

Riley glanced toward the kitchen. The dad part of him wanted to go to the kids. See how they were doing—comfort them. That was not his job right now. His task was to figure out what happened. Bennett would take care of the kids until child services arrived. He met Blake at the front door, and they hiked down the sidewalk.

"Did you learn anything?" Riley asked.

"This has happened before."

"What?"

Blake was on the verge of tears. "The kids freaked the first time. EMS came and resuscitated the parents. They refused to go to the hospital. The mother told the girl—she's six—what to do if it happened again. That's how she knew to call 911. Because Mom and Dad were fine last time, the kids thought nothing harmful would happen. They don't understand why the paramedics didn't get their parents to wake up again since it worked before."

"Were you able to find any relatives?"

"Bennett found a contact list by the phone. It looks new. Mom probably made it after the first scare. The dad's sister is on her way from Helena."

"I sent Gibson to Missoula with a bag of pills. I think it's OxyContin. But I've got a feeling these aren't from a pharmacy."

Riley and Blake sat across from two paramedics in the ambulance station. One paramedic, Adam, poured coffee and sat down next to his partner, Kathy.

"Thanks for the coffee," Riley said. "Didn't I see you at Franklyn's fire?"

Adam nodded. "Yup, we were there."

"That must have been an awful call for you two tonight."

Adam nodded. "I've never been to a double overdose before. We were busting our asses to get everything done. Luckily some of your guys were there and did compressions and grabbed the equipment we needed."

"The kids were watching TV with their parents dead on the couch," Riley said.

"Yup," Kathy said. "We arrived at the same time as the troopers. When we entered the house, it appeared like the adults were sleeping, and the kids were enjoying cartoons. As we got closer, we could see the parents were ashen, their lips blue. At first, I thought of carbon monoxide poisoning, but the kids weren't affected and the blue lips didn't fit either. I pulled the dad onto the floor and checked his eyes. There aren't a lot of reasons a young adult would be unresponsive, and with two adults, I figured overdose. The dad's pupils were pinpoint—I thought opioids. Adam had the mom on the floor and checked her pupils were pinpoint. Neither had pulses. We got the troopers to do compressions. We gave Naloxone intramuscularly into their thighs, then started an intravenous. We gave Naloxone through the IV. The cardiac monitor showed asystole—flat line—for both. The troopers kept doing compressions, we ventilated and gave additional Naloxone. We also gave epinephrine to try to start the heart. Nothing worked. After twenty minutes, I called an emergency doctor in Great Falls, and he gave the order to discontinue resuscitation. We were going to clean up, but a county deputy said you wanted the scene left as it was."

"Do you go to many overdose calls?" Blake asked.

"I wouldn't say we go to a lot." Adam leaned toward Blake and shrugged. "But it's increasing. Last year it was drunks on the weekend, then we started seeing some heroin overdoses. Over the last three months, we've had an increase in Oxy overdoses. We never responded to Oxy overdoses at all last year."

"Now we're getting them nearly every day," Riley said.

"Opioids are the drug of choice for sure," Adam said. "The addicts get pissed when we take away their high with Naloxone. They don't care that they weren't breathing. We're seeing more violence directed at us."

"I thought the paramedics were the good guys," Blake said.

"Not to the addicts," Adam said. "The hospital has had a rise in opioid overdoses. Some overdose patients were left on the sidewalk outside the emergency entrance. They found others unconscious sitting in chairs in admitting. The emergency doc says there's something new and powerful out on the street."

"If you gave Naloxone, why didn't it work?" Blake asked.

"We give Naloxone to reverse the effects of an opioid overdose—OxyContin, Percocet, heroin, morphine, and fentanyl. Those are the main opioids. They cause respiration to slow and then stop. If we give Naloxone within the first couple of minutes of unconsciousness before they stop breathing, it will probably work. But if more than about four minutes have passed—the brain can survive four minutes or less without oxygen—then nothing will revive the patient, including Naloxone."

"The kids told me their parents had overdosed before," Blake said. "Why would they take a chance?"

Kathy nodded. "When we got back here, I entered my EMS report into our computer system. The parents' names appeared two other times. Both for overdoses. It's hard to understand the addict's mind. The need to take the drugs defies all other logic, like staying alive for their kids."

"That's horrible," Blake said. "Those poor kids."

"Stuff with kids is the worst part of this job," Adam said.

Blake sighed. "I don't know how you do it."

"I could say the same to you," Adam said. "Investigating deaths or dealing with scum. We're well trained and have excellent drugs and equipment. We do our best and move on to the next call. If you'd like, I could give you a tour of the ambulance."

"That would be great." Blake followed Adam out to the ambulance.

"You'd better keep an eye on your partner," Kathy said. "Adam is on the prowl."

Riley grinned. "She can take care of herself. He's fighting a losing battle."

A horn sounded, then a voice came over the speakers. "Great Falls Medic 1 and Medic 2. Range Road 1 Township 7. Multiple unconscious, repeat, multiple unconscious patients. Time out 1934."

"Like the last call?" Riley asked.

"One way to find out," Kathy said. "Follow us."

Kathy joined Adam at the ambulance as Blake met Riley at their SUV. When the ambulance sped out of the station, Riley pulled in behind. The ambulance's red lights lit the darkness and bounced off windows as they raced east down Main Street.

"Did you enjoy your private ambulance tour?"

"Adam is proud of his job."

"Uh, huh."

"Seriously, it was interesting."

"And the tour guide?" Riley grinned.

Blake pulled up the call on the computer. "That's the farm where we found the guns. What the hell's going on?"

Riley shook his head. "I don't know. I've never seen anything like this. In Chicago, this happened a few years ago with heroin addicts who bought from the same guy. The heroin was more powerful than usual, and there were dozens of opioid overdoses. The users still had the needles in their arms."

"The mom and dad didn't have any track marks," Blake said. "A seemingly normal, respectable couple who overdose while their kids watch TV."

"Not heroin, but it sounds the same," Riley said. "I've got an uneasy feeling about this."

"We'll find out in a few minutes."

The ambulance headed down the dirt driveway. Riley dropped back so he wasn't in the cloud of dust. He parked fifty feet from the house leaving room for the another ambulance enroute. As Riley exited the SUV, an MHP cruiser raced by and parked behind the ambulance. Gibson jumped out and followed EMS into the house.

Dumbass. A noise behind the house caught Riley's attention. "Blake, go with EMS and help. I see lights behind the house on the path to the barn. I'm going to check it out."

"I'll come with you," Blake said.

"No, EMS will need help until another ambulance arrives."

Riley stayed in the house's shadow, then followed the path to the barn. The trunk of a car was open—the trunk light providing some illumination. Then the back-passenger door opened, and the interior light came on. Riley noticed a man set an ice cream bucket on the back seat. Riley pulled out his gun and held it to his chest as he stepped closer. A second man put a large silver object into the trunk. When Riley stumbled, the men spun and spotted him.

"Police! Don't move."

One man grabbed the bucket. They raced around the side of the car and sprinted down the rutted wagon path into the darkness.

Riley sprinted after them, activating the mini-mag flashlight on his gun. They were following the path that led to the decrepit granaries. Riley had the advantage following the lighted path.

One suspect swerved off the path into a stand of trees—the other continued down the trail. Riley followed into the trees, branches slapping his face and twigs snapping underfoot. Riley was catching up as they broke out of the trees into an open field.

Gotcha, Riley thought as he closed the gap. As they sprinted across the field, the suspect peered over his shoulder a few times, which slowed him. He glanced back again, stumbled, and fell to the ground.

Riley stood over him.

"Don't fuckin' move." Riley stepped closer, shining the flashlight on the supine figure. "Show me your hands. Now."

"I broke my ankle."

"Like I care. Sit up and show me your hands."

The suspect rolled into a sitting position. Riley shone the flashlight on the suspect's face and smiled. "Hello, Lou. You don't know how delighted I am to see you again. Do you have any weapons?"

"Shit, no."

"Not even a knife?"

Lou's head dropped. "Yeah, front pocket."

"Slowly take the knife out and toss it to my feet."

Lou complied.

Riley grabbed the knife. "Onto your belly, arms outstretched." When Lou was lying flat, Riley holstered his gun, dropped a knee into Lou's back, then pulled out his handcuffs. Riley slapped a cuff on one wrist, then pulled the arm down to Lou's back. He pulled the other arm down and snapped on the cuff. He grabbed Lou's shirt and hoisted him to his feet.

"Fuck, that hurts my ankle."

"Walk."

"Screw you. I want an ambulance."

"They're busy." Riley shoved Lou. "Get moving."

When they got back to the car, Riley slammed Lou over the hood. "Don't move." Riley opened the back door.

"Hey, dipshit." Lou laughed. "You lose something? You're the stupidest cop around here." Riley slammed Lou's face into the hood.

"Careful, you'll slip." Riley dragged the groaning Lou back toward the house.

The front of the house was lit up like a Christmas display. A half-dozen police cruisers, three ambulances, and a firetruck crowded the lane. An ambulance swung a U-turn and raced away.

A couple of sheriff's deputies approached—a typical pairing. An older, seasoned cop with a rookie. The rookie stared nervously at Riley, his hand near his pistol. Riley recognized the older guy.

"Hey, Dunbar." Riley pulled out his badge. "Briggs, DEA. Can you put him in your cruiser and keep an eye on him?" He nodded over his shoulder. "I caught him loading a car down by the barn. There was another guy who got away. Can you get your K9 out here and see if they can track him?"

"Sure thing, Briggs," Dunbar said. "You been inside yet?"

Riley shook his head.

"Fricken' mess. Unconscious folks everywhere."

"I'll head there. I need someone to stay with that car."

"No problem," Dunbar said. "Barnes, you think you can handle that? Was it something you learned at the academy?"

Barnes nodded, stepped around Riley, and headed to the car.

"Kids these days," Dunbar said.

"Roger that," Riley said. "I've got my own junior-high recruit. I'd better see how she's doing."

Faith Bennett came out of the house and held the door open for the paramedics carrying a stretcher. They were using a bag to breathe for a large male patient. As Bennett passed Riley, she raised her eyebrows and shook her head. "He's critical. I'll follow them to the hospital and keep continuity in case he doesn't make it."

"Don't follow, give them an escort. When you get to the hospital, check on the patient the first ambulance transported and call me. Where's Blake?"

"She's inside." Bennett sprinted to her cruiser.

Riley hiked the steps two at a time, through the door and into the living room. Paramedic supplies littered the carpet. Paramedics were working on a patient on the far side of the room. They taped IVs in both arms and a firefighter held the IV bags. Another firefighter was doing chest compressions. A paramedic eyed Riley and slowly shook her head.

A yellow blanket covered a body close to the kitchen. Blake headed over. "I followed the paramedics into the house, and we found four people unconscious. With Gibson, there were only four of us, so we each went to one person and checked for a pulse. I couldn't find a pulse on my guy, but jeez, I'm not a paramedic. Kathy didn't get a pulse either, so we left them and helped with the two who had a pulse. Adam and I worked on a large guy. I did whatever Adam said. I don't know how long we were there. Then another EMS crew arrived with four firefighters. Kathy had them take her female patient. They rushed her out of the house. Then Kathy helped Adam. She sent me to get a yellow blanket and put it over the guy on the kitchen floor. I watched the ambulance race away and raced back into the house. After I'd put the blanket on the guy, I stepped back and watched. The firefighters helped get their patient on a spine board and carry him to the ambulance." Blake held up a hand. "I'm still shaking."

"Blake, slow down. You're talking a mile a minute. Take a few deep breaths. This scene is screwed up, no doubt about that. Do you need to take a break? Get some fresh air."

"No, I'll be okay. It's just—" She shook her head.

"Good thing you're a special agent and not a paramedic," Riley said. "Let's do some special-agenting." He headed over to the covered patient and pulled back the blanket. He let out a low whistle. "That's Anthony Hart from the gun bust."

Blake nodded and pointed to another yellow blanket. "That's Melissa Springfox. What did you find?"

"Two guys were loading stuff into a car. When they spotted me, they bolted, then split up. One got away. I've got K9 coming to track him. I caught one of them—Lou Reynolds."

Riley and Blake headed down the lane to the barn. "Follow me." Riley pulled out latex gloves. "You'd better put some on."

"I had them on when I was helping the paramedics, they insisted."

"Smart."

They stepped into the barn. It had changed since their last visit.

In the center of the main floor, a kitchen table was expanded so it could hold at least eight people, but there were no chairs, dishes, or cutlery—it wasn't used for meals—it was set up to process drugs.

One end of the table held an empty one-gallon bucket that looked like an ice cream pail.

"And that," Riley pointed, "is the product—acetyl-fentanyl. Someone got away with another pail while I was chasing Reynolds. "What did they teach you about fentanyl at the FBI academy?"

"Not a lot. They said to call the DEA if you had questions."

"Well, I'll tell you what I remember from when I was awake in class. It's one hundred times more powerful than morphine and even more powerful than oxycodone. If they were mixing fentanyl into the pills, that could be the reason for the overdoses."

"How do we find out?" Blake asked.

"Tomorrow, we will go to the medical examiner and see what the autopsy showed. I'll courier some pills to the crime lab in Missoula tonight. We'll go there tomorrow as well and get the results."

"Do they steal fentanyl from the hospitals?" Blake asked.

"That's what people think. It comes from China or Mexico. Imported illegally, just like cocaine or heroin."

"Is a pail of fentanyl expensive?" Blake asked.

"Worth seven to ten thousand dollars. When it is mixed into pills, the street value of that pail would be hundreds of thousands of dollars."

Large mixing bowls were next in line with a four-gallon pail of green powder. The bucket was two-thirds full. A faint green outline on the table suggested another bucket had been sitting there. A scale and boxes of sandwich bags were off to one side. On the floor, a box was half-filled with baggies.

"This is a workstation to make pills," Riley said.

"Fake pills?"

"Yup. The green powder means they were making fake OxyContin. We need to back out and get a hazmat team in here." He pointed at the pail as he stepped out of the kitchen. "Binding powder and coloring, mixing bowls and the final product." He pointed to the outline on the table. "That's where the pill press was. We need to back out and get a hazmat team in here."

"Did they hide the pill press?"

"It's not hidden. I know where it is." Riley led the way out the back door to the open trunk of the car. "Shine your flashlight in here."

Blake's flashlight shone on a stainless-steel object with a wheel on one side and a spout on the front.

"That," Riley said, "is a pill press."

"How many pills would it make?" Blake asked.

"Hell if I know. Too fuckin' many. They wouldn't need a lot of fentanyl in each pill." Riley shook his head. "Tens of thousands, I'd guess. Five dollars a pill—fifty thousand dollars for every thousand pills. Practically pure profit."

"That's not all profit, though," Blake said. "This setup must cost a lot."

"Not as much as you'd think," Riley said. "Most of the expenses are one time. The pill presses cost between five and six thousand dollars. The die to stamp the pills to appear like Oxy, about one hundred dollars. The scale, maybe one hundred. For about seven thousand dollars, you're set up to press pills for years and make buckets of money. You'd be able to sell pills as fast as you made them."

"What went wrong today?"

"If the mix was wrong and there's too much fentanyl, you've got unconscious or dead users," Riley said. "Lou knew they had screwed up. He was getting out of here as fast as he could."

"Who was the other guy?"

"I'd put my money on Noel Bourget. If they weren't wearing gloves and masks, they might have inhaled or absorbed the fentanyl. When we were here a few weeks ago, this stuff wasn't here. It's a recent operation. I bet that's what Bourget of the Red Demons was doing here. They might have tested their product."

"Is the overdose of the husband and wife related?"

"My guess is they got some first pills off the press." Riley's phone rang. "Briggs." He listened for a moment. "Thanks."

"Who was that?"

"Bennett. The two overdoses EMS transported died."

CHAPTER FIFTY-ONE

FRANKLYN SLUMPED ON THE COUCH, SOCK FEET ON THE COFFEE table. Eva was curled up beside him, sipping from a wine glass.

"You haven't touched your wine?" Eva said.

Franklyn glanced at the full glass. "I'm not a wine guy."

"Right, rodeo champs must drink beer."

"Do you have any beer?"

Eva shook her head.

"Rum?"

"Sorry. No rum."

Franklyn stared at the wine goblet on the table. He groaned as he leaned forward to grab it. He sipped and did his best to smile as he choked the warm liquid down.

"See, it's not so dreadful." Eva drank a mouthful, swirled it around, and then swallowed. "You can taste the berries, like a homemade jam."

Franklyn forced a smile and took another sip.

"Is your back sore?"

"My entire body is sore. I didn't get a great sleep."

"You should sleep here."

"That's an option." He grinned. "Although sometimes we don't get a lot of sleep."

Eva punched his arm. "I'm serious. You should stay."

"Maybe. Riley Briggs said I could stay with him. Paulette offered me a bed."

"I'm sure she did."

Franklyn glanced at Eva, cocked his head, then increased the volume on the TV. ESPN was showing the rodeo highlights.

Eva snuggled close. "Where was this rodeo?"

"The Little Big Horn Stampede PRCA Rodeo last weekend."

"Did you compete there?"

"All the time."

"Did you win anything?"

Franklyn dropped his feet to the floor and set the wineglass on the coffee table. "I had some luck there."

"Like what?"

"Bareback champion five times. Steer wrestling champ six times. All-round cowboy five times. I have a shoebox full of buckles in the camper. Thankfully they didn't burn."

Eva sat. "Seriously?"

"Yup. I did the same at every rodeo in Montana, Colorado, Wyoming, and even in Canada at the Calgary Stampede. I competed in the National Finals Rodeo in Las Vegas four times."

"Huh. You were kinda important."

"Were?"

Eva tilted her head to the side. "You're not rodeoing anymore."

"Too early to put me out to pasture. You never know. I might enter the Fort Benton Rodeo."

"Not this year. Not with the way you're moving." Eva laughed. "I didn't know they had a seniors' rodeo."

Franklyn frowned and glared. No. Not this year, not ever. Not even at the smaller rodeos. That part of his life was behind him.

"Are you okay?" Eva asked.

"Yeah, why?"

"You zoned out for a minute. You seemed miserable."

"When you said my rodeoing days were over, I didn't like it, but you're right. My mind says keep going, but my body screams *what the fuck*."

Eva slid her fingers across his cheek. "You're soaked in sweat. Are you okay?"

"My body has seized." He rolled off the bed, slipped into his jeans, and headed to the bathroom. "Save my spot."

He closed the door and sat on the toilet. The sweat was pouring off him. He grabbed a towel and wiped his forehead and face. His hands shook, and he felt a cold wave pass over him. He leaned forward, his head in his hands. The world spun, and his vision blurred. He reached into his pocket and pulled out the bottle of Oxy that had been in his truck. He'd cut back to two pills a day, and already he was in agony.

His throat tightened, and his vision blurred. *Oh, shit.* He dumped out the pills—one wasn't going to cut it. He swallowed two.

He stood and leaned over the sink, running icy water and splashing his face several times. There was no way the pills could kick in that fast, but he felt better. Maybe it was knowing relief was coming.

He tossed his jeans on the floor and climbed back into bed. "Where were we?"

"Maybe you need a hot shower and massage."

"The shower at the arena never gets hot, and Ember is a terrible masseuse."

"Who said anything about the arena?"

CHAPTER FIFTY-TWO

THE VOICES SOUNDED FAR AWAY, MUFFLED. SOMEONE GRABBED HIS shoulders and shook. Weird. *I don't care.* Then something scraped down his chest. *That hurt.* Still, he didn't care.

Someone was blowing air into his nose and mouth. Something was over his face. Then he felt the stab in his thigh. *That should have hurt.* It didn't.

The voices were clearer. *A couple of guys?* Then a higher-pitched voice. *Eva?* There was a stab into his arm. This one he felt and groaned. With his other hand, he tried to grab the object in his arm.

"Easy, Franklyn. We're paramedics. That's an intravenous in your arm. I'm giving you Naloxone."

Paramedics? What happened?

He waited for another stab in his arm, but nothing happened. Then the fog lifted. A paramedic stared at Franklyn. "Welcome back."

"Where am I?" Franklyn asked.

Eva's face came into view. "At my house."

"What happened?"

"The paramedics think you swallowed too many of your medication. You overdosed."

"That's not possible. I've been taking Oxy for years."

"How many did you take?" the paramedic asked.

"Two. I always take two."

The paramedic nodded. "I have to ask. Is it prescription Oxy?"

"Of course …" Then Franklyn wasn't sure. "I think so."

"Either it is, or it isn't," the paramedic said. "There've been a lot of overdoses on fake Oxy. Are you sure it was your prescription?"

"The pill bottle is in my jeans." Franklyn sat and rubbed his eyes. "I'm okay." He glanced at the paramedics. He was relieved to see they weren't the Speargrass paramedics. The patches on their shirts said Great Falls EMS.

"We'll stay a few minutes. If that isn't prescription Oxy, we need to take you to the hospital."

"No, I have a prescription. You can check with my doctor."

The paramedic held out the pill bottle. "Yeah, we found it. That prescription was for two months of pills, but you filled it one month ago."

"I'm in a lot of pain from rodeo injuries. Sometimes I take an extra one or two."

"All right, Franklyn. I need you to sign this report saying I offered to take you to the hospital, but you refused."

"Do you have to do a report?"

"Afraid so. Especially since we administered the Naloxone. With the rash of overdoses, we're keeping close track of responses."

"This doesn't go public, does it?"

"Nope. This is a private medical record."

"I'd appreciate it if this was kept quiet. I'm embarrassed enough as it is." Franklyn signed the form.

The paramedic nodded. "I'd suggest you see your doctor tomorrow. You're lucky your girlfriend called us in time. Next time we may not get here quick enough."

CHAPTER FIFTY-THREE

Riley and Blake headed to the Great Falls Medical Examiner's office first—forensics in Missoula would be next.

"I got a call from the K9 officer this morning," Riley said. "No luck with the track. The second guy got away."

"Do you still think it was Bourget?" Blake asked.

Riley frowned. "Has to be. I know Lou Reynolds isn't smart enough to plan this." He parked in front of the ME's office.

Riley showed his badge at reception. "We're here to talk to the medical examiner about the overdose deaths last night."

"Name?"

"Tony Hart. Melissa … not sure of the last name."

"Springfox," Blake said.

"She's finishing with Hart. Head back to Suite 4."

Blake followed Riley down the hall.

"Ever been to an autopsy?" Riley asked.

"Just at the FBI academy."

"If you're going to puke, don't do it on the body."

Blake glared at Riley. "I'll be just fine. I'm not sure I can catch you when you collapse, though."

"Not going to happen." Riley tapped on the door to Suite 4, then opened it. "Riley and Blake, DEA."

"Come on in, Riley. I'm done."

Riley opened the door and the odors of the autopsy room rushed out. Disinfectant, dried blood, stomach contents, and intestines. No matter how many disinfectants they used, it wasn't enough. No matter how many times you came here, you never got used to it. They stepped into the autopsy suite—all stainless steel and shiny. The medical examiner pulled off a hood and face shield and shook out her long blond hair. "Haven't seen you for a while, Riley. Have you stopped killing bad guys?"

"Yeah. The last one I shot in the shoulder."

"Deliberately, or poor aim?"

"Bad aim," Blake said.

"I like her," the coroner said.

"My partner Leigh Blake, FBI," Riley said. "Dr. Sonya Churchill, medical examiner, and all-around ballbuster."

"I remember a time you didn't mind that."

Blake glanced between Riley and Sonya.

"About the two ODs," Riley said.

Sonya smiled. "Okay, flirting is over. All business. Body number one, Anthony Hart. His heart stopped."

"Is that a medical conclusion?" Riley glanced at the body.

"It is," Sonya said. "It stopped for lack of oxygen because he stopped breathing."

"Jeez, Sonya, get to the point."

"You used to be so much fun." Sonya sighed. "Hart had massive amounts of opioids in his system. Enough to kill him about three times."

"And Melissa?"

Sonya grabbed another chart. "Melissa Springfox. Same thing. She's got enough opioids to kill her five or six times over."

"Pills?"

"There's evidence of pills in the stomach, but also trace amounts in the nose, mouth, and on her hands. I'd say they were handling some pure stuff."

"That fits," Riley said. "We found a pill press."

"The good news is we know where they were exposed," Sonya said.

"That's good news?" Blake asked. "What's the bad news."

"Because they had pills in their stomachs, that means they made at least one batch of pills. Did you find pills at the scene?"

"Yes," Riley said. "We also seized pills at a double overdose early last night."

"They are next on my autopsy list," Sonya said. "The hospital is reporting an increase in opioid overdoses this week. If these guys got a batch onto the street, you better be ready for an overdose epidemic."

"We also seized an empty pail of fentanyl."

Sonya closed her eyes. "Oh, no."

"Why is fentanyl worse?" Blake asked.

Sonya strode over to her desk and grabbed a chart. "The drugs we are talking about are opioids. There are many drugs in that category. Some are natural, like heroin from a poppy. Others are synthetic, meaning manufactured in a lab."

She set the chart on an empty stretcher. The diagram listed ten different opioids.

"If we say morphine is the baseline and give it the potency of one, then codeine and Demerol are 1/10th the strength of morphine. Moving up the diagram, oxycodone is 1.5 times the strength of morphine. Heroin is five times the strength of morphine."

"Does that mean heroin has a greater potential to be a lethal overdose?" Blake asked.

"You can see the relative potency, but even at five times the strength of morphine, if the dose is consistent, it will not cause death in most overdoses."

"But the street dose is seldom consistent," Blake said.

"Correct. However, fentanyl is one hundred times the strength of morphine."

"That's what Riley said.

"For once, he's right." Chamberlain winked at Riley. "Do you see the problem?"

"If someone thinks they are taking oxycodone, and it has fentanyl, even a minute amount, it could be lethal," Blake said.

"It can be a threat to anyone who comes into contact with it. Fentanyl can be absorbed through the skin or accidentally inhaled. In 2015, a New Jersey police officer had shortness of breath, dizziness, and slowed breathing after coming into contact with fentanyl."

"Just contact or inhaling? Not ingestion?"

"Correct. Just a quarter milligram—0.25 milligrams—can kill you."

"How much are 0.25 milligrams?" Blake asked.

"A typical baby aspirin tablet is 81 mg," Sonya said. "If you cut that tablet into 324 pieces, one of those pieces would be equal to a quarter-milligram. It gets worse."

"What can be worse?" Riley asked.

"There are two more powerful opioids. Carfentanil at 1000 times the potency of morphine, and Sufentanil at 10,000 times the potency."

CHAPTER FIFTY-FOUR

THEY CAUGHT A COMMUTER FLIGHT TO MISSOULA. IT BEAT THE SIX-hour round-trip driving. A cab dropped them in front of the forensics lab fifteen minutes later.

Riley showed his badge at reception. "I need to talk to someone about test results."

The receptionist nodded and grabbed her phone.

"I've only been in forensics once before," Blake said. "I got yelled at because I touched a counter."

Riley chuckled. "The forensic team are a special breed. They appear human, they talk like humans, but they don't get along with other humans. They prefer to stay close to their pack."

"That's cruel," Blake said.

"They also live up to every stereotype of a lab rat. Not the cool TV CSI forensic investigator, but the bubbly liquid in a beaker over a Bunsen burner scientist."

The man who headed over to them was no exception—five-foot-ten, a hundred and twenty pounds, skinny as a barber's pole and the same color, without the red stripe. He wore a white lab coat complete with pocket protector bulging with pens, and thick, dark-framed glasses.

"You can't be in here," he said.

Riley read the name embroidered on the lab coat. "Darvin, I'm Special Agent Briggs, DEA. And my partner, FBI Special Agent Blake. I sent pills to your lab last night from some overdoses. We need to get the results."

"You sent them last night?" Darvin asked. "We haven't opened last night's evidence. We're months behind. Come back in eight weeks." He spun on his heels to leave, but Riley grabbed his arm.

"You don't understand," Riley said. "Four people died last night. Others are in ICU and probably won't live. A mother and father died in front of their kids. Let me spell this out for you. It's likely, hell, 99.9 percent certain those pills are lethal and sold on the street. I need them analyzed now."

Darvin pulled away. "That's not the protocol. We analyze everything in the order they arrive. Eight weeks at least."

"Get your supervisor or manager over here," Riley said.

Darvin's thin lips formed a straight line and curled slightly at the corners. His eyes grew wide, and his eyebrows raised. Riley didn't know whether to laugh or be creeped out.

"I *am* the manager, and I have a lot to do." Darvin opened the door. "Have a pleasant day."

The door slammed behind them.

"What are we going to do?" Blake crossed her arms. "We can't wait for eight weeks."

"We won't." Riley pulled his cell phone out of his jacket pocket and headed down the hall.

Twenty minutes later, the door opened, and Darvin stood in the doorway. If possible, he appeared paler than before. "We're currently doing the tests. We should have something for you in half an hour." Darvin slunk back into the lab.

Blake stared, open jawed at Riley. "How did you do that? Who'd you call?"

"I can't give away all my secrets."

"MacDonald?"

Riley laughed. "That's funny. Not old MacDonald. He's got no juice."

"Must have been someone high up."

Riley grinned. "The highest."

"The president?"

Riley smiled. "Okay, not that high. We know a guy who owes us a favor, and I called in that favor."

Blake studied Riley's face for a clue as they sat in silence. "Ah. Major Leavitt's wife."

Riley's head bobbed a few times, and then his chin rested on his chest. He slept for an hour.

Riley awoke to the electric click of the door lock. The door opened, and Darvin stepped out.

"The testing was more complicated than I thought," Darvin said. "When we got the first results, we thought it was an error. So we started over."

"What did you find?" Riley asked.

"Both tests came out the same. Those pills are off the charts for fentanyl. We've never seen a batch of pills like that. I called the CDC. They didn't believe our results."

"Why are the pills so powerful?" Blake asked.

"Until you find the pill maker, we can't be sure. Best guess is they mixed it wrong. They possibly confused microgram with milligram."

"That's deadly," Blake said.

Darvin nodded. "That mistake means the pills are 1000 times more powerful than they should be. How many pills did they make?"

"I have no idea," Riley said. "But we attended two deaths earlier last night. The pills are on the street."

"Heaven help us all," Darvin said.

CHAPTER FIFTY-FIVE

RILEY LED FRANKLYN DOWN THE HALL TO A CONFERENCE ROOM. HE opened the door and followed Franklyn into the room. He eased into a chair and grimaced. Riley sat across from Franklyn.

"You okay?" Riley asked.

Franklyn shuffled. "Yeah. The aches and pains are intense today. Some days are better than others. Today is one of the unmanageable ones." He tossed his Stetson on the table and forced a smile.

Riley scrutinized Franklyn. Something wasn't right. Sure, he'd beat up his body in rodeo, but this was the first time Riley had seen Franklyn appear this ghastly. "Are you sure?"

"I'm sure. What do you have for me?"

Riley set two thick file folders on the table in front of Franklyn. "That's everything I have on the drugs, including the overdose deaths on Wednesday. The autopsy and toxicology reports are there."

Franklyn slid a thin folder across the table. "Here're my

report on the overdoses the night the paramedics were assaulted."

"How are the paramedics?"

"They're back at work, but Pam is considering a new job or a new career. After their assault and my house burning, who can blame her."

"You know, I still can't get the smoke smell out of my clothes," Riley said.

"Ah, your pretty-boy suit got dirty."

"You know fashion goes beyond a Stetson and pointed boots."

Franklyn shook his head. "Nah, you're the one who lacks any fashion sense."

Riley grinned as he adjusted the cuffs of his shirt and flicked a phantom piece of lint off an arm. "I can let you read the files here. You can take notes, and you can't take them with you and no copies. Understand?"

"I thought we were on the same side."

"Everything this task team does is confidential. My boss is a stickler. Like I care, but I'm already on double-secret probation."

Franklyn glanced at the folders. "This will take a while."

"Take your time. Coffee is at the front counter. If you're still here at noon, I'll buy you lunch." Riley stood and headed to the door, then glanced back. Franklyn wiped the sweat off his brow with his shirt sleeve.

Franklyn followed Riley to a table in the back corner.

"Lunch is on me." Riley plucked the menu off the table.

Franklyn glanced at the menu and tossed it on the table.

"You boys ready?" the waitress asked.

"I'll have a Coke, light ice," Riley said. "And the steak sandwich—medium rare, and fries."

The waitress glanced at Franklyn.

"I'll have the chicken soup and ginger ale."

Riley's eyes grew wide. "I'm buying, and you're having soup?"

Franklyn smiled weakly. "I might have a touch of the flu. I'll take a rain check on the steak."

"Nope, one-time offer. Did you find anything of interest in the files?"

"We've got the same problem, toxic pills." Franklyn frowned. "We're dealing with the same shitheads."

"That's why we have to work on this together," Riley said.

The waitress set their drinks on the table.

Franklyn sipped the ginger ale. "You arrested a guy with the pill press, and the other one got away. Do you know who he is?"

"He's a ranking member of the Red Demons," Riley said. "They're trying to get into the drug and gun market here."

"I thought the Warlords were the larger biker gang in Montana."

Riley grabbed his Coke and swallowed a long drink. "They were, but where there's money to be had, and where there's dirty money for the taking, competition appears."

Franklyn grabbed a napkin and wiped his brow. "So, white boys are making drugs and then selling them on the rez."

Riley shook his head and set the Coke down. "Not just white guys. The overdoses in the drug house had Indians."

"Sure, they were there doing the dirty work." Franklin's jaw clenched. "It's the white boys that got them into this."

"Where the hell is this coming from?" Riley asked.

"I'm frustrated and disappointed. What's happening to my heritage?"

Riley leaned across the table. "I know you care, and the white boys leave their hands dirty. Don't lose hope because you can make a difference."

Franklyn nodded. "You're right. Too right."

Riley sat back and folded his arms across his chest. "I hear you have first-hand knowledge."

Franklyn's eyes widened. "What?"

"Don't BS me, Franklyn." Riley hit the table with his fist. He leveled a cold, hard stare at Franklyn. "I read the paramedics' report."

Franklyn focused his attention on his Ginger Ale. He rubbed at the condensation on the glass. "That was a mistake."

"It was fricken' stupid." Riley's spittle sprayed the table. "What were you thinking?"

Franklyn told Riley about his Oxy use and that the doctor wouldn't refill the prescription. That he was in withdrawal and wasn't thinking clearly—two extra pills in a day didn't seem like they should have the effect they did-top powerful.

"Jeez. We're brothers. You should have come to me."

Franklyn shook his head, not meeting Riley's eyes. "I couldn't. I'm ashamed."

They sat in silence, Franklyn with his head down and shoulders slumped.

Without glancing up, he broke the silence. His voice was soft and hesitant.

"I know how I got here, but how did my people get here?"

"It happened over decades," Riley said. "When something takes that long to get entrenched, there are no overnight solutions. No amount of money will fix this. No amount of sitting at the table and discussing will help."

Franklyn sat back and folded his arms across his chest. "So, we continue to abuse each other, kill each other?"

Riley leaned back and spread his arms. "I'm not saying that. I'm saying there isn't a quick solution. In my opinion, searching outside the rez for an answer is wrong. Your people must fix this from inside. If that means going back to the traditional ways, then do it. But do it soon. The elders know the culture, but they're dying. When they're gone, so is any hope of returning to a proud people."

Franklyn nodded. "It's easier to blame outsiders, but there comes a point where we need to stand and defend our ways."

"You're an honorable man, Franklyn, and the tribe needs you."

Franklyn stared straight ahead as he drove back to the rez, mulling over the conversation with Riley.

Have we done this to ourselves? Franklyn didn't believe that. *But we haven't done ourselves any favors either.* Riley was right on a few points. Hell, Franklyn was dealing with his staff following Indian time every day. It was hard to find reliable workers.

A lot of the homes he went into were falling apart and overcrowded. The kitchens stocked with soda and potato chips. The kids were awake to all hours of the night playing video games. There was alcohol and drugs, minor parental supervision, and no discipline.

Then you'd go to a decent house. Riley would call it a normal home. It was clean, well maintained, there was food, and the kids well behaved. This house was different. Why? Typically, it was the house of the chief or councilors.

Men fought for the power of being chief, not always for the benefit of the people, but for the control. To guarantee his family would have jobs if they supported him. If they didn't, he'd cast them out.

Some of his tribe were educated outside the reserve, either through the foster system or with relatives living in a town or city. They came back to the rez and started businesses. They contributed by providing a service, hiring local workers, giving back. The rez needed companies. Local jobs would give hope. Right now, there was no hope.

The anger was replaced with absolute despair. How could he have any impact? How could he make a difference when he was challenged at every turn? They'd already shown him he was alone, an outcast, an apple.

If he quit, what would he do? He was a washed-up rodeo cowboy and likely be a failed sheriff.

The survival instinct was powerful, and it was telling him to keep driving. An hour south, he'd be in Helena. The Montana Highway Patrol would take him back. Less stress. Safer.

But Franklyn knew he would stop on the rez. He'd never backed down from a two-thousand-pound bull, and he wasn't about to back down now. They'd picked a fight with the wrong guy. One man could make a difference. Franklyn wanted to be that man.

He wasn't so stupid that he thought he could do it on his own. He'd need help from his brother.

He'd wanted to be a cop twenty years ago. He had that chance, and he wanted to do it right. He needed to make a choice. He could do as the chief asked, or he could continue to do it his way, whatever the consequences.

Franklyn sighed. One person against the world. *Can one person make a difference?* Franklyn remembered the quote. *The only thing necessary for the triumph of evil is for good men to do nothing.*

He couldn't stand by and watch this reservation continue to crumble.

CHAPTER FIFTY-SIX

FRANKLYN PARKED BEHIND THE ADMINISTRATION BUILDING. HE strode toward Jesse, who was sitting on the sidewalk drawing. "Whatcha doing out here, Jesse?"

Jesse scratched his arms. "Got kicked out."

"By whom?"

"Paulette. She says I'm drunk and loud. She told me to get out. She's mean."

"Are you drunk?"

"More high than drunk." Jesse scuffed his shoe against the ground. "She can't stop me from sitting here. I'll sell some of my drawings."

"What are you working on today?" Franklyn glanced over Jesse's shoulder. "Looks like an Indian Chief."

Jesse shook his head. "I swear, you ain't no Indian. It's Sitting Bull."

Franklyn nodded. "Sure, I see it. Excellent likeness."

"You're shitting me."

"If you're high, where'd you get the drugs?"

"At a party."

Franklyn sighed. "I had that figured out."

"Okay. I woke up outside, sitting by a tree."

Franklyn's eyes narrowed. "Who had the drugs?"

"Some chick."

"Did you buy any?"

Jesse stared at his shoes and shrugged. "I bought some pills, and they gave me some new stuff."

"Why'd they give you drugs?"

"You don't know shit as a cop. They give you free samples of new drugs. Then when you like them or get hooked, they sell to you."

Franklyn nodded. "What's the chick's name?"

"I don't know." He flipped through his sketchbook.

"That's bullshit. Where did she get them?"

Jesse fidgeted with the pencil in his hand and stared across the parking lot. "How would I know?"

"You can't tell me or won't tell me?"

"I can't. I won't."

Franklyn leaned against the wall. "Why not?"

"They'll kill me."

"Who?"

Jesse glanced up, and his shoulders sagged. "The brothers."

"Lamont?"

Jesse stared at his feet again.

"What's the name of the new drug?"

"They called it Apache."

"Apache?"

Jesse shrugged, scribbling. "Sure, give it a cool Indian name, and it will sell."

"What is it?"

"Don't know, but they say it's potent. Different from Oxy. Better."

"Meth?"

"How would I know? I swallowed the pills first, and the next thing I remember is waking up next to a tree, like, wasted. I took the Apache, and everything was clear. I had tons of energy."

Franklyn straightened. "Have you taken it before?"

"Nope. It's new." Jesse's hair hung over his eyes as he sketched.

"I gotta go," Franklyn said. "Take care of yourself."

"Hey, Franklyn. I hear they make it here on the rez."

CHAPTER FIFTY-SEVEN

Riley woke with a start—someone was outside the house. He swung his feet off the bed and grabbed his pistol from the nightstand.

He slipped out of the bedroom and silently followed the sounds. His physical reaction had been immediate—his brain slower catching up. The sound came from the front door. Someone breaking in? Were they coming after him like Franklyn?

Then his brain registered. It was someone banging on the door. If they were coming to kill him, they wouldn't knock. If it was a home invasion, they wouldn't knock either.

Still, his senses were tingling. He stepped silently to the door, quietly slid back the deadbolt, and flung it open, pistol pointed.

Riley was staring at Blake, who stepped back and drew her gun. "What the hell, Riley?"

"I heard noises and thought someone was breaking in." He lowered his gun.

"I was knocking."

"I know that now."

Blake re-holstered her gun. "I phoned you a dozen times. I've been pounding on the door for minutes."

"The volume on my phone was low. How did you know I was here?"

"Oh my god. Do you think you and Regan are a giant secret? Everyone knows." Blake's eyes lowered. "You sleep in the buff. Good to know. You might want to put on some clothes. All hell's breaking loose."

"Give me a minute." He dashed back to the bedroom. Regan was asleep. How could she sleep through this? He grabbed his clothes off a chair, dressed, and slipped on his shoes as he raced out the door. Blake was leaning against the car, arms folded across her chest. She shook her head as he approached. "Get in. I'll tell you what's happening."

Riley buttoned his shirt as Blake peeled away.

"What time is it?" Riley asked.

"Three in the morning."

"What happened?"

"About midnight dispatch got the first call in Great Falls. An overdose. An hour later, every ambulance in the city was dealing with overdoses. In some scenes, there were two or three. Then it got crazy—dispatch was flooded with 911 calls for overdoses. The paramedics stopped at the entrance to the hospital, unloaded their stretchers, grabbed a spare, and responded to the next call."

"Oh, god."

"Then overdose calls came in from Speargrass. Same thing. Multiple patients. There were no ambulances available anywhere near here. They transported some patients in firetrucks and police cars. Dispatch sent out a call to all ambulances around to help both Great Falls and Speargrass. Helena sent everything they had. It was chaos."

"How many overdoses?"

Blake shook her head. "Maybe two dozen. The hospital called in all staff. Then it got worse."

Riley turned to Blake, trying to imagine something worse. "What's worse than two dozen overdoses?"

"The paramedics and the hospital ran out of Naloxone."

"They ran out? How is that possible?" Okay, running out of a lifesaving drug was worse.

"Most of the patients needed multiple doses."

"What did they do?"

"They got the governor to declare a state of emergency, and he ordered the medivac helicopters to bring Naloxone in from Helena and to go to surrounding hospitals and collect all they could."

"That leaves those hospitals with limited supplies."

"Right. If this batch of drugs was distributed outside of Great Falls and Speargrass, EMS and hospitals farther away will be screwed."

"Which scene are we going to?"

"Too many scenes." Blake whipped the car around a few slow-moving vehicles, then drove on the wrong side of the road. "We're going to the hospital."

Blake followed Riley to the emergency department triage desk. "We need to talk to your emergency department director."

"We're soverwhelmed," the triage nurse said.

"I know, this is urgent."

"Can I tell her what it's about?"

"Sure." Riley showed his badge. "Riley and Blake. We're investigating the overdoses."

The triage nurse glanced past Riley and pointed.

A tall lady in her late fifties with blond-gray hair strode toward them. "I'm Heather, charge nurse. How can I help you?"

"If we can speak in private, please?" Riley asked.

"We're swamped, can this wait?"

"I will take a minute or two."

Heather led them to a coffee room.

"Are any of the ODs regulars?"

"Since we stopped prescribing Oxy, there's been some people in here a few times."

"What do you mean, 'we stopped'?" Blake asked.

"The doctors agreed to stop prescribing Oxy. Most stopped, or at least reduced the number of prescriptions."

"Some doctors still prescribe Oxy?" Blake asked.

Heather hesitated. "Look. They're excellent doctors. It's a challenging decision deciding not to prescribe opioids. People are addicted. We stop prescribing but don't provide any counseling or alternatives. That creates problems. Tonight is a horrible reminder. Before, we'd see the occasional opioid overdose. Since we stopped—well, reduced—prescriptions for Oxy, the addicts have to get their fix elsewhere. Now they buy Oxy on the street."

"Real Oxy is in short supply, and addicts have turned to fake pills laced with fentanyl," Riley said. "The unintended consequence of keeping Oxy off the market is that fentanyl is the problem."

"Exactly. Tonight, around midnight, it started with four overdoses from a party in Great Falls. That's a lot to see at one time, but we managed. Then paramedics were calling in from Speargrass and the rural area saying they had unconscious patients. Within half an hour, we were overwhelmed. Some were dead when they arrived. We couldn't continue to resuscitate them because there were too many patients on the brink of death."

Riley nodded. "Leave the dead and focus on those you can save."

"Right. Within an hour, every paramedic crew had used all their Naloxone and had to borrow from us. Just as we administered the last Naloxone, the first medivac helicopter arrived with one hundred ampules."

"How many patients did you have?" Riley asked.

Heather shrugged and pursed her lips. "I don't have a clue. Twenty? Maybe more."

"All unconscious?" Blake asked.

"Most were. Some were lucky. The paramedics reversed the effects of the opioid. One EMS crew brought two unconscious, not-breathing patients in at the same time. This is new for them … and us."

"We'd like to talk to one of the overdose patients," Riley said.

"Sure. Jesse is your best bet. He's a regular opioid user, so it didn't hit Jesse as hard, and he's recovering." Heather gave them directions to the ICU. "I'll let them know you are coming."

A nurse met them as they headed down the corridor. "I'm supposed to help you. I'm Olga, an ICU nurse."

"Riley and Blake," Riley said. "How are the overdoses?"

"Two will be okay, they're conscious. One is unconscious and on a ventilator. We keep the ODs here until they're breathing on their own, then transfer them to another floor. Four died in the last hour and another one who won't make it."

Riley shook his head. *Damn.* "We're here to talk to Jesse."

"I was just about to ship him out of here. He's overdosed more times than I can count. He's one of the lucky ones. His tolerance for opioids is higher than others."

"Where did EMS find him?"

"There was a huge party on the rez. Speargrass EMS got called for someone who was drunk. When they arrived at the party, they found six unconscious patients. Speargrass EMS left with three patients. None of them breathing. The paramedic used all his Naloxone on them. Two died in the emergency department. One responded to the Naloxone and started breathing on his own. He's a regular messed up from years of drugs, alcohol and household products. He'll take whatever he can get. He's generally talkative—you might have some luck with him. He's down the hall, follow me."

Olga stopped and pointed. "Bed four. Be quick. I will need that bed real soon."

"Thanks."

Riley and Blake entered the hospital room for four patients. A mid-twenties Indian sat on the bed, drinking orange juice. A meal sat on the table in front of him.

"Jesse?" Riley asked.

"Who the fuck wants to know?" Jesse went back to drinking the juice.

"Special Agents Riley and Blake. We're investigating the overdoses."

"What makes you special?" Jesse grinned, the missing gaps in his gums outnumbering his teeth.

"We're narcotics cops," Riley said.

"I don't talk to cops, especially narcs."

"You do today." Riley moved the tray of food away.

"Franklyn's the one cop I trust. Even when he arrests me."

"Franklyn Eaglechild?"

"Yeah. You know Eaglechild?"

"He's my brother," Riley said.

Jesse laughed and stretched for the orange juice. "Franklyn ain't no brother of a white cop."

Riley held up his hand in the three-finger scout salute. "Scout's honor. True story."

"You don't look Indian."

"I'm not. He lived with my family when he was a teenager. We played hockey together. We rodeoed."

Jesse laughed. "That explains it."

"Explains what?" Riley asked.

"Why he's an apple," Jesse said.

"What does that mean?" Blake asked. "Apple?"

Jesse stared at Blake. "You don't know about Indians, do you?" Jesse chuckled. "Apple. Red on the outside, white on the inside. That's Franklyn. He looks Indian, but inside he's white."

"Tell me about last night, Jesse," Riley asked.

"What's to say? It was a party."

"Yeah, I had that part figured out. Someone died from that party. The emergency department is filled with overdoses from the same pills we think you had at your party. More will die. You were lucky."

"Yeah, I'm lucky. I'd rather be dead."

"Why's that?"

"I'm an Indian addict. No one cares if I live."

"What about family?"

"They kicked me out years ago."

"Why'd they do that?"

"Cuz they said I stole from them."

"Did you?"

Jesse smiled. "All the time." He laughed.

"Jesse, help me out. Tell me about the party."

Jesse cocked his head and stared at Riley. "You really Franklyn's brother?"

"I am."

"Okay. There's always a party. The place changes, so the cops can't find us. 'Cept sometimes Franklyn finds us. Last night we're out by the river. It's hard to get to. You have to drive across fields for about two miles, then hike down a hill to the river. It's a spot we use a lot. The river takes a sweeping turn, so there are places where the water is slow and shallow. Sometimes teens swim there."

"Do you swim there?"

"Yeah. The one bath I get. Besides, the chicks swim nude. That's exciting."

He could use a bath now. "Tell me about the party last night."

"Everyone brings stuff, you know, pills or whatever. For the last few weeks, there have been green pills. They were okay at the start, but they must be making them more powerful because people fall out."

"Fall out?" Blake asked.

"Yeah, they just rolled over on the spot asleep."

"Did anyone die?" Blake leaned closer to the bed, then stepped back.

"Nah, not then. I heard some were hard to wake up."

"Let me get this straight," Riley said. "Someone brings pills and sells them."

"Not always. When they first showed up, they gave the pills away."

"Who showed up?"

"A few weeks ago, the Lamont brothers brought a few white dudes to a party. They gave out free stuff. They did that for about a week, then started charging. We were hooked. We didn't have a choice."

"Were the white dudes there last night?"

"Just the Lamont brothers. They've been to every party this week. They're giving out the new stuff for free. Meth."

Riley nodded. "Soon, they'll charge for the meth."

"Oh, yeah. Guaranteed."

"What was different last night?" Riley asked.

"I don't know, man." Jesse shrugged. "Same as usual. They brought the pills, and we bought them. You buy pills before they give you the free meth. I bought the pills but got the nods quick. It was like I was watching myself, you know, like from above."

"What's the nods?" Blake asked.

"That's the sedative effect of the narcotic," Riley said. "Were the pills different?"

"They appeared the same. But it wasn't Oxy. No way." Jesse shook his head. "Happened too quick. Got the nods right away. Then I remember fighting with a paramedic."

"Why?" Blake asked.

"They took away my nods, man. I was out of it. Then I'm in the fuckin' ambulance. But then I went out again."

"Who arranged the party?" Blake asked.

"The Lamont brothers?" Riley crossed his arms.

"Ah, man. I can't tell you." Jesse slipped his tongue into the gap in his teeth. "They'll mess me up again."

"What happened?"

"They beat me. That's why I ain't got no front teeth."

"What did Franklyn do about the assault?" Riley asked.

"Nothin'. That was before he got there."

"So, the drug dealers living in the trailers arrange the parties?"

"Ah, shit." Jesse slid his fingers through his long greasy hair.

"How do you know where the party is going to be?" Riley asked.

"I'm a dead man if I tell you."

Riley stared at Jesse, arms folded.

"They like the western movie set. They figure they won't have trouble with the cops, so the parties are going to be there for a while."

CHAPTER FIFTY-EIGHT

FRANKLYN WIPED THE SLEEP FROM HIS EYES AS HE SWUNG ONTO THE highway. The radio was busy. EMS was heading to another overdose. The fire department was responding to a grass fire. Lefebvre was heading to the overdose with EMS. Who knew where Crow was? Franklyn needed to hire another officer or two.

Now, in the early morning, there was a party out by the quad. Just another night on the rez. Why he thought he'd get a full night's sleep escaped him. He hadn't had a full night's sleep since he arrived.

He drove off the highway, sped down the hill toward the quad, and peered into the darkness. If there was a party, he'd see a fire—no such thing as a party without a bonfire. The two just went together. He remembered that from his youth. Fires were a significant part of the culture like pow wows and sweats.

The quad was in darkness, not a campfire in sight. He drove

around, shining the spotlight onto the baseball diamonds, into the dugouts, and around the bonfire pit—nothing and no one.

He eased out of the SUV and hiked around the quad. No evidence anyone had been there recently, not for a week at least. *They must have a new party spot.*

He shut off his flashlight and wandered back to the truck. He waited for his eyes to adjust to the darkness, then lay on his back. The coolness of the earth seeped through his clothes. It relaxed his aching muscles. As his eyes adjusted, he spotted thousands of stars. He felt at peace here. Something he'd been lacking for a long time. He was home. He'd spent most of his life running, traveling, searching for peace, and here it was. He wasn't religious, but there had to be a plan and a mastermind behind the plan. Was it a god, a Great Spirit, the ghosts of ancestors? He didn't know. What was his part in the plan? Was he back on the rez for a purpose? He smiled, thinking the purpose couldn't be to piss people off. That's what he was doing. He was sure he was doing the right thing, the ethical thing, the stuff that would make the rez better. But he was one man. A man with few friends—a few Indian friends like Paulette, Calvin, Preston, Silas. And the white Eva and Riley.

He inhaled a deep breath, glanced at the stars, then struggled to his feet. He moved like the tin man from the Wizard of Oz—needed oil. Or rum. Or Oxy.

He stumbled through the darkness to the SUV, pulled himself in, and grabbed the mic.

"Dispatch. Nothing out here at the quad. No one's been here for a week. I'm heading back to town. I'm available for another call."

"Roger, Sheriff."

He hung a U-turn in the field and headed for the hill. From the left, in his periphery, he glimpsed motion.

The sound of twisting metal and shattering glass echoed through the cab. Fabric exploded into his face before he smelled electrical burning and powder.

His head shattered the side window. He was suspended upside down by the seatbelt, slammed into the seat, then suspended again. The sequence repeated several times.

The steering wheel crushed into his chest. After another roll, warm blood flowed over his eyes, and coppery fluid filled his mouth.

Another roll and the roof collapsed. The SUV floated, then came to a rest, hard. His head was out of the window and pressed against the cold dirt and grass. He willed his eyes to stay open. He willed himself to stay conscious.

He failed.

CHAPTER FIFTY-NINE

LEFEBVRE YAWNED AS HE ENTERED THE OFFICE. "BOSS IN?" HE asked Paulette.

"Nope, haven't seen him," Paulette said.

"Must have slept in."

"Boss has never slept in," Paulette said. "What did he go to last night?"

"It was one hell of a night. We were all going to overdoses. Speargrass EMS went non-stop, and Great Falls had dozens of overdoses. Boss went to a party complaint at the quad, but he said there wasn't a party, and he was available."

"When was that?" Paulette asked.

"About 3:30 this morning."

"You didn't check on the boss?"

Lefebvre stood straighter. "Why? I was with EMS at an overdose, and we were busy."

"Did you hear him book off at home?"

"He'd cleared from the call. I, uh, didn't check."

Paulette was on the phone. "His cell goes to voice. Try the radio."

"Sheriff Eaglechild, HQ, what's your twenty?"

No answer.

"Sheriff Eaglechild, HQ, what's your twenty?"

No answer.

"Still sleeping?" Lefebvre asked. "Feeding the horse?"

Paulette typed frantically on her computer.

"What are you doing?" Lefebvre asked.

"Pinging his phone. See where he is."

Lefebvre crowded behind her, staring at the computer. A map came into focus, then a flag appeared on the map.

"The signal is from the quad," Lefebvre said. "He's back out there."

"Or never left," Paulette said.

"I gotta go check," Lefebvre said.

"I'm coming with you."

Lefebvre's truck bounced and twisted on the rough rocky road. He lost control as they headed down the hill to the quad, the back end fishtailing. He fought the steering wheel, getting control at the bottom of the incline, where they spotted the destroyed SUV on its side.

"Oh, no." Paulette's hands flew to her mouth. "No, no, no."

Lefebvre slammed the truck into park and sprinted to the SUV. He peered in the front window where the windshield used to be. Franklyn was lying still, blood everywhere. Lefebvre heard Paulette step behind him.

"Is he okay?"

"Go to the truck, call EMS, then bring the first aid bag."

Paulette didn't move.

"Now, Paulette, dammit. I need your help. EMS, then first aid kit."

Paulette stumbled back to the truck.

Lefebvre crawled over the glass and metal into the cab beside Franklyn. He stretched out his fingers and tentatively touched Franklyn's neck. Warm. *Good.* He fumbled around until he could feel a carotid pulse. He pressed, holding his breath. The pulse was there, faint and fast.

"Tell EMS to hurry. He's alive, but he's messed up."

Paulette knelt next to him. "Of course I told them to hurry. You know they'll hurry, just like you rush to back them up. They'll be here as fast as the ambulance will go. Tell me what to do."

"Okay. First, we don't move him. I figure the truck rolled a bunch of times. At least he was wearing his seatbelt. Better than having the SUV roll over him. He's breathing, that's good. But I haven't got a clue what I'm doing."

"Don't they teach you first aid and stuff?"

"Sure, but it's not like this. If I see EMS going to a call, I go slow and follow them, so I don't get there first and have to do something. This is what they do. Not me."

"What about checking where he's hurt?" Paulette suggested.

"Sure, I can do that." Lefebvre crawled farther into the SUV. "He's breathing well. I don't see any significant bleeding. He's got lots of cuts to his face. His nose looks broken."

"Check his chest," Paulette said.

"I can't. He's wearing his ballistic vest. In the middle of the night, he still put his vest on. It undoubtedly helped when he was thrown against the steering wheel. I can't check his legs, they're pinned under the dash. We're gonna need fire here to do an extrication."

"Already asked for that," Paulette said.

Lefebvre raised an eyebrow. "I thought you didn't know what to do?"

"I'm not stupid," Paulette snarled.

"Speargrass Fire might not show."

"That's why I asked for Fort Benton Fire." Paulette wiped her palms against her pants, breathing fast.

"Smart lady," Lefebvre said. He squeezed her shoulder and nodded.

Paulette spun at the crunch of tires.

"Over here," she shouted, then smacked her forehead. Nowhere else for EMS to run to. Pam Taylor placed hand on Paulette's shoulder. "We'll take good car of him."

Paulette did a double take when she saw the bruises to Pam's face.

Eric Kennedy knelt next to Lefebvre. "How is he?"

"Unconscious but breathing. Face cuts, broken nose, but he's trapped."

Kennedy got to work. "Okay. Slide out—let me check. When Fort Benton Fire gets here, tell them they need to flap the roof."

"Flap the roof?"

"They'll know what it means."

Fort Benton Fire made quick work of cutting the posts where the front window had been and folding the roof back. With room to work, Kennedy directed the firefighters as they slid Franklyn out of the SUV onto the spine board. Kennedy kept control of

Franklyn's head and neck in case there was a spinal injury. They lifted the spine board onto the stretcher and carried it to the ambulance.

Taylor had intravenous lines hanging from hooks, oxygen ready, and bandages and splints laid out on the bench seat.

"I need a driver," Kennedy said.

"I'll do it," Lefebvre said.

"That would normally be okay, but you've got a crime scene to manage. I'll take one of the firefighters."

Lefebvre faced Chief Wilson. "Who's your best driver? I need smooth and fast."

"I'll do it," Wilson said.

"Go slow until you hit the highway," Kennedy said.

Taylor sat on the airway chair at the head of the stretcher and applied an oxygen mask, the leads for the cardiac monitor, and assessed Franklyn's facial injuries.

Kennedy applied a tourniquet and started an intravenous line on the inside of the elbow.

He stared at the heart rate and rhythm on the monitor. "He's in a tachycardia, but it's not critically high. His blood pressure is low. I can't find any obvious internal or external bleeding. His stomach is soft to touch."

"Why is he unconscious?" Taylor asked.

Kennedy shook his head. "Hard to say. He got bounced around a lot. We have to suspect a head injury. How are his pupils?"

Taylor shone the penlight in each eye. "They are mid-sized, and both react."

"That's encouraging. We'll monitor his vital signs. When we get to the highway, we'll use the lights and make time. I'll call ahead, so they're ready for us."

Franklyn's condition was unchanged as they raced to the hospital. Eric used the time to splint Franklyn's left forearm.

They were entering Great Falls when Franklyn's hand swatted at the oxygen mask. Taylor leaned over him. "Franklyn. You're in an ambulance. You were in an accident. Stay still."

"No … get up … I can't move."

Taylor placed her hand on his chest. "Franklyn. Please listen. Stay still. We have you on a spine board."

"Pam?"

"Yes. Eric is here, too."

"Pain … everywhere."

"It was a horrific crash."

"Can't see. I'm blind."

"No, not blind. Your eyes are swollen. There's blood around them. They'll clean you up at the hospital, and you'll be able to see just fine. We've got you. Trust us, okay? Please."

CHAPTER SIXTY

RILEY SPRINTED INTO THE EMERGENCY DEPARTMENT AND FOUND Heather. Her shoulders sagged, and there were bags under her eyes. "Where's Eaglechild?"

"He's in the trauma room. They're still assessing him. I can let you know when you can see him."

"It's okay. I know the way." Riley brushed past and headed down the corridor.

"Agent Briggs, wait—"

At least a dozen emergency staff surrounded Franklyn. A doctor at the head of the bed gave orders.

"Blood pressure?" the emergency physician asked.

"110/72."

"Getting better, keep the IVs running."

A paramedic headed over to Riley. "Eric."

Riley glanced at Eric, then back to Franklyn.

"Yeah, I remember." Riley watched the nurses as they worked.

"Do you know who did this?" Eric asked.

"I have my suspicions. Tell me what they're doing."

"Sure. A bunch of things are happening at the same time. They'll keep him immobilized until the X-rays are back. They need to be sure there aren't any neck or back fractures. While they wait for the X-rays, they're getting his blood pressure up. It's close to normal. They'll watch his pupils. They're a reliable indicator if there is a brain injury. They'll send him for a CAT scan."

"That doctor any good?"

Eric nodded. "He's the best in Montana. Mark Stossell."

"I noticed most of the emergency staff here a few hours ago. They must be exhausted."

"They're like us, work until the job is done. They know Franklyn is a cop. None of them will leave until they know he'll be okay."

"What about the X-rays?" Stossell asked.

"I just put them up," an X-ray tech said.

Stossell headed to the X-ray screen and asked the tech. "What do you see?"

"You want to know what I see?"

Stossell nodded.

"The neck and spine are clear. Everything else is okay."

"I concur," Stossell said. "Okay, people, the neck and spine are clear. Let's release him from the spine board torture device. Keep him flat until we know the blood pressure is stable."

Stossell glanced at Riley. "Should you be back here?"

Riley showed his badge. "I'm investigating the accident."

"Just stay out of the way," Stossell said.

Riley glanced at Eric.

"He's a business-like, no-nonsense guy."

"When can I talk to Franklyn?" Riley asked.

Eric shook his head. "Not anytime soon. They'll be doing tests for hours and likely sedate him."

"This afternoon?"

"You could see him, but he won't know you're there. I'd say tomorrow morning is your best bet."

"Damn. I need to talk to him. How do I get ahold of Calvin Lefebvre?"

"I can call him for you."

"Tell him to meet me at my office in an hour."

CHAPTER SIXTY-ONE

CHIEF FOX STORMED INTO THE CASINO SECURITY OFFICE, SLAMMED the door, and threw his Stetson on the desk in front of Balam. "What the hell were you thinking?"

Balam rolled a toothpick around his mouth, reclined in his chair and put his feet on the desk. "Taking care of a problem."

"We talked about this." Fox's jaw clenched. "Unbelievable. You have no idea what you've done."

"You said you didn't want to know what I had planned."

Chief Fox's jaw clenched. "I was clear I didn't want attention here."

Balam shrugged and waved a hand. "Eaglechild is out in the early hours of the morning and rolls his truck. These things happen."

"There's no way I can keep the feds out of this."

"You worry too much. Eaglechild is out of commission for weeks. Fort Benton's fire chief told me Eaglechild was in serious condition, unconscious and all. Anything Eaglechild thought he knew or any leads he had are long gone. We've moved everything to a location hard to find and harder to get to. We have people patrolling. If the cops get within a mile of us, we'll know. Besides, you've got Hiram Crow on the inside. He'll know what's happening."

"Eaglechild keeps Crow in the dark."

"Sure, but with Eaglechild in hospital, you should announce Crow is acting sheriff."

The chief pulled out a chair, sat, and rubbed his chin. Then a grin formed. "You might be right. I leave Crow as sheriff, even when Eaglechild gets healthy. I can use his injury to let him go."

"He won't leave without a fight."

"Maybe. With the right incentive, he'll go quietly."

"I don't know." Balam shook his head. "He's not a quitter."

"For a hundred thousand, he'll take the cash and run."

"That's a lot of money."

The chief nodded. "It is, but what has he cost us in a month? What have your mistakes cost us? You underestimated Eaglechild. Better to get rid of him now when we have the chance. We let him go because we're worried about his health."

"Hey, remember, I didn't want him hired."

"Apparently, his addiction issues weren't as severe as we were told."

"What if the Great Falls Hospital gives him the okay to come back to work?"

"Then we insist Eaglechild sees the doctor at the health center."

"What makes you think the doctor will go along with this?"

"Let's just say he owes me a favor or two." Fox grabbed his Stetson and headed to the door. "What table should I go to?"

CHAPTER SIXTY-TWO

THERE WAS A KNOCK AT THE DOOR. RILEY GLANCED UP FROM THE map on his desk. Blake stood in the doorway.

"Boss, Deputy Lefebvre is here."

"Great, bring him in."

Riley stood. "Lefebvre, thanks for coming. Have a seat."

Blake sat in a second chair.

"Eric said you needed to see me," Lefebvre said.

"That I do." Riley pointed to the map. "We got lucky. I know where they've moved their drug production."

"You're kidding. How?"

Riley filled Lefebvre in on his talk with Jesse.

"Out of the blue Jesse told you this?"

"Not that simple," Riley said. "Once he gets going, he's a talkative chap. Jesse is so messed up he doesn't know which side he's on. The thing is, he's practically invisible. He's around the drug dealers, and he's around the admin office, but no one takes notice."

"What do you mean around the admin office?" Lefebvre asked.

"He sells drugs at the admin office."

"Sure, we've never … no, Jesse?"

Riley lifted one shoulder in a shrug.

"Well, I'll be damned. The little snake."

Riley pointed to the map. "He says the Lamont brothers have moved their drug operation out to the movie set."

"We've got a bunch of those," Lefebvre said. "This is a popular rez to film westerns. There's a whole western town we always chase kids out of. That would be too obvious."

"Jesse said it was by the river."

"Oh, he means the fur traders' village. A few log cabins, lean-tos, and a large drying shed. That's an excellent location. They could make pills or cook meth, and no one would know."

"We need to get out there. Do some surveillance. Show me where it is."

"Not easy to get there." Lefebvre put his finger on the map.

"That doesn't appear hard," Blake said.

Lefebvre laughed. "Sure, on the map it looks flat." He pulled out a pen and made an X. "Here's the closest road." He drew a line across the map. "This is prairie grass for a mile. Wide-open, no cover." At the end of the line, he drew a circle. "Here's a steep hill, practically a cliff. It drops off real fast. There's one road down the hill. They'll have guys just over the side of the cliff. They'll see us coming before we get off the road."

"You mentioned a river," Riley said. "That's an option."

Lefebvre nodded. "Yeah, just not a suitable option. Upriver are some class-four rapids. Every year we get called to find kayakers who've failed to negotiate the rapids. Most of the time, we find them downriver a few miles—dead."

"So, we come from downstream," Riley said.

"You're in decent shape, but there's no way you could paddle against the current. And if you want to use something with a motor, like a Zodiac, they'd hear you. Sound travels well out there."

"Helicopter drop would be out," Blake said. "Way too noisy."

"There is one option." Lefebvre scratched his neck.

"What's that?" Riley asked.

"Horseback."

"Are you kidding?" Riley's eyes bulged, sure Lefebvre was joking.

"Hundred percent serious. We'll be able to get close. There're a few herds of wild horses roaming over the rez. The guys guarding the place won't bother with the sound of horses. Especially at night when the horses come to the river to drink."

Riley shook his head. "I'm not sure about that."

"Can't ride?"

Riley glared at Lefebvre. "I can ride. I … I just haven't ridden in a few years."

"How many years?"

Riley crossed his arms. "About twenty."

Lefebvre laughed. "It's like riding a bike—you never forget."

"I haven't ridden a bike in about twenty years, either."

"What about you, Blake?" Lefebvre asked.

She shook her head. "Never ridden a horse. Dirt biking, now that's my sport."

"Dirt bike would be too noisy," Lefebvre said. "Too bad, though. It would be perfect."

Riley slumped back in his chair. There weren't any other options. They had to check out the place before the raid. He couldn't remember the last time he'd ridden a horse—before he became a cop. Possibly a rodeo he and Franklyn had entered. Franklyn winning a buckle and Riley eating dirt. *At least I was a skilled hockey player.*

"Where do I get a horse?" Riley asked.

Lefebvre whooped. "All right. Hell, I can get you a dozen horses."

"Maybe one that's friendly."

"Nah. I figure you need one to match your disposition, you know, one with attitude."

"Just when I was starting to like you," Riley said.

"What about me?" Blake asked.

"This isn't the time to learn how to ride," Lefebvre said. "No offense."

"Offense taken." Blake glared. "What am I supposed to do?"

"You'll be at the command post," Riley said. "Monitor our progress and get resources if it goes to crap. Have Gibson and Bennett ready to swoop in."

"Swoop in?"

"Think of it as backup." Riley smirked. "If it makes you feel better, think of yourself as the cavalry coming to my rescue."

"Now, I'm offended," Lefebvre said.

"Great. Hours sitting in a car with that pig Gibson," Blake said.

"Make him sit in the back. You and Bennett can share girly stories."

"Screw you, Riley."

CHAPTER SIXTY-THREE

Riley stomped into Franklyn's room and stood at the end of the bed. "You look like shit."

"Oh great, the glee club president is here. I'm not supposed to have visitors."

"I'm not a visitor. I'm the po-lice. I go wherever I want." Riley pulled up a chair and sat. "Seriously, you look like shit."

"I'll take your word for that."

Riley glanced at the monitors and intravenous lines. "How long are you going to be in here?"

"A couple of days."

"Injuries?"

"Nothing serious. Broken nose. That should give me the roguish good looks I've always wanted."

"Maybe the roguish part."

Franklyn raised an eyebrow. "You checked the mirror lately? You're no prince charming."

"I try to look better after a fight than the other guy."

"Not if the other guy is a truck."

"Good point. I thought you rolled your truck."

Franklyn shook his head and groaned.

"Are you sure you're okay?" Riley asked.

"It hurts when I move ... or breathe." Franklyn slid higher on the bed. "It was a setup. I went out to the quad on a party complaint. No one was there. No one had been there for a week or more. As I was driving home, I was T-boned. Perhaps an F350. Something that size."

"I need to get forensics out there."

"Probably too late. Lefebvre and Paulette trampled the scene, along with paramedics, Fort Benton Fire, and the tow truck."

"Where'd they take your truck?"

"Lefebvre says your impound lot."

"I'll send forensics to examine your truck. Your chief sent out an email last night."

"About how distressed he is that I was hurt? Or upset I lived?"

Riley leaned against the bed. "Not even close. Hiram Crow is acting sheriff."

"That's why I need to get back. Crow will undo everything."

"What can I do?"

"Help Lefebvre."

Riley nodded. "Already done. We met yesterday afternoon. I told him about a drug dealer who overdosed from your rez that I interviewed."

"What's his name?"

"Jesse."

"Jesse Ranger? Is he okay?"

"He's going to be fine. He's one of the lucky ones."

Franklyn nodded. "He's not a dealer. He's an addict and will take anything he can get."

"He admitted to me he's a dealer," Riley said.

"Maybe more of a trader than a dealer."

"Crap, you don't know?"

Franklyn squinted. "Know what?"

"Jesse has been dealing drugs in your admin office for years."

"Jesse?"

"Yup."

"Right under my nose. The bastard."

"He gets his stuff from the Lamont brothers. He hangs around during the day under the buffalo head and deals. He's popular."

"Paulette warned me about him. I tried to be his buddy and help him when I could."

"You were played, my friend."

Franklyn sighed. "Everything goes back to the Lamont brothers."

"They're backed by the Red Demons motorcycle gang. That makes this huge."

"Do you have a plan?"

Riley nodded and smirked. "You bet I do. Lefebvre and I worked it out yesterday afternoon. We're riding out tonight to get the lay of the land."

"Riding?"

"Yeah. Horses."

Franklyn laughed, then started coughing. "Don't make me laugh—it hurts. When did you last ride?"

Riley shrugged. "Doesn't matter."

"When are you taking them down?"

"If we get the info we need tonight, then tomorrow night."

"I want to be there."

"I'm not sure that's a good idea."

"I'll rest today, but you've got to break me out of here tomorrow."

"Breaking who out?"

Franklyn and Riley faced the door as Eva stepped in and headed to the bed. "Oh my god, you look horrible."

"Nice to see you, too."

Eva sat on the bed and kissed his forehead. "I came by earlier, and you were sound asleep. Why didn't you call me when you were awake?"

"Cuz, you'd worry."

"Right. And I didn't worry when I found out what had happened." She punched his arm. "You're an ass."

"I've been telling him that for years," Riley said.

"Eva, this is my brother, Special Agent—in his mind—Riley Briggs."

Eva smiled. "I've heard so much about you. Nice to finally meet you. Do you know who did this?"

"I'm investigating the accident."

"My money says it's those sons of bitches, the Lamont brothers," Franklyn said.

"We don't know that yet." Riley stood. "I've got things to do. See you tomorrow, Franklyn."

"Be here early," Franklyn said.

Riley nodded and headed out the door. He stopped in the hall and glanced back. He had the feeling he'd missed something.

CHAPTER SIXTY-FOUR

NEAR MIDNIGHT, IN COMPLETE DARKNESS, RILEY PARKED BESIDE A horse trailer. Lefebvre had the horses saddled, and they grazed on the sweet grass. Blake parked her SUV beside Riley's.

A barking black shape raced around the trailer toward Blake.

"Pax, out," Lefebvre commanded.

Pax stopped a few feet from Blake, hackles up, growling softly. Lefebvre grabbed Pax by the collar. "I said, out. They're friendly."

Blake stepped forward, and Pax sniffed her hand.

Riley grabbed two duffel bags from the back of his SUV and hauled them past Pax to the horses. "Keep the dog away from me."

Lefebvre glanced at the bags. "Jeez. I should have brought a packhorse. Do you realize we're just checking things out? The battle is tomorrow night."

"*Prepare for the worst* is my motto," Riley said.

"Well, it looks like you're prepared for Russia invading. What the hell is in those bags?"

Riley pulled out his ballistic vest loaded with spare magazines, flashbangs, and a tactical first aid kit. He pulled out a second vest and handed it to Lefebvre. "Can never be too cautious."

Lefebvre lifted out a magazine and held it out to Riley. "What do I do with this? Throw it at them?"

Riley grinned and hauled an M4 assault rifle out of the bag. "Got you one of these."

Lefebvre lifted the rifle and held it like it was fragile China.

"Do you know how to shoot that?"

Lefebvre nodded as he swung the M4 around to a shooting position. "Yup. I learned at a gun club."

"Let's hope we don't have to." Riley reached into the other bag, selected a plastic case, and handed it to Lefebvre. "Night vision goggles."

"Whoa," Lefebvre said. "Riding in on horseback with an M4 and night vision goggles. This day couldn't be better."

"Do you need a moment to clean up?" Blake asked.

Lefebvre ignored Blake and headed to the horses.

Riley slid earbuds and a jawbone microphone in place. "Riley to Blake, test, test."

"Loud and clear."

"This will take a few hours. I'll stay in contact."

"What if they spot you?" Blake asked. "What if it goes to crap? We need a code word."

"Okay, 'Blackhawk Down.'"

Blake rolled her eyes. "That's the best you have?"

"How about 'Broken Arrow'?"

"They're getting worse. Enough with the movie quotes."

"I liked the movie 'We Were Soldiers.'"

Blake shook her head. "Whatever. Just don't get killed. I hate paperwork."

For nearly an hour, they followed a cow path through the woods to the river, then headed south. Pax jogged ahead, tracking scents.

Riley swayed with the movement of the horse, frequently standing in the stirrups trying to relieve the ache in his butt.

More than once, he caught Lefebvre glancing back and grinning.

Riley pulled out his phone and activated the GPS. "We're getting close."

"I could have told you that." Lefebvre rolled his eyes. "Another quarter mile and we'll be at the cliff on the north side." He led them away from the river, up a hill, and stopped. The trees thinned and offered a view of … darkness.

"I can't see a thing," Riley said. "Time for the night vision goggles. There's a switch on the right."

"Oh, wow." Lefebvre's voice cracked with excitement. "Everything is green. These goggles will take getting used to."

"There's a glow to the south," Riley said. "A campfire?"

"They've got it going well."

"Watch for traces of light around the camp." Riley's eyes searched the darkness from left to right. "That'll be the sentries smoking."

"They'll either be smoking, drinking, or sleeping."

"There might be others farther out into the woods. We might not see them all."

"Pax will let us know if there's anyone there."

"Great, a barking dog."

"He won't bark. I trained him better than that."

"He barked at me."

Lefebvre shrugged. "He doesn't like you. He's an expert judge of character."

"Feeling's mutual." Riley keyed his mic. "Blake, we're to the south and above the camp."

"Roger, that."

"They've got a huge fire going. With all the trees, it's difficult to tell how many there are. We're going to go closer."

"Don't be an idiot," Blake said. "A general number will do."

"This is as far as we take the horses," Lefebvre said. "We'll go on foot. Pax, come."

Thank god. Riley gingerly stepped out of the saddle and slid to the ground. He stretched his back and willed his thighs to return to a normal range.

Pax trotted over to Lefebvre, who attached a leash. "If we stay up here, we'll see the fur traders' camp and anyone on the lookout on this side of the river."

They tethered their horses and headed out on foot.

"We're moving closer on foot," Riley said.

"You're an idiot," Blake replied.

Pax led them farther up the hill for about ten minutes, then stopped in a clearing. With their goggles, they could see the outlines of cabins and a large drying shed. Images in green moved around the fire. By Riley's count, there were a dozen near the fire and at least six walking around the camp. He scanned the immediate area. Once his eyes adjusted to the darkness, he would search for sentries. Along the river, he spotted five green figures—three were smoking. In the trees to either side of the camp were two sentries, one on each side. It was impossible to see through the trees to the east side and the cliff.

"I want to get closer," Riley said. "Let's head down the hill to the river."

"You sure that's a good idea?"

"I need to know who we're dealing with. The Lamont boys and their gang just standing around because they were ordered to. Or the Red Demons providing serious protection."

"Pax, heel," Lefebvre said.

They shuffled down the hill and stopped at a rock outcropping about one hundred feet above the river.

The group around the fire pit passed something around—a bottle or a pipe. Their voices carried across the river.

"This is bullshit. We work our assess off making pills, and all we get is booze."

"You think you've got it awful, try cooking meth all day. My lungs are fucked."

"Screw this. I'm going to slip a few pills out. Have my own party tomorrow night."

"Are you crazy? Remember what happened to Max?"

"He ain't here no more."

"Right. Do you think Max just wandered off? He stole some pills, and the next day he's gone. Coyotes are still picking his bones."

"Well, it's still bullshit."

Three of the sentries came out of the woods, heading toward the river. "I gotta piss."

One of the men unzipped his pants and peed into the river. "All I do is piss when I drink that watery booze they give us."

"Gotta be patient, man. They promised us drugs or cash if we worked for a week. Monday morning, we'll have more drugs or cash than we can use. If we take the drugs, we'll make descent cash selling what we don't need."

"Hey, do you see something across the river?"

"No, you're seeing things."

"I see, ah shit. Red eyes. There's a wolf or bear or something across the river."

"Give it a shake and zip it up. Let's head to the fire. Wolves hate fires."

Riley watched the men head back to the fire. The Red Demons' crest glowed green in Riley's goggles. "I've seen enough. Let's get out of here."

They scrambled up the hill to the horses. Riley swung into the saddle. "Blake, we're on our way back."

Lefebvre unleashed Pax. "Take us home, buddy."

CHAPTER SIXTY-FIVE

Riley gingerly rolled out of bed and slid on a pair of shorts. He waddled toward the bathroom. His ass was numb, his thighs cramped, and his back spasmed.

Regan's eyes followed Riley's painful walk. "You're moving like an old man."

"I don't think Lefebvre could have picked a wider horse." Riley leaned against the wall and arched his back, which crackled and popped. "Ah, that feels better." He lifted his knees toward his chest. "I feel like someone made a wish, grabbed both my legs, and pulled. I'm not sure my legs are still attached to my hips, and my nuts are up in my chest."

Regan laughed. "I made sure that was not an issue."

"Not for long. We'll go back in by horseback tonight."

"Poor baby." Regan wiped imaginary tears from her eyes. "Take a long hot shower, or maybe a bath."

"Alone?" Riley frowned.

"Wouldn't want your nuts to hurt more."

"I'm willing to take that chance."

"Maybe when you don't walk like you're eighty."

"Eighty—watch this." Riley did a few squats, then quickly straightened his right leg. "Damn, a thigh cramp." He danced around the room, trying to get the cramp to release.

Regan rolled on the bed with laughter. "Did you have fun on your boy scout trip?"

Riley massaged his thigh. "What do you think? It's difficult to get to, but not well protected. The guys they have around the camp aren't experienced and couldn't give a shit. They won't be a problem."

"Are you taking them down tonight?"

Riley nodded. "I'll call Deaver and get SWAT with us. We'll meet tonight at dusk and plan it out. We'll hit them in full darkness."

"By the book, Special Agent Briggs. I don't need any crap from Judge Leery on Monday or Dalton Frey picking apart your less-than-stellar methods."

Riley saluted. "Yes, ma'am."

Regan sat and let the sheet fall. "Come back to bed and let me massage your cramps."

CHAPTER SIXTY-SIX

Riley, Blake, and Lefebvre exited the elevator and headed to Franklyn's hospital room. They zipped past the nursing station —no one paid attention.

Riley stopped. The others bumped into him.

Franklyn glanced over. "Oh, hey. I didn't expect you *this* early." The sheets rustled, and Eva's head popped up next to Franklyn's shoulder.

"Give us few minutes," Franklyn said.

Riley and the others scattered.

"I didn't know about them," Lefebvre said.

Riley cocked his head. "And you call yourself a cop."

Lefebvre shrugged. "I don't pay attention to that romantic stuff."

"No girlfriend?" Blake asked.

"No."

"I'm not surprised," Blake said.

"Here's your chance," Riley said. "We need to distract the nurse down the hall while we sneak Franklyn out. Maybe you can get a date."

Lefebvre headed down the hall.

Riley glanced at Blake. "What?"

Lefebvre was back in thirty seconds. "Not gonna work."

Riley glanced down the hall. "What? Why?"

"The nurse is a guy," Lefebvre said.

Riley shrugged. "Maybe you still have a chance."

"Oh my god, Riley," Blake said. "You're such an ass." She headed to the nursing station.

Then Eva came out of Franklyn's room. "If you change your mind, you can stay at my place. I'll provide twenty-four-hour nursing." She smiled at Riley as she passed. "He's all yours. I have to rush off. Nice to see you, Riley. See you later, Calvin."

"She's in a cheery mood," Riley said.

"That's the first time she's ever talked to me," Lefebvre said. "First time she's called me Calvin, that's for sure."

Riley glanced down the hall. Blake and the nurse were engaged in deep conversation with Blake blocking the nurse's view of the hall. Riley stepped into Franklyn's room. "Okay, lover boy, time to get out. Blake bought us a couple of minutes."

Riley supported Franklyn as they rushed down the hall and around the corner. Lefebvre had an elevator waiting.

Inside, Franklyn slumped against the wall. "I need to catch my breath."

Riley nodded. "Lefebvre, we're going to need a wheelchair."

"No, I'm fine," Franklyn said.

The elevator doors opened, they dragged Franklyn to the exit and outside. Lefebvre opened the back door of Riley's SUV.

They shoved Franklyn onto the seat and then jumped in. Blake sprinted out the front door and slid into the passenger seat.

"Good timing," Riley said. "How's the nurse?"

Blake held a piece of paper with numbers on it. "Lefebvre, it's for you."

CHAPTER SIXTY-SEVEN

THE COLEMAN LANTERNS CAST AN EERIE GLOW THROUGH THE TREES. Riley adjusted the closest lamp to see the map laid out on a table in front of his SUV. "Screw this." He pulled out a LED flashlight, clicked the button, and held it in his teeth. "Thash bitter."

"You sound drunk," Blake said.

"The drool verifies it," Franklyn said.

Riley pulled the flashlight out of his mouth. "You got a better idea?"

"Sure." Blake held her flashlight over the map. "There, you can see and talk, and the map doesn't get soaked in your spit."

"You just thought of this?"

"Nah. I've had my flashlight out for a while. I wasn't sure if you'd pull out your grandpa reading glasses or ask for help."

Franklyn laughed. "I could listen to her mess with you all night."

"If you jerks are finished laughing, how about we make a

plan for arresting the Lamont brothers and anyone else they're working with."

"Yes, sir, my commander," Blake said.

"Yup, watch this all night," Franklyn said.

"Based on what Lefebvre and I observed last night, and from some great photos from Google Maps, we know where the fur traders' camp is and what the terrain is like. As much as my butt wants to drive there in my comfortable SUV with heated leather seats, we go on horseback. That way, we cut off their escape on the river or into the trees. When they see us, they'll backtrack and head up the hill and flee across the field into the waiting arms of SWAT."

"Aren't they supposed to be here by now?" Blake asked.

Riley checked his watch. "Yeah. They should have been here twenty minutes ago. Blake, call them. And bring the warrant back."

"Sure."

"It better be an FBI warrant," Franklyn said. "I don't need another talking to by the justice or the chief."

"It's better than an FBI warrant. It's signed by the governor."

"What's better than that."

Riley grinned. "It is signed by the state Attorney General."

"How did you manage that?" Franklyn asked.

"Connections."

Riley pointed to the map. "SWAT will fan out across the field. Once SWAT is in position, we'll make some noise from across the river. When the shitheads ascend the hill to get away from us, SWAT will be there. They're bringing powerful lights and will illuminate the hill as they come over the crest."

"You think three of us on horses is enough?" Franklyn asked.

"It would be great to have more, but on short notice, who are we going to get that we trust? I know the SWAT members don't ride. Blake has never been on a horse. That leaves you, Lefebvre, and me. If we make enough noise, they'll think there's a major attack coming their way. I'll throw some flashbangs and make a lot of noise."

"All right," Franklyn said. "How close did you two get last night?"

"We got close enough to see them around the fire and to see three Red Demons come down to the river to piss."

"The bikers didn't see you?"

"Nah. We were above them. The sentries were spooked when they glimpsed the eyes of Lefebvre's dog. They thought it was a wolf."

"That's close."

Blake set her phone on the table. "SWAT got lost. They're about four minutes away. I'll be back in a few. I've got a couple of things to prepare."

Lefebvre's boots crunched on the gravel. "Horses are saddled and ready to go."

Paulette came out from behind Lefebvre, leading a horse. "Diesel is ready. He's champing at the bit."

"What are you doing here?" Franklyn asked.

"I came out with Calvin to help with the horses."

"It's dangerous here."

Paulette placed her hands on her hips. "More dangerous than it is for you with your injuries? I can hold my own."

"She will help me here at the command post," Blake said.

"Great, you're in on this, too."

"You sure you're up for this, boss?" Paulette asked.

"Damn straight," Franklyn said. "I've ridden in worse shape than this."

"Sure, but not sober," Riley said.

"Screw you."

Riley lifted a duffel bag onto the hood of the SUV and pulled out three plastic cases. "Night vision goggles."

"Sweet," Lefebvre said. "I love these."

"I'm not wearing those stupid things," Franklyn said. "I can see fine in the dark."

"You'll be wishing you were wearing them when the first tree branch knocks you out of your saddle and onto your ass."

"Ain't gonna happen."

"Take them anyway." Riley tossed the goggles.

Franklyn snatched the case out of the air and lobbed it back to Riley.

"Fine," Riley said. "I've got an M4 for each of us and a few hundred rounds of ammunition."

Lefebvre slid an M4 out of the duffel bag, cleared the action, then grabbed a handful of magazines.

Franklyn eyed the M4 in Lefebvre's hand. "Nice and fancy, but I brought my own." He reached down to a bag at his feet and groaned. "Oh god, I'm not sure I can make it back up." He grabbed the table and pulled himself upright.

"You okay, boss?" Lefebvre asked.

"Yeah. I hurt in places I didn't know I had places. Tylenol isn't cutting it. Lefebvre, lift that bag for me."

Lefebvre grabbed the bag. Franklyn reached inside and pulled out a lever-action rifle.

"The museum know you stole that?" Riley asked.

Franklyn held the rifle toward the light and rubbed the wooden stock. "Good enough for six generations, good enough for me."

"Great, great grandfather?" Riley asked.

"Back further than that. A souvenir from that skirmish you whites call Little Big Horn. We call it the Battle of the Greasy Grass."

"It still works?" Riley asked.

"It does, but that one is in a safe place. This one is a replica, but it works."

Blake came out of the shadows and set what appeared to be a giant spider on the truck hood.

"What the heck is that?" Franklyn asked.

"A drone."

"A what?"

"A drone. I fitted it with a FLIR TIC."

"You're talking some weird language," Franklyn said.

"It has fur?" Lefebvre's face contorted.

Blake laughed. "FLIR is a company that makes thermal imaging cameras. It picks up body heat from humans and animals."

"You can't use it," Riley said. "It will be too noisy."

"It's not that loud. Sounds like a swarm of bees."

"I don't know," Riley said.

"I'll wait until you are ready, then I'll launch it. Last night I didn't have a clue what was going on. You're not the best at giving updates. I can't be command here and not see what's happening. Trust me, this will work."

Four black SUVs stopped about twenty yards from them, sending clouds of dust their way.

Riley headed to the first truck. "Where's Deaver?"

"His wife is having a baby." Taggert lifted his chin. "I'm in charge tonight. I've got four to a truck, sixteen of us, and three K9."

Riley's jaw clenched, and his neck tensed. "Good for you. Come over to my truck, and I'll explain the plan."

Riley pointed to the map. "Here's the camp. I'll come from the south. You guys set up a perimeter in this field. I'll make noise with flashbangs. That should drive everyone away from the camp and up this hill. Once the druggies crest the hill, you'll be waiting in ambush. Hit the lights, they'll be blind, and you can arrest them. The Cascade County Sheriff's deputies will have a half-dozen vans to transport the suspects."

"Will any of the shitheads fight?" Taggert asked. "Do they have guns?"

"Here's the problem. Some of the guys with guns are Red Demons. We know of three, but I'm sure all the sentries are Demons. That could be a dozen or more. They'll likely start a gunfight. The rest, about another dozen, is a mix of Indians and low-level drug dealers. I doubt they're armed. They won't fight. Use less-lethal force unless you absolutely have to shoot. Beanbag rounds would be the best. K9 can take down anyone who runs. They'll like that."

"Jeez, thanks, Riley. I didn't know I could use less-lethal or K9. How about you worry about your sorry ass, and I'll direct *my* team."

"I'm not starting a pissing match with you. If this goes sideways, you guys need to make the *right* decision. Shooting low-level drug dealers or Indians would be devastating."

CHAPTER SIXTY-EIGHT

PAX LED THE WAY THROUGH THE DARKNESS ON THE SAME TRAIL they'd used the previous night. Lefebvre, Franklyn, and Riley followed behind on horseback. The pace was slower.

Riley kept a close watch on Franklyn. They shouldn't have busted him out of the hospital. He was in no condition to sit on a couch watching TV, let alone go on an hour-long trail ride into who-knows-what. More than once, Riley was sure Franklyn would fall from the saddle. But each time, he pulled himself upright. Asking Franklyn if he was okay was a waste of time. He grumbled and told Riley to mind his own business.

Riley keyed his mic. "Blake, it's Briggs."

"Briggs. Wow. I wouldn't have guessed."

"You're bored."

"Good guess."

"We're nearly at the river. Is SWAT in place?"

"They're running late. Taggert underestimated the distance, terrain. And hauling the lights. Give them another fifteen."

"Roger."

Lefebvre held up his hand, and they reigned in the horses. They were on the hill overlooking the river. "Even larger fire than last night." Through the still night, they heard voices and laughter. Not enough to make out the words, but they were having fun.

Riley swung off his horse and headed to the edge of the hill. Through the night vision goggles, Riley surveyed the scene. There were more green shapes moving than last night. He keyed his mic. "Blake, looks like we've got about thirty bandits."

"That's too many. I'll radio for backup."

"Great. Have EMS move to your position."

The radio clicked twice in acknowledgment.

"You guys heard, SWAT isn't ready yet," Riley said. "Time to spread out. Franklyn, you stay here. Lefebvre go downstream about a quarter of a mile. I'll take a position in between. Wait for my command, then make a lot of noise. Flashbangs first, then your pistols. We need them to think we're attacking."

Franklyn slid off his horse and groaned as his feet touched the ground.

Riley headed over and grabbed Franklyn by the arm. Franklyn twisted away. "Let go. I'm fine."

Riley backed away, hands up, then mounted his horse. He nodded to Lefebvre, and they scrambled down the hill to the river and headed downstream. Riley stopped at a bend in the river where the water was shallow enough to cross.

Lefebvre saluted and continued downstream.

Riley tethered his horse to some shrubs, then knelt behind a boulder. This was a perfect location. He had an unobstructed view of the party across the river and could see downstream to where Lefebvre would be. Across the river, to the left, a sandy hill rose to the field. "Blake, we're in position. Give me an update on SWAT."

"SWAT is still crossing the field. Taggert gets pissed off every time I radio him. Let him tell us when he's ready."

Riley swore under his breath. "You can send up your toy whirlybird. We need that when we start shooting. Up to you to find the ones who get away."

"Isn't that amusing. Is this your way of saying, *Good thinking, Blake*?"

Riley rolled his eyes and clicked the mic twice.

Lefebvre said he was in place. The voices from across the river were clearer, a mix of males and females.

Riley's eyes roamed from the fire to the hill behind—the direction SWAT would be waiting. The top of the hill burst with light. He flung the night vision goggles off and rubbed his eyes. He closed them tight. When he opened his eyes, everything was blurry. He heard screams of panic. When his eyesight returned, a mass of people was heading toward him. He tossed three flash-bangs onto the sandhill. Other flashbang explosions echoed down the valley. That stopped the charge, and the stampede swung as a group and bolted from the blasts.

The buzz of bees sounded overhead. "You've got three guys coming toward you."

"What happened?" Riley asked. "And who is this?"

"It's Paulette."

"Where's Blake?"

"I'm not sure where she went."

"What's going on with SWAT?"

"I don't know what happened. Taggert told me SWAT was in place—then the field lit up like mid-day."

Asshole.

"Oh, crap," Paulette said. "Two suspects are heading downstream toward you, Lefebvre. Riley, another will cross the river between you and Lefebvre. Franklyn, stay where you are. The third person is still on the other side of the river. I'll let you know when he crosses."

Franklyn sat with his back against a tree. His breath came in gasps, and pain burned throughout his body. It was worse than any of his rodeo injuries. Hell, it was worse than all of them combined. He sweat profusely, despite the cool air.

He crawled to the edge of the hill and scanned the far side of the river. After a few attempts, he spotted the moving figure. *Don't need any goggles.* In another hundred feet, the suspect would be across from Franklyn.

The shadowy figure continued along the river in front of Franklyn, then farther upstream. Franklyn pushed onto his knees and groaned in pain. He used the rifle to pull himself upright. The waves of pain flashed again. He squinted across the river and upstream. The dark figure was crossing the river close to Franklyn.

Using the rifle as a crutch, Franklyn staggered across the hill.

After a dozen steps, he was gasping for air, which increased the pain in his chest. He stumbled on for another dozen steps, then leaned against a tree.

This was as close as he would get. He lifted his rifle and held it against his side with his right arm. His breathing slowed, but the pain remained.

His eyes darted across the hilltop, searching for the escaping suspect.

Behind him, a tree branch snapped. He slid his back around the tree and peered into the darkness. Fifty feet away, he spotted a crouching figure, moving from tree to tree. He pushed against the tree until it supported his back, then raised his rifle.

Thirty feet away, the figure stepped out into a clearing.

"Stop right there," Franklyn said. "I have a rifle pointed at your chest."

Riley spotted the suspect wading across the river downstream. A rocky outcropping stood between Riley and the suspect. There was no way to catch him by running down the river. Riley sprinted to his horse and swung into the saddle. He guided the horse uphill. The horse stumbled in the soft sand. At the top of the hill, Riley veered left, and they galloped in pursuit. Riley hunched over the horse's neck, branches slashing at him. He hoped the horse could see where he was going because Riley couldn't. A branch had knocked the night vision goggles off. The horse raced on. When they reached the point where Riley thought the suspect had crossed, they slowed. He searched the night.

"Fifty feet to your right," Paulette said.

Riley swung his head to the right and glimpsed the suspect crawling along the river toward boulders. Riley quietly slid from the saddle. He was within twenty feet when the suspect ducked behind the rocks.

Riley jogged through the trees. His boot caught on a root, and he fell, hitting the ground hard.

His M4 rattled into the bushes. Then bullets peppered the surrounding ground.

He rolled behind a tree, heart racing, breathing rapidly. The shooting stopped.

He leaned around the tree, but there was only darkness. His eyes adjusted. He could make out the outline of boulders, but that was it. He had no clue where the suspect was. Riley drew his pistol and peered into the darkness.

A twig snapped to his left, he spun but couldn't see anyone. Another twig snapped—closer this time. He glimpsed a blur of movement to his left and rotated, gun ready.

Two deer raced past. He exhaled, then icy steel pressed against his neck.

CHAPTER SIXTY-NINE

"STEP TOWARD ME, SLOWLY," FRANKLYN SAID.

The figure stepped closer, rifle at his side.

"Drop the rifle."

"Franklyn, I'm here to help."

Franklyn recognized the voice. "Crow?"

"Yeah. Don't shoot."

"What the hell are you doing here?" Franklyn asked.

"I followed you."

"That's bullshit. You were across the river at the party. You're part of the drug dealing. No wonder there were never any arrests. You made sure of that."

"You've got it all wrong." Hiram Crow held his hands out, the rifle hanging by its strap at his side. "I've always had your back. Balam is the guy mixed up with the Red Demons. He's the one you need to arrest."

"Why should I believe you?"

"I can prove it out. Give me a chance. Lower your gun."

"You say you followed me. How did you know we'd be out here?"

He shook his head. "You're not going to like this."

"Try me."

"Eva told me."

Franklyn stilled. "You're lying. You're trying to save your skin by blaming Eva."

Crow shook his head. "I wish I was lying. She works for the chief."

"We all do." She'd warned Franklyn about the chief. She'd been there for him when he was injured.

"Not like she does."

"What do you mean?" Franklyn felt a lump in his stomach and a wave of nausea. His mind thought Crow was full of bullshit. His body told him otherwise.

Crow stepped closer. "He assigned her to you. Right from the start, her job was to get close, any way she could, and report back to him."

Franklyn had a vision of Eva with the chief. "That's a damn lie."

"Did she ask you about the drugs and the dealers? Did she ask you what you were going to do about it?"

The blood drained from Franklyn's face, his stomach in a violent spasm. This couldn't be true. He'd never given her the details … but enough that the chief could figure it out. Then it hit him. "I know you're full of shit. I told Eva this morning at the hospital about the raid tonight. If she was working for the chief, why didn't he tell everyone to clear out."

"She came to the office needing the chief, but he wasn't in," Crow said. "She said she had important information for him. I told her to tell me, and I'd find the chief. She told me about your plans for tonight. That's why I'm here."

"I believe the first part that she told you. But you're here to stop me. If I get killed during the raid, no one would be suspicious. You'd get to stay sheriff—that promotion would stick if I'm dead, right?"

"If I was trying to stop you, would I come alone?"

"Maybe what you say is true, maybe you're lying. I'm not taking any chances. Drop the gun and get on your knees."

Crow set the rifle on the ground and slowly knelt.

Franklyn stepped within five feet. Even in the dark, Franklyn could see the anger in Crow's eyes. Franklyn lowered his rifle. As he reached behind for his handcuffs, waves of pain shot through his back. He staggered and used the gun to keep himself upright. When he stood, Crow's rifle was aimed at him.

Before he could react, the muzzle flashed.

"You're a pain in my ass."

Riley froze with the icy steel pressed into his neck.

"With your right hand, slowly unholster your pistol and drop it to the ground."

Riley's brain raced for options. He had none. Trying to take the gun away would get him a bullet in his brain. That was going to happen anyway. Better to go down fighting. He wasn't religious, but he said a prayer. He asked God or a higher power to protect his kids. To watch over them. To help them deal with the loss of their dad. What the hell was he thinking? He'd find a way out. He slid his pistol out of his holster and dropped it to the ground.

"Nice. Hands on your head and slowly turn around."

Riley rotated and recognized the gunman. "Hello, Graham Keane. Or should I call you Noel Bourget?"

"Noel will be fine. Not that it will matter to you. I had a first-class setup here. Yet at every step, you messed things up. The sheriff wouldn't have figured this out."

Riley heard the buzzing overhead.

Bourget gazed toward the sound. "What the hell is that?"

"Deer must have stirred up a wasp nest in the grass. They'll attack when they find us."

"That's the stupidest thing I've heard. Wasps don't nest in the grass."

"Okay. If you say so. They sound angry. The buzzing is getting louder. They're close."

Bourget swung an arm over his head. "Maybe you're right. Start walking to the river."

The buzzing diminished. They walked a few hundred feet, then Bourget said, "Stop here."

Riley halted.

"Time is up for you, Mr. Special Agent Man. Turn around. I'm not going to shoot you in the back. I want to see you die for screwing up our operation."

Riley slowly turned to face Bourget. He was out of options.

The buzzing sound swelled until it was over their heads.

"Motherfucker." Bourget swung one hand wildly above him.

Riley watched Bourget fight the invisible swarm. His gun wavered, and Riley calculated how fast he could cover the ten feet. Not fast enough. But you never know.

He stepped forward. Bourget stopped swinging his arm and aimed at Riley. "I'll deal with you first, then the wasps."

Riley glared at Bourget. "Do your best."

Bourget grinned, and his head exploded. The rifle shot echoed through the woods.

Riley glanced at the body, then swung to his right. Branches snapped as Blake stepped into the clearing.

"You waited long enough, taking the shot," Riley said.

"I had this problem with trees and branches. You couldn't have stopped at a worse spot."

"Sorry, I made this hard for you. Nice shot."

"Is that your way of saying thank you for saving your life?"

"I had a plan."

"A good one?"

"No. I was going to die."

"That's a horrible plan."

"Best I could come up with. How'd you get here so fast?"

"I rode my dirt bike. Paulette was monitoring the three of you. She was calling you, but you didn't answer."

Riley reached for his radio—it was gone. "Didn't realize I'd lost it."

"Pax took down Torin Lamont, and Lefebvre got Zeke Lamont. Lefebvre's fine."

"What about Lonnie Lamont?" Riley asked.

"We're not sure," Blake said. "Looks like he got away."

"Damn."

"You were the one who needed help."

"Why didn't you shoot when the drone was first overhead?"

"That wasn't supposed to happen. Paulette is still learning to use the drone. She didn't mean to get that close. I was too far away."

"If Bourget killed me there, you had no shot."

"Roger that."

CHAPTER SEVENTY

When the muzzle flashed, the boom of the rifle followed. Franklyn heard nothing other than the ringing in his ears. His hands roamed over his chest—no blood. Had he died? No, he was still standing. Crow sprinted past. Franklyn spun and took a few hesitant steps. Crow pulled out a flashlight. Franklyn followed the beam. Lying on the ground was Balam, with a bloody wound to his shoulder.

"What the hell?" Franklyn staggered over to Balam.

Crow pointed to the rifle on the ground next to Balam. "He had you in his sights. The coward was going to shoot you in the back."

"Fuck you, Hiram," Balam said. "I was saving the sheriff from you. He's full of shit, Franklyn."

Franklyn barely heard the voices through the ringing in his head.

"I heard what he said about Eva. That's not true. She loves you."

Franklyn glanced from one man to the other.

"Crow is the chief's boy. You know that. He's the dirty cop."

"If I need to make a choice, I'm going with Crow."

"You're making a big mistake, Franklyn. He'll kill you as soon as you turn your back."

"I'll take my chances. Crow cuff Balam." Franklyn staggered backward, collided with a tree, and slid down the trunk.

"The chief is going to have your ass," Balam hissed. "You're done here."

Crow pulled out his cuffs and knelt by Balam. He placed one cuff, then wrenched Balam's injured arm behind his back.

"You're a fucking traitor," Balam yelled.

Crow stood and headed to Franklyn. "You gonna be okay?"

Franklyn shook his head. "I'm in rough shape."

"No problem." Crow reached down and lifted Franklyn to his feet.

Bushes snapped. Crow swung his rifle in the sound's direction. Diesel stepped into the open.

"Lean on me," Crow said. "I'll get you on your horse."

CHAPTER SEVENTY-ONE

RILEY GUIDED HIS HORSE ACROSS THE RIVER. BLAKE RODE HER DIRT bike farther upstream and they met up at the fire.

Riley slid out of the saddle and hit the ground with a groan. "If I never ride again, it will be too soon. I'm not gonna be able to sit for a month."

"Poor baby," Paulette said.

"Where's Lefebvre?"

"He's gone to get the horse trailer," Paulette said. "We'll load the horses here. I don't want to hear any more complaining about your tender parts."

"Not a lot we can do until daylight," Riley said. "I'll get forensics and a hazardous material team here at first light. Where's Franklyn?"

Blake shrugged.

"Didn't he come back with you?" Paulette asked.

"He's on the horse."

They watched Crow lead a horse toward the fire. Franklyn swung loosely in the saddle. Another man staggered behind.

"Franklyn's not doing well."

Paulette and Riley raced to the horse and slid Franklyn to the ground.

"I'll radio for the paramedics," Blake said.

"Come on, Balam," Crow said. "Let's find you a high-quality jail cell."

"I thought Hiram Crow was on the dark side?" Riley asked.

"I was wrong," Franklyn said. "He saved my life." He smiled at Riley. "Turns out, we make a decent team."

"Sure, like The Lone—"

"Don't even think that." Franklyn glared at Riley. "I can still kick your butt."

"Not tonight. You'd go down crying."

Paulette held Franklyn protectively in her arms. "Maybe you can tone it down, you know, for one night."

Riley grinned. "Sure, I'll go easy on the old cowboy. It's been a crazy month since he rode into town as the new sheriff. Is this what we can expect?"

"Maybe, if I still have a job after this. How many did we arrest?"

Riley shook his head. "We don't have the full count yet. There was a lot of confusion when SWAT lit up the night. No way to know how many escaped. Last I heard on the radio there were three Red Demons shot, none serious, and nine others arrested. About a dozen with beanbag bruises. A few raced into the trees, and the rest surrendered. About thirty give or take."

"That's a good roundup," Franklyn said.

Riley scanned the gathered cops. "Where's Taggert?"

"Last time I noticed him, he was with his team at the drying shed," Blake said.

Riley glanced at Franklyn. "Looks like you're in capable hands. I've got some overdue business." Riley headed over to the drying shed with Blake trailing behind. Taggert and four of his team stood outside the police tape in front of the drying shed.

"Pill press and meth lab inside," Taggert said. "Like shooting fish in a barrel. Perfect mission."

"Perfect? You idiot. You used the lights too soon. That wasn't the plan."

"Don't get your panties in a knot," Taggert said. "Some may have escaped, but I have their pill-making operation. We'll find the others."

"The problem is that the four top suspects rushed at us and we nearly got killed. Another is missing."

"If you're worried about four guys coming at you, it's reasonable they tossed you out of SWAT. You're not man enough."

Taggert didn't see the punch that connected with his jaw. He was unconscious before he hit the ground.

Riley shook his hand after hitting Taggert.

"Oh, crap, Riley," Blake said. "There's gonna be hell to pay."

Riley glanced at the four SWAT members. Reliable witnesses. He was screwed. But it was worth it.

One of the SWAT members stepped toward Riley. He was sure he was about to be arrested.

"We'll take care of Taggert. He must have run into a tree or something. We found him unconscious."

Riley's eyes widened. "You're kidding."

"He put us at risk. For what it's worth, we miss you. Now, get the hell out of here before he comes to."

Franklyn groaned as the ambulance bounced over the rough field.

"I'll give you morphine for the pain," Pam said.

"No, no morphine."

"It will ease the pain and spasms. I can give fentanyl."

Paulette glanced at Pam and shook her head.

Pam put the drugs away.

"You need to know," Franklyn said weakly.

Paulette leaned close.

"About Eva." Franklyn told Paulette what he'd learned from Crow. Paulette held Franklyn's hand as he drifted into a restless sleep.

Franklyn awoke as the ambulance pulled into the emergency entrance. The back doors of the ambulance opened, and Pam jumped out.

Eva rushed to the door. "Franklyn, are you okay? I was worried."

Eric pushed her back as he and Pam slid the stretcher out and onto the ground. Eva wedged her way back to the head of the stretcher. She reached out and stroked his face. "Oh, Franklyn."

A hand grabbed her arm and yanked her back.

"You'd best leave, now." Paulette glared at Eva, arms crossed over her chest.

"Why would I do that?" Eva stared down at Paulette.

Paulette lowered her arms, and her hands balled into fists.

"If you don't, I'm gonna rip out your hair and gouge out your eyes."

Eva stepped back. "What?"

"He knows."

"Knows what?"

"About you and the chief and the spying. Maybe you should run back to your boyfriend and tell him it didn't work." Paulette stepped toward Eva, who backpedaled.

Eva glanced from Paulette to Franklyn. Her jaw trembled and her eyes were downcast. Eva slid her hand over Franklyn's arm. Eyes ablaze, she glared at Paulette, then and stalked away.

CHAPTER SEVENTY-TWO

CHIEF FOX HEADED DOWN THE STAIRS TO THE CELLS—TWO WERE occupied. One with a huge, sleeping Indian, the other with Balam. When he spotted the chief, he jumped off the cot and raced to the cell bars. "Chief. Am I glad to see you. I can't stay here any longer."

Fox nodded. "Unfortunate events last night."

"Crow sold us out. No way the cops found us by accident."

"Yes, sold out for sure." The chief pursed his lips. "How would Crow know what was happening?"

"Eva came to tell you about the raid but told Crow instead."

"That's what you say."

"You think I sold us out? That's crazy. If I did, why would the cops put me in jail."

"Oh, I'm not saying you told the cops. I'm saying you are incompetent. You made mistakes along the way. You misjudged Eaglechild."

"Don't pin that on me. Eva did the background check. She

said Eaglechild would be easy to influence. I said, don't hire him."

The chief nodded.

"Even Silas Powderhorn told you not to hire Eaglechild."

The chief nodded again. "Yes, Powderhorn was against it. That's interesting."

"I told you he'd be trouble, but you didn't listen."

"Leroy, do you think this is my mistake?"

Balam held out his hands. "No, that's not what I'm saying. We can still make this work. Get me out of here."

Fox leaned close to Balam. "It can't work, not now. I trusted you to know what the cops were doing. You fucked that up. Now I have to start over. Build everything from the bottom up because you are incompetent."

"I'll fix it." Balam clutched the bars, as if he would pull them out of their frame. "I'll take care of Eaglechild. He won't be lucky again."

"Yes, kill the sheriff." Fox chewed a lip and shook his head. "And what do you think his white friend will do?"

"They'll never find Eaglechild. There's a wolf pack south of here. Kinda funny, at Wolf Creek. They'll tear the body to bits and drag the bones for miles."

"This mess does need to be cleaned up." The chief swung away from Balam and nodded slightly to the man in the next cell.

"Goodbye, Leroy," the chief said over his shoulder.

CHAPTER SEVENTY-THREE

A WEEK LATER, FRANKLYN STARTED WORK ON A NEW HOUSE. Paulette helped with the measurements and pounded the stakes. Franklyn checked the plans a couple of times to make sure he had dimensions right. Then he used a spray can to mark the ground between the sticks with red paint. He didn't want to take any chances the backhoe operator would misunderstand what he wanted.

Earlier in the week, the operator had scooped the remains of the burned building into a dump truck and hauled it away. Monday, he'd be back to dig the hole for the foundation.

Franklyn surveyed their work. "Morning sun on the front porch, sunset on the back deck."

"You have a great imagination," Paulette said. "I see a hole and prairie grass."

"You have a limited imagination."

"I'm practical."

A swirl of dust headed toward them—the cloud hid the dark

SUV heading their way. Ember headed toward the truck, growling, hackles up.

The truck skidded to a halt, the dust cloud continuing over Franklyn and Paulette. They averted their faces. Riley exited the truck. "Sorry about that."

"I doubt it," Franklyn said.

Ember stalked toward Riley, growling.

"Why does he still hate me?" Riley lifted his arm, producing a case of beer. "Forgive me?"

"Only if they're cold."

"That they are."

Regan slid out of the passenger seat, and Blake from the seat behind Regan.

"Party time," Regan said.

Franklyn raised an eyebrow, mouthing to Riley, *The lawyer?*

Riley smirked.

Franklyn glanced behind him. "I'd invite you in, but … the place is a mess."

A Speargrass SUV pulled in beside them. Lefebvre and Crow exited the truck.

"I hope you don't mind us crashing the party." Lefebvre pulled a cooler from the back of the SUV, set it by the fire, and opened the lid. "Everything we need for a weenie roast."

Crow carried over two lawn chairs. "It's either that, or we have to arrest you all because of the beer."

Riley waved a hand. "I've got pull with the sheriff."

Franklyn struggled to his feet. "If we're having hot dogs, we'll need some wood for the fire."

"We've got it, old man." Riley and Blake gathered wood and soon had a roaring fire going.

Paulette glanced at the cooler. "That's not a lot of beer."

"Damn, you're right." Riley jumped up, headed to his Yukon, and brought back another cooler filled with beer. "Backup."

"You never have a backup," Blake said.

Riley grabbed another beer. "There are special occasions."

They sat around the fire drinking beer and roasting hot dogs.

"How's your arm?" Regan asked.

"Good as new." Franklyn raised his arm, then groaned.

"Hard to make that old arm new," Riley said. "How many times did you break it?"

"How many beers did you bring?"

"Three dozen."

"Well, not that many." Franklyn smirked.

"It's not the arm pain that's the problem," Paulette said. "Tell them."

Franklyn nodded, then stared at his hands. "I'm gonna need help from all of you. I got a problem with prescription opioids. Like many others, they were prescribed to me repeatedly and in sizable dosages. I need to beat this. It won't be easy."

"Are you going into treatment?" Riley asked.

"No. Well, yes." Franklyn's shoulders slumped and his right hand shook. "I'm working with an elder. With his help, I will beat this the traditional way. He'll be my guide."

"Good for you, Franklyn," Regan said. "Anything you need, let us know."

"There is one thing. I'm worried Riley will get in trouble when I'm not around."

"Not my problem." Regan shook her head.

"Why're you staring at me?" Blake poked a wiener stick into the fire. "I don't babysit."

Paulette shrugged as she put marshmallows on her stick. "Don't know the guy."

"I can't tell you how much that hurts." Riley passed around more beer.

Riley dropped Blake off at her house, then drove off.

"Do you think Franklyn will be okay?" Regan asked.

"He'll come through this," Riley said. "He's one tough sucker. But he's going to go through hell for a week or two, maybe more."

Reagan swiveled in her seat to face Riley. "Please check on him."

Riley glanced at Regan. "I can't. Elder Powderhorn is taking him into the hills, away from everything and everyone."

"That will be hard," Regan said. "I admire his courage. Who's going to handle the sheriff's duties?"

"Hiram Crow. He proved his loyalty to Franklyn. They want the same thing for their people."

"Won't Chief Fox object to Crow?"

Riley turned off the reservation and onto the highway. "I'm sure the chief wants Crow gone. Especially since he knows Crow is not his lackey. But Chief Fox had already appointed Crow acting sheriff after Franklyn's accident. The chief must be careful. With one sheriff dead and another injured within two months, it won't appear right to appoint someone else sheriff."

"The chief will need to watch his step."

"Damn rights," Riley said. "I'll be watching every move."

"I'd love to lay some charges on Chief Fox." Regan sat back and stared out the window. "Thanks to you, I have plenty of work. The arrest of the Lamont boys, Noel Bourget, and the Red Demons will keep me doing trials for a year or more."

"I have nothing I can make sick on the chief, yet," Riley said. "I know he's behind this, but he's made sure he's clean. My hope was for Balam to come clean in a plea deal."

"But he's dead."

"He died in jail under suspicious circumstances." Riley shook his head. "Apparently, he hit his head on the jail cell bars and fractured his skull. Bleeding on the brain."

"You don't believe that bullshit."

"Of course not," Riley said. "The Dr. Chamberlain says it was several blows to the head."

Regan cocked her head. "Not self-inflicted."

"Nope. If it was, that's the worst case of suicide I've ever seen."

"What about the guy in the next cell?" Regan asked.

"Enoch Fox. He said he was sleeping." Riley glanced at Regan and grinned. "When Enoch awoke the next morning, Balam was on the floor. Fox yelled for the guards. The paramedics said Balam had been dead for hours."

"Does Enoch have a record?"

"Drunken bar brawls that he frequently won."

"A history of assault?"

"There were charges for assault, but none of them went to court. I ordered the case files so I can review them."

"So, he's walking away from murder?"

"Only for now. I'm not giving up. But he's not talking, there are no witnesses, and the cells are a forensic slush pond. Judge Leery didn't give me a chance to interview Enoch before Leery released him into Chief Fox's care."

"Because he was Fox's grandson?"

Riley raised his eyebrows and snorted.

Regan reached over and took Riley's hand. "I'll stay at your house tonight if you want."

"I hoped you say that." He squeezed her hand. "Remember, I have to go out late tomorrow morning."

CHAPTER SEVENTY-FOUR

RILEY PARKED OUTSIDE THE RESTAURANT, INHALED THEN EXHALED, and headed inside. A hostess met him. "Table for one?"

"I've got a reservation. Briggs."

"Got it. Follow me."

She led him to a booth toward the back. That worked fine for Riley.

"Can I get you anything while you wait?"

Rum and Coke. "A Coke, light ice, please."

He checked his phone. No messages. He was ten minutes early.

A waitress brought his Coke. "Do you want anything while you wait? An appetizer?"

"Nothing yet, thank you."

Riley grabbed his Coke, leaned back, and took a drink. Every time the door opened, he glanced up, his heart skipping a beat. Families, couples, and occasionally someone alone came in. His shoulders slumped, and his stomach flipped. Why was he so anxious? He drank again. *Why can't this be rum?*

That was a hell of a month. Seeing Franklyn after so many years had been outstanding. But it didn't take long for Franklyn to put his foot in it. Just like when they were kids. They could have killed him at least three times. He was always lucky. At least that's what Riley told himself when Franklyn beat him at a rodeo.

Thinking about rodeos reminded him how much his butt hurt—no more horses.

He lifted his glass, stopped halfway, then set the glass on the table as he stood with an enormous smile.

"Hello, Daddy." Chris and Robyn wrapped their arms tight around him. "It's late, but Happy Father's Day."

CHAPTER SEVENTY-FIVE

FRANKLYN SAT CROSS-LEGGED ON THE GROUND. HE HEARD THE HISS of steam as water flowed over the hot stones. Heat rolled over him in waves. Sweat stung his eyes and gushed from every pore.

He opened his eyes and rubbed the sweat from his face with the back of his arm. When Franklyn was about ten, he remembered his grandfather performing sweats. His grandfather gave him the honor of assisting the firekeeper by keeping the fire going.

He glanced at the dome over them. Traditionally, the dome was covered by skins. Instead, blankets covered the branches. An opening in the dome faced the fire. Four heated rocks were positioned to represent north, east, south, and west.

Silas Powderhorn sat motionless and cross-legged across from Franklyn. Franklyn couldn't tell if Silas was breathing. Franklyn had tried to let go of everything in his head, to find a spot of peace and calm. He'd accomplished that for a time—about ten seconds.

This was long overdue. Addiction does strange things to your mind. You know you need to stop, but you can't. You know you need to ask for help, but you won't. When friends try to help, you push them away. Today he followed the path back to the start of the addiction. As the rodeo injuries piled up, the pain increased from dull aches in the morning to searing pain most of the time.

Because he was always following the rodeo circuit, he didn't have a family doctor. So, whatever town he was in, he'd find a clinic and get a new prescription. Soon he'd graduated from Tylenol 3s to OxyContin. It was easy to get. Doctors were prescribing Oxy like candy. Tell them you are a rodeo cowboy, describe a few serious injuries, and you left with a month's supply. Sometimes you got a two-month supply, so you were ahead of the game. The addiction started gradually, one in the morning to get the aches out. Then another at night so he could sleep. Sometimes one mid-day to keep the pain away. Before long, he was taking at least four a day.

While he was on the rodeo circuit, getting the prescription was easy. In 2016, deaths from opioid overdoses skyrocketed. The primary culprit was fentanyl, but fingers were pointed at physicians who had over-prescribed opioids like OxyContin. Suddenly, it was near impossible to get a prescription for opioids, and no option other than Tylenol Extra Strength . He'd panicked when he realized he was on his last medicine, and he fought the temptation of the illegal pills. Sometimes you have to hit rock bottom, but even the accidental overdose didn't push him to get help.

Franklyn knew there were tough days ahead, but with Silas as his spiritual guide, he'd beat the addiction—even if it meant a sweat every day. Heck, he could afford to lose a few pounds. He needed to do this—for himself, and Speargrass.

AFTERWORD

As my regular readers know, I am passionate about writing the Brad Coulter Thriller Series that began in 2010. After three Coulter Thrillers, my writing path led me to an opportunity that deviated from the Coulter Thrillers. In 2016 I challenged myself to write an 80,000-word novel in 40 days and *Speargrass: Opioid* took on a life of its own. I was writing like a madman and by thirty days I was ahead of schedule. Then I hit a wall—hard!

I realized that the novel was missing a character and without that character the plot was one-dimensional. So, I created the Riley Briggs character. The challenge was to fit the Briggs scenes throughout the novel and have Franklyn and Riley interact. I could see the two characters fitting together, like fingers interlocked. Easier said than done. I put the novel aside and committed to getting *Crisis Point* completed and in print. I accomplished that in April 2018. By then I was writing *Outlaw^{MC}*. Prior to the *Outlaw^{MC}* launch, I had already completed the first draft of *Wolfman is Back.*

In summer 2019, with *Wolfman is Back* in final edit, I pulled *Speargrass-Opioid* out of the computer files and worked on it again. Within a short time, I had over 120,000 words. My novels are usually 81,000-86,000 words. On review, I realized that now I had too many plotlines, so I cut drastically.

I always save chapters I cut in a file called orphan chapters. They may come back to life in a future novel.

So, you might ask, "Why Speargrass?"

I am a big fan of Craig Johnson and his Longmire series. Robert Taylor as Walt Longmire in the TV series is brilliant. That was the spark for the idea.

And personally, as a paramedic, I have witnessed the effects of the Opioid Crisis from the front lines, both in cities and as it ravaged Indigenous reservations. I have done CPR on overdose victims and administered naloxone to counter the effects of opioid overdoses. I have seen the panic in the eyes of the family as they watched our attempt to save their loved one. Too often we were too late. I responded to a call where parents had overdosed and died while their children played in the next room.

Opioids don't play favorites. Regardless of your ethnicity, your socio-economic situation, single or married, young or old, it doesn't matter. Oxycodone, Fentanyl, and all opioids can prey on anyone.

With Walt Longmire in my head and an opioid crisis, I was well on the way to a plot. Speargrass is a fictional Reservation in Montana. Now I had a setting. My goal was to show that the opioid crisis hits everyone—residents of the City of Great Falls, the rural area and the Speargrass Reservation. Even the good guys, our heroes, like Speargrass' new Sherriff, aren't immune to the damage wrought by the Opioid Crisis. Drug dealers don't care who they sell to, as long as the customers are paying. Tragically, the threat of death from contaminated street drugs doesn't lessen the addict's need.

How did we get here? That could be a novel in itself. Drug companies said Oxycodone was safe. Physicians overprescribed. Patients liked the pain relief. Then the opioid crisis hit. Physicians stopped prescribing opioids, making it impossible to get legal opioids. The unintended consequence was that the addicts turned to dangerous street drugs.

Why? There are too few available (and affordable) addiction treatment centers. For most addicts, if at this very moment they wanted to get treatment, they couldn't. There are no openings, and few alternatives to get help. Franklyn's own struggle with severe pain and resultant opioid addiction, and his path to finding community-based treatment to help him through, highlights that not only can addiction happen to anyone, but that getting help isn't easy.

And that, my friends, is how *Speargrass-Opioid* became a novel.

Will Franklyn and Riley be back? I think so. I have plots for three more Speargrass novels. The ultimate decision is up to you, the reader. Let me know your thoughts on *Speargrass-Opioid.*

In case you are wondering what Brad is up to, don't worry. Novel four, *13 Days of Terror* and novel five, *Goddess of Justice* are on their way!

Credits - I have an exceptional team ...

Valerie West

Valerie has supported my writing right from the beginning. Since March we have been spending all our time together-me writing and Valerie teaching from home. It took some getting used to, but we worked it out and the novels continue to flow.

She's always my first Beta Reader and provides just the right amount of critique and encouragement. I'd be so lost without her.

Jonas Saul

Jonas Saul is the New York Times bestselling author of the Sarah Roberts series. In 2018 I attended a panel he was on and some of his comments hit me dead on. After the panel ended, I waited to talk with him. I'd just published my first novel, Crisis Point. From that first talk I'd found an awesome writing mentor. A little over two years later my sixth novel is in editing process. Jonas set a path and a challenge for me-so far I'm on track.

Thank you, Jonas for mentorship and friendship.

Taija Morgan

Taija is an awesome editor. I need to find a bigger and better word, because she's more than awesome. Her edits are outstanding, her comments are thoughtful, her suggestions are always bang on. She not only edits but teaches through her comments. The best part is her comments throughout the manuscript. "I love this scene." "I didn't see that coming!" "You had me laughing out loud." Comments like those mean so much to a writer. Thank you, Taija, for your professional edits, but also for teaching me to be a better writer. Hopefully that comes out in each successive novel.

Travis Miles, ProbookCovers

Travis created all the book covers for my novels. His designs are outstanding. Readers frequently comment about the high quality and creativity in his designs. They certainly stand out amidst other novels.

Jennifer Cockton - Onlineforauthors-keeps the web page up to date, manages all things social media and reminds me the newsletter is due.

(You can sign up for my newsletter at DwayneClayden.com or email me at dwayneclayden@gmail.com).

Sheila Clayden - Mom

My mom is my biggest fan (sorry, Susan Sturgeon). She taught me to read, shared her love of reading and is the first to let everyone know I have a new novel out.

Beta Readers

I have a great group of Beta readers that give me early feedback on the plot and characters. Each provide their unique perspective, which collectively gives me the direction I need.

Bill and Susan Sturgeon—Bill, a retired Calgary Police Sergeant, and Susan, retired RCMP, provide feedback everything policing. Susan is my second biggest fan and shouts out to everyone she knows (and some she doesn't) that they should buy my novels.

Janna Hart. A new Beta Reader. I worked with Janna for several years and she was keen to review Speargrass. Her input was very valuable and I appreciated her perspective.

Colleen Peters has hung in here as a beta reader from the start with Crisis Point. She's an avid readers of crime thrillers and always provides great perspective on the plot and characters.

Bob Modray. Bob was a a fan from the first novel, Crisis Point. We had many discussions about writing over the past few years. I'm excited that he has agreed to be a Beta Reader. Thanks Bob!

Lori Craig. My police training classmate and great friend. From her vast experience with First Nations her ideas and suggestions were so very valuable.

Jason Johnson. Jason works for the Montana Department of Justice with twenty-two years experience as sheriff, undersheriff and coroner in Montana, USA. Jason spent a great deal of time teaching me about state politics, law enforcement, the legal system and the relationship between law enforcement and American Indians. Any errors in my understanding are mine, and not Jasons.

A Final Note to My Readers

There is significant trepidation in starting a new novel with all new characters in a new setting. I hope that Franklyn and Riley are characters you want in more adventures.

There were challenges regarding terminology for American Indians (US) and First Nations (Canada). Speargrass-Opioid is set in Montana, so I used terminology that is accepted in the United States, which differs in some instances to terminology accepted in Canada. Any errors are mine and not a reflection on Beta Readers, editors or proofing and will be corrected in future editions.

Some days the words don't cooperate and an email from you reminds me why I'm doing this, and I push on.

Thank you for your fantastic support.

Dwayne

ABOUT THE AUTHOR

Dwayne Clayden uses his knowledge and experience as a police officer and paramedic to write crime thrillers.

His first novel, **Crisis Point**, was a finalist for the 2015 Crime Writers of Canada Unhanged Arthur Ellis award.

Outlaw^MC and **Wolfman is Back** are the second and third novels in the in the Brad Coulter Thriller Series.

Dwayne's short story, **Hell Hath No Fury**, was published in **AB Negative**, an anthology of short stories from Alberta Crime Writers.

His vast experience working with emergency services spans over 40 years and includes work as a police officer, paramedic, tactical paramedic, firefighter, emergency medical services (EMS) chief, educator, and academic chair.

Dwayne is a popular speaker at writing conferences and for writing groups, providing police and medical procedures advice and editing to authors and screenwriters.

The co-author of four paramedic textbooks, he has spoken internationally at EMS conferences for the past three decades.

The Brad Coulter Thrillers

CRISIS POINT

OUTLAW MC

WOLFMAN IS BACK

13 DAYS OF TERROR

GODDESS OF JUSTICE

DwayneClayden.com

dwayneclayden@gmail.com

facebook.com/DwayneClaydenAuthor
twitter.com/dwayneclayden
instagram.com/dwayneclaydenauthor
linkedin.com/in/Dwayneclayden
goodreads.com/dwayneclayden
amazon.com/author/Dwayne%20Clayden